SANCTUARY

Tugging Iola along, I circled the lake, staying beneath the cover of trees.

Ahead of us, I heard more guards coming from the direction of Fountain Avenue. They were flanking us, like a pair of pincers. And there was nowhere for us to go.

My eyes darted from side to side, desperately searching for a way to escape.

I didn't even notice the massive copper arm bearing a torch until Iola and I ran past its concrete base.

Bartholdi's colossal limb glistened against the heavens. "Liberty Enlightening the World" was far from finished, but it was already majestic enough. Its electric torch, now dimmed, reached toward the sky, waiting to be ignited by the dawn.

Along the base of the Liberty statue were some paintings showing what it would look like upon completion. Iola lingered over them, pointing excitedly. I was more interested in the door at the base of the statue. There was no lock on it. . . .

Avon Books are available at special quantity discounts for bulk
purchases for sales promotions, premiums, fund raising or educational use. Special books, or book excerpts, can also be created to
fit specific needs.

For information, please call or write:
**Special Markets Department, HarperCollins Publishers, Inc.,
10 East 53rd Street, New York, NY 10022-5299.
Telephone: (212) 207-7528. Fax: (212) 207-7222.**

THE
BLACK
MARIA

A Mystery of Old Philadelphia

MARK GRAHAM

AVON

TWILIGHT

AVON BOOKS, INC.
An Imprint of HarperCollins*Publishers*
10 East 53rd Street
New York, New York 10022-5299

Copyright © 2000 by Mark Graham
Inside cover author photo by Fauzia N. Graham
Published by arrangement with the author
Library of Congress Catalog Card Number: 99-96775
ISBN: 0-380-80068-3
www.harpercollins.com

First Avon Books Printing: March 2000

AVON TRADEMARK REG. U.S. PAT. OFF. AND IN OTHER COUNTRIES, MARCA REGISTRADA, HECHO EN U.S.A.

Printed in the U.S.A.

WCD   10 9 8 7 6 5 4 3 2

In memory of
William Graham
and Martha McCleary Graham,
who were there.

ACKNOWLEDGMENTS

To Andrea Gottshalk, archivist at the Fairmount Park Commission, for the time she generously spent taking me through a private tour of Memorial Hall. Ms. Gottshalk allowed me access to the archives of Fairmount Park and to a rare panoramic photograph of the Centennial Exhibition. These were instrumental in helping me visualize the grandeur that was the Centennial.

To Tom Gaughan, Director of the Trexler Library, Muhlenberg College, and Kristin Harakal of the Interlibrary Loan department, who made it possible for me to acquire numerous rare guidebooks to 1876 Philadelphia.

To my editor, Jennifer Sawyer Fisher, for her acumen and advice.

To my parents, Kenneth and Michele, for their support and love.

And to my wife, Fauzia, for the gift of her being.

SPELLBOUND, I WATCHED the Tunisian girl dance.

The sight of her bare brown feet and ankles held my attention. I was not used to seeing the ankle of a woman. A respectable woman, that is. It was as stimulating as the coffee I was drinking out of a dainty porcelain cup.

The coffee was as thick and strong as brandy. It gave enough of a kick to get a dead man going.

I was sipping it in a dome-capped room that was covered with odd designs—arabesques I heard a nearby party call them—and furnished with tables, chairs, and even divans. At one end was a platform with exquisite Oriental carpets draped over it. The girl moving over the carpets was an exquisite piece of work herself.

Like the rest of the attendants and musicians, she wore her native garb—a far cry from what the society ladies considered all the go.

There was no bustle or even a trace of a corset. The beaded jersey she wore gave a generous view of certain areas that so-called ladies kept under lock and key. Half of her legs were on brazen display—the plain white skirt tucked up just below her knees to facilitate movement. Around her waist was a bright red sash, its tassels bouncing every time she moved, accentuating her hips.

Her dark, curly hair was partially covered by a plain

1

blue scarf. Not like the miniature flower patches our gentlewomen wore on their heads. She was a young girl, perhaps seventeen or eighteen years of age. The face was as comely as any you'd see on Chestnut Street.

In her hands were two scarves which she weaved through the air with the hypnotic allure of a snake charmer.

A girl who could have been her little sister, her head capped by a fez, poured me another draught.

I watched the dancer shift her hips, stamp the carpet, and flutter her arms. I concentrated on her loveliness, hoping I could use it to blot out all the ugly things I would have to look at to-night.

Some of those ugly things were hard to ignore, being deep inside me.

For a moment I thought how nice it would be to go to Tunisia. I wasn't quite sure where it was. In Africa somewhere. It would be nice to go there and hide. Perhaps with this dancing girl for company.

We could sit around all day, far removed from the world, and pic-nic on a sand dune. She could feed me pomegranates.

I sighed with contentment.

My eyes locked on hers and I sent her a silent message that I'm sure she did not receive.

It was nice to at least pretend that there was still something innocent and beautiful in the world.

There was only so much human evil and misery a body could stand.

After two years as a detective with the Philadelphia police, I'd about reached my saturation point.

I needed a vacation to Tunisia. Or anywhere.

It was bad enough being forced to wade through the muck of a typical beat. But to play chaperone to a bunch of swells out to chase the elephant—that was too much.

That was just what I had to do to-night.

Vainly, I tried to get back that feeling of peace.

It was too late. The spell was broken. The music ceased, the girl stopped dancing.

A hand gripped my shoulder.

"Detective McCleary?"

Turning away from the girl, embarrassed, I faced the young man.

He was a dude. That much was obvious from his attire. He wore an orange plaid suit with a tomato red necktie. As he sat down, he doffed a sporty-looking derby. His cuff-links and the stud in his cravat gleamed with real gold.

I twigged he was about twenty or so. Dark brown hair, well oiled, was just beginning to recede from his intelligent-looking brow. The mustache he wore was long and dark, a thin disguise of his youth. His eyes were watery and his complexion sallow, the look of a consumptive or a dipsomaniac. I hoped it was neither, because it was a pleasant enough face, even handsome.

The boy smiled at me amiably.

But I was not in a good mood. I had a feeling why he was there.

"What do you want?" I growled at him, taking a last sip of bitter coffee dregs.

"You *are* Wilton McCleary, aren't you?"

I nodded.

"Well, that's capital!" The young man beamed. "You know, I've been looking all over for you. Captain Heins said you might be in the Japanese Bazaar, so I checked there first. No luck. I checked Main, Machinery, the Art Gallery. Then I finally asked a member of the Guard if he'd seen you. He told me you often came here when you were off duty."

"Why not?" I said defensively. "It's a clean place. Good drink and good music."

The young man eyed the dancing girl as she stepped off the stage.

"I see what you mean," he said.

"Well, what can I do for you, sir?"

"I'm sorry! I forgot to introduce myself. The name is King. David J. King. At your service."

His slightly moist palm clasped mine.

"So you're the reporter," I said.

"None other!" he replied sanguinely.

"Which paper are you with?"

"The *Bulletin*! Just started there Tuesday last."

The *Evening Bulletin* was my paper of choice. It had a little bit more color to it than the *Ledger*. And it was run by the Republican Party.

I knew a few of the reporters there—all young fellas like this one. They'd been more generous to me than the others had during the whole case.

The Eddie Munroe case.

It was my first assignment as a detective: to find a boy kidnapped from his home in Germantown.

Instead I found a killer.

As far as the rest of the world knew, I never found the boy.

Worse, I was responsible for killing a man who might have revealed the boy's whereabouts.

Things went well for me until that became public knowledge. An acquaintance of mine named Bunker whom I'd sent to the penitentiary made sure the press got wind of it.

When no one ever found the boy, it didn't take them long to blame me for it.

Two years later, the world was still speculating whatever happened to Eddie Munroe, the little boy from Germantown.

His name remained in the head-lines. There was a song written about him called "Bring Back Our Darling."

It was a well-known fact that Wilton McCleary had not brought back our darling. That he'd in fact ruined the chances of ever finding Eddie.

Cap Heins had fought hard to keep me from being

thrown off the force. It wasn't easy. People quickly forgot about all the collars I'd made. And the property I'd recovered. All that mattered was that I let Eddie Munroe get away.

Some nights I'd lie awake wondering if the young murderer I let go was going to turn into a respectable citizen or keep on killing. I might never know. In a way, I didn't want to.

That act of mercy had helped him—as well as me—go on living.

But sometimes I wasn't sure I liked the life I'd held on to.

I had made a sacrifice. My life for his.

If I had destroyed myself, at least I knew that another person was saved.

But I would never know if he was worth saving.

That uncertainty had been eating away at me like a cancer for two years.

Heins had seen I was about to snap. When he was given the position of Chief of Detectives at the Centennial, he brought me with him. It kept me out of the city, away from the scamps there. I'd been looking forward to some fresh air.

But now they had me lined up for a slum sociable.

I must've looked as gloomy as I felt.

David King asked, "Are you all right, Detective?"

"Sure, sure," I said. "What time is it?"

King pulled out a fancy, engraved hunting case watch. It was worth at least thirty-five dollars.

For a reporter, he was pretty well-off.

"It's half-past four," he said.

"Why don't we get out of here and walk around Main for a while?"

"Splendid! That'll give us time to talk before the big event to-night."

"Talk about what?" I said, standing up and pushing my chair in.

"I want to write a column about you. A personal history sort of thing."

"Now why," I said, putting on my boater, "would anyone want to read about me?"

"Oh, Mr. McCleary, I think the public would find your life very interesting."

I merely snorted.

"Don't be so modest. You're a famous policeman."

"Infamous, more like it."

"Well, now's your chance to change peoples' perceptions. We'll show them how sharp you really are—how exciting and demanding your job is."

"Mr. King," I said impatiently, "why in blazes would you want to do that?"

"I'm a police intelligence writer, you see."

The young man hurried after me as I headed for the door.

"And, uh, my father, Hiram King—"

"On the Centennial Board of Finance?"

"The same. My father asked your Captain Heins if I could tag along with one of the detectives on his regular beat. Captain Heins recommended I accompany you."

"Good old Cap. Always did have a soft spot in his rather hardened heart for me."

"And when Heins told me a little bit of your personal history—and the fact you'd be going to Shantyville tonight, I rushed out after you."

We paused at the door, listening to the sound of the musicians who'd just started up again.

"You mean you didn't know about me or the Eddie Munroe case?"

"To be perfectly honest, no," King said. "I've been abroad for quite some time and just returned a few months ago. When the Centennial commenced. My father sent for my sister and me and I thought it would be a good step to get on one of the papers here. I'm a writer, you know."

"Is that so?" I said, staring at the glass in the door and adjusting my necktie.

"Yes, though I haven't been able to publish my own work just yet. Thought I'd have a go at reporting. Especially police intelligence. It's very exciting. Don't you think?"

That got a snort out of me. I turned away from the stage, catching a last glimpse of the dancing girl.

Then we walked out of my little Tunisian haven and back into a far different world.

The International Exhibition, 1876.

The greatest spectacle Philadelphia—the Republic—maybe even the world—had ever known.

IF THE WORLD had seen a greater spectacle than the Centennial I certainly hadn't heard about it.

The day I shot dead one of Eddie Munroe's supposed kidnappers, Mayor Stokley laid the foundation for the Centennial Exhibition in Fairmount Park. Construction commenced soon afterward, and all through '75 the Grounds attracted hordes of visitors awed by the magnitude of the project.

The Centennial took up about two hundred and fifty acres not far from the west bank of the Schuylkill. If you peered from the other side of the river, you'd see the Centennial's iron peaks and gaily painted walls gleaming like a fairyland. Each morning when I came over the bridge at Fortieth Street, the sight of the Grounds took my breath away.

This was more than a fair or an exhibition. It was a fantasy city, a vast, splendid jewel of progress set in Philadelphia's own little pocket of Arcadia.

It was the Union's birthday present to itself. From firsthand experience I knew the price we'd paid to survive. The country, like some of us who fought in the war, still bore the scars. But you never saw any old wounds at the Centennial. There were only a few tips of the hat to the

8

past. Enough to placate those of us who'd ensured this anniversary with our blood.

The rest was new. Magnificent, unbridled newness. That was us, the United States. If there'd been any doubt that we were coming of age after sowing our wild oats in a four-year tour of hell, those doubts were now allayed.

The Republic was focused on the future. On taking its place as one of the great nations of the world.

It wanted the rest of the world to know it, too.

The aim of the Centennial was to showcase machines, art, education, agriculture, textiles, and every other sort of item that men grew or manufactured.

Joining the frolic were thirty-six other nations. Of course Great Britain, France, the German Empire, Austria-Hungary, and Italy were there. Then there were even more outlandish countries: Hawaii, Hayti, the Orange Free State in Africa, Turkey, Tunis, Peru, Ecuador, Liberia, Russia, China, and the most exotic of all, the one that everybody made such a fuss over: Japan.

In five huge exhibition halls these and other nations displayed the fruits of their industry and agriculture. There was enough space on the grounds to accommodate sixty thousand people.

They came—from all over the Union and the world—to gawk and take pride in the accomplishments of their Republic, their state, their town.

Like any dream it was too beautiful to last. The dates for the Exhibition were set from May 10 to November 10.

That day, September 5, 1876, the crowds were still pouring in.

Never in my life had I seen such a throng of people—not even the one time I'd been in New York City during the war.

There were all types: farmers, dudes, sports, mechanics, ministers, nurses, nuns, domestics, soldiers, and droves and droves of respectable families, their dolled-up kids scampering here and there, munching that pop-corn stuff or taking huge drains from the soda fountains.

On most of their faces was a look of something akin to shock. The place was so big, so full of stuff, that it would take a lifetime to absorb it all.

David King and I halted outside the Tunisian Cafe, breathless ourselves. The afternoon was waning but the crowds weren't. People had a way of staying until the last possible moment, which was usually sunset.

That left us with several hours to kill before the fun began that night.

We decided to go for a stroll down Fountain Avenue, one of the main thoroughfares in the wedge-shaped grounds. Right at the corner there was a model of Paris, built on top of the street. A scaled-down Seine wound through exact miniature replicas of every notable building in that city. Boys and girls, their long hair, skirts, and straw hats making them indistinguishable from one another, had to be restrained from leaping into Paris and doing more damage than the Prussians ever hoped to do.

Skirting past the kids we made our way down Fountain, past the Pennsylvania State Building, the Turkish Cafe, the *Boston Herald* Pavilion, and the Vermont State Building.

It was a pleasant day for a stroll, despite having the reporter for company.

The *Bulletin* had said that morning that the temperature would be in the low seventies. I was glad to see September arrive. Only now was I beginning to feel comfortable in my linen suit and straw hat. There'd been some days in July where my collar would be as limp as a soggy rag. So far to-day I hadn't even wanted to loosen my necktie.

Though I did wonder if in the next century of progress some far-sighted genius might do for clothing what others had done for, say, farm machinery—that is, make it easier on us poor men so we didn't have to sweat so much. I wouldn't have dreamed of going outside on the most humid day of July without my jacket and vest on. After all, I didn't want to get an inflammation of the lungs. Yet every now and then I'd think about the Red Indians and wonder if it might not be more comfortable to go around bare-chested.

If anyone had dared to do that in the Quaker City they'd have been arrested. After all, life wasn't just about being comfortable. There were more important things to consider—like decorum.

A cooling breeze was coming from the Schuylkill and bore with it a host of other smells. The most delicious was the smell of pop-corn, which made my mouth water. My first day as a detective on the Grounds I'd tried it. They told me the Red Indians had been eating it for years. I wondered what took us so long.

There were all sorts of smells coming from the dozen or so restaurants on the Grounds. My personal favorite was the Southern Restaurant—where I found that Southern cooking was quite unlike the gruel I'd been fed in Andersonville. I didn't go to the Trois Frères French place too often. Someone told me *trois frères* meant three brothers, and from the prices I'd say each one was charging you separate.

We reached the end of Fountain Avenue and came to, appropriately, a fountain.

The Catholic Total Abstinence Fountain, to be precise.

A statue of Moses on a miniature Sinai stood in the center. Four notable Catholic Founding Fathers did their best to look noble on their own pedestals. At the base of one I took a drink of water spewing out of a lion's mouth. I wiped my moist neck and brow and replaced my straw hat.

Then David King looked up the Avenue of the Republic and said, "Magnificent, isn't it?"

It surely was. On our right Machinery Hall sprawled for fourteen hundred feet. After that came Main, which seemed to stretch into infinity. Main was two thousand feet long and five hundred feet wide. It was the largest building in the world and we were very proud of it.

Stepping over the tracks of the West End Railway which serviced the Grounds, David King and I headed for the shadow of Machinery's flag-festooned iron arcade. As I looked up to the sky I saw clouds of dense, black smoke skirt across like thunderclouds. They were from the three annexes on the other side of Machinery, all of them large enough to be works themselves.

The reporter seemed to perspire a lot. He was wiping his pale brow with a silk monogrammed handkerchief.

For a moment we silently scanned the crowds.

Then King said to me, "I could sit here all day and watch them."

"What?" I said. "Machinery and Main? Yeah, they're pretty spectacular."

"No!" he almost shouted. "I don't mean the buildings. I mean the people. The whole Centennial is so ersatz. So contrived. But these men, women, and children are the genuine article. From all over the Union. Every walk of life you can picture. Here they are. They're real, Detective."

What was he talking about? I wondered.

I didn't have to ask him. Like most reporters and writers I'd ever met, he had an inordinate desire to hear himself talk.

"They don't notice when you watch them. Every now and then you can spot a private look. One meant only for themselves. That's what I like, Detective. Finding something men hide in themselves come unexpectedly into the open. That's reality. That's what I'm looking for. The secret things, the hidden things."

"Is that what you find writing for the *Bulletin*?"

"Sometimes. We've civilized ourselves so much that we forget who we really are. Savages beneath a thin veneer of morality. Don't you think so?"

I smirked impatiently and said, "I don't know about the thin veneer. But I've seen plenty of savages."

"That's the modern nineteenth century for you. Look at them all. They walk so orderly, so calmly from place to place. But underneath there's all this simmering energy."

"And you like that?" I said, eyeing the reporter. He was squinting at the people as if he were trying to see through them.

"No," he said. "I don't like it at all. It frightens me actually."

"You know what, King? You're a queer one."

"Yes," he said, raising his chin and smoothing his mustache with a smile.

In spite of myself I was beginning to like this kid. I got the feeling he maybe didn't take himself as seriously as I'd thought.

And it was better to listen to him than to stand around and wait for a dip to make a touch. After a month of arresting pickpockets, I was tiring of their company.

I always had a soft spot for the educated. Maybe because I'd always wanted more schooling myself. But the war had gotten in the way of that.

Like David, I was also interested in people. I met plenty of them every day, though usually not under the most pleasant circumstances. Some of my best acquaintances were people I arrested time and again.

"So you like reality, huh?" I said. "Well, you'll get some to-night, I reckon."

"That's exactly what I wanted! The *Bulletin* wanted me to cover the sights and sounds of the Centennial. Bah! As if there hasn't been enough printed about the Exhibition. So I told them I was going to do a profile of a guard on duty. I wanted to look at the dark side of the moon, you know?"

"The world of tramps, pickpockets, and confidence men?"

"Yes! That's it! That's why I had Father get me a job as police intelligence reporter. Because I wanted to see the secret things, the hidden things."

"The stuff your mother told you not to do?" I smiled.

"My mother was dead before she could tell me to do anything."

My smile disappeared.

"Sorry. I didn't—"

"It's all right. It was a long time ago, when I was still in short pants."

I left it at that and said, "You're not planning some kind of . . . what do they call it? Sensationalism?"

"You mean, do I plan to expose the sordid details of the Quaker City? And the Centennial?"

"Ha! There's nothing sordid about the Centennial. I can tell you that. If any place in the world is clean, it's here. We've got the criminal element bottled up tight."

"Can I quote you on that?" King said, pulling out his pocket tablet.

"Well, sure," I said uneasily.

"Now, when you say the Centennial I take it to mean you are not referring to without the Grounds?"

I chuckled and shook my head.

"I thought not. Listen, can you tell me what we're going to see to-night?"

"Whatever you're looking for, Mr. King. But I'd be careful."

"Oh?"

"There are a lot of people who would be very unhappy if you look too closely over there in Shantyville."

"I expected that. My story will be watered down, I assure you," he said with a weary tone.

"I don't care what you do," I said defensively. "But

there are some other parties who would. You get my drift?"

"Of course. Rest assured, I don't plan anything sensational. I just want to see it."

Genuinely curious, I asked, "Why would an educated boy like you be interested in all that stuff?"

"Because! It's what they—" he gestured to the Centennial buildings—"don't want us to see. Reality."

Looking at the magnificent buildings, I said, "I don't care for reality. I've seen enough of it. I prefer the Centennial."

"That's because you're not an artist, Detective. Every artist seeks for, above all else, truth. Not the truth of clergymen. Not the sentimental claptrap of the masses. I'm talking about truth."

"What is truth?" I said, laughing at the biblical allusion I'd made.

The reporter stared at the crowds. His watery eyes looked almost feverish.

"Truth is whatever frightens you the most," he said.

David pulled out a cigar, lit it, and puffed away.

I thought on what he'd said to me, and how intensely he'd said it.

I liked the idea that he wasn't afraid to see things that most folks wanted hidden. He made it sound almost heroic to go and live in that cheap, sordid world—the world I lived most of my life in.

Maybe he was only saying that because he'd never seen it.

Well, to-night he'd get his chance.

Then we'd see how much truth David King could stand.

As we stood there, music erupted from the sky—a cascade of bells, their pleasant ringing signalling visitors it was time to exit the Exhibition.

Each day the chimes rang three times—morning, noon, and sunset. Professor Widdows, the musician in charge of the bells, always had an eager audience to watch him hammer away.

Their silvery cadence interrupted David's gloomy thoughts. I could see him stare heavenward with a serene expression. For a moment the chimes drowned out all the other sounds of the Centennial—the bellowing chimneys, the churning machines, the blare of locomotives rolling into the depots outside the Grounds.

David and I decided to part for a while. He told me he had some things to discuss with his father. I reminded him where we were supposed to gather for that night.

Then I walked down the Avenue of the Republic, taking deep breaths—as if to capture the day and not let it go.

I never tired of walking about the Centennial. It was easy on my feet. They'd decided to pave it not with the usual cobbles or bricks but with a new material called asphalt. The result was luxurious to say the least—nice level walkways sparkling a deep black. On hot days you

16

could smell the tar in them and it had a good, clean smell of newness to it—like everything else there.

With some time on my hands I headed for the American Newspaper Building. I cut across the clay ground which passed for grass (and which we were supposed to prevent people from walking on). Taking the loop that wound behind the Pennsylvania Building, I skirted the artificial lake and came to a two story frame building that looked like a railroad terminal in a big city.

Stepping inside, I went to the long table stretching down the middle of the great hall. On the table were arranged current copies of every paper published in the United States. I picked up the *Bulletin* and settled down in a divan set near one of the many side chambers, where hordes of pigeonholes contained back editions of each paper. A few journalists were clustered around the table, guffawing at some backwater editorial.

Looking at the head-lines, I was glad once more to be nestled away in the Centennial.

TURKISH BARBARISM—
ATROCITIES IN BULGARIA
SKULLS AND SKELETONS IN HEAPS

The article made sure to note that dogs were having a field day with the remains.

Some religious maniacs in Missouri had beheaded a man. They followed one Cobb, who believed he was Christ and that women should live in adultery to be purified.

I thought on the implications of that for a few moments and moved to the presidential election news.

More junk about Sammy Tilden. I didn't know who was the bigger humbug. Him or Rutherford Hayes. I didn't want to vote for either of them.

Yellow fever was raging in Savannah.

I didn't have much sympathy for Georgians. I'd seen

what their hospitality was like at Andersonville. But I wouldn't wish the yellowjack on my worst enemy. Well, maybe I would.

Grant was still making a fuss about the incident in Wyoming.

Lately I'd been thinking on that incident quite often. There was something kind of meaningful in it.

A bunch of redskins had massacred Federal troops under General George Custer. It happened at a place named Little Big Horn.

Custer was killed June last. When the Fourth rolled around we still hadn't heard about it. We celebrated Independence Day at the Centennial and slapped one another on the back, glorying in our progress.

I pictured the two scenes on a stereograph. On one side you had the Centennial with its innumerable machines proving man's superiority, how bright our future was.

On the other side you had a bloody field covered by scalped corpses, each one so full of arrows they looked like pin cushions.

Two different worlds—one civilized and hopeful, the other savage and damned.

Two worlds in one stereograph, in one country.

It made me laugh, if you could call that joyless chuckle laughter.

At the bottom of the page someone had taken an advertisement. It said: "A woman with a fresh breast of milk wishes a place as wet nurse."

There seemed something absurd about that in light of the rest of the news. Maybe it was even hopeful.

I'd had enough of the world by then.

I replaced the paper and headed back outside. The crowds were dwindling, herding themselves to the various turnstiles ranged along Elm Avenue.

I wound about the lake, listening to the calming sound of the large fountain in its center. Soon I came upon a curious exhibit. It was a gigantic copper hand holding a torch. A platform was built beneath the torch's flame. I'd walked up through the hollow arm to take in the view a few times.

A Frenchman named Bartholdi had built it, along with a fountain that stood right inside the main entrance between Main and Machinery. From the illustrations at the base of it, one could see that eventually a whole body would be built to go along with the torch-bearing arm. All out of copper. It would be the tallest thing I'd ever see. The idea was to put the statue up in New York Harbor. He was calling it, *Liberty Enlightening the World.*

Emerging on Belmont Avenue, I headed east toward the Main Annex. I had a friend there.

Most of the Annex was taken up by every type of carriage under the sun: stages, broughams, barouches, sleighs, drags—as well as wheels, hubs, whiffletrees, harnesses and every other sort of carriage hardware.

My favorite was the Pullman car. It was like a hotel suite on wheels with a boudoir and library car with luxurious gas lighting, satin-upholstered seats, and velvet curtains. There was even a Brussels carpet on the floor.

But the most popular item in the Annex was a humble looking traveling carriage with a floor about five feet from the ground. It was obviously old-fashioned, mounted on high, awkward springs and attached to four life-sized wooden horses. The wheels were as high as a full-grown man. A placard told you whose it was: "Washington Carriage."

It being the Centennial and all, there was a lot of fervor about Washington. Aside from being the subject of half the statues on the Grounds, his face was everywhere from badges to guidebooks to murals to sheet music.

I quickly noticed a young member of the Guard, dressed in his elegant uniform complete with brass buttoned wool jacket and forage cap. He was lounging against the footman's cushion at the back of the carriage.

His eye was on a visitor who wasn't minding the placard on the carriage that said "Hands Off."

As the villager stepped onto the driver's seat, the guard got off his cushion and said, "Hey! What are you doin' up there?"

"Nothin'," the farmer replied with a sullen look, putting his thumbs behind his suspenders.

"Well," said the guard, "do nothing down here on the floor or I'll make you think a mule is loose around here somewhere."

"Consarn yer everlastin' . . . !" the farmer said. "Is this a free country or arn't it?"

Taking a step toward the man the guard said, "You'll get a free clubbing if you go up there again!"

"Well, I'll be goldarned! Jirk a man around for a little thing like that!"

With a disgusted wave of his hand the farmer made his exit.

I clapped my hands.

The guard turned around with a snarl. When he saw me the snarl disappeared and a smile took its place.

He said, "Oh, it's you, Mack."

"Hiya, Tad," I said.

"I've had it for to-day," the Guard said.

"How 'bout some dinner at the American Restaurant?"

"Suits me."

There were some late nights when I couldn't catch a train or car back to the city so I'd have to stay at the Grounds. Every member of the Centennial Guard was required to stay in the barracks but there was some room left over for those of us from the city who needed a place to sleep.

Thaddaeus Schmoyer's bunk was next to mine. Over the past month since Heins had appointed me as detective here, I'd gotten to know Tad pretty well.

He was a young fellow, just nineteen, and eager to do a good job. He was hoping that if he succeeded at the

Centennial, a place might open for him with the Philadelphia police.

Many nights I'd lie there listening to him talk about his parents, whom he missed a great deal. They were from up north in Lehigh County. His father was a schoolteacher. He told me they were the kindest people you'd ever meet. I believed him.

They'd adopted him from an orphans' asylum when he was still an infant. Even though they led a quiet life, Tad had always longed for the big city and its excitement. So when construction began on the Centennial, he'd spent his savings on a train ticket to Philadelphia and gotten a job as a carpenter. He'd driven in many of the nails holding the floorboards of Main together.

Once the buildings were completed he wrangled his way into the Guard, after catching a man trying to make off with some silverware from the French section.

He was an easy kid to talk to and was impressed with me. Every night he'd ply me with questions about what detective work was like. I told him it was usually incredibly boring and quite rarely dangerous. Naturally he wanted to know all about the Eddie Munroe case. I told him what I could.

His curiosity didn't stop there. Tad gave me the equivalent of a good backroom sweating every chance he got. We must have gone over my entire career as a police officer. I guess I liked the audience. With Tad I could forget for a little while how much of a pariah I'd become.

When we got to the American Restaurant, we convinced the chefs to prepare a meal even though the Exhibition had closed for the day. They were only too happy to oblige. Like most merchants, they knew the value of keeping coppers happy.

Of course, it went without saying that we would not pay for our meal. That was just the way things were.

"The copper's credo, Tad. Hear, see, and say nothing. Eat, drink and pay nothing."

"Really, Mack?"

I stared at him for a moment in disbelief. The kid seemed crestfallen.

"No, Tad. I was just kidding you."

"'Cause I heard a lot of the boys talkin' like that."

"Well, don't you listen to 'em."

"I won't, Mack. I don't fancy getting dirty like that."

"You'd be surprised how dirty people can get when they wallow in the sewers all night long."

Tad took that silently, nodding. Then he said, "I think you can do what we do without wallowing in a sewer. You can kind of walk along the edge of it without taking a dip."

"That's true. But you have to concentrate to keep your balance. Lots of people don't have the patience for that. Or the willpower."

"I do," he insisted.

There was something innocent about him that appealed to me. His face was young-looking and his closely cropped blond hair was the color mine had been when I was a shaver. Tad was like a younger version of me. One who'd seen less of the world and its ugliness. One who'd never lived through a war.

I hoped he'd never lose that willpower of his. No matter what he saw.

In no time the waiter brought out our dinners. Tad had oyster soup, a slab of roast beef, some green beans, and rice pudding.

My meal was on the light side. I had the typical Philadelphia dinner and my personal favorite: broiled chicken and waffles.

As we stuffed our faces, Tad asked me if our card game would continue that night.

"Sorry. I have to go to work."

"I can keep you company if you have to stand guard somewhere."

"No, 'fraid it's not as comfortable as that. I won't even be on the Grounds."

"Where then?"

"Shantyville."

The waiter walked by just then and must've seen the distasteful look on my mug. I had to quickly reassure him that it wasn't over the food.

"How come you're going to Dinkytown, Mack?"

"It's a long story, Tad."

"I ain't going anywhere," he said, slurping his pudding.

"You ever hear of a slum sociable?" I asked him.

"What's that?" he said, wiping cream from his valiant attempt at a mustache.

"Chasing the elephant with a copper for a chaperone."

"Huh?" Tad said squinting at me across the table. "Why would someone goin' slumming want a copper around?"

"It's a big fad with the swells. They got the idea from the English. I guess they're tired of parading their boodle in front of each other. So now they want to go to the slums to show off their camel shawls and diamond-studded cuff-links. After the ball or the opera or what have you, the idea is to go for a trip through the dives, with yours truly guarding their sanctity. They've been doing it in York for a while, I hear. The bulls up there take them to the disorderly houses, gambling hells, and bucket shops. Almost as much fun as a trip to the Zoological Gardens."

"You sound bitter, Mack."

"I don't like it a bit. Make me go through those dives with them like I'm running a freak show or something. What I'm actually doing is advertising the underworld sewer better than any steerer I ever heard of."

"I guess they pay for this."

"You bet. The tips I get are all right. Sometimes I can make a week's pay in one night."

"Well, that's something."

"Yeah."

The bitterness hadn't left my voice.

I drained the soda water I'd ordered. It was made by a man named Hires. I saw him make it at one of the pavilions the other day. He called it root beer.

It was sweet enough even for my sweet tooth and took the edge off my simmering anger.

I told Tad about David J. King wanting to write a newspaper story about me.

"That's great, Mack! Maybe you'll get a little respect now once people see how you operate."

"Maybe. But sometimes I think the less people know about me the better. It makes my job easier if I don't stand out too much. Anyway, this King is just going along for the ride to-night. He won't be able to write about much of what we see anyway."

Tad nodded solemnly, not quite understanding what I meant.

What a greenhorn. Poor kid. He'd learn.

"Still seems like an okay duty to me," Tad said. "Get to sit around saloons and watch rich folks make asses of themselves. What happens if they do anything illegal?"

"Not my problem. Remember what I said. See and hear nothin'."

"You mean you weren't kidding?"

I smiled a little sadly, standing up from the table. Then I bade him a silent goodbye.

I **WALKED OUT** the main entrance, crossed Elm Avenue, and entered Shantyville.

This was the other side of the stereograph.

Most of it wasn't so terrible. Just tawdry and cheap. Beyond Girard the park began again. Next to its verdant trees, Shantyville stood out like a sore.

The wedge the developers had carved out between Elm, Belmont, and Girard was as dense as any block in the center of the city.

It depended on the Centennial for its existence. All along Elm Avenue, right across from Main, it stretched like an elongated, murky parasite.

Shantyville was as impermanent as the rest of the Exhibition. Most of the buildings were the flimsiest kind of frame shacks. A few were brick, all of which had been painted as bright red as an engine. Not that you could see the buildings anyway. They were obscured by a host of signs and flags of every size suspended from the flat roofs. They were flat to allow more space for patrons to take in the spectacle of the Centennial and Elm Avenue—which was a sight to see in its own right.

The crowds in the Grounds were nothing compared to the throng on Elm Avenue. It was as chaotic as the night of an election. People of every size, age, and color prom-

enaded under the blaring gas-lights, the shadows of the
flags above floating over them like an army of ghosts.

Above, on the roofs, people were laughing, screaming,
shouting, arguing, and making merry. Music erupted from
all quarters—from the soprano and alto at Operti's Trop-
ical Garden to a ribald bunch of drunks moaning a song
that I figured was in German.

There seemed to be a million people out to-night. Their
necks craned above to read the gargantuan letters embla-
zoned over the storefronts:

**BALLOON RIDES 15 CENTS
OIL WELL
REDWOOD TREE
VARIETY SHOW
GRAND EXPOSITION HOTEL
15 CENTS ONLY—
THE FAT WOMAN, 602 LBS.!
ALLEN'S ANIMAL SHOW—
THE LEARNED PIG, FIVE-LEGGED COW**

The number of restaurants beggared description. Most
of them were also hotels and saloons to accommodate
every class from tramp to swell. Many of them catered
specifically to Germans. The sound of their brass bands
and the stink of their sausages were hard to miss.

The fumes of restaurant kitchens, human sweat, and
smoke from cigars, gas-lamps, pipes, and chimneys
swirled over Shantyville in a thick cloud. Behind every
window you could see someone moving around or watching the street below.

Everywhere you looked there were saloons, catch-
penny and variety shows, cake and fruit stands, cheap
Johnnies, peddlers, and any other sort of game to help a
greenhorn part with his three-cent coins, nickels, and
dimes. A giant calliope at Tuft's Soda Fountain on Belmont cut above the din like melodic thunder.

It was as harmless as a country fair. At least from a first look. But I'd been past the storefronts. I'd taken a peek at some of the variety shows and the buildings that lay hidden behind the row along Elm Avenue. I didn't fancy poking my head in there. Not that I was afraid of anything happening. It's just that the sights always made me respect mankind a little less.

My rumination came to a halt when someone right behind me said, "The many men, so beautiful! And they all dead did lie: And a thousand thousand slimy things lived on; and so did I."

It was David King. He had an elegant walking stick capped with a copper boar's head. His kid leather–gloved hands rested on it now. The reporter wore his derby cocked at a rakish angle. He'd changed clothes, donning a more conservative black suit and vermilion cravat. The shoes looked like they'd just been blacked.

I looked down at mine and tried to brush the dust off them.

I said, "That's not too far from what I was thinking of this whole mess. Did you write that yourself?"

"I?" He chuckled. "You flatter me, Detective. No, in fact, those lines were written by Samuel Taylor Coleridge. From 'The Rime of the Ancient Mariner.' It's one of my favorite poems."

"How about that?" I said. "A little gruesome but it reminds me of me."

"I thought it would. I memorized the whole poem once. I used to think quite a lot of Coleridge and De Quincey and the rest of them."

"But not anymore?"

"No. I've gone beyond them."

I laughed at his serious expression. He straightened his spine with a languid gesture. Then a smile slowly crept across his wan face.

"Now I'm content to draw on what I see around me for my inspiration. Look at these people, McCleary! Have you seen any panorama more bizarre, more colorful than this one?"

I had, but in places this kid wouldn't understand—on the battlefield and in prison.

"Sometimes when I walk along Elm Avenue I've stopped in front of that museum there and watched the crowds gawking at the Fat Woman. I've stood there for hours and hours that seem like an instant and an eternity at the same time. I find those vapid faces so inexplicably fascinating I can't pull away my gaze."

This kid was a little too smart for me. I guessed artists were like that. Had to act a little eccentric to keep up appearances. David's father, Hiram King, had enough money to allow for eccentricity.

David pulled out a cigar and started puffing blue smoke into my face. Beneath the haze he said, "So? Where are we to rendezvous with the party?"

"Right in front of the Transcontinental Hotel over there on the corner. In fact it looks like they're waiting for us."

"Should I keep my occupation a secret?"

"That might be a good idea. After all, they're here to have a good time. With a reporter around they might become a little self-aware."

"That wouldn't do, would it?"

"No it wouldn't. Since they might not tip me if they don't enjoy themselves."

"Ah, you're a cynic, aren't you?"

"Why not? There's a percentage in it. Let's go."

This was the third time I'd conducted a slum sociable. Heins always made sure I got the assignments. Maybe he thought I needed the extra money.

The crowd to-night was the usual. A half-dozen of them, four men and two women. All of them were overdressed, like they were going to pay a call on royalty. They wanted people to see them and know how fancy they were. Their baubles were brazenly displayed—from gold watch chains to ivory cameos.

After all, it was my job to make sure no one put a touch on them. It was nice to know they had so much faith in me.

No sooner did I introduce myself to them than they were plying me with requests.

"Can you lead us to a quiet game?" one asked.

"Yes," said another. "We'd like to fight the spotted animal."

He smiled at his friends, who appreciated his wittiness.

"If you're looking for a faro bank you'll find one in just about every saloon from Belmont to Forty-first Street. But I wouldn't advise it. They're full of sharks who'll fleece you for every three-cent coin you've got."

This didn't deter them. They weren't going to believe the word of a mere policeman.

One of the women said, "Oh no you don't, Bertie. You promised me a look around first."

"Yes, my pet," the man said with a groan.

One chubby fellow fluffed his burnsides and hid away his pince-nez. He'd be heading straight for the nearest bawdy house, I figured. Funny that it didn't occur to him that the girls there didn't care how he looked. They didn't have much of a choice.

I had a list of places to take the folks. The lower the places the better, just so long as no rough stuff happened. By this time most of the owners of the dives knew I was a copper. I didn't expect any funny business.

The list was very specific. I was to take them along Viola Street, the dirt path behind the row facing Elm Avenue. This was where Shantyville got a little seedier.

We ducked between Murphy's Oyster Saloon and Allen's Animal Show. There was a narrow dirt alley there called Tischner's Lane that led eventually to the back of Tischner's Restaurant on Belmont.

Emerging on Viola Street, I led them first to Schutzen

Hall, where we walked in as a fight was winding down. Two German women were grabbing each other's hair and kicking with all their might. One of them flew into a table, nearly knocking over a lady in our party. The lady squeaked with delight and said in a high voice, "My, she's a savage brute, isn't she?"

The bartender was screaming at them in their language to cease and desist. He came out from behind the bar with a base-ball bat ready to do some damage.

Before he'd taken two steps one of the Valkyries stopped him with her meaty fist. The folks in our party cheered. This was high entertainment for them.

I turned to David and shook my head. His face was calm and impassive. I couldn't tell if he was shocked, thrilled, or bored.

The two pugilists had fallen to the ground. My party gasped in horror and delight when one of the women grabbed a lager-beer bottle and cracked it against the sawdust-covered floor.

The bottle was poised in the air, ready to come smashing down with the force of a German Krupp gun.

I walked quickly behind the woman with the bottle and withdrew my club from beneath my long coat.

As she was bringing the bottle down, I gave her nob a good tap.

The club bounced off her skull with a hollow sound. The bottle dropped out of her hand. She fell to the planks with a thud that shook the tables.

After helping the bartender off the floor I made my way back to the party.

"If anyone wants a faro game, there's one in the back, I think."

There were no takers.

Our next stop was Blanchette's Amazon Theatre.
We heard the music from the street.
Stepping inside we saw four men in blackface rolling

their eyes and flashing their teeth. They capered about the stage singing what I took to be some old plantation melody. A slightly out of tune violin screeched in accompaniment to the quartet.

They didn't do so bad a job with the singing either, and a few of the colored men in the audience nodded their heads approvingly between sips of whiskey. Colored and whites mingled freely, shocking the sensibilities of one of our females.

The ladies and gents in my party were taking in the atmosphere, polluted as it was. The sawdust was hard-put to soak up all the tobacco juice people were spitting. The language was as foul as the air. There was no fighting but there was plenty of bawdiness. Women sat on tables, flashing their ankles for everyone to see. That drew the eyes of my chubby friend.

"Look, Bertie," said one lady, rubbing her gloved hands together. "That woman's smoking. Isn't she vile?"

"Delightful, my pet. Absolutely delightful."

She wrinkled her nose in disgust but kept gawking just the same.

Suddenly Bertie recoiled as someone bumped into him.

"Oh excuse me," the man said and hurried away.

But he wasn't fast enough.

"Come back here, Bill," I called after him.

The shabby-looking file came back dutifully, his shoulders hunched and hands folded in a mockery of contrition.

"My apologies, Mack. I dint know these were wit you."

I nodded and held out my hand.

William put a gold watch chain in my palm.

"Is that everything?" I asked him.

Smirking, he handed over a sporty-looking gold pocket knife.

"Okay, get lost."

Bill said, "Sure thing, Mack. See ya around."

I handed the watch chain and pocket knife back to Bertie.

His wife or mistress or whoever she was started patting herself down, just to make sure everything was there.

I steered them toward the back room as the minstrels were stepping off the stage. A well-fed young lady in tights sprang onto the gas-lit platform. Most likely she was an acrobat. That was a nice way of putting it. She made her body do all sorts of interesting things.

When the bruiser at the doorway saw me he reluctantly got out of the way.

"What's this? Just a hallway?" David asked me.

"No," I said, "Wait a moment."

In no time a door opened and a woman crept out, hitching up her skirts. A man followed her, buttoning his trousers.

The swell folks tittered.

"What do they do in there?" Bertie's gal asked me.

"I'm sure your husbands could tell you," I said.

"Now, just a minute, my good fellow," Bertie said. "Don't get impertinent."

I stared at the man and cracked my knuckles. His indignant pout withered.

Right next door was the Oriental Saloon.

This dive was a novelty, even for me.

There hadn't even been a Chinaman in Philadelphia that I knew about before '70. That was the one who started the laundry on Race Street. There were a few more of them there now.

The Chinamen in this place weren't the Philadelphia variety. They were from California and the Far East, working at the Chinese Bazaar in the Centennial. When they were off duty they repaired here for a bit of the old country.

At first they tried to keep me out. They were like that, very defensive of their territory. Knowing what was going on upstairs I understood why. They got quiet when I showed them my star.

The ladies and gents stared with wonder at the Celestials. They'd probably never seen one before. They were quaint in a way, with their foreign-looking costumes and haircuts. They clustered around tables playing backgammon or some sort of checkers game. Someone had told me the stuff they were drinking was called ginseng. I didn't know what it was but I figured it wasn't alcoholic. With what they had upstairs they wouldn't need booze.

One thing anyone could see was that they were inveterate gamblers. Piles of greenbacks shifted across the tables with amazing rapidity.

"Aren't they adorable little creatures!" one of the ladies said.

"They're little, all right," said the chubby man.

"Don't their eyes look so funny! How can they see with them?"

"I wonder why they wear their pyjamas in a saloon?" And so on they went. When their gawking was reaching an end I said, "You'll be wanting to see the upstairs."

The steps were so small and close together the ladies' heels got caught a few times, sending them reeling. We reached a portal with a canopy stretched over it in place of a door. I waved the party through and followed them in.

The room was very quiet. Kerosene lanterns and candles provided enough light to see the five Chinamen stretched out on the floor. Nestled among them were three American women. They lay there like lizards taking a sunbath.

A thick cloud of smoke wrapped around us, making my eyes water.

"What is that smell, Detective?" one of the ladies said, breathing deeply.

"Opium," I said.

They gasped with joy.

We watched as the men, reclining on their sides, were serviced by young boys who supplied the opium. The pills resembled pieces of mouse dung.

The Chinamen were adept at the complicated process of smoking their poison of choice. I'd only watched them do it a few times and wasn't quite sure of all the steps.

After popping the pills into the bowls of their pipes, they held it over a nearby lamp until the pill started melting. Then they sucked the opium smoke inside them and kept it there for as long as possible.

It was soon too much of an effort to sit up. They collapsed to the cushions beneath them and fell into a stupor.

Some of our party were shocked that American women were lying between the Chinamen in very familiar positions.

"Don't get the wrong idea," I said. "They weren't seduced from the streetcorners. These girls are professionals."

The ladies stared wide-eyed. Their expressions alternated between pious indignation and a lustful titillation.

There was something sensuous about the languid whores draped over the Chinamen. They seemed so damn comfortable.

"You ever been in a joint like this?" I asked David.

His expression hadn't changed. It made me wonder if he'd been around more than I'd thought.

"I hear," he said, "about them. I'm sure it would gratify you ladies and gentlemen to know that those young boys supplying the pills also supply other favors to the clientele."

"Eh?" the fellow named Bertie said.

"They're catamites, my dear fellow."

I pulled David aside and said, "Are you kidding me?"

"That's what I hear."

For the first time that night I was shocked.

"I didn't know they did those kinds of things here!"

"Of course. But still it's all very quaint, isn't it?"

David's smile was hard to read. I couldn't tell if it was ironical or not.

That bothered me.

I supposed opium smoking was harmless enough. In fact, the pharmacists said it cured everything from diabetes to tuberculosis to head colds. Opium was in every baby syrup I'd ever heard of, to keep them from crying. If it was good enough for babies then it should be okay for grown men. It couldn't be worse than booze and that was still legal, notwithstanding the Women's Christian Temperance Union.

The opium joint was very quiet. The only noise was the sound of men sucking on their pipes.

The smoke was getting to me. I herded the swells outside to the relatively fresh air.

Then we headed for our last stop.

The freak show.

WE WENT BACK to Elm Avenue by way of Tischner's Lane. After traveling the space of a few squares we came to the Museum.

This was not quite the kind of entertainment one would expect after visiting Memorial Hall, the art museum of the Centennial.

Humans were on exhibit here. Specifically, the Wild Children of Australia, the six-hundred-and-two-pound Fat Woman, a collection of pure and unadulterated Man-Eating Feejees, the Wild Men of Borneo, and a Beautiful Circassian.

In place of Old Glory, huge pieces of canvas jutted from the flat roof, each bearing a portrait of a freak on display. A light breeze set them billowing. My party watched the Fat Woman undulate on the canvas and sneered.

Flags drooped halfheartedly over the entrance. The gaslights were turned off now. It looked like the Museum was closed for the night.

I knew better. The door gave when I pushed and I went inside.

There was a vague animal smell in the darkness—a dank, human stench. The kind you encounter in especially old and run down shanties. Which was quite a feat considering the place had gone up only a few months ago.

I'd visited P. T. Barnum's Museum in York once during the war, not long before it burned down. If the exhibition of freaks could ever be made genteel, it was there,

This was a more lackluster version.

Just inside the door was a large hall. Kerosene lanterns provided the only illumination. Gas-light was too upscale for this dive.

In the middle of the room was a simple platform with a curtain drawn across it that looked as if it were looted from a low sort of dance hall.

We took a seat on some plain benches arranged in three rows before the platform.

David was snickering beside me.

"Seems like an anticlimactic way to wind up the evening."

"I have my orders."

"Oh?"

"You think I just picked these dives out of my hat?"

I wasn't going to tell him where I got my itinerary from. I was sure he could figure it out for himself.

Of course I got my orders from Heins. I wondered if the places he'd picked were ones that paid a good deal for the privilege.

The funny thing was when he gave me the list he pretended that he didn't know anything about it. That someone else had made the list. Someone above him.

Who? I wondered. Colonel Clay, the head of the Centennial Guard? He seemed like a straight arrow to me.

In the end I didn't really care where the list came from. I just did my job. Asking too many questions had got me into trouble before. I was tired of that kind of trouble. And I was afraid of it too.

David seemed restless. He shifted positions in his seat several times.

"The other places were so . . . gaudy with vice. The only thing sinful about a museum is its shabby artifice."

I shook my head at David and said, "I think it's pretty appropriate. After all, this is what we've been doing all night with the swells, taking them through a big freak show. So they can gawk and leer at poor slobs who're too weak or stupid to resist acting like animals. What do the swells get out of it? They get to reassure themselves that they aren't so rotten. There's always somebody worse. Makes 'em feel better. But I'm telling you, whoever goes to a museum to laugh has more ugliness in them than the freaks."

"That's quite a speech for a detective. I'm impressed with you, McCleary. You can be articulate when you want to. Well, I hope you don't think I'm like them," David said, making a hurt face. I couldn't tell if he was genuine or not. He was too aware of his gaunt, good looks and used them for all they were worth.

"Of course not, King," I said. "You came along to uncover those hidden things you were telling me about."

"Yes," David said, encouraged. "So you understood me. I'm gratified to hear that."

I understood him, all right. At least I thought I did.

David wasn't so different from me. He was attracted to evil.

So was I.

Evil was a state of being that I had to visit every now and then. It was a dangerous place to visit. It wasn't always easy to make an exit. You had to fight your way out, tooth and nail. That fight was what kept me breathing.

But there were others who didn't exit, didn't even want to. They settled in very comfortably and made a home there.

I hoped David wouldn't be one of them. In his youth he saw evil as something deliciously secret and epic.

He didn't realize it was much more like this freak show—deceptive and cheap.

I hoped he would learn.

A door slammed somewhere and startled me.

The curtain rustled as someone took his place behind it.

Then the owner, whom I had already met, appeared on stage. He hadn't bothered showing up out front where he usually stood with a freak to draw people inside. From the previous nights when I'd visited he knew we were a captive audience.

His bald head glistened like a crystal ball. The pince-nez perched on his bulbous nose gave him that scholarly air. I bet he called himself Professor. They usually did. He was certainly the equal of any college-educated rhetorician. Like most public speakers, especially politicians, he crammed more falsehoods in his speech than there were stars in the firmament.

As he approached us on the floor, I said to the party, "Get your nickels out."

"That's right!" the Professor cried, passing his hat to the party. "All for the insignificant sum of one dime, two nickels, ten coppers, one-tenth of a dollar—the price of a shave or a hair ribbon—the greatest, most astounding marvels and monstrosities gathered together in one edifice. Looted from the ends of the earth! From the wilds of darkest Africa, the miasmic jungles of Brazil, the mystic headwaters of the Yan-tse Kiang, the cannibal isle of Antipodes, and the frosty slopes of the Himalayas! Sparing no expense, every town, every village, every hamlet, every nook and cranny of the globe has been searched with a fine-tooth comb to provide for you cultured ladies and gentlemen! May I present to you, the daughter of a prince, rescued from unholy bondage in the slave marts of Constantinople! From the barren steppes of the Caucasus comes this Venus of Circassia, a daughter of a now-lost tribe surviving since the dawn of men! Doomed to serve as odalisque in the sultan's harem, prized above all others for her Circassian white beauty, the purest of all races! Ladies and gentlemen, feast your eyes upon Zalumma Agra, the Star of the East!"

Suddenly a woman slid onto the stage.

The first thing I noticed was the enormous snake curling around her shoulders and encircling her waist. The Professor informed us it was a python.

I'd never seen a snake so big in my life.

The ladies held gloved fingers to their mouths in disgust.

The reaction of the gentlemen was slightly different.

Their attention was naturally drawn to the young lady as well as the snake. Her costume was about the size of an overgrown corset, and it displayed the sort of anatomy a corset was designed for. Tights covered her generous legs, as sinuous as the snake wrapped around her. Nevertheless, from the shifting of men's legs in the audience, I figured her looks were doing their job.

The most bizarre part of her costume was her coiffure. Actually it was more like an explosion of hair, sticking straight off her head like some African savage's frizzy locks.

Her face was attractive enough, though not quite as beautiful as the Professor suggested. Which was to be expected since this girl, I had a feeling, was not a genuine Circassian. An Irishwoman down on her luck, more likely.

She didn't talk but moved around the stage, letting her reptile friend go wherever he wanted to along her body. As the snake writhed about her, she contorted her own body, hissing softly, her lips parted, teeth showing.

It was quiet enough that I could hear the fat man in our party panting.

The Star of the East had a little bit more polish than the whores in the Amazon Theatre. She never took her costume off, though it made little difference. We got the picture anyway.

The Professor gave a little story about her capture. Plenty of details about her being in chains on the auction block. Once she got in the harem things got juicier.

It sounded like a paraphrase of *The Lustful Turk*, a well-known pornographic novel I'd confiscated many times in my career. Naturally I'd read a few pages of it, just for curiosity's sake.

After she'd twisted her body in every possible lewd angle and position, Zalumma Agra began to speak. Her broken English was very deliberate. At least she tried.

The purring tone she used made every sentence sound suggestive.

"I cry and cry in harem. I stay for ten year. There *hundred* other girl with me. We try escape but is impossible. If we try run away he catch us and *punish* us."

I looked around at the men and saw their foreheads glistening with sweat.

"What can we do? Bey do *whatever he want with us.* There nothing to do in palace where we stay. Just . . . *talk* . . . to other girl. And smoke . . ."

She took a deep breath through her nostrils. Her dark eyebrows arched themselves seductively as she pierced us with suggestive eyes.

". . . *opium* and dream I far away . . . that I have *everything I want* . . ."

The lights went out, the curtain fell down.

Alas, the Professor told us, the beautiful Circassian's command of the English tongue was such that communication was difficult. Fortunately, the Professor had spared no expense in preparing a volume for the modest sum of twenty-five cents that further detailed the Circassian Beauty's story. With illustrations, he was quick to add.

The men without female companions had already dug their quivering hands into their vest pockets for two bits.

"Well," I said to the party, "that concludes our evening. I'm sure you'll want me to accompany you back to your various hotels so you can get to sleep."

They all politely declined. My sarcasm was a little too subtle for them.

I herded them out the door. David King and I watched

as they scattered in different directions, shaking my hand as if they were touching a plague victim. At least I got a few hefty greenbacks out of the transaction.

"The fat fella will be heading back to the Amazon Theatre directly," I said.

David nodded and said, "That lady seemed interested in the Oriental Saloon."

"Maybe. And we know what those others wanted. To buck the tiger. They'll find a game soon enough."

A few of the men lingered about the freak show, as if they hoped to catch another glance of the Circassian Beauty. They were scrutinizing the pamphlets detailing her adventures.

Something fell out of one of the booklets and the swell hurriedly picked it up. With a weak smile, he walked quickly past me.

"I wonder what that was," I said to King.

"What?" he said, preoccupied with a still-bustling Elm Avenue.

"That piece of paper that fellow was in such a hurry to retrieve."

Curious, I decided to go back into the Museum and ask to see one of those booklets. But when I tried the door I found it was already locked.

"That's queer," I said.

"Circassian Beauties must sleep too," David said.

Ignoring him, I started walking down Elm.

"Where are you going, McCleary?"

"Don't you have to go somewhere, King? The slum sociable's over. Now I'm back to work."

I unbuttoned my coat and took my club out.

"Back to work, eh? You think that paper was suspicious. Capital! I'll go with you."

With a groan I waved for him to hurry up. We rounded the end of the square and ducked through Viola Street till we were behind the Museum. There were woods interspersed between the hotels and saloons. The Museum had a miniature backyard, the trees vying for space with a backhouse and a tin-plated hovel that looked like sleeping quarters or a kitchen.

Bits of lard and rotten food scattered across the ground gave off a vile stink. David held a handkerchief to his face. I'd been accustomed to bad smells for years. Once you've smelled a human carcass or a gangrenous leg about ready to be sawed off you can handle your run-of-the mill offal.

David went ahead of me to rap on the back door with his cane. I was going to try the door to the hovel.

Then I heard him gasp.

There was someone else at the back door to the Museum, someone who'd been concealed by the shadows of the nearby trees.

Whoever it was turned slowly away from the door and stared at David for a good twenty seconds.

Then the stranger sprang at my reporter friend with more ferocity than a wild man of Borneo.

David and his attacker sprawled off the doorstep and landed right at my feet. I took my club and stuck it beneath the stranger's jaw. Then I gave it a good yank.

With both ends of the nightstick in my hands I eased the maniac off David.

I kept the club jammed in his Adam's apple, like a garrote.

When he stopped grunting with rage and began wheezing I let up.

Then I kicked him on his stomach.

"Now what the hell's that all about?" I growled at him.

He lifted his head out of the dust and eyed me with fear.

My hands were still gripping the club.

"I can do a lot more damage than that," I said. "So get up slowly and don't even think of dusting off."

He did as I told him. David had picked himself up as

well and was busy brushing dust off his expensive suit-coat.

"You all right, David?" I said.

"Yes, thanks."

The two of us looked at his attacker, who'd risen agonizingly to his feet.

There wasn't much light back here. Just a glimmer from a candle or lantern at a window.

I could tell he was a young man, not much older than David.

He was about my height, a little on the thin side. His clothes were the plainest you could get. An ill-fitting vest covered a much-stained shirt. There was no collar around his neck. His pantaloons needed a hemming and looked like they'd been salvaged from an almshouse.

Despite all that he didn't look like a ruffian. He ran a trembling hand through flax-colored hair and mustache. The sensitive-looking face winced at me.

His eyes glistened in the bluish light of the moon.

It took me a moment to twig what was the cause.

They were tears. The fellow was crying.

"Now, what's all this?" I said, embarrassed for him. I was afraid I might have clobbered one of the half-wits from the museum.

Then the fellow spoke. There was no need for me to worry. He was no idiot.

"Just keep that club away from me and I'll leave you alone."

Curiously he wasn't looking at me at all. His gaze was reserved for David King.

"What're you doing back here?" I said.

"What business is it of yours?" he asked with a sneer, wiping away his tears.

"I'm a city detective," I said, pulling out my star. "So wipe that smirk off your face and answer me."

"I was looking for a friend," the man said.

"I see. So you must've thought this fella here was your

friend. And you were so happy to see him you nearly beat him to death."

"No," he shook his head. "My friend has four legs."

"Four legs? What kind of friend are we talking about here?"

"A porker. He's the learned pig at Allen's Animal Show. I take care of him. Feed him."

"Well, I don't think he'd be payin' the Feejees a call. They're man-eaters."

The young man lost his patience. "He escaped, damn it! I've been chasing him for hours. I thought he might have wandered back here. I smelled the food. So I was looking around for him when you two creeped up behind me. I thought you were going to attack me so I attacked first."

"That was a good strategy. Almost got your head caved in."

"What are you going to do with him, McCleary?" David asked me. He was returning the young man's stare. For a man who'd just been attacked, his voice was certainly poised.

"Well, we can take him to the magistrate and you can charge him with assault. How's that?"

"No, please!" the young man said, looking at me for the first time. "Look, I didn't mean anything by it. It was a mistake. I'm upset and you fellows surprised me. I apologize. I really do."

David narrowed his eyes and said, "Why don't we forget about it, McCleary? I can't be bothered with a magistrate to-night. I've got a story to write for to-morrow's edition, remember?"

I turned to the reporter and said, "You take it pretty well. Most folks don't care for that much reality. Not when it smacks 'em in the face."

David laughed and said, "I don't want to make any trouble for this fellow. He made a mistake. I'm satisfied with that. I'd advise him to be more careful in the future about who he puts his hands on."

With a tip of his hat, David said, "I'll see you to-morrow morning, McCleary. I suppose we chased the elephant down to-night, eh?"

"We did at that."

I waited until was David was gone.

The young man went over to the doorstep of the Museum and turned his face to the shadows.

"Well, what am I going to do with you?" I asked myself aloud.

I heard the young man sigh. When I walked closer I saw his fist clenched and still trembling. There was another sigh that sounded more like a sob.

Maybe he was just a maudlin drunk on a bender.

But no, his speech had been too precise. Too coherent.

I listened to the sounds of Shantyville on the other side of the Museum. The manufactured gaiety of whores and swindlers and suckers.

There was nothing artificial or booze-induced about this young man's sorrow.

He seemed to need someone to talk to at that moment, and not just about the pig.

I said, "Maybe I can help you look for your four-legged friend."

WITHOUT TURNING HIS head, he said to me, "You mean you aren't going to arrest me?"

"No. It was a simple misunderstanding. But why don't we go over to Allen's Animal Show, just to put my mind at rest?"

"What do you mean?"

"I want to know for sure you are who you say you are."

"I see."

He sounded hurt again.

"We can look for the porker on the way there. We'll take Viola Street down."

"All right."

He saw I was staring at his downcast face and said, "I've had a bad day."

"That makes two of us. What's your name, by the way?"

"Uh, Wilson. Jesse Wilson."

"Pleased to meet you, Jesse. My name's Wilton Mc-Cleary."

When I stuck my hand out he shook it, surprised and then relieved.

Soon afterward he began to talk, as if he hadn't had a soul to listen to him in ages.

47

He told me his life's story. It wasn't a happy one.

It began when I asked him how he'd ended up at Allen's Animal Show.

Like Tad Schmoyer, he'd done construction work at the Centennial.

"You live around here so I'm sure you know how many laborers they needed to raise the Grounds. I heard about it from where I was staying and decided to come down and make a little money. I worked underground because I was used to it, carving out pipelines for gas and such. Afterward I searched around for a place to stay because I liked it here. I mean the Centennial. I didn't want to work in the city just yet. It was more fun out here. I met the man who ran the Animal Show one day at Doyle's Tavern and he offered me the job of taking care of the animals."

Pretending to look for his pig in a dark corner, Jesse averted his face.

"I . . . needed the money. I'd spent what I'd made drinking. Didn't have anywhere to stay. Allen fixed me up with a place to sleep behind the building there, where the animals live. I didn't mind that too much. All I had to do was keep the pig and the cow fed and sell tickets now and then."

I kept my mouth shut, afraid that anything I said would sound like I was talking down to him.

The silence had the same effect.

"I don't care if I'm not working some steady job in a mill somewheres. Beats what I was doing before."

"What's that?"

He paused for a moment, looking into another dark alley for shelter from my questions. Despite his reluctance to answer, I got the feeling he was looking for someone to talk to, someone to unburden himself to. You get a nose for that after being in the back room long enough, waiting on men to confess.

After a while he said, "Oh, I've been all over the place.

Worked on the canals and in the mines. That was hard work, the mines. Does something to you to have to work in the dark day after day, you know?"

I nodded. I thought I had some idea what that was like.

"But I didn't mind all that much cause I could always think of . . ."

As he turned to me his face passed through a beam of moonlight. His expression was suddenly one of bewilderment and loss.

"My mother and father died way back. Of yellow fever. I'd been alone my whole life after that, shuffling from almshouse to asylum. When I was seven and old enough to work I went down into the mines. In that dark pit. That was how it was for years and years till I met *her*. And then there was no more darkness. You understand? I loved her so much. I loved them both."

Then, his voice quivering, he said, "I still do."

His lip twisted with bitterness and then grief. I watched him, trying to peel away the years of loneliness, toil, and pain that disfigured his boyish face.

Jesse stopped in the middle of Viola Street and inhaled deeply. He closed his eyes and shook his head like he was casting some spell on himself that would make him forget where he was.

It was then I began to think there was something a little unhinged about Jesse.

His emotions raged through him, out of control. He'd displayed his grief to me so openly, so unashamedly. It wasn't the way you expected a man to act.

Especially not with a stranger.

I'd always been taught to bury my feelings inside, to be a cool and placid lake to the world. Let the muck settle far beneath, invisible.

Control. A man needs control. Every man does. Or things start falling apart.

Jesse Wilson was long past caring about whether he

was respectably composed. A Shantyville swineherd. A shoddy, modern prodigal son.

It made that muck within me churn.

His craziness was infecting me. I got the feeling that I was looking at some moonlit reflection of myself, slightly distorted.

I knew I had to help him somehow and that it would also mean helping me.

So I kept listening.

"Jenny kiss'd me," he said, his voice taking on a weird, unworldly tone.

"She did?" I said, without asking who Jenny was.

The boy didn't notice me now.

"When we met," he continued, almost chanting. "Jumping from the chair she sat in. Time, you thief, who love to get sweets into your list, put that in! Say I'm weary, say I'm sad, say that health and wealth have miss'd me. Say I'm growing old, but add . . ."

He hung his head, whispering again, "Jenny kiss'd me."

We stood there for a few minutes, silent, remembering different things.

Then I put my hand on his shoulder and patted him toward the direction of Allen's Animal Show.

Shantyville was beginning to get a little quieter. Some of the gas-lamps had been extinguished and the revelers were dwindling from the streets. A few flashy carriages wheeled past us, escaping back to the city, to their wives or husbands, to their pretense of respectability.

Allen was not too happy to be roused from sleep. When he was informed that his prize porker had flown the coop, his curses shook the flimsy walls.

If Jesse wanted a roof over his head, Allen told him, he had better find that pig by daylight when the show opened.

It was about one in the morning and I had gone beyond

the point of exhaustion by now. I volunteered to help Jesse look for his charge.

We'd already searched Viola Street pretty thoroughly. I suggested we split up, with Jesse walking along Elm and me heading down toward Girard and Columbia avenues.

Jesse shook his head. He didn't like the idea of splitting up. I decided he just wanted to have someone around to talk to.

We came out by Tischner's Restaurant and headed north to Elm. Then we walked slowly, in the shadow of the Main Building. There were plenty of alleys and crevices for a pig to poke its nose around in.

As we walked, Jesse explained to me exactly what a learned pig was.

"What Allen tells folks is that the pig can add, subtract, multiply, and divide. He gives it an equation and the pig taps his hooves to give the right answer. He shifts from one hoof to the other depending on how many digits you got, understand? One night Allen got drunk and felt like showing off how he trained the pig. It's pretty easy. He already has the equations worked out in advance. Then he teaches the pig to tap his one hoof a certain number of times. Then the same with his other hoof. Afterward he feeds it. So the pig knows the only way he's gonna get fed is to tap his hooves just so. And that's all there is to it."

I said, "What about the five-legged cow? Does it do any calculations?"

"No. It just sits there in a hay pile. All I have to do with that thing is feed it and clean its mess and put some salve on the fly bites. Not much of a spectacle that one."

"All a bunch of humbug," I said.

"Yeah. But the kids like it. You should see the way their eyes get all wide when the pig scratches out how much three plus four is. I mean, those little ones probably don't know that themselves."

I laughed.

"The men and women who believe it are suckers. But I don't blame the children. I even think it's good for them."

"What?"

"Believin' in somethin' fantastic like that. I am a firm believer in the fantastic. It's the only way I can account for my life."

"Your life isn't that fantastic, Jesse. It was just hard and maybe a little lonesome. There are plenty of lives like that."

He pursed his lips in a smile and said, "I'll allow that. I think with most of 'em their lives are like a cage, one they build. Well, I didn't build mine. But I'm breaking out of it. You don't often get the chance to leave once you've wandered in."

"Leave where?"

"Hell, of course."

Suddenly I was worried that this boy was talking about suicide. Maybe he wanted me to talk him out of it tonight. But sooner or later the time would come when there wouldn't be someone to talk him out of it.

I didn't like to think this poor kid who somehow quoted poetry would end up on a noose for someone like me to cut down.

"Where is that damn pig of yours?" I said nervously, wanting to get him talking on something else.

"We've checked just about everywhere," Jesse said. "All except the woods behind the Museum, where I first ran into you."

After a couple squares' walk we came to the front of the Museum again. Jesse stared at the freakish portraits and murmured, "Back where I started from."

"What made you come here first?" I asked.

For a moment he was at a loss for words.

Then he said, "Like I told you, there was that offal out back."

He didn't quite convince me. I decided not to press him on it, at least not yet.

We cut between the freak show and the hotel next to it, down a muddy alley.

As we walked along the edge of the copse I heard something rustle in the bushes.

"What's that?" I said, pointing.

A lumbering shape was creeping through the brush a few rods off from a backhouse.

Jesse squinted into the woods and said, "I don't see anything."

"Look where I'm pointing. Close to the ground there, about three rods away."

"Yeah! I see it now! Teeny! Hey, boy! That you?"

I had my club out, just in case we were mistaken and it was something more dangerous, like a stray dog.

We both stumbled over rocks and gnarled bushes full of thorns. Despite our blundering, the creature didn't run off.

Jesse began to run, crying, "That's him, McCleary! I recognize him now! That's him!"

Soon I could see the pig myself, its shiny black hair covered with brambles and burrs.

I almost ran into Jesse as he stooped over to pick something up off the ground.

"What is it?" I asked him.

"My lucky day! Probably a three-cent piece. Well, at least I can say I'm not broke now."

He held the coin for me to inspect it.

"Looks like you're still broke," I said. "There's a hole in the center of it. Probably a token for the shooting gallery or something."

Jesse shrugged, pocketing it anyway.

He stepped a little closer to the pig, more careful now. We didn't want to scare it off.

"Well . . ." I sighed, putting back my club.

My words were suddenly cut short.

Jesse had begun vomiting.

His brow deeply furrowed, Jesse clamped a trembling hand over his mouth. Then he viciously kicked the pig away from him.

By the time I reached Jesse he was murmuring the Lord's name.

The pig had been sticking its nose in something on the ground. The light wasn't so good. I had to squat down to see what it was.

Then I said the Lord's name myself and made a quick, silent prayer.

A meager blessing for this dead girl. At least, I thought it was a girl.

"Get out of the way, Jesse. You're blocking what little light we got."

I pushed him backward and examined the corpse.

She, I was sure of at least that now, was a young girl. Maybe thirteen or fourteen.

Her cheap dress was soaked with still-moist blood.

The skirt was pulled up over her waist. Her unmentionables were ripped to shreds and covered with dark stains.

The basque was unbuttoned and also cut to pieces.

She hadn't just been stabbed. She'd been hacked to death. I counted at least a dozen wounds.

The weapon protruded from her neck. With a grimace I yanked it out and held it at different angles till the light hit it.

When I pulled it out I thought Jesse was going to faint. Then he said, "Is that what . . . ?"

"Looks like it," I said.

At first I thought it was some queer sort of ice pick. But the handle wasn't the same.

It was more like a gigantic darning needle with a sharpened edge. There was some foreign-looking design on the top of it.

"Look like anything you've ever seen?" I asked him.

I don't think he even saw the needle. He was still staring at the dead girl.

"Christ, there's a lot of blood," he said.

"Christ didn't have anything to do with it," I said.

Her legs and arms were flung at haphazard angles, like a doll thrown aside by a child in a tantrum.

The worn-down heels on her boots made me flinch with pity.

Her face was untouched except for a black eye that looked too old to have happened that night.

It was a plain face. Perhaps it had been pleasant-enough to look at when there'd been life in it.

A bonnet covered her dark hair. The ribbon reached below her round chin, in a bow. There was a thinner, uglier ribbon at her throat, where the needle had slashed, deeply. The coup de grace.

The killer had his sport with her.

I thought it must have taken her a long time to die.

She'd tried to fight for her life. I could see the nicks on her knuckles and palms.

I raised myself up and felt my body stiffen, inside and out. My head swirled and I reached out to Jesse to steady myself.

We said nothing. I watched the clouds skirt overhead. Their slow, serene movement brought me no peace.

NO ONE HAD seen or heard anything. We woke up the people at the Museum and questioned them several times. They had nothing for us.

If a two-hundred-pound educated pig could make its way there without anyone noticing, so could a murderer and his victim.

Heins had shown up for a brief spell, sent for the coroner's wagon, and commanded us not to speak to the press about it. It was pretty clear why.

When the coroner arrived, Cap gestured with his gloved hand, beckoning me aside. We stood just a few rods off from the body. No one had bothered to cover it up yet. The city coppers who patrolled Shantyville and the Centennial Guard were too busy gawking at the corpse. Some shook their heads with disbelief. Others made jokes about the corpse's occupation and rated her attractiveness.

Heins was on his second segar. He scratched at his collarless neck, took his broad-brim hat off, and spat.

"We need somebody to run it through," he said.

"You know it has to be me," I told him.

"Need you inside the Grounds. Been too many touches going on in there. Need your sharp eye."

"The hell you do!" I said.

Then, lowering my voice, I began to plead.

"You got plenty of dicks who have every pickpocket spotted. It's just that a bunch of them don't make any pinches. Otherwise they wouldn't get their percentage."

"Well, now there's some truth to that, I don't deny it. I didn't have much say in who they hired before me. You know I gave a few of the worst ones the boot. That ain't the issue, anyway. I got my reasons for keeping you on the Grounds."

"Like what?" I asked, exasperated. "So you can make damn sure I never work a worthwhile case again? Is this more penance for Eddie Munroe? Will I ever stop paying for that?"

"I don't know," Heins said quietly.

"Sure you do, Cap. Just like I do. The answer is no. Not after the outcry against me in the papers. That got you believing you'd made a mistake—in making me a D in the first place and then putting me on Eddie Munroe. When things didn't work out, when we didn't get the answers everybody wanted, it made you look bad. *I* made you look bad. So you decided to ease me out. Put me on shit duties like the depots and parades. Hoping I'd get sick of it and muster out. That way you wouldn't have to constantly be reminded that you failed."

"The only failure I made was letting you run wild with the Munroe case!"

"Maybe," I whispered, hanging my head. "Maybe I would have been better off never hearing about that boy."

We said nothing for a while. I listened to Heins drawing the smoke into his mouth.

Finally he spoke.

"Listen," he said placatingly, "this ain't gonna be a big to-do, anyway. If you want a chance to make good again this ain't for you. 'Cause we're gonna bury it, understand? I got my orders from the top."

"The Board of Finance, you mean?"

Heins said again, "The top, Mack."

Could he mean the Gas Ring? I wondered. The leaders

of Philadelphia's political machine? They pretended to be a plain old board of directors for the city gas company. Everybody knew otherwise. They were the bosses.

I couldn't think of anyone else who would have that much pull.

He wouldn't confirm or deny suspicions. All he did was gesture at Shantyville and say, "There's a lot of money tied up in this place."

"So?"

"So they don't want that supply running dry, understand? This ain't your shot at public redemption, boy. This is going nowhere. We're going to investigate it. Quietly. By the time we find the bastard and bring him to trial the Centennial will be over and it won't matter anymore."

He put a thick hand on the back of my neck and said, "Mack, you know I take care of you the best I can. That's why I want you far away from this and on the Grounds with me."

"So I can keep giving slum sociables?"

"I have nothing to do with that. I got my orders too. They wanted someone discreet to conduct 'em. I said you were the man. That's the end of that story."

"No it isn't," I said, throwing his arm off me. "Who are 'they'?"

"Good coppers know when not to ask so many damn questions. This time I'm askin' you to keep your trap shut, understand? For me?"

"Show me the percentage in it."

Staring into his eyes, I gave him the most callous look I could muster.

It was no surprise to me that Heins didn't look hurt.

"I told you I'd take care of you, huh? Listen, you show up at the Judges' Pavilion to-morrow morning at ten and I'll have something you can sink your teeth into. Something juicy."

The conversation came to an end when the coroner's assistant called for Heins. The body had been loaded on the wagon.

There was no use going over the area in this darkness. They'd have to wait for dawn. In the meantime Heins had two bulls stand guard over the woods.

I hoped they wouldn't expend too much manpower in combing the brush. They would come up with nothing.

Not even the murder weapon.

That was in my pocket, wrapped up tight.

My little secret.

I'd known all along that nothing was going to be done, that Shantyville's dirty business had to be protected.

Up to the point of our talk I'd been deciding whether to take the murder weapon out of my pocket and toss it on the ground, pretending to discover it.

Heins made up my mind for me.

I had stopped trusting him a long time ago, when he decided that saving face was more important than our friendship.

Now I was looking out for myself.

And for the murdered girl, whoever she was.

I made Jesse promise to say nothing to anybody about the girl. He was willing to go along with that, especially when I told him I'd need his help. That was on the way to summon the other coppers. I let him go before I brought them into it. The only person who knew about Jesse was me.

The kid was still shook up when I brought him and the learned pig to Allen's Animal Show. He didn't want to shake my hand goodbye. I'd never seen anyone more spooked.

It was nice to meet someone who could still be upset by a stranger's death. Someone who didn't make smart remarks on her looks or her clothing or her hairstyle, like the other coppers had done.

I only hoped he would be all right. He was a sensitive

kid and I wasn't sure he could handle the experience of viewing a murdered girl's body.

After bidding him a hasty goodbye I'd gone back on the Grounds to the barracks. Tad was snoring fitfully in the bunk next to mine.

I couldn't get to sleep for hours. I was thinking about the dead girl. About what the killer had done to her.

The needle stayed where it was in my jacket. Tomorrow I'd try to make out what those designs were and where it came from.

Eventually I must've fallen asleep because the next thing I remember was the dream.

It was one of those dreams that seemed so real. Just like everyday life.

I was walking around the Centennial, near Memorial Hall. I tried getting into it but the doors were locked from the inside. So I wandered to the Art Annex, directly behind it. Couldn't find my way in. I headed for the castle-like building right off Lansdowne Drive.

The Burial Casket Building.

Its door was unlocked.

Inside the light was dim. There wasn't a soul there but me.

My steps on the wooden planks echoed ominously.

There were coffins everywhere, lining the walls, piled on the floor, and displayed in the heavily carved showcases you saw everywhere at the Centennial.

Only the finest examples of each company were on exhibition. I saw redwood, mahogany, and cherry caskets covered with silver and gold handles and nameplates.

Everything seemed just as I remembered it.

Until I saw the Egyptian sarcophagus.

This weird artifact, an ancient coffin holding an embalmed corpse, was a very popular fixture at the World's Ticket Office. It didn't belong here.

At the same time, it very much did belong.

I was attracted to the strange designs on it—birds and

beetles and bizarre-looking men and women with animal heads.

I'd been reading Charles Dudley Warner's travel serials in the *Atlantic Monthly*—the one called "Mummies and Moslems and My Winter on the Nile." Maybe that's what attracted me to the mummy case.

I knew the creatures on it were gods of some sort. Inside I knew there would be a mummy, wrapped in bandages and covered with jewel-encased clothes.

All I knew was I had to take off the lid. It was wooden and rather heavy. I laid it carefully aside.

Then I shouted with surprise and horror. I'd been expecting to see a golden mask. Instead I saw a face. A familiar one.

It was Jesse Wilson. Just the way I'd last seen him— his blond hair carelessly parted, his eyes wide open just like they'd been when he saw the dead girl.

I touched the face to see if it was real. I could've sworn it was. But as soon as I touched the skin it turned to wax. I felt around the jaw line and realized it was a mask. With a light tug I pulled the waxen mask off so I could see the mummy.

Instead I came across another familiar face. David King's. His eyes were narrowed and his rakish mustache curled around a sardonic smile. When I touched his too-real skin it also became wax.

By now I was terrified, but I could not stop. I knew that I had to peel away every face until I got to the real one, the mummy.

Beneath David's face was one I barely recognized. I'd never truly seen it in life, just in a handful of photographs. But the flaxen curls and round, plump face were unmistakable.

With a shriek I tore away at the waxen mask so like the face of little Eddie Munroe.

At last I came to the face of the true mummy, the inhabitant of the sarcophagus. There were bandages wrapped around his face that I painstakingly unwound.

Toward the end I held one hand in front of my face to ward off the sight. I removed the last loop of soiled bandage. Lowering my hand I looked at the face of the mummy. That was when I started screaming, loud enough to wake the whole barracks. After they'd told me to shut up and were back asleep, I still had my eyes wide open.

I didn't plan to sleep any more that night. I was afraid I'd see the mummy's face again.

Afraid because it had not been a mummy's at all, but my own.

I WAS AT the wash basin before the rest of the boys even woke up. The tiny mirror showed my sleep-hungry face. Black circles radiated around my bloodshot eyes. My mustache needed a slight brushing, and a shave might've been nice. But I didn't have the time for a barber.

I changed my unmentionables and put on a new plaid, single-breasted morning suit. I'd just bought a sporty le petite necktie at the French corner of the Main Building the other day and tied it around the fresh collar I put on.

After I ran some oil in my hair, I brushed the soot off my straw hat and adjusted it on my head in front of the mirror. I'd bought this hat from an English firm also exhibiting at Main.

I wound my watch, slipped it in the vest, and buttoned my jacket—satisfied there was no telltale bulge.

I had my barker with me to-day.

I was at the main entrance by opening time. There was only an hour till my meeting with Heins, so I figured I could pass the time by the turnstiles.

There were thirteen entrances and exits all around the Exhibition but this one got the most traffic. It was conveniently located between Main and Machinery, directly below the Grand Plaza and Bartholdi's Fountain. Right across Elm Avenue was the Pennsylvania Railroad Passenger Depot.

This morning I couldn't see the depot. It was like some foreign shore, made invisible by a vast ocean. In this case the ocean was of people and the animals and machines they traveled on.

Elm Avenue was teeming with a chaotic swarm of humanity unlike any we Philadelphians had ever seen. Parasols, flags, and banners bearing the date 1776 bounced up and down, swooped and fell like insects skirting over a tremulous lake.

There was a riot of color and sound. Women paraded their most fashionable dresses—carmine, vermilion, garnet, and navy skirts and jerseys of gingham, camel's hair, cashmere, and Henrietta cloth swishing over the asphalt entrance. There was finery and ornament decorating every inch of them—wooden beads, Chantilly lace flouncing, striped bows, brocades of silk, puffs and pleats, and bustles bursting from corseted waists.

The men were in their best too—in velvet collared frock suits of cassimere, serge, and a few seersuckers despite the recent autumnal coolness. Their glistening top hats bobbed up and down in the throng.

They came from all directions on every kind of vehicle imaginable. Most seemed to arrive on the streetcars. The poor horses could barely move with all the passengers inside. Rumps piled out the windows and back of every stage. Gigs, broughams, four in hands, and hansom cabs went every which way, darting across the locomotive and streetcar rails whenever convenient. The drivers hurled oaths at one another, the horses snorted and neighed, locomotives whistled, and visitors to the Centennial sent up a polyglot din.

Chinamen, Frenchmen, Britishers, Irishers—there were all kinds mingling in the crowds. Foreign soldiers in dress uniform with shiny caps, buttons, and epaulets rubbed shoulders with skull-capped, pig-tailed Celestials and fez-wearing Turks dressed like the Zouaves I'd often seen during the war.

Some were fascinated by the foreigners. Others were upset by them. I saw more than a few women jerk their skirts from a Chinaman's way lest he pollute their virtue with his touch.

As soon as they descended from their transport, the visitors were assaulted by hordes of vendors and hucksters—some licensed and many more not—selling flags, hats, buttons, and guidebooks. It was easy to spot these fellows since they each had about a half dozen miniature flags stuck in the ribbons of their hats. They were annoying but at least patriotic.

I went into the crowd to get my breakfast. There were plenty of things to choose from. I didn't fancy waiting around in the packed hotel restaurants so I approached the vendors. They were everywhere to be found.

"Hot sassidges and sandwitches, gentlemen?" one man cried.

It seemed an appealing enough idea to me.

The sausage man was shabbily dressed and looked like he'd stuck his face in a smoky oven for too long. He was wheeling a portable kitchen in front of him that was little more than a long tin box. When I drew near he poked a fork into a compartment filled with hot coals and brought out a smoking bit of sausage. From another compartment he took two slices of bread and from the third one some mustard. Without asking he splayed the mustard all over my breakfast and handed it to me, mumbling, "That's fifteen cents, sir."

I gave him three nickels and he tipped his hat to me.

The sausage was gone within a minute. It tasted something like leather but I wasn't picky. Food never made that much difference to me. After spending a year eating hardtack, anything seemed good.

I passed on some ready-made waffles. Within the space of a square I came across six people of various ages selling "fresh-roasted California Centennial peanuts," dried apples, and those curiously twisted pretzels that I loved despite their tasting at times like cast-iron.

I bought a few from a dyspeptic-looking German who kept bellowing, "Bretzels, bretzels; fresh bretzels!" even as he served me.

On my way back to the entrance I was wondering how I could wet my whistle. There were some lemonade boys singing their songs to attract customers.

Each one had different words, some to popular tunes.

The one closest to me had a good ditty:

"Don't be afraid! The best lemonade! Made in the shade and as cold as ice can make it!"

As I approached he added, "Only five cents a glass."

Nearby a competitor cried out suddenly, "Two glasses for five cents!" but I'd already made up my mind.

"How can he afford to sell it that low when sugar is so much a pound?" I asked the kid.

"Well, you see, sugar grows right up the street here, so there's plenty of it."

I nodded solemnly and replaced the glass.

Going back into the Centennial, chewing my pretzel, I thought, That's exactly what Heins was talking about last night. Can't keep the people from their sugar.

I wondered if they would be scared off from their sugar by a little thing like murder.

The people in the dives wouldn't, probably. But the respectable folks who went to the Centennial and who tacitly condoned the other seedy side of Elm Avenue might get upset. They didn't mind having to live next door to the sewer. Just as long as they never heard about it or smelled it. If they did, they might have to stop ignoring it and clean it up.

That would be just too bad.

Pretty soon I'd taken a position against an oak tree in the courtyard immediately past the entrance.

The Centennial Board had made things much easier on

the visitors when they'd decided to drop their policy of accepting only fifty-cent notes for the admission price. I remembered the lines of disgruntled men and women who had to go to the Centennial Bank to make change each morning.

This particular entrance had four gates, each manned by a keeper who controlled the turnstile. The keeper put the money received in a box under the counter that could only be opened by bank officers with the proper key. Nevertheless, a copper was always on hand to make sure there was no trouble with the money or with gate-crashers. One man trying to get in without paying had been arrested the previous day and sentenced by the magistrate to three years in Moyamensing. Considering all that was being allowed in Shantyville I thought the penalty a little harsh.

I watched couples promenade past me, their arms linked, the ladies' pale complexions shielded by parasols. They looked ahead of them with eager excitement, exclaiming where they would go first. Little boys in sailor suits and straw hats had to be restrained from dashing off. Little girls in gingham and calico dresses, their long, carefully combed hair hanging down their backs, tugged at their mother's sleeves, imploring them to hurry up.

Many people halted just inside the gate and consulted their guidebooks. Inevitably, a crowd began to form, with people still piling into it from the turnstiles.

That crowd was ripe ground for the buzzer's touch.

I stayed where I was, right past the gates where all could see me.

Especially the pickpockets. That morning I saw four of them walk nonchalantly through the turnstiles. In no time they'd be bumping into people right and left, lifting leathers, watches, purses, you name it.

They had their specialties. Some were mollbuzzers, who preyed specifically on women. Others went for gentleman's watches. A few novices practiced the "kinching lay"—bouncing into children and grabbing whatever pocket change the little shavers had on them.

I'd been leaning against the tree for about ten minutes when I spotted a familiar buzzer.

There was nothing that special about him. Which was a good thing, because a pickpocket never wanted to stand out in a crowd.

His plain black suit wasn't the newer cutaway style. That would've given him less space to conceal things. The straw hat he wore was tipped a little too far over his brow. It was his attempt at disguise.

Before he was even out of the turnstile I was standing in front of him.

"Morning, Bill," I said with a smile. "I've been seeing a little too much of you lately."

His cheerful expression disappeared.

"Come over here, I wanna talk to you."

He followed me over to the oak tree.

"What's in your pockets, Bill?"

"Nothin', McCleary. Just some change for the Public Comfort Building."

"Not likely, Bill. Cough it up, now."

Bill knew me well enough. I'd saved him from riding the Black Maria once. I thought he might be a good mouth-piece to have. There were plenty of buzzers at the Centennial. In exchange for not pinching him I sometimes asked him to point out others of his profession. They always knew one another.

He dropped an engraved watch in my hand then looked me straight in the eyes.

I didn't buy his look of contrition. Scowling, I snapped my fingers.

Bill dropped another watch and chain into my palm.

"You've been a busy beaver," I told him.

"I take pride in my work," he said sullenly.

I stepped aside and said, "Looks like it's gonna be a beautiful day. Nice seein' you, Bill."

"Likewise."

Poor Bill. He was probably wishing he'd run into some other coppers—the kind who, once they spotted him, just asked for a few coins to let him go.

I dropped the watches in my coat pocket. When I went to meet Heins I'd take them to the desk sergeant. I'd have to fill out a report and then we could put them in the drawer with the other stolen and recovered articles.

I made my way through the Esplanade between Main and Machinery and took a moment to admire the bronze figures of Light and Water by Bartholdi. Staring into the fountain's pool I caught sight of my face and smirked at what I saw.

Straightening my necktie and brushing my mustache, I walked past the triangular beds of grass and flowers to the Avenue of the Republic. Directly across was the Judges' Pavilion, a handsome wooden building with four flag-topped towers. The roofs of the towers and the hall itself jutted outward, propped up by delicate-looking wooden buttresses. I could see people leaning out the many windows, peering at the already crowded avenue. From inside I heard cheers and applause. Each day there were awards and medals given inside for the best threshing machine, the best statue, the best saw, and whatever else was on exhibit.

I was about halfway across the avenue, at the base of the Washington statue there. The door to the Public Comfort Building was in my sights and I happened to stare at it.

Despite the change in her dress, I recognized the woman who was exiting at that moment and coming toward me.

She wore a bustle skirt now in place of the tights. A flower-bedecked hat covered the frizzy hair.

Her movements were businesslike—a far cry from the sensual writhings with her reptile friend from the night before.

I wondered what the Circassian Beauty, the Star of the

East, Zalumma Agra was doing at the Centennial.

Suddenly I remembered the piece of paper that had fallen out of the pamphlet describing her exploits. The one the swell seemed anxious to avoid showing me. I thought now might be a good time to ask her about it.

She turned west down the avenue. It looked like she was going into Machinery.

Like the Main Building, Machinery Hall was a colossal structure, fourteen hundred feet long and three hundred and sixty feet wide. It was more or less a one story building, the roof being seventy feet high along the wide avenues inside and forty feet high over the side aisles.

It was painted a light blue and had about as much ornamentation as the typical mill, which wasn't much. Some people objected to the design, calling it too plain, while others, who were sick and tired of the modern taste for excess, complimented its purely utilitarian exterior.

At the east and west entrances were festooned towers with galleries, just to relieve the monotony of the elongated blue mass.

The Circassian Beauty joined a throng entering the more toned-down entrance on the avenue. I followed her in.

Inside, the hall was alive with humming and clicking sounds. Along the two immense avenues and side aisles was every kind of mechanical device. The machines shimmered in an ethereal glow, thanks to the massive skylights overhead. In the center of the building, the Corliss Engine glistened like a monstrous idol.

It was a forty-foot-high double-acting duplex vertical engine—one of the marvels of the Centennial. I watched its massive, fifty-six-ton flywheel revolve, awed by its size and power. The Corliss Engine was what kept all the other machinery in the hall in motion—a leviathan heart, made of iron.

For a few moments I stared at the gigantic engine, feeling a shiver pass through me. It was a beautiful creation and somehow a symbol of everything we hoped to be: massive, powerful, efficient and relentless.

Its beauty was hard. There was nothing fanciful about it, no decoration to make it less or more than it was: a perfect machine. All that mattered was its size.

A symbol of America's dawning industrial might. Something we could all take pride in. The rest of the nations could stand at its feet and gape in wonder.

But I still preferred to worship a different sort of god.

I was waiting for the Circassian Beauty to step out of the water closet by the entrance. She'd entered it first thing. Now, as she emerged, I followed her through the American section of the hall.

We passed gas meters, barrel-making equipment, automatic shingle-makers, saws, moulding machines, and blast furnaces.

She didn't seem to have any specific destination in mind. Nor did she seem particularly interested in the machinery. I got the feeling she was killing time.

Waiting for an appointment?

With whom?

Why did I even care? I asked myself.

Because that piece of paper intrigued me.

And I was interested in who she was here to see. If anybody.

Of course she had just as much a right to visit the Centennial as anybody else. As much a right as anybody respectable, I added.

That's what's bothering you, isn't it? I thought. That somebody from Shantyville should be over here in the Centennial.

The collision of worlds bothered me somehow. It was the copper in me—the part of me that was immediately suspicious of people who were outside their place, their station, or their neighborhood.

That was the way my copper's brain worked, even if I

didn't always like it. People belonged in certain places and they weren't supposed to stray.

It was an ugly way to feel. I didn't like it.

But I'd made a lot of good collars with that attitude.

There was perhaps another motivation that I wasn't admitting to myself.

The Circassian Beauty was a not altogether unattractive woman. The few times I'd seen her perform I'd caught myself wondering what her real name was, where she came from, why she was working in a museum.

Just out of idle curiosity, of course.

Maybe she reminded me of the Tunisian dancing girl.

I was close enough to take in the shape of her legs when she walked in front of the blowing machine, which unexpectedly burst out a wave of warm air, much to the delight of spectators.

Womens' skirts were inevitably blown aside just enough that you could get a decent look at their ankles, at the very least. There were more than a few young boys waiting around for just such an eventuality.

Zalumma Agra walked into the blowing machine as if she knew what was going to happen. When her skirts flew up, she made a pirouette to the boys and men who were watching and then walked right past them all. They blushed and lowered their heads.

It was only mid-morning and I'd already done a good deal of walking. My legs were beginning to ache. I would've liked to sit down but the crowds were getting thick and I didn't want to lose her.

I thought of approaching the woman and getting it all over with, but I still had this idea she was going to meet somebody. I decided to be patient and wait to see who it was.

She stopped in front of a loom weaving corsets. I kept my eye on her reflection in the nearest showcase window. There was a contraption behind the glass that I'd never heard of before. It looked like some large, queer sort of spinning top bolted to a little stand. The end was hollow, like the tiny horns fire chiefs use to holler at their men over the roar of the fire. I wondered what use it might have. Since it was in a neglected corner next to some magic tricks I figured it wasn't that important. It was called a telephone.

The girl wound past hordes of looms making everything from carpets to drawers. She stopped to look at Howell & Brothers of Philadelphia and their newest wallpaper designs. Nearby was a bon-bon making machine where she bought some candies.

The sound of negroes reached us over the mechanic hum. They were demonstrating how chewing tobacco was made, though most people were there just to listen to their quaint songs. They were singing a hymn when I passed by, something about a chariot. I couldn't stop to listen. The girl was moving on.

She stopped to join a crowd gathered around a man operating what the sign called a type-writing machine. It was the tiniest printing press I ever saw, but it seemed impractical. With all the keys it would take forever to find the right letter. I thought I'd just as soon use a pen and a good nib. For fifty cents the operator would do up any message you gave him. It was a big novelty and there were plenty of people waiting in line to get their special message printed on the new toy.

I wondered if the girl was going to have her message printed. If perhaps she had a young man somewhere who didn't know about how far she'd fallen in the world, or what she was doing to support him.

I snickered at my attempts at cheap melodrama. All I wanted to do was make her more interesting. Perhaps if she had been in her costume—the tights and the snake.

The girl was disappointing me. She wasn't doing anything suspicious.

I followed her down the south transept and into the Hydraulic Annex.

There was no drone of machinery here. Just the pleasant, natural sound of running, trickling, bubbling water.

In the middle of the annex was an enormous tank, one hundred sixty by eighty feet, full of Schuylkill water pumped in by the Centennial Water Works. From a smaller tank about forty feet above the other came a breathtaking cataract, eighteen thousand gallons a minute.

On all sides of the larger tanks jets of water streamed from a host of pipes, making what had to be the greatest fountain ever created.

The girl took a seat in one of the benches set up at the north end of the large tank. A group of sailors leaning over the railing leered at her. Maybe it was the way she crossed her legs—most unladylike—displaying a portion of her calves.

I took a seat next to an old man and what I hoped was his granddaughter. They were sharing a pair of field glasses and taking in the cataract, walls, and ceilings. With the floral decorations on the rafters it was like a flooded Gothic cathedral made of iron.

I was glad the girl had finally decided to sit down. With some relief I eased into the bench. The waterfall was truly beautiful. After all the machinery it was nice to see something natural, even if it was brought to us by mechanical means. I watched the mist rise up to the vaulted ceiling, and listened to the bubbling echoes bounce from wall to wall.

The man-made cataract was mesmeric, soothing. I fought the desire to close my eyes and just listen to it. For an instant I gave in.

Instead of seeing an after-image of the waterfall I saw the girl's face. Not the Circassian Beauty's.

I was staring at the murdered girl, into her sightless eyes.

With a start, I jerked my head up and took a look at the water, hoping to banish the sight.

But it lingered there, beneath the constant motion of

the cataract—like a ghost image in a spirit photograph.

It was then I realized that I was wasting my time with this museum freak. I had more important things to do.

Just as I was getting up to leave I noticed that the Circassian Beauty had left her seat. She was standing on the other side of the tank now, staring down into it. Her boot was tapping impatiently against the wooden planks.

Another man was rapidly approaching her. I wondered if this might not be the person she was supposed to meet.

If it was her lover she had fallen pretty low. He looked about forty-five. His figure was lean and well-clothed in a navy frock suit. A scarlet bow-tie gleamed at his throat.

He bumped into her backside, one hand reaching out to steady her. She turned her head and looked at him with disdain. Bowing profusely, he tipped his hat and hurried on.

I waited a few seconds to see if she noticed.

It had been a masterful touch, the work of a veteran mollbuzzer.

When he'd bumped into her his free hand had darted right into the pocket of her skirt and lifted out what buzzers called a leather—her billfold.

I made sure I spotted the face of the pickpocket: a nose like a bull terrier's, ill-kept mustache, and gray-stubbled jowls. Thick dark eyebrows arched over truculent, deep-set eyes. I'd remember this customer.

As if he'd startled her out of a dream, the Circassian Beauty started walking out of the annex at a quickened pace. I didn't think she was aware she'd been robbed. There was nothing frantic about her movements. More like she'd spent her free time and now had to attend to business.

Right outside the entrance she made for the West End Railway Station. I sighed with relief. Maybe she was tired of walking and wanted to take in the rest of the Centennial sitting down. The West End line was the Centennial's private railway, with four miles of track covering the whole Exhibition.

I followed her into the station, paid a nickel, and climbed onto the platform. After surrendering my ticket to the guard there, I made sure not to look at the girl, hoping she wouldn't remember me from Machinery.

Soon we were chugging along at eight miles an hour, quick enough but not so much you couldn't take in the sights.

I took off my hat and let the meager but welcome breeze cool my sweating brow.

We wound past the Catholic Total Abstinence Fountain and then up to State Avenue, where the various states had their official headquarters. Crossing Belmont we skirted Agricultural Hall, a massive dark brown building of wood and glass shaped like a medieval church with the appropriate towers, turrets, rose windows, and even iron crosses. Inside it was more like the world's greatest barn and grain elevator—with all sorts of food and farm equipment on display.

The Circassian Beauty got off at the station right across from Agricultural Hall's main entrance, in front of the American Restaurant.

I waited in the crowd on the platform for a few seconds and followed her north. She went into the first building on our right, the offices of the Elevated Railway.

There was a crowd of about a dozen waiting to ride over the Belmont Ravine to Lauber's Restaurant. Though the restaurant was a popular one, I figured plenty of them were there just to ride this peculiar car.

It was unlike any other railway I'd ever seen.

There were three rails, one upper and two lower, set in a triangular position. Resting on the center rail, the car had a set of horizontal wheels on either end to make it run more smoothly on the tracks. A tiny engine with a diminutive stack did the pulling.

I gave the ticket-taker a three-cent coin and hopped into

the car. There were three compartments to choose from—
one above and two below, on either side. I followed the
girl, entering through the door set in the middle of the
car. She took a seat to one side of the stairs leading to
the compartment above. I took the other side, poking my
head over the steps and watching her through the railings.

We waited a few minutes for more people to get on.
There was no longer any room inside. People were cram-
ming themselves on the outside stairs and on the metal
railings.

With a whistle from the back, the car began moving on
its elevated tracks, the tree-covered valley directly below
us.

I heard people shuffle their feet above me and, as the
train started moving, I saw the girl step outside, even
though we'd been instructed not to.

She opened the door and immediately ran into someone. I saw him from behind.

With the way she was putting her arms around him, I
figured they were acquainted.

Then she turned with him to face another man, leaning
against the railing.

I recognized him well enough.

He was a stout, acerbic looking gentleman. Bright white
hair with a tinge of yellow in it curved over tiny ears and
around thick jowls. His mustache was prodigious. The suit
that elegantly draped his bulk would've cost me a month's
pay.

The man didn't bother removing his hat for the lady.

I wondered what she and her unknown companion were
doing talking to a big bug like Hiram King. There was
too much noise in the car for me to hear what they were
saying.

He was on the Centennial Board of Finance and thus
one of the heads of the whole Exhibition.

That was about as much as I knew about him. And that
he was David King's father.

The girl slipped her hand into her pocket and then began patting her own posterior, frantically.

I think it dawned on her then.

Whatever it was that had been there, it was something she wanted Hiram King to see.

From his sullen expression, I got the feeling he didn't want to see it.

My face was stuck against the window. I felt my nose start to bend. I wanted to hear what they were saying.

It was no good. They were very close to one another, keeping their voices down. Hiram King leveled a threatening index finger at them and shook his head. The girl's companion started pointing his own finger, which soon became part of a clenched fist.

I got up from my seat and made for the door.

Before I could throw it open, they made their move.

With a snarl of rage I could hear from inside, the unknown man grabbed Hiram King by the shoulders and tried to hurl him off the side of the car, into the valley thirty feet below.

Hiram King stumbed backward, careening off the edge.

I opened the door quick enough to hear his scream.

The train came to an abrupt halt that sent me sprawling.

As I slammed into the metal platform I felt my teeth bite down on my lip. I brushed the blood off with chafed fingertips.

The girl and her companion were scrambling over the side of the front steps. The man had already jumped to one of the lower rails. A cable attached there stretched to the ground below.

The girl had one leg over the metal railing when I shouted, "Don't move!"

She turned to face me, her eyes full of panic.

From below I heard someone shout, "Hattie!"

That was when I noticed the hands clinging to the lowest step, perched well over the rails and into the abyss.

Soon a bald head, gleaming with sweat, appeared over

the edge. I could hear Hiram King moaning with desperation as he struggled to pull himself up.

As the girl froze, watching me like a hunted animal, I saw King's fingers slowly peel away from the step. I could hear him grunting with terror as his hand lost its grip.

I lunged forward, my hand outstretched. King's hand let go as soon as I wrapped my own around his wrist. One of his gold cuff-links popped off and went sailing down.

I helped him get another hand onto the stairs and then began pulling him up. His boots scrambled in the open air as I tucked my arms under his and heaved. It felt like the veins would burst in my forehead. He was a little on the heavy side.

I got him about halfway up. Then he fell over the bottom step and onto the platform. With wheezing, painful breaths he drew his two inflexible legs over the side. He lay on his back, breathing frantically for about a minute. Everyone in the top compartment had his head craned out the tiny windows, shouting at me.

"They're getting away! Do something!"

But there was nothing I could do now. The Circassian Beauty or Hattie or whatever she called herself was about halfway down the cable by now, swinging from one hand to the other like a seasoned acrobat.

I peered over the railing and watched her go. My heart felt like it had jumped into my throat and was ready to explode. I wiped my eyes and didn't mind if the cuff got soiled.

There was a rivulet at the bottom of the valley that wound its way to the Schuylkill. A skiff waited for them on the banks, hidden by a pile of willow leaves. The man looked above, waiting for the girl to reach the ground. When they were both safe, they clambered into the skiff and began to paddle furiously for the Schuylkill. Soon they were lost beneath the canopy of trees.

I walked over to Hiram King, who was still flat on his back, breathing like an asthmatic.

Then I leaned over the side of the car, squeezing the metal railing as hard as I could.

Staring down into the valley, I tried to stop the pounding in my head by looking at the trees there. It didn't work. I tried looking at the clouds, watching their movement.

It was no good.

Something inside me was deeply disturbed. Not so much by Hiram King almost being killed. People killing and getting killed was something I was unfortunately accustomed to.

This time I was more upset about who had tried to do the killing.

I'd seen him when he looked up the ravine at the girl on the cables.

It had hurt me somehow to recognize the disheveled face of my young friend, Jesse Wilson.

9

WE RODE BACK to the grand plaza, Hiram King speechless the whole way. I asked him if he needed my help to get to where he was going next. I thought any questions I had about him and the Circassian Beauty and Jesse could wait until he got used to breathing again.

When we were let off in front of the Judges' Pavilion, King turned to me, smoothing down his tufts of white hair.

"What is your name, sir?"

I told him.

"I need not inform you that I am forever in your debt. I don't forget anyone who does me a favor. And saving my life is one hell of a favor."

King gained back some of his composure. He pulled a cheroot from his vest pocket and lit it with a quivering hand.

"May I ask how you are employed, Mr. McCleary?"

I thought on how many school-aged boys dreamed of this moment. Saving the big boss's life and then getting offered a job and maybe his buxom daughter's hand in marriage.

"Why are you smiling?" he asked me.

I shook my head and said, "I'm a detective."

"At the Centennial?"

"Yes."

"So you know Captain Heins of course."

I nodded.

"Well, let's go over to the station-house. I was supposed to meet him there anyway. Then I can let him know what you did for me. We'll see what that does for you."

"Thank you, but you don't have to trouble yourself."

"No, I insist," he said, sucking in his generous belly. "I want to help you in any way I can."

I let him take me to the station-house without another word. I knew what it felt like to be indebted to someone for your life. You felt a sort of awe and fear of them. They had had the power that you hadn't—the power to give you life. You wanted to pay them back quickly so you could forget what that powerlessness had felt like.

The guard at the entrance to the station-house saluted me when I showed him my star and deferentially escorted King and me into Cap's office.

Heins was seated at his large desk, the same one that had once been in City Hall. It was still covered with reports, receipts, and rosters, scattered chaotically across the blotter. He was just dipping his nib in the ink bottle when Hiram King cleared his throat.

Cap looked up and said, "Well, Mr. King, sir. I wasn't expecting you for another half an hour. And McCleary. Just who we wanted to see."

Hiram King drew back slightly and eyed me up and down as if seeing me for the first time.

"This is the man, Heins? The one you told me about?"

"Yes, that's him," Cap said, smiling at me with a proprietary air. "Don't worry, you can trust him implicitly."

Hiram King smiled and said, "Of that I have no doubt. You see, this man just saved my life."

His version of the story was interesting, to say the least.

"I was riding on the prismoidal railway when two ruffians, a male and a female, assaulted me on the platform. For the purpose of obtaining my billfold, I should think."

Heins sat up and waved us to the two armchairs before his desk.

"When I told them where they could take themselves, the ruffian flew into a rage and damn well threw me off the train. I came this close to breaking every bone in my body, especially my neck. Luckily I had managed to hold on to one of the steps at the front of the car. Mr. McCleary helped pull me up."

"You let the two of them get away, Mack?" Cap said reprovingly.

Hiram King defended me.

"He had no choice, Heins. It was either that or let me fall to my death. I'm satisfied with his judgment."

"No doubt, no doubt. Well, did you get a good look at these scamps?"

I cut in and said, "I did, sir. One was a woman employed at the Museum on Elm Avenue. She's the Circassian Beauty there. The other was a man named Jesse Wilson who tends the learned pig at Allen's Animal Show."

Cap beamed and said, "You see, Mr. King? What did I tell you? He's sharp, this boy."

King shifted his bulk from one side of his chair to the other. Then he looked into my eyes for a few moments and said, "Yes, he's certainly sharp."

"Just the man to look into this matter for us, I should think," Cap said.

"Indubitably," King replied. "You mind telling us how you got that information?"

I felt my palms getting damp.

"I've seen them in Shantyville during the past few nights. I know pretty much all the people who work along Elm Avenue."

They seemed satisfied with that for now.

"Did you, uh, bring the letter?" Heins asked.

King nodded, drawing it out from the pocket of his

striped waistcoat. He tossed it on the top of Heins's desk, then watched it as if it might start moving.

"Read it, McCleary," Heins told me.

I got up and sat on the edge of Cap's desk. I picked up the letter and started to read.

"Wait a minute," I said, looking at the words with surprise.

They weren't written by any human hand. That much was sure.

The letters were printed out in a perfect line across the paper.

Now I knew what that type-writer machine was good for.

"This was written on that machine . . ." I mumbled.

"Yes," Heins said. "The type-writing device in Machinery Hall. We've already questioned the man who operates it. He doesn't remember anyone handing him such a bizarre message."

"What about the operator himself? Could he have written it?" I asked.

"No," said Hiram King. "I've had him investigated already."

"How many people would know how to use this machine?"

"A handful. It's brand-new, being exhibited here for the first time. The operator's the only one who has access to it during the day."

"Someone else must have access to it too, then."

"Yes, that's something you're going to have to look into."

I nodded gravely, though I was ecstatic. This was, like Cap had said, something juicy.

The note said:

I've found you Hiram King. I will do to you what you tried doing to me. God damn you to

hell. "My eye shall not pity; it shall be life for
life."

B.F. (ha ha)

The anger seethed off the page. I wondered what King
had done to deserve it. He was a rich man, which told me
he was probably no saint.

"B.F.?" I said, dangling the letter across my knee.

Hiram King shrugged. "Haven't the slightest bloody
idea. Obviously he's some kind of madman."

"Maybe a former employee? What exactly is your line
of business, sir?"

"I owned part of the Philadelphia and Reading Railroad
for quite some time, till all that unpleasantness. Now I've
bought into a pharmaceutical firm here in the city."

"By the unpleasantness you mean the Molly Maguires?"

"Yes, damn them."

The Molly Maguires were by all accounts a band of
murderous Irish thugs who had subjected the respectable
owners of the Reading Railroad and various coal mines
to murder and mayhem for some years. Recently one of
Pinkerton's operatives had infiltrated their gang. A few of
them were waiting in the Carbon County Jail to be
hanged.

I'd read up on the subject a bit in the papers. From
what I understood, the Molly Maguires were doing what
they did because there was no other choice. They were
living the life of slaves, maybe worse. Forming a labor
union was a sure ticket to the penitentiary. So they'd decided to get what they wanted through violence. Unfortunately, it hadn't worked out for them.

"B.F.," I said to myself, getting up from the desk and
wandering about the room. Heins offered King a segar.
The two of them spat out their bits into the cuspidor and
began filling the room with blue smoke.

I was remembering the previous night.

Jesse Wilson had said something to me about working in the mines. That his life had been hell. That he'd been in a cage but was about to break out of it now.

I'd thought he was talking like a suicide. Now I had another point of view.

Walking over to a corner I bowed my head and silently chastised myself.

I'd spent the whole night wandering around Shantyville with this kid. The one who tried to kill Hiram King and who most likely had sent this letter. No doubt Jesse Wilson wasn't his real name. King hadn't reacted to it.

What bothered me the most was that I would never have expected that kid to do what he did. There had been such a tenderness in him, such vulnerability. I had to admit that my heart had gone out to him, that I'd wanted to help ease that pain that he didn't bother hiding.

How could I have been so wrong about a person? I wondered. I, the big detective, the shrewd judge of men's characters. Why had I let myself get flim-flammed like that?

Maybe he had a reason for hating Hiram King. It didn't matter much. The letter was one thing. Attempted murder was another.

I was going to find him, I had no doubt of that. He'd been a fool for confiding in me last night. Now I could use that information to track him down and put him back in that cage he was trying to break out of.

I was angry and looking forward to the job.

Most of the anger stemmed from feeling betrayed somehow.

I buried the sentiment and turned to King.

"You have any idea why a freak show beauty and a swineherd would want to kill you or your family?"

"I suspect, Mr. McCleary, that this is the work of the Mollies. I know their cowardly tactics. They're trying to scare me from testifying at their comrades' trials. They want those men free so they can keep fomenting revolution upstate. But I won't let them. No, sir! No matter what the cost I'll see that those villains get what's coming to them."

"Make no mistake, Mr. King," Cap said. "We aim to help you do just that. But we have to look after your safety here at the Centennial. Whoever this Wilson person is, he somehow got on the Grounds and used the typewriter for that letter. Then he mailed it from the Centennial Post Office. Now to-day he followed you to the prismoidal railway. He seems to know his way around here well enough."

I wanted to tell them how—that he'd worked on the construction crews here. But that would mean admitting that I'd met him. I wasn't sure I wanted to do that yet. Not before I thought things out some more.

David King and I had caught Jesse creeping into the Museum. He was meeting Hattie, the Circassian Beauty, there, no doubt. Probably to plan for this morning.

Then we'd surprised him. And he sprang at David, almost throttling him.

His explanation had seemed reasonable last night. This morning, I had a better one.

Jesse had recognized David King somehow. All the anger I'd felt coming off that page had focused on the son of this hated man.

The question was, did David recognize Jesse, whoever he was? It didn't look that way to me last night. But that wouldn't stop me from asking.

Maybe David might be able to tell me why two people would be so interested in seeing his father come to an unpleasant end.

"Does your family know about this letter, Mr. King?" I asked.

"I've told them about it. I thought it was best they should know. But they haven't had a look at it."

"I thought this might be like Mr. King says," Heins

said to me. "A threat to scare him off from the Molly Maguire trials coming up. But after this morning I think it's more than a threat. I think the maniac is just out for blood. And aims to get it. We're gonna have to be careful with this one, Mack."

Damn right I'm going to have to be careful, I thought.

I knew a whole lot of things that I wasn't supposed to.

I knew who Jesse was and knew that he'd assaulted David.

I knew that King hadn't been the victim of some Centennial garroters. He had met them there. They had brought something for him to see. At least they tried to bring it.

Hiram King had known them well enough. I wondered why he was lying about it now.

It might be interesting to hear what exactly he knew about this Jesse Wilson. It might help me explain the coincidence of Jesse being around when I'd discovered a dead girl. A murder that the big bugs were anxious to pull the wool over.

Jesse had picked up a token from the woods where the girl was killed. At first I hadn't thought much of it. But now I wanted very much to find that token. I thought maybe Jesse had a good reason for picking it up.

Perhaps the token didn't happen to just be lying there. Maybe he was trying to hide it by not trying to conceal it from me—making me think it wasn't important.

Had Jesse killed the girl? I wondered. Did he have the audacity to take me there and gloat while I examined the work of his hands?

If he had, Jesse would find I could quote Deuteronomy as well as he did. And I could put it into practice too.

10

THERE WAS A knock at the door.

Before Cap could say anything David King walked in, nodding at me with a smile.

Seeing Hiram King in the armchair beside me, David bowed to him and said, "Good morning, Father."

"Good morning, my boy."

From the doorway came a rustling sound. I turned my head and saw the woman there.

I tried not to stare.

"Mr. McCleary," David said to me. "I have the pleasure of presenting you to my sister, Miss King."

"How do you do, miss," I said and bowed slightly.

David's sister put a white-gloved hand on her skirt and did a graceful curtsy.

Her head was inclined so that her eyes did not meet mine. That would have been too forward for a lady like this.

From the way she walked and held herself and from her society manners, I knew she was a well-bred girl.

The excessive formality made me nervous. Lucky I hadn't held my hand out for a shake. She would've known I was low-class then.

Miss King was as stately a piece of femininity as any I'd ever seen. The clothing added to the overall effect.

Her walking costume was especially elegant—with a burgundy-colored polonaise over a white flannel bustle skirt, trimmed with velvet ribbon, bows, and buckles. A straw hat faced with velvet and beads and trimmed with hyacinth flowers perched over her intricately curled dark brown hair.

It was hard not to notice the effect of the corset on her already fine figure. I hoped she didn't see me blush.

She said, "Hello, Father," to the man beside me.

He said nothing, giving her a curt nod.

For a moment I saw her lips curve downward. Her eyes flashed in anger.

When I offered her my chair, she rustled her skirts over and sat down, nodding at me. She was all smiles again.

I was so taken with her that I didn't even notice the other fellow who followed her in.

The girl spoke to him without turning her head around.

"Bert, could you find somewhere to put my parasol?"

"Of course, Miss Elsie," the man said, moving past me.

I recognized him well enough. He was one of the other dozen detectives employed by the Centennial to keep a watch over the place.

His name was Pemberton Pierce. I'd never heard anyone call him Bert before. He wasn't the kind to encourage familiarity.

I'd worked with him a few times at the turnstiles. He had a sharp eye for pickpockets and had plenty of their mugs committed to memory. When I tried talking to him he merely grunted. I had to learn what I could from some of the boys at the barracks.

They told me Pierce had been an operative for the Big Man, the Pinkerton Agency. It was no secret that the Big Man was far more efficient, ruthless, and dependable than city police departments, much to our shame. Most banks would never have thought of relying on city coppers to protect their bags of greenbacks. Hiring Pinkerton detectives out of their own pocket ensured a modicum of loyalty and honesty.

The Big Man had money and resources that city police could never hope to have—with mouth-pieces and detectives in every state of the Union, all interconnected. It was a good organization. But the individuals were just as easily bought as coppers were. Except they made no secret of it. The Big Man owed its loyalty to whoever was paying him. Coppers were at least supposed to be honest.

Maybe that was just a lot of sour grapes. I envied the Big Man's operation, like any honest copper would. They were better at our job than most of us were.

It bothered me when I saw the boys fawning over Pierce, asking him all sorts of questions. They would've given their eye-teeth to work for the Big Man.

I had nothing against Pemberton Pierce myself. Especially since he wasn't working for the Big Man anymore. At least that's what I heard.

Apparently he'd been working for Mr. King back up in Carbon County for years, breaking strikes and policing the mines. When King had come down for the Centennial he'd brought Pierce with him, appointing him as one of the few detectives on the Grounds.

He'd made some good collars, from what I heard. But he gave himself airs around the boys. Made them feel small by reciting his exploits—the many guns he'd collared and the exotic places he'd traveled to.

Tad Schmoyer told me that he'd talked with Pierce one day while they were both at the magistrate's court on the Grounds. Tad had just tried for a little friendly conversation and happened to inadvertently mention me. He was proud of being my friend. I think it tickled Tad to know someone who'd been in the papers. Thankfully it didn't matter to him that I'd been lambasted in those same papers.

When Pierce heard my name spoken, Tad told me,

he snickered and said, "They oughtta put that cow out to pasture."

Tad had been a little offended and asked him to explain his remark.

Pierce said, "I read all about that McCleary. How he messed up the whole thing with the kidnapped boy. I think it's a disgrace. But what can you expect from a city copper, huh? Now, if I'd been on the job . . ."

Naturally that bit of intelligence hadn't warmed me up to Pierce.

It was kind of gratifying now to watch him fawn over Miss King.

When she asked for him to take her parasol, he dashed across the room and took it in his hands like it was a newborn babe.

Miss King probably had a notion that his interest in her was more than passing. But she pretended not to notice.

I wondered if she was interested in him. I suppose Pierce was handsome in a gruff sort of way. He was a bit older than I was, slightly taller, and less muscled. His angular, clean-shaven face could have appealed to the fairer sex.

"McCleary."

David was speaking to me but I hadn't been paying attention.

I raised my eyebrows and said, "I'm sorry, David."

"Quite all right, my dear fellow. When we're through with this interview I should like to show you the article I wrote for the evening edition. I'll think you'll be impressed."

"By all means."

"Now, Father, will you tell us why you brought us all here?"

Heins said, "That's okay, Mr. King. I'll tell them."

Cap told the three of them about what had happened on the prismoidal railway that morning.

"My God, Father! You could've been killed! McCleary, I do believe you're a hero."

David smiled and clapped me on the back.

Miss King clasped my hand in hers and said, "You have our most profound gratitude, sir."

Pemberton Pierce was trying hard not to fume at me. I gave him a little wink.

"The ordeal has only just begun, I'm afraid," Cap told them. "Your father informed you of the letter. We think it might be the work of some Irish terrorists from upstate. McCleary spotted the two who tried to kill your father this morning. What did you say their names were, Mack?"

I repeated their names and occupations. There was no reaction from the King siblings. Pierce said, "I'll go have a look at the Museum and the Animal Show. Maybe they were fool enough to crawl back to their holes."

He was acting very gallantly. Miss King didn't look in the mood to swoon, however.

"I don't understand," she said. "Why would anyone want to kill *you*, Father?"

Then, surprisingly, she began to laugh.

It was more like a cackle. For a moment her genteel facade dissolved and something wild and a little frightening stood in its place.

"Mind your tongue, Elsie!" Hiram King said, nearly drawing himself out of his chair.

To the room he said, "My apologies to you, gentlemen. My daughter is of fragile health. This business with the letter has, I fear, played havoc with her nerves. Isn't that right, Elsie?"

The girl, still chuckling, said, "Perhaps you wish me to *convalesce*?"

She made the word sound obscene.

David, rubbing his hands together and smiling with embarrassment, said, "How about a stroll, eh, Elsie? With our fine detective here. Would that make you feel better?"

Suddenly the girl was quite eager. "Oh, Davy, could I?

You know I haven't seen the Japanese House yet."

There was a childish tone to her voice now. Her beauty, so statuesque at first, now seemed vulnerable.

"Father, do you mind?" David asked.

Hiram King shook his head.

"Well then!" David said. "That's all arranged. Can we meet in a few hours at the newspaper building, McCleary? So I can read you my story?"

"Sure thing, David."

Miss King was out of her chair. Before I turned to leave I said to Cap, "Instructions?"

"You take Miss King for now, McCleary. You've earned a little relaxation time. After that I want you to help Pierce here look for traces of those two in Shantyville."

"That won't be necessary, Captain," Pierce said. "I'll handle that myself."

Heins bristled for a moment. He'd never liked insubordination.

He was about to open his mouth when Hiram King said, "It's all right, Heins. I trust Pemberton to do a thorough job. Perhaps Mr. McCleary could be employed elsewhere."

"Doing what?" I asked.

"Making sure my daughter is safe."

"Why, Father. I'm shocked at your depth of affection."

Hiram King narrowed his eyes at her. That look had a mighty sharp edge to it.

"If that is all right with you, Heins."

It was a statement, not a question.

"Well," Cap said, "I agree your daughter needs protection. What about David, here?"

"I think Pemberton can keep an eye on him when he's through across the street. How about it, Bert?"

Miss King had gotten out of her chair. She was looking at me expectantly.

I took the parasol from Pierce's begrudging hand.

"Enjoy it while it lasts, Mack," Heins told me. "When you're through with your promenade I want you to take Miss King back to wherever she's staying and we'll put a guard at the door."

"And then what?"

"Go over to Shantyville and see what the Big Man missed."

Pierce took a threatening step forward.

Heins ignored him. He got up from behind his desk, stood right in front of me, and said, "See what you can do with this. I'm hoping it'll be enough to make everybody forget about what happened with the kid."

I nodded grimly and helped Miss King out the door.

11

RIGHT OUTSIDE THE entrance to the station-house was a Centennial rolling chair. Many visitors hired them with or without a uniformed attendant to do the pushing. For sixty cents an hour, the chairs were a little dear, but many preferred to pay rather than walk here and there over the two hundred and thirty-six acres of grounds.

Miss King sat herself on the rattan-backed iron chair as I took my position behind the two large rear wheels.

With a push I started us off. As we rounded the bend at the Centennial Medical Office, I asked her, annoyed at my awkwardness, how much she'd had a chance to see of the Centennial.

"Blessed little."

I couldn't see her face but she sounded frustrated.

"Don't you, uh, have anyone to escort you during the day? What about your brother?"

"My brother?" she snorted. "He's much too busy for me. Quite like our father."

"Seems funny that he would work so hard when your father has so much . . . I mean . . ."

"So much money?" she said, understanding me to my embarrassment. "It was father's wish that he get some sort of employment. And David has always held a fascination with policemen and police work."

She turned her delicate head around and said, "He speaks quite highly of you, sir."

"I'm honored."

"He said you were very . . . real. Those were his words."

"Real?" I thought about that for a moment. "I'm not sure what that means."

"Oh, that you're the genuine article—not a pompous buffoon like Bert."

"I got the feeling he was rather close to you."

"He's impertinent. But I can't get rid of him. Father has seen to that. Whenever I take some air Bert has to follow me about, like a lovelorn cur."

I laughed and said, "He seems very devoted to you and your family."

"Bert? Devoted? To our money. Certainly not to us. Father's had him around forever. Since the war. Were you in the war, Mr. McCleary?"

"I was, miss."

"Call me, Elsie. People I like never call me that."

"All right, Elsie."

"I like you, by the way."

I lowered my head.

"I mean," she said, "I like what I've heard about you."

"What have you heard?" I asked.

I noticed that I was wheeling her chair very, very slowly. The Japanese Bazaar was only a hundred rods away. I wasn't in a hurry to get there.

"That you're very courageous. Father found that out this morning, didn't he? David told me about the fight you stopped in that vile place the two of you visited."

"He told you about that, did he?"

"Oh, David tells me a lot of things. I know more about David than he knows about himself."

"Well, he's a fine young man."

"He is now."

"I guess the trip abroad did him some good. Got his wild oats sown."

"David hasn't ever gone abroad, Mr. McCleary."

I wheeled her over to the side of the asphalted road and sat myself on a bench there.

Facing her, I said, "Your brother told me he'd been abroad right before he came to the city."

Elsie fingered her parasol nervously.

"I've blundered!" she said, raising a gloved hand to her lips. "That was a secret father didn't want me to tell."

"Did something happen to David?"

"He went away—to the country—for his health."

The words were chosen carefully.

"Is David a consumptive?" I asked her.

It might explain his leaness, pallid skin, and glazed eyes.

"Father wouldn't want me to talk about it."

She seemed to like that idea.

I waited for her to say more. I had the feeling I was getting in the middle of a domestic quarrel that I had no business in.

Obviously Elsie had some kind of score to settle with her old man. Hiram King had treated her with undisguised contempt in Heins's office. I saw how much it had hurt her. I'd heard the hatred lingering behind her sarcastic remarks to him.

But I didn't like the idea of her using David to get back at her father.

If he had consumption, that was his own affair.

"Can I trust you, Mr. McCleary?"

Elsie looked straight at me for the first time. Her demure expression altered suddenly, becoming fierce and intense.

In the station-house she had seemed so aloof, so lady-like. Now she was being especially forward and blunt with me. The switch in personality was abrupt. Her voice had a frantic pitch to it. There was something about the way she was looking at me that made me think she might be a little mad.

For an instant I wondered if Elsie might not have written the death threat to her father. Just to watch him squirm.

But that would make no sense. Jesse Wilson and Hattie had acted on their own. And they were not the types to make the acquaintance of a society belle like Elsie.

To calm her down, I said, "Of course you can trust me, Elsie."

"I think—no—I know that they both detest me. So much so that they might want me dead. Yes, I think they might very well wish me dead."

Ah, I said to myself. So this is how it is with her.

"Who?" I said to humor the poor soul.

But she didn't answer my question, as if she hadn't even heard it.

"They tried to kill me once. I knew too much. But I lived. If you can call this living."

It seemed especially sad to me that so comely a girl was so far gone.

"What are you saying, Elsie? You're young and very beautiful and I should think you've got a lot to live for."

It was futile, I knew, to try to reason with someone like her. That didn't stop me from trying.

"Young? I'm a hundred thousand centuries old."

I laughed and said, "You look like you're not a day over twenty."

"Twenty-six. But that doesn't matter. They took my life a long time ago and buried it in some secret place. And I've never been able to find it since."

"Maybe you're just looking in the wrong place. Maybe there are others who could help you find it."

I noticed she was weeping. With a nervous hand I dug into my pocket and pulled out a handkerchief, holding it to her nose.

She blew into it and shook her head. Then she gave me

a startled look, like she was seeing me for the first time.

"You must think I'm quite mad."

"No, of course not," I lied.

"I wouldn't have told you about them except I heard David talking about you and I thought you might understand me."

She put her hand on mine, her brow furrowed. With her lips pursed in consolation, she said, "He told me what happened with the boy. That it was your fault he was never found."

I let her hand stay where it was. Suddenly it was easy to overlook her madness.

But I had no wish to discuss Eddie Munroe.

Elsie persisted.

"I think you must've tried very hard to solve that case."

"Can I tell you a secret, Elsie? Will you promise not to tell?"

She nodded eagerly.

"I *did* solve that case. But no one can ever know that. Do you understand?"

It felt so good to admit that to someone.

"It's a secret that has to stay a secret."

"But it hurt you, hurt your reputation."

"Yes, it did."

I chewed on my lip and felt the back of my throat getting hoarse.

"But," I said, "if I can help your family that old stuff might not matter anymore."

"We have our secrets, too, Mr. McCleary. Everybody does."

"What does that mean, Elsie?"

"It means that I know how you must feel, having the past like a chain around you. Like a dark hole you're thrown into, a prison that you can't escape from."

"Is that how you think I feel?"

The girl shrugged and said, "That's how *I* feel. I've

been in the prison so long I wouldn't know what the outside world looks like.".

"Now, now, no more of that," I said with a grimace. I wiped her tears off and said, "Why don't we go see some of the outside world right now, okay? The Bazaar is just down the corner here."

I needed some time to let things cool down. In spite of myself, I found that I was seriously thinking on what she'd told me. Some of the things she told me were truly disturbing but I couldn't tell if they were realities or phantasms.

But when a beautiful girl told you someone was trying to kill her, you paid attention, no matter how mad she appeared to be.

I thought Elsie King might indeed know some dangerous things.

As I wheeled her to the Bazaar I was forming questions in my mind.

We reached our destination and stepped into another world and another time.

Inside the enclosure we found ourselves in a Japanese garden. A large crowd was gathered there, as usual.

"So many people, Mr. McCleary," Elsie said as I parked the rolling-chair and helped her to her feet.

"There always are," I said. "People can't seem to get enough of the Japanese."

Which was hardly surprising, for their exhibits were far and away the most novel at the Centennial.

Many of the people, including myself, had never seen a Japanese person before they arrived to construct their buildings.

There were plenty of Japanese here now, scurrying about inside in their native costumes. Elsie viewed them with delight.

"They're so tiny! And look, their robes are so colorful, so gay!"

I smiled, enjoying the wondrous look on her face.

We took a walk around the building, admiring its design.

"I've never seen anything like it," Elsie said. "It has no doors."

"No, just those moveable panels on the sides."

"What are they made out of? They look so thin!"

"Paper of some kind, I imagine."

She shook her head. "That wouldn't do for this climate."

"No," I said. "Neither would all that carved unpainted wood. The humidity wouldn't be kind to it. But it's a pretty piece of work just the same."

"Those tiles on the roof, there's some sort of design on them."

"Yes," I said, trailing off, suddenly remembering the needle in my pocket.

Elsie and I stepped into the building and perused the items on display. Like most of the other exhibits at the Centennial, these goods were for sale.

She drew me over to a painted screen with some scarlet cranes and purple iris flowers on it. The background was a flowery jungle, half enshrouded in mist. Another drawing nearby showed a few houses and trees beside water that vanished into hazy scenery like an opium dream.

"Look how the landscape hardly has any color," Elsie said, fascinated. "But it's not black or white. More like veiled moonlight without shadows."

The girl inhaled and said, "Ah, it's so pretty. The wandering airs they faint on the dark, the silent stream. The champak odors fall like sweet thoughts in a dream."

"Is that poetry?"

"Yes, these beautiful things make me feel poetic. It's been a long time since I've seen something beautiful enough to think of verse."

Her head tilted forward, the hyacinths on her hat quivering.

She said, "Music, when soft voices die, vibrates in the memory."

I felt I was losing her again but she raised her head, looking at the Japanese screens, and said, "These make everything else at the Centennial look vulgar."

There were many others who shared her opinion. Perhaps they liked Japanese art because it was so different from our own. Delicate, understated, and somehow timeless.

Elsie bought one of the screens and a fan, which she began using as soon as we exited the Bazaar.

"Thank you so much, Mr. McCleary. My whole soul feels refreshed now."

"I'm glad to hear it," I said, giving her a gentle smile.

I wheeled her back to the Judges' Pavilion, where she would meet her father.

Before I let her go, I said, "Elsie? What you were saying earlier? About being in danger . . ."

The fan started fluttering in front of her face.

She waited for me to say more.

"You don't have any idea who might be writing those letters, do you?"

The girl shook her head, giving me a blank stare.

"Your father said he hadn't shown you the letter, just told you about it, right?"

"That's correct."

"So you've never heard of B.F.?"

"I don't understand."

"B.F.," I repeated. "The letter writer printed his initials at the end. Do you know anyone with those initials?"

I watched her eyes dart back and forth, as if she were reading pages inside her head.

Then the fan came in front of her face. She said, "I don't feel too well, Mr. McCleary, you'll have to excuse me."

I'd seen her face behind the fan. There'd been a look of recognition there.

Before she could turn away from me, I gave her arm a tug.

She didn't look offended, just surprised. I pulled her away from the entrance to the shade of a nearby oak.

"Listen to me carefully, Elsie. If you know anything I want you to tell me. Remember the information that you thought someone might want to kill you for? Well, you can tell me about it. You can trust me, right? Remember you asked me and I said you could trust me."

Listening to myself, I thought I sounded like a mother instructing an infant. It was the only way I could keep the insistence out of my voice.

"I don't know what you're talking about. I say queer things sometimes. But nobody ever listens. They don't mean anything anyway."

"Look, Elsie. I don't know what kind of game you're playing. But I can tell you this. Someone is out to kill your father and probably you and your brother. I saw this person."

She was wavering. I thought I might get her to talk if I threw her something in return.

Hesitating, I finally said, "I saw him last night."

"Who?"

"The man who pushed your father off the train! I met that same man last night in Shantyville. He told me his name was Jesse . . ."

"Jesse," she said softly. Her eyelids started to flutter. It looked like she was going to faint. I wasn't sure if she was faking it or not but I eased her down to the ground.

"Do you know him, Elsie? Who is he? How do you know him?"

Covering her ears, she began to shake her head, violently.

"No," she said. "It's not possible."

"What isn't? Elsie, you have to tell me what you know. It could save your life."

Then, before I even knew what I was saying, I blurted out, "One girl is dead already."

Right after I'd said it I wanted to kick myself.

Elsie jumped on it right away.

"What do you mean, a girl is dead?"

Her gloved fingers dug deep into my arm and squeezed with a surprising strength.

We stared at each other silently, our breaths labored now.

With a sigh, I said, "This man Jesse and I found a dead girl in Shantyville. Nobody knows about it, but I think she might've been killed by this Jesse person. The same man who tried to kill your father."

I was surprised by her next question.

"What did the killer do to her body?"

The memory made me flinch. Before I could try to evade the question she said, "Stabbed her? Many times. And then . . . cut her throat. Am I right?"

Her voice was suddenly lifeless.

Now I was the one who felt faint. I asked her how she knew that.

Elsie began to shake her head. She stood up, her fists clenched.

"No, I don't believe you. You're a liar, Mr. McCleary. Father put you up to this, didn't he? To drive me mad? Isn't that right? Wouldn't you all like to see me go mad? Wouldn't that make things so much easier! Damn you all!"

The girl dashed away from me.

I got up off the ground and tried to pull her back.

"Take your hands off me!" she cried. "Right now! Or I'll scream so loud the whole fair will hear!"

She was already loud enough to attract the attention of several visitors, who grimaced at the spectacle.

It was the kind of attention I didn't especially need.

"I'm not trying to drive you mad, Elsie," I said calmly. "I only want to help you. I want to keep you safe."

Still shaking her head, she picked up her skirt and ran up the stairs to the Pavilion. The sound of her weeping trailed after her.

I didn't mind letting her go. This was not the time or the place to give Elsie King a thorough sweating. I could bide my time.

But sooner or later I would have to make her talk.

I was looking forward to that.

Turning away from the Pavilion, I took the needle out of my pocket. It was time to find out what this thing was and where it came from.

Tad Schmoyer was on duty at the Art Gallery. I decided to find him there and have him help me out. He'd relish the chance to do some real police work.

At first I was merely walking toward Memorial Hall. Then, as I began to think, I started running, the air stinging as I sucked it in.

I thought on Jesse and the talk we'd had, how much I'd taken to the boy.

And what he'd done to the girl.

What he might do to Elsie King.

I thought on Jesse and despised myself. Because I didn't want to believe what was staring me in the face. I wanted to deny it like Elsie had, but for different reasons—because I'd liked talking to the kid, because I pitied him. Because he reminded me of me.

I picked up my pace until I was breathing in groans, my feet pounding the asphalt, my teeth gritted with rage.

12

THE ART GALLERY, Memorial Hall, was across the Avenue of the Republic from Main. Gigantic bronze horses held in check by metallic amazons guarded the entrance. Off to one side was a large statue representing the Navy. On the other was one of a lioness in her death throes, defending her cubs. What the two had to do with each other was anyone's guess.

Memorial Hall itself was one of the fancier buildings, made of granite with a roof of iron and glass to let the natural light in on the paintings and sculpture. There were plenty of arches and columns. The guidebooks called it the modern Renaissance style.

Its dome was quite magnificent, rising one hundred fifty feet above the ground and topped by a large ball supporting a figure of Columbia. That statue was usually the first thing I saw as I came across the Schuylkill to the Exhibition.

I walked through the iron doors bearing the coats of arms of all the states in the Union. Once inside I began searching for Tad. He wasn't in the south vestibule, with its colossal, disproportionate bust of George Washington. There were plenty of other people milling about though. This building got the most visitors except for the Japanese Bazaar.

107

He wasn't in the central hall either. Crossing right beneath the dome, I passed the patriotic statuary without a glance.

From there I began searching the narrow galleries, the purple wainscoted walls covered with thousands of paintings.

I tried the American wing first. Most of our country's great artists had at least one canvas on display. You could barely see Albert Bierstadt's paintings, there were so many people crowding in front of them. By accident, I stepped on a young lady's skirt. This was a common problem for women in crowds, since their dresses reached to the ground and trailed behind them like coronation robes. I tipped my hat in apology and caught a smile for my efforts.

Finally I made it to the hall where Rothermel's *Battle of Gettysburg* was hung.

It was a gigantic canvas, taking up practically the whole wall.

The scene was Pickett's Charge, and the Union was making mincemeat out of the Rebels. I bet it made our Southern friends' blood boil. I hoped it might.

For a few moments I stayed where I was and surveyed the gory spectacle.

Looking at the men gesturing majestically as the balls struck them, I wondered how my life might have changed if I'd been atop that ridge. Perhaps if I'd made it through the second day I might've been killed on the third. Perhaps I would've lost a leg or an arm or been blinded.

There were times when I wished that I might have been killed and spared the horrors I went through at Belle Isle and Andersonville.

But the Almighty had other plans for me. As I stood there I offered a prayer for those fallen men and for the boy who had fallen there—the old self of mine, lost on a field dyed with blood and sown with death.

I nearly jumped when someone said behind me, "Hiya Mack."

I whirled around suddenly and saw it was Tad Schmoyer.

"Didn't mean to startle you," he said, laughing. "What brings you over here?"

"I was looking for you," I said.

"Been here all day. Don't mind Memorial Hall. Kinda interesting. All the pictures, I mean. Gives your brain somethin' to do instead of just standing around."

"Where're you guarding to-day?"

"I'm down in Italian Sculpture," he said, trying to keep his expression solemn.

"That must be very nice for you," I said, smiling. "A good view down there."

"Well, I'll allow that." Tad broke into a wide smile. "And it's educational too."

"If you're studying female anatomy. I take it you've also studied our home-grown work as well."

"You mean that *Premier Pose* by Roberts? Sure have!"

That was the statue that got the most attention in the Hall. It showed a woman shrinking from exposing herself in the studio of an artist. Her efforts at protecting her modesty were, much to our delight, slightly halfhearted.

"But I wonder," he said to me gravely, "what's the difference between one of them artistic nudes and the statues of women in their underthings you see in saloons?"

"Well, this stuff's art."

"Ain't those naughty-looking saloon things art too?"

I shook my head. "If a nude's in an art gallery or in a swell's house it's art. If it's in a saloon it's indecent. Get it?"

"No."

"I don't either," I said, laughing.

Tad looked over my shoulder and suddenly shouted, "Hey you!"

I turned to see a man pointing at one of the paintings with his cane.

Tad strode over to him and said, "What's the matter with you? Can't you read?"

He pointed to a sign at the bottom of the painting that said, "Do Not Touch with Canes or Umbrellas."

"No," the old man said, probably meaning it.

"I see," Tad said. "Well, just look at 'em, don't poke 'em. Understand?"

We walked back to the Gettysburg painting, Tad muttering about people not being able to keep their hands to themselves.

"You take this pretty seriously, don't you?"

"Why not? It's all I do all day. Gets kinda boring standing around."

"Believe me, I know."

"At least here there's some scenery to take in."

"The statues?"

"No, the live ones. I play a game by myself sometimes but it's better with another fella. Whenever a gal comes into the room we try to claim her first, if she's handsome. You know, like that one over there?"

He gestured to an attractive young girl reading a guidebook.

"I say, 'Claim her.' And each gal gives you one point. Now, when it's just me I sort of rate them to myself, on a scale of one to five. And I try to make a certain amount of points by the end of the day."

"That gal over there looks like she's chewing the cud."

"Oh, that's just that chewing gum stuff. It's a big fad now."

"Looks mighty unseemly for a gal to be workin' her jaws like that. I'd have to make her rating pretty low."

"I ain't that picky."

I shook my head sadly.

"My boy, you are in some dire straits."

Tad began to chuckle.

"It is kinda silly, ain't it?"

"Yes. The work of a mind nearly burned out by boredom. Listen, Tad. How would you like to do something real? Get your hands dirty?"

"Sure thing!" he said eagerly. "Are we gonna do some detective work?"

"That's right. I need you to help me collar a file."

"A file?"

"What kind of copper are you, Tad?" I said with mock reproval. "A buzzer, a file, a dip. A pickpocket, I mean."

"Is that all? We're just gonna collar him?"

"Not all. First we have to find him. But there's more."

"Tell me."

I sighed and looked into his youthful, earnest face.

I found myself repeating the question Elsie had asked me.

"Can I trust you, Tad?"

He looked almost hurt.

"Of course you can, Mack! When haven't I been square with you?"

"I need your help on something big. Remember how late I got in last night?"

Tad nodded.

I told him why I'd been late.

"How come we haven't heard anything about this?" he said, indignant.

"Because somebody wants it kept quiet. Remember what I told you about the copper's credo? See no evil, hear no evil. Shantyville has to look respectable. It's making plenty of money and has to keep on making money."

"But I thought you said somebody was running it through?"

"Oh, sure, Tad. Running it through to the wastepaper basket. I'm the only one who aims to do anything about it. So what do you think? Will you help me?"

The boy was wavering. It was quite a risk to take.

I understood his hesitation. There was no guarantee that

we would profit from our investigation. Quite the contrary. If I went poking my head into the wrong places I could lose my job. And Tad might lose any chance he had of getting one.

I thought it might help if I went into the details of the killing. Tad was a part of the younger generation. The wholesale carnage of war hadn't inured him to the ugliness of murder.

"Now wouldn't you like to help me find the bastard who did that?"

The boy stiffened his upper lip and nodded. With a satisfied grin I slapped him on the back.

Then I pulled the needle out of my pocket.

"You want me to darn your stockings too?" Tad asked.

"I pulled this out of her neck."

He winced.

"See those markings on the top there? Looks kinda Japanese. I think maybe we should go to the Bazaar and see if those fellows have seen this before."

"Can I see that for a second?" Tad asked.

I handed him the needle, which he accepted gingerly.

Shifting around till he was directly beneath a skylight, Tad held the needle up to his squinting eyes.

"Mack, I've guarded practically every part of this Centennial. Been to all the exhibits in Main, plenty of times. Seen all the countries. And from what I seen of Japan this don't look Japan-made."

Before I could call his expertise into question, Tad said, "But these here designs—they look more like letters to me. Chinese letters. I seen 'em all over China's exhibit."

I held out my hand for the needle and looked at the designs myself. Maybe he was right, maybe they were letters.

"Why don't we go see, Tad? You know any of them Celestials?"

"I know one who works at the Chinese Court at Main."

"Good. Let's go."

"Uh, Mack. Wait a minute. I can't just leave my post, you know."

"Sure you can. Plenty of guards around to keep the umbrellas off the paintings. I'll square it with your captain. What's his name?"

"Mulford."

"Oh yes, you were telling me about him."

"He's a son of a bitch, Mack. Pardon my language."

"Well, if you don't feel right . . ."

"Of course I do! It's just that Mulford has it in for some of us. He's a real tyrant. Makes us go with him to dinner on Elm Avenue at this shanty that his second cousin owns. The food is godawful, Mack, I tell you. But if we don't eat our dinner there he threatens us, says he'll give us the boot. Can he do that?"

"Maybe. If Colonel Clay doesn't look into it."

"Ha! The Chief of the Guard? We're the last thing he wants to bother with."

"Well, don't worry about Mulford. I'll make sure Heins straightens him out."

Tad nodded reluctantly and followed me out of Memorial Hall.

Crossing the Avenue of the Republic, we walked by the gigantic soldier statue in front of Main and into the cavernous interior.

One of the two enormous organs on either end of the hall was piping away. It sounded like Bach but I wasn't sure. We came in at the tail end of it. There was a great deal of applause, the echo of which thundered from rafter to rafter.

I'd been in Main plenty of times but I still got lost. That was easy to do in the largest building in the world, with a total area of twenty-one and a half acres.

There was so much to see here, so many things. It was like every object in the world had been collected and placed in beautifully carved showcases each more fanciful than the last.

We walked past line after line of showcases displaying books, Yale locks, postage stamps, floor cloths, silk goods, cutlery, porcelain, pig-metals, watches, breech-loading guns, fire-proof safes, mechanical toys, ready-made clothing, telegraph apparatus, needles, fruit stands, glassware, a peacock feather made of six hundred diamonds by a man named Tiffany, sugar-coated pills, perfumes, folding beds, and piano-fortes.

That was just the American section.

The temptation to stop and gape was overpowering. We hastily made our way to the Chinese Court at the end of the aisle.

It was by far the gaudiest exhibit in the Hall.

Tad told me the portal over the entrance was from something called a pagoda. Besides the queer carving and garish paints there were four ugly dragons on top, curled up like sidewinders.

There were more joss-houses like this scattered all over the exhibit, ornamented with the most brilliant colors. All the showcases were done in the Chinese style, as gay and odd as the pagodas.

Tad and I weaved our way through displays of silks, gold cloth, embroideries, inlaid tables, and of course plenty of China ware, all of excellent quality.

Next to a group of vases that reached up to my midsection were some fine porcelain tiles with Chinese monsters on them. There were coins there as well with writing on them that I now realized was much like the scratches on the top of my needle.

Stepping carefully through the heaps of cotton prints, stockings, Chinese shoes, hats, trunks, toilet boxes, native paper, and the like, Tad finally came upon his friend.

Like the other Chinamen at the Centennial, this one was in his native garb—knickers like the kind Washington wore, with those soft black Chinese shoes, and a loose-sleeved waist that could've passed for a large child's pyjamas. On his shaved head a little cap was perched, a pig-tail dangling behind it.

He was showing a vase off to a lady ensconced in a rolling-chair. She held tinted pince-nez to her wizened face and pursed her lips in concentration.

Tad called out to him, "Hiya George!"

The Chinaman scanned the crowd with his almond eyes. Finding Tad, he smiled and said, "Hello, Mr. Schmoyer."

Handing the vase to one of his comrades, the Celestial bowed to Schmoyer, who laughed and shook his hand.

"This here is George, Mack."

I bowed to the man like he had done to me and said hello.

George struck me as an odd name for a Chinaman to have. I said so.

"Nobody say my name too good," George said. "So when I come here I think of name Americans know how say. And I see your George Washington everywhere. So I think George good name."

I said that it certainly was and complimented him on his English.

"Oh I speak lot of English. Live here, live there, meet many people."

"George told me he worked out west on the railroads for a few years."

"Well, how do you like the eastern part of America?" I asked him.

"Like it very much! Very nice place, friendly people."

He was smiling the whole time and so were we. It was queer to talk with a man from the other side of the world. For many of us at the Centennial, this was the first and only time we would ever get that chance.

But the novelty wore off when I thought on the business we needed to take care of.

"George," I said, "I'm a policeman like Tad. He told

me you might be able to help us identify this article. I'd appreciate any help you can give us."

I took the needle out of my pocket and handed it to George.

The Chinaman examined it for only a few seconds. Then with a scowl he said, "Not know what this is."

"Wait a minute," I said to him. "Maybe if you looked at it carefully. See there's some kinda writing on top. A few letters. That mean anything in Chinese?"

"Not know."

The man looked inexplicably embarrassed.

"C'mon, George," Tad said. "You can't tell me that ain't Chinese."

"That not language I speak at home. From other part of country."

George hastily handed back the needle and said, "Must go now, so sorry."

I let Tad grab him by the arm and drag him behind a nearby pagoda.

"What's your hurry, George?" I said to him, pushing my face into his.

He looked frightened now.

"Know nothing, please. Not want trouble."

"Trouble?" I said, looking at Tad with a mock expression of surprise. "Who said anything about trouble?"

I rested my arm on his slumped shoulder, my hand drawing around the back of his neck.

I applied some pressure.

Tad grinned and said, "You're not bein' square with us, George. I thought we were friends."

"Sure," the man said, desperately grinning. "We friends. Good friends. Yes, yes."

"Friends don't lie to each other. You know what that word means? Lie?"

"Not know what you want," George whispered.

I pointed my finger and inch from his face and said, "I

want you to tell us what this needle is and where it came from. Don't give us any more trouble. Or we'll give it right back."

He shook his head and said, "Not want no trouble for anybody."

His next words came out in a snort. "I see police in California, I see police on railroad. They all the same. Like rest of people. They make trouble for us, always."

"Look," I said, "I'm not trying to make trouble for you Chinamen here. All I'm concerned with is this needle. But I will make trouble for this Chinaman right in front of me if he doesn't help me out. And if he does help me then I'll help him whenever I can. Because friends do favors for each other and I'd kinda like to think of you as my friend."

I'd released my grip by that time and withdrew from him.

It took him some time to think about it.

"You promise you not make trouble if I tell you?"

"If I can help it. Now what is this damn thing?"

George sighed and said, "That yen-nock."

"What?" I said, not understanding it.

"Yen-nock," George said slowly and a little loudly, as if the louder he spoke the easier it would be for me to understand.

"What's that mean?"

"Use it make afuyong."

He made his arm rigid, held his hand cupped and sucked in his breath.

"You know what he's talking about, Mack?"

I was about to shake my head when suddenly I remembered something from the previous night.

A scene at the Oriental Saloon.

"You mean opium, George?" I said.

"Afuyong," George said, nodding his head enthusiastically. "Yen-nock take chan du, put on fire then into pipe. Then he go puff puff."

"Chan du?"

George held his thumb and forefinger together.

"Look like mouse shit."

My memory of the Oriental Saloon wasn't too clear. There had been a lot of smoke and I wasn't too interested in the goings-on. But I remembered the tiny opium pills that the boy servants carried around with them on trays.

I was beginning to understand why George had been so reluctant to tell us what the yen-nock was. He had been protecting his Chinese brethren, the seedier ones who patronized the opium den. I didn't know why he would care for the likes of them. Perhaps it wasn't for them at all that he feared. He knew, as I did, how easily the actions of a few could taint—and hurt—a great many. Especially when people were looking for the slightest excuse to despise you.

"No hurt you, little smoke," he said apologetically.

"I don't know about opium, George. But this—yen-nock—hurt somebody. Does it look familiar at all? Belong to a friend of yours?"

George pointed to tiny scratches in the tip.

"These letters," he said. "I never see yen-nock like this. Made of silver, see?"

"What about the letters?" I said. "That spell somebody's name?"

"No name. Just sounds. Like two letters. One say like your B. The other say like your F."

"B.F.?"

My voice was slightly tremulous.

George nodded, smiling again. He saw the change in my expression.

I put my hand on his shoulder and said, "Sorry if I upset you, George. Let's get out of here, Tad."

My companion thanked George and we parted good friends.

I walked under the four dragons at the entrance and

stared up at them. They flashed their nasty teeth and tongues at me. I grimaced back.

"B.F.?" Tad said. "What does that mean, Mack?"

"It means I have a chance to make up for letting a killer go. Have you ever seen a pig do arithmetic?"

13

MY FRIEND PLIED me with questions the whole way to
Elm Avenue. I answered him the best I could. So much
for what Heins called my discretion.

It was a great relief to be able to confide in someone
else what I was thinking. So often I tended to work things
out for myself, resenting anyone's intrusion. This time
was different. There was something personal about it.

When Tad asked me why I hadn't suspected Jesse Wilson of anything, all I could answer was, "Because I liked
the kid."

I wasn't sure why I had liked him. Worse, I realized
that I still did, and that it bothered me a great deal that I
was going to have to put the pinch on him.

I found myself hoping that this B.F. and Jesse were not
the same person, though I knew that was a stretch. It was
pretty clear that the one who sent Hiram King that death
threat was also the person who'd killed the young girl in
Shantyville.

Was it possible that Jesse had a completely different
dispute with King, unrelated to the poison pen letter?

Sure, I thought. That's possible. It's also possible that
women will get to vote someday.

But not too likely.

One person sending you death threats and another one

120

trying to throw you off trains was too much rancor for one person to bear.

So what was the connection between Hiram King and this dead girl?

I had a feeling that answer was waiting for me in Shantyville.

That Bert Pierce had already surveyed the place was no account to me.

I wanted the chance to ask my own questions.

The Animal Show was a long shot. I told Tad to go to the place by himself and ask Allen if he'd seen Jesse since this morning.

"Learn anything you can about Jesse and then meet me at the Museum," I said.

Tad smiled with boyish anticipation, like he was about to buy himself his first ice cream soda.

"You won't be disappointed, Mack."

I told him I was sure I wouldn't be. Then I left him and headed east on Elm till I got to the Museum.

By the time I made it to the entrance I was ready to sit down again. My body reminded me how much walking I'd been doing.

I sat on the steps leading to the model of the Pennsylvania Oil Well, a contraption invented for sucking petroleum out of the earth. It was a popular draw with the Shantyville crowd.

The Professor was not out on his platform. Instead his assistant was doing the honors, talking so fast it made my head spin. He managed to put more forty-dollar words in a sentence than you'd see in the whole *Congressional Record*.

Beside him was a little man, wearing striped underwear beneath a curious set of overalls.

The Professor's assistant proclaimed him, "Plutano, the Eighth Wonder of the World! The Wild Man of Borneo!"

Plutano's long hair was carefully groomed. So was his goat beard. He didn't look too wild to me.

"Plutano and his brother Waino are two atavistic specimens of a bygone savage age, captured only after a desperate conflict where one man lost his life, torn limb from limb! It took the assembled brawn of four men to subdue these fearsome scions of a lost race, who are so wild and ferocious that they could easily rend a tiger to pieces! Though dwarfs in size they exhibit herculean prowess in feats of strength, lifting many hundred pounds their weight or throwing the most scientific six-foot athlete with ease!"

As he began soliciting nickels and dimes, I stepped around the building, heading for the back entrance where David and I had surprised my quarry the previous evening.

The door was open now and I walked into a dimly lit room. It was a makeshift kitchen, a pot of soup boiling on an iron stove that belched clouds of foul smoke, thankfully masking the even fouler miasma of the soup.

The Professor was seated at a long table set up between two doors leading to the hall outside and a water closet.

There were two other diners with him. I couldn't help staring.

They were children, I supposed. At least they were dressed like children. The taller boy had a skirt on over his tight-fitting drawers and a linen shirt. The girl wore a plain brown dress with girlish puffs at her short sleeves.

Their hair was shaved quite close to the skull, no doubt to show off their deformities.

To be kind, I would have called them imbeciles. Others more cruel would have used the word "pinhead."

They were eating quietly, their table manners certainly no worse than the Professor's.

When he saw me, his eyes blinked behind his thick spectacles. Then with an exclamation that startled the two children, he cried, "Ah! Look who's come for a visit! Mr. Detective!"

He didn't offer me a seat.

"I do believe we're not due for another payment till the first of October," the Professor said, slurping up something that I hoped was a potato.

"I'm not here for your money," I said with obvious distaste. "I'm looking for the woman called Hattie."

The Professor's magnified eyes blinked a few times.

One of the children grunted. They were both looking at me, fascinated. I managed a weak smile.

"How remiss of me!" the Professor said. "I forgot to introduce you. May I present Hoomio and Iola, the Wild Australian Children."

Then, as if he couldn't help himself, the Professor launched into his usual slew of words.

"These specimens belong to a distinct race hitherto unknown and undreamed of by civilization! Their strangely shaped heads have been fashioned by nature to enhance their struggle for survival in their far-off land."

I interrupted him by saying, "How in hell could the shape of their head make a difference?"

"Ah! You see they are adapted—you understand that concept, don't you? I thought so, sir. You have a keen intellect, anyone can see that. Scientific men like yourself can surely see why their heads would need to be foreshortened as it were, for creeping invisibly through the tall rank grass of their native plains. Then, sighting their prey, they spring upon the sleeping game and dispatch them with the utmost celerity. When the first white men spotted these two they were thought to be kangaroos. They were lured into the way of a lasso with a raw carcass for bait—at great expense and certainly at great risk—for these living artifacts have the sharpened teeth of the worst sort of jungle predators. Notice the similarity in their visage with the ferocious monster ape, the ourang-outang."

The Professor turned to pet the boy, Hoomio, on his shaved head.

Iola grinned at me and said something indecipherable. Once again I smiled at her.

"I'm very happy to meet you," I said to them, feeling more than awkward. I was not used to being around people who were so crippled. And they were obviously people, not monsters, like this idiot was saying.

I did not like the fact that I could not help staring at them. For that reason I had never liked Museums.

All I wanted to do was get out of there.

"I can see you don't want to talk about Hattie. But why don't you just try telling me where she is? Or the last time you saw her?"

"Hattie? Hattie, who?"

His thin lips coiled in a smile.

"The beauteous Star of the East," I said, mimicking his high-pitched voice. "The Circassian Beauty. The one I saw here last night. Where is she?"

"I'm sorry, Mr. Detective but I can't help you. If you're interested in a private viewing of her many . . . talents, I suppose we could accommodate, but as you can see I'm still in the middle of my supper."

My patience had worn thin. I reached over to his bowl of soup and sent it crashing into the stove. Then I hooked my boot around one of the legs of his chair and gave a tug. The Professor's gangly body sprawled onto the floor.

The two children were very upset, hugging each other and muttering in their own, unique language.

"I'll ask you nicely, one more time," I said to the man scrambling to get to his feet. "Where is Hattie?"

He told me to do something I won't repeat.

"You could learn something from these so-called wild animals," I said, gesturing to the terrifed children. "They have manners."

I planted my boot on his chest with as much force as I could muster.

His breath came out in a groan.

"Now, seeing as how you appreciate natural history, I'm sure you understand the concept of a state of nature. That's what they call the wild, where there are no laws, no civilization. That's what we have here, right now. A state of nature. And I am the predator and you are the prey."

I slammed my boot into him again. He began to gasp, his eyebrows upturned pitifully.

Hoomio and Iola were hiding under the table now, embracing each other for meager protection.

I said, "Your skinny little neck looks adapted mighty well for wringing. Maybe I'll try it."

"All right, damn it. All right. That bitch ain't worth it," the Professor sputtered.

"Well," I said, leaning on his sternum.

Flinching with pain, he said, "I ain't seen her since this morning. That's the truth so help me! She said she was goin' to Ullman's down the street for a bite to eat. She didn't come back."

"Aren't you curious at all what happened to her?"

"What do I care? There are plenty of girls who'd die for a chance to work in my show. A damn sight better than where they're at, that's for sure."

"How'd you come across Hattie in the first place? By the way, what's her last name?"

"Anderson. Henrietta Anderson. Who knows if that's her real name? Probably ain't. None of them go by that. I saw her working at one of the beer gardens June last. You know what I mean by working," he said with a leer.

"I'm sure I do."

"I offered her the job because I thought she could use the money. I wanted to give her a break."

"You're quite a philanthropist. What did she give you in return? Or are you too bashful to go into the details?"

"I never laid a finger on her! Which is not to say that I couldn't have. When she wasn't working she'd sit in her room half-naked smoking hop. She'd just lie there for hours. I coulda done anything and she wouldn't have cared. Probably wouldn't have even noticed."

"What was she smoking? Hop, did you say?"

"You know. Dope. Opium."

"Was she . . ." I tried to remember the word, ". . . habituated?"

"Oh yes. She probably had her old man get it for her."

I described Jesse Wilson.

He didn't surprise me by answering, "Yep, that's him all right."

Anger was making my hands tremble. I jammed them in my pockets and said, "Did he also smoke opium with her?"

"How'm I supposed to know? You think I drilled a peephole through her door?"

"I wouldn't put it past you. How long was this boyfriend coming around?"

"I don't know. Pretty much since she's been with the show. Mind you, he never gave me any trouble. Never tried getting her to dodge work. It was just afterward . . ."

"He hogged her all to himself. Is that it?"

"In a manner of speaking," the Professor said. Unrequited lust lit up his face with memories. "She was a handsome piece."

"What do you mean, was?"

"Just a figure of speech, damn it! You coppers are always readin' into things."

"You have any idea where she went?"

"I don't know and I don't care. There're plenty more where she came from! I'll have a Beautiful Circassian in her place within a few days. I just hope . . ."

He bit down on his lips, three words too late.

"What do you hope, Professor?"

"N-nothing."

I'd been relaxing my heel a little bit. Now I reminded him it was there.

"Okay, okay. I was just afraid if she was gone I wouldn't get that extra money anymore."

"What extra money?"

"You don't know?" he said, looking at me incredulously. His voice was accusatory. I didn't like the implications.

"Why the hell should I?"

"You're the one who brings the swells here at night. Don't you wonder why?"

I took my boot off his chest and started pacing around the room, nervously stroking my mustache.

Whatever came next, I had a feeling I wasn't going to like it.

"Why don't you tell me?" I said cautiously.

"The extra money for showing the Circassian Beauty to the swells and passin' those guidebooks around without lookin' in them."

"You mean you don't supply those yourself?"

"No! Not with Hattie. She had her own made up for her. I don't know where. I never asked."

"Why would someone be interested in showing Hattie off to the swells?"

The Professor began to hesitantly raise himself to a sitting position.

"It's not like she does anything extra for them," he said. "I'm always around to watch. Maybe she talks that harem bit up for them a little more than usual. She doesn't throw in that stuff about opium for the usual customers."

"So why for the swells?" I asked myself aloud.

Then I said to the Professor, "Who gives you the money?"

"A boy. Comes the morning after you or the other coppers do. A different boy each time. The first time I just got a message saying some people were coming that night and that if I showed them Hattie and none of the other freaks I'd find it worth my while."

"And you haven't seen anyone else since then? No letters?"

"Nothing. Just the parcel with the money. Except this morning."

"It didn't come?"

"No, and it usually does by this time. Maybe because Hattie ran off they won't be paying me anymore."

He seemed more hurt by that than by anything I'd done to him.

"Where's Hattie sleep?" I asked him.

"Upstairs, first door on the right, but you won't find anything. I looked already, when she didn't come back from Ullman's."

"There a key?"

"The door's open. At least it was when I checked this morning. Though I haven't been up there the whole afternoon. Been busy out front."

I went over to the huddling children and said, as gently as I could, "It's all right now. You can stop hiding. I won't hurt you."

The Professor shouted at them to do what I said.

Their shoulders hunched, the two of them got out from under the table and sat down in their chairs, smiling at me with buck teeth.

The smiles disturbed me.

It was a look of pure, defenseless innocence.

I hadn't seen anything like that for a long time.

It reminded me of how far from innocence I myself had strayed.

I could've asked why I was taking those men and women through Shantyville. I thought it was just for their perverse amusement. I never wondered why certain establishments were on my list and others weren't. Cap was the one who gave me the list, and I figured he was sending me to those who'd paid for the privilege, like a hotel pays a hack driver.

It had never occured to me to ask who gave Cap the list. I hadn't cared. My sensibilities were not shocked by a Chief of Detectives more or less doing advertising for the underworld. That was pretty much standard among city coppers, who didn't hesitate to skim the profits off of any fancy houses, gambling hells, or blind pigs in their district.

After all, a fellow had to make a living.

That was what most other people did, whether they were coppers or not.

I let them order me into Shantyville and led those swells to their cheap, seedy thrills like a slavish dog.

Only now was I realizing how wrong, how stupid I'd been. How terribly weak.

Looking at those two children, I thought maybe there was still time to atone for the worst thing I could've ever felt. Despair.

I stared at the poor imbecilic children and thought with a blaze of insight or madness or whatever that they were God Himself watching me.

When I thought that to myself it sounded crazy. But that's how I felt.

I could feel Him looking through their eyes, smiling through their lips.

I knew then that I had lost nothing that was worth anything to begin with.

I felt myself smiling back at them.

Then I walked outside and took the half-rotten staircase to the second story, where the Museum's exhibits spent their nights.

I was feeling especially good, like I had just washed my body from the inside out.

The door was indeed open, though the windowless interior was dimmed.

My hand fumbled in the dark for the lantern.

Out of the darkness, another hand grabbed my own as the door swung shut.

A fist pounded the side of my head.

It was a hard fist, made even harder by a pair of knuckle dusters. I couldn't see them but I could certainly feel them.

I let the darkness pull me in and threw my own fists

into it. A few times I felt them land on something that wasn't shadow.

We fought silently in the dark for about a minute. I tried getting my barker out of its holster but we were too close. I could smell his sweat and his reeking cigar breath.

Then I found the lantern. Or rather, it found me.

It crashed into the back of my head and sent me careening into what I supposed was a table.

I fell to the floor, not unconscious but stunned.

The brass-encased fist reached into my pockets while I lay in the darkness, groaning. They took whatever was there.

Without warning, a foot crashed into my neck. I rolled over, crying out with pain.

Footsteps clattered behind me. I tried to turn around in time to catch a glimpse of at least a silhouette. But my neck had other ideas.

The door had opened and shut before I could even remember what my name was.

In the dark I searched my pockets. It took me a few moments to realize what was taken. Just one thing.

The needle. The yen-nock.

I put my head back on the ground and cursed.

Then I heard the door open, slowly.

He was coming back to finish me off. An afterthought. That's all I was.

A sliver of light creeped toward me.

This time I had my barker out, aimed at the doorway. My thumb brought back the hammer.

I didn't bother warning him.

I thought I might enjoy shooting a man, just this once.

14

My FINGER NEVER found the trigger.

It was Tad's face that peered from behind the door.

As soon as he saw me, he rushed over and tried to get me to my feet.

"What in hell happened to you?"

"There was someone here when I came to give a look."

"Did you see them at all?"

"No, it was too dark."

I slowly stood up, kneading the muscles of my neck.

"Anything bleeding?" I asked Tad.

He gave me a good look and said, "Nothing I can see. You need to straighten your tie, though."

I left the cravat dangling from my unfastened collar.

Moving my head from side to side was extremely painful. Looking straight ahead of me, I began stumbling for the door.

"Was it Jesse?" Tad asked.

"Who else? He took the yen-nock."

"The wh—? Oh, you mean that Chinese needle."

"Ripped it out of my pocket."

"That wasn't very sporting, was it?"

"No. Neither was the kick in the neck he gave me. Or the knuckle dusters."

As I walked I could feel bruises erupting on my back, ribs, and arms.

My head throbbed with pain where he'd first hit me. My eyeballs felt like they were still rattling.

"Did you see anyone coming out of the building?"

"No," Tad said. "I just got here though."

We gave the room a looking over. There was nothing for us.

It suddenly occurred to me that Tad might have some information.

"What did Allen tell you?"

We began our descent down the rickety stairs.

"Not much. Just that Jesse had run out to get some breakfast and never came back."

"Did you ask him about where Jesse came from, how long he'd been there, that sort of thing?"

"Of course I did, Mack. He told me Jesse'd been there since the opening of the Exhibition. Jesse was on the crew that built the Animal Show, and a few weeks later Allen saw him at Doyle's Restaurant looking pretty destitute. Jesse said he didn't have a job now that construction was finished on Elm Avenue. So Allen let him take care of the pig, as a sort of favor."

"Why would he do Jesse a favor?"

"I asked him about that. He said Jesse reminded him of his son. Died at Chickamauga."

I laughed mirthlessly.

"Jesse has that quality."

"What do you mean?"

"That innate quality of the confidence man to make you trust him. I don't know how he does it. Isn't there some kind of story about a monster that takes on the shape of someone you love in order to gain your trust? So it can kill you then?"

Tad whistled, "Sounds like a story I never want to read."

"I've just lived it."

For a moment I was lost in my own thoughts. We were at the bottom of the staircase.

"You want to go in and ask them some more questions?"

"No," I said. "The Professor told me he hadn't been up there all afternoon. I believe him. I don't think he'd try to fool around with me after our talk. Jesse must've gone there and waited for me to show up. Or maybe I just surprised him doing something else."

"Covering his tracks?"

"Could be. We won't know until we catch him."

"Do you think we have a chance?"

"Oh yes. He's still here in Shantyville, the fool. If he had any sense he and his moll would've been halfway across Jersey by now."

"So there's something he must still be looking for."

"Let's hope he didn't just find it in my pocket."

Tad helped me walk back to Elm Avenue. From there we headed to the Centennial, so I could take advantage of the Medical Department.

Most of the way there, Tad was talking. There wasn't much else that Allen had told him about Jesse.

He'd never seen a person answering the dead girl's description with Jesse. Nor had Allen mentioned Hattie Anderson. It would've been hard to miss someone with her hair-dress. I asked Tad if Allen had said anything about Jesse smoking opium. He hadn't. Jesse didn't even smoke tobacco. Just drank, and a great deal at that.

I wondered if it was a drunken rage that had caused the girl's death. Hadn't Jesse seemed queer that night? Was he still drunk when he pushed Hiram King off the train?

That made me think of Hattie. And more importantly, Hattie's leather, the one she got buzzed from her in the Machinery Annex.

To find the buzzer, I'd need a talk with Bill. It would take some looking, but I was sure I'd find him at work somewhere in the Centennial.

"You want to come with me to look for a buzzer?" I asked Tad.

"No," he said, disheartened. "I better get back to my post. Griffin probably noticed I wasn't there. He'll give me hell, I reckon. And so will Mulford."

"No he won't. Like I said, I'll take care of him."

"You don't know Captain Mulford. He doesn't answer to anybody. Colonel Clay gives him free rein. We all know he's a corrupt bastard but nobody says anything. I can't believe I'm even telling you this."

"What? You think I'd repeat it to anybody?"

"No! It's just, I'm worried if he finds out I said anything."

"What's the worst he can do to you?"

Tad gave me a grave look and said, "Well, one man in our company is dead."

I stopped in the middle of the wooden sidewalk and said, "Come again?"

"He died last week. You know, they gave us explanations like oh, it was some sort of debility or miasma or something. The sewer pipes leaking into our water give off an awful stink. Some fellas think it was the food he makes us eat at his cousin's slop-house."

"Why would Mulford want to kill anybody?"

"I don't know, Mack!"

He had my arm in a tight grip. His voice was down to a frantic whisper.

I let Tad pull me over to a narrow alley between two restaurants.

"I'm getting scared, that's all. That's why I don't want to talk about it with anybody."

"How about letting go of my arm, Tad? All I need is another bruise."

"Oh! I'm sorry, Mack."

"That's okay. Now why don't you give me a little more on this Mulford. What exactly does he make you do?"

He had me hooked now. I'd got the scent of something.

"Well, I told you already that he makes us eat where he tells us. When we're on leave with our families he still makes us pay for meals we don't even eat. Some of us can't help but complain."

I smirked and said, "Not much of a motive for murder. Maybe those fellows really did have something wrong with them. Wasn't there a story in the papers about a sewer pipe near the barracks leaking gas?"

"Wait. There's more. Mulford has a staff of six. One man to black his boots and clean his room, a clerk, a bugler, and four sergeants—three of which do absolutely nothing, while the fourth, Griffin, is as tyrannical as the captain."

"That's a little excessive, but hardly criminal."

"Well, it's no surprise why his staff is so large. All cousins of his. That costs the Board of Finance nine dollars a day! Just so he can have his flunkies around."

"The board must get something out of it. Can you think what that would be?"

"I have my suspicions, Mack. But I can't prove nothin'."

"Tell me."

His eyes darted from right to left, searching for would-be spies. There was no one around except a waffle vendor, whom I called over and bought a stale waffle from. I was famished and didn't care if it was petrified. As Tad began to talk I found my chewing getting slower and slower until I'd stopped entirely, just standing there with my mouth open.

"There are some nights where we're ordered to stay away from certain posts. I mean those of us in the Fifth District. We have some guards patrolling the grounds while others are stationed at the various entrances. Well, there've been two nights when Sergeant Griffin's come along and told me to leave my post at the Art Gallery's entrance and go to the Photography Building. It's happened to some of the others too."

"You never asked why?"

"None of us did. You think we want to just stand around there in the middle of the night? I made sure to check up on where I'd been the next morning. You know, see if anything had been taken. But nothing ever was. Why would anyone want to steal art, anyway?"

"Some people think it's valuable," I said, now gulping down my waffle. "Who takes your place when you leave?"

"Griffin, I think. At least he's the one who relieved me those few times."

"You think there's something suspicious about that?"

"Don't you?"

"Maybe. Are there any other buildings they order you away from? Like Main?"

I was thinking about that death threat and how it was made without anyone knowing about it.

Tad disappointed me by saying, "Far as I know it's only the Art Gallery."

The scent was getting faint. I was beginning to think that Tad was just grousing about his superior officers to me, afraid of getting hell from them for following me around.

I was more interested now in how someone might get into the Main Building to use the type-writer.

I asked Tad if it were possible.

"You'd have to get past the guard at the entrance."

"Who's stationed there, usually?"

"A fellow by the name of Copper. Eric Copper. He's been caught sleeping on duty a bunch of times. When he's not sleeping he's usually lousy."

"With drink?"

"That's right. He and Sergeant Griffin both get bottles passed to them through the fence when they think no-body's looking. Then they stand around and trade stories about the girls at the Amazon Theatre. I heard one of the boys say that Copper isn't much of a copper. I thought that was a good one."

I wondered if anyone had talked with Copper about the death threat. Perhaps he would've seen someone enter Main. Would've if he hadn't been passed out from drink. It was something worth looking into. At least I could satisfy myself as to how the letter had been written so secretly.

"Tad," I said, "it sounds to me like your superior officers are less than exemplary. But don't go blaming any deaths on them. None of what you say sounds too dirty."

"But what about them ordering us from our posts at Memorial Hall?"

"So what? Maybe they don't have the manpower to cover both places all the time, but they want a body outside the Photography Building now and then."

Tad rubbed his slender mustache and pondered that.

"I suppose that could be."

"Don't worry yourself over Captain Mulford. I told you Heins will take care of him. Trust me, you won't even lose a day's pay over this. And you did good work. Wonder what o' clock it is?"

I pulled out my own watch and flipped open the lid.

"Two forty-seven o' clock. Plenty of time. Let's go back to the grounds. I'd like you to make the acquaintance of an unsavory friend of mine."

15

TAD AND I had taken up a position a few rods away from a bench set in front of Agricultural Hall.

I spotted Bill wandering around with two colleagues of his. Neither man was the same buzzer who'd put the touch on Hattie that morning.

The three of them split up well before Bill hailed the man standing in front of the bench.

He was an elderly gentleman with a long beard and a top hat over his silver hair. His well-worn suit would've been fashionable in the days of the Buchanan Administration.

From the way he had the map of the Centennial pressed against his spectacles, it was clear he was lost.

"What's the matter, sir?" Bill called to him.

"Eh?" the man said.

"You lost?" Bill said.

"Speak up! Hearin's not so good."

Bill had to practically shout, "Need any help findin' someplace?"

The old man nodded and said, "That's mighty white of you. Can't seem to find the Brewery Building."

"The Brewery Building? Well now, let me see."

Bill took a position to the left of the old man. Meanwhile, another man, one of Bill's friends, approached the two.

"You two lost?" he said.

"Lookin' for the Brewery Building," Bill said.

"I think I can help you."

The other buzzer got to the old man's right. Bill and his fellow dip were both pointing at the map now, darting their fingers from one point to another and giving him the rattle—that is, talking up a storm.

"Yes, the Brewery Building. Nice exhibit there."

"No mistaking that," Bill said. "I tried the English pale ale there the other day."

"Oh, I prefer the Milwaukee lager-beer."

"Rochester is better."

"You think so?"

"The appartus are very remarkable," Bill said to the old man, who kept nodding at the two pickpockets.

The third buzzer had joined the other two by now, going behind the old man and pointing over his shoulder at the map.

With all their pointing and pattering the old man had his mind fully occupied. His eyes were constantly directed to the map, where three different hands drew his attention.

The other three hands were deftly whisking into his pockets.

"They're pretty good," Tad said.

"They get plenty of practice. All they do is wait for some lone person to pull out a map and start looking for someplace. Then they pounce."

"The one you called Bill is starting to leave."

"Yes, he's got the old man's pocket watch in his vest by now. All right, let's pinch them. I'll handle Bill and the fellow in gray. You take the third one. Don't be afraid to use your club if he gives you any trouble."

They saw Tad's guard uniform while we were a few rods off.

"Cap your lucky!" Bill cried out. The other two under-stood the flash phrase meaning to run away. They split up and dashed off in three directions.

Tad took his club off his belt and threw it at the buzzer in gray.

The club landed in the crook of his neck, right behind his ear. The man whirled around and then fell on his rump.

I had to exert more effort.

Bill was far ahead of me when I started running after him. He headed into Agricultural Hall, figuring he might lose me there. It was a good thought.

I ran through the cathedral-like entrance, my heart be-ginning to pump extra fast.

Once inside, I scanned the white-washed nave from wall to wall, truss to truss.

Beneath the bewildering network of trusses and beams was a vast array of showcases and displays with hordes of people winding around them. I had my work cut out for me.

With my pace close to a trot I went through the display of plows at the left of the entrance, walking further into the American section.

Bill was nowhere to be found among the threshers or meat-packers' machinery. A large crowd was gathered around a machine called a self-loading excavator that dug up the ground, took the load of earth, and deposited it in the desired place. I didn't see Bill working the crowd so I went on, past the automatic binders, power cornshellers, grain-drills, cultivators, and sulky plows. I got a few stares from visitors when they saw my scowling expression. Per-haps I was muttering a few profanities without being aware of it.

Agricultural Hall was enormous and Bill might easily have made his way out by now. I was hoping that he hadn't—that he had decided instead to play a game of hide and seek with me and was hoping I'd simply lose my patience.

But I wasn't going to give up. I needed his help to find Hattie's mollbuzzer. That leather was going to make things much clearer for me. I had to have it.

I stopped by a working cider-mill grating five hundred bushels of apples per hour. I dropped a nickel on the counter and received a tasty glass of cider. It was so good I had another.

Rolling the sweet taste around in my mouth I looked down the south side of the court, past the ice cream freezers, churns, and wooden ware. I tried to think where the greatest crowd would be. That was where Bill would try to blend in.

The aquaria, I decided. That was the place.

It was a ways off from where I was. I trotted off, moving faster than anybody else in the building, attracting the suspicious looks of the few guards who were pacing back and forth.

I went past huge stacks of biscuits, seeds, African coffee beans, a mammoth California grape vine, showcases of mustard, canned meats, and a plum-pudding stand with a huge stuffed cow on top of it.

Back in the nave, I came across a gigantic windmill built in the old style, with a peaked roof and an octagonal stone tower. There was a picture-perfect family taking it in, the patriarch leaning against his silver-capped cane, his wife's arm linked in his own, with a little girl in a straw hat covered with ribbons pointing at the old mill that looked so much like something from a storybook.

It would've been a good place for Bill but he was nowhere around.

On the eastern side of the nave were tall glass showcases displaying some amazing animals I'd read about but never seen: a Bactrian camel, a thirteen-foot-high giraffe, and casts of monstrous fossils—skeletons of long extinct mammals as tall as trees. I couldn't resist taking a peek at them.

The aquaria were nearby, a set of thirty-five tanks. They

were all large, one being about twenty feet long by seven feet wide and four feet deep. People stood on all sides of the glass tanks, pressing their faces against them, and making all sorts of surprised, admiring, or horrified ejaculations.

The large crowds were fertile ground for the pickpocket. In fact, I'd collared more than a few here since the summer began.

I made my way from tank to tank, peering through the murky water to the people on the other side.

In between us I saw king-crabs and horse-foots. There were graylings from Michigan and Oswego bass, black-gill sunfish, suckers, long-finned chubs, fresh-water eels, drumfish, toadfish, rock bass, and moon-eyed fish.

Suddenly the fish spread away, and I could see clear through to the other side of the tank.

Bill's sallow mug was staring right back at me, like a nightmarish reflection.

I was already moving before his face could register surprise.

Bill was struggling to get through the crowd when I reached him.

A few ladies gasped as I yanked Bill by the scruff of his neck over to the tank. His face slammed against the glass, attracting curious stares from the salmon.

"Ruffians! Someone get the guard," I heard a dowdy, black-clad Quakeress say.

"Don't bother," I told them. "I am the police. Now just step aside and let us through."

When they heard Bill's cornucopia of profanity they were more than happy to make way.

I had him in a good policeman's grip, with my left hand on his left wrist. His palm was tilted upward and his arm straightened. My right hand twisted under the upper part of his arm and grasped his waistcoat. My two arms made a stiff lever that would dislocate his shoulder or break his arm if he gave me any more trouble.

Bill was well aware of that.

"Let's march," I told him.

"I didn't do nothin', damn it. You can search me. I dare you to, you big ugly bastard. There's nothing on me. Son of a bitch! Is this a free country? I'm gonna talk to your fucking chief and get your ass thrown out on the pavement for this! I'm gonna—"

His next words came out as a shriek. I'd given his left arm a little tug.

"Now why don't you just shut the hell up, Bill. I'm not in the mood."

I walked him out of Agricultural Hall to the bench where Tad had the gray-clad buzzer in bracelets. My young friend was scribbling fiercely in his memorandum book. The old man was still there and cackled with delight when he saw the two of us emerge.

"Well I'll be gosh darned! You got the little stinker! I do believe he took my watch."

"Where'd you stick the watch, Bill?" I said.

"Go bust yourself," he said with a sneer. He had to look good in front of his friend.

When I tugged his arm again it brought him to his knees.

"It's . . . in my . . . stocking . . . damn it!"

I pulled the little pocket watch and chain out of his left stocking and handed them to the old man.

"There you go, sir. Why don't you go with Officer Schmoyer to the station-house so you can sign a complaint."

Tad replaced the memorandum book in his back pocket and said, "You find the other one, Mack?"

"No. But I hooked the fish I was looking for."

"Are you gonna come back to the station-house with us?"

"In a little bit," I told him.

The three men headed off and I sat Bill down on the bench.

"What're you smiling about?" I asked him, taking off my straw hat and giving my forehead a wipe.

"You ain't gonna run me in after all. I didn't think you would."

"What do you think this touch rates? A two-spot? Maybe three?"

"Which one you talkin' about? My touch or the one you're makin' on me now?"

"That's funny, Bill. Let's add a little gravity and say that I can make sure you'll get two years at Moyamensing. How does that sound to you?"

The pickpocket shook his head with disdain.

"Two years inside. Or you can tell me how to find a buzzer I'm looking for."

"Oh, so that's what you want! I won't peach on anyone to the likes of you."

"I thought we had an arrangement, Bill. A sort of understanding."

"I've already had to pay two coppers a percentage today." He spit and said, "Eight dollars they stole from me!"

"Easy come, easy go, Bill. Your financial affairs don't concern me. I want a name."

I described the pickpocket who'd stolen Hattie Anderson's purse.

"Forty-five or so. Gray mustache, big, round nose. Puffy whiskers. Wears a navy frock suit and a red tie. Mollbuzzer. Sound familiar?"

"Maybe. But you're gonna have to do better for me. How about those eight dollars your copper pals already skimmed off me to-day?"

"Not a chance. Tell me this fellow's name and where to find him and I might just escort you to the exit instead of the magistrate."

I gave him a few seconds. Then I hauled him to his feet and said, "All right. I'm running you in."

"No! Wait! I think I've seen him around. Grand Central's his moniker. On account of he used to work in York. I don't know his real name. I think it's Pete something."

"Where do I find him?"

Bill rubbed his tangled hair and said, "Well, I wouldn't know about that."

"Maybe you'll come up with some ideas from here to the magistrate's."

I took him by the arm again and started walking him to District Court Number Twenty-three, on the other side of the grounds.

I was tired of walking so we got on the narrow-gauge car and rode it down to the Avenue of the Republic.

We didn't say a word to each other the whole ride.

The closer we got the more sweat began to appear on Bill's forehead.

The train stopped in front of the Judges' Pavilion and we got off.

The court was just a few rods off.

"I heard the food at Moyamensing's pretty good. If your stomach's made of brass. And the neighbors are friendly. Real friendly."

"Okay, okay!"

Bill began to blubber.

"Don't send me back there, please! I'm beggin' ya. I'll tell ya whatever ya want to know. Just don't send me back. I was there for sixteen months and it almost killed me. I saw a man get hanged once. It was horrible! I had nightmares for weeks! Don't send me back, please!"

He was clutching me by my lapels. I swatted him away.

Bill clutched his hands together in a prayerful expression and said, "His name's Pete O'Grady. Lives in the Southwark Hotel, next door to the Newark Beer Saloon on Viola Street."

"The one by the Amazon Theatre?"

"Yeah. A whole bunch of us room there. That's how I know him. He lives on the floor above me. We got the same fence. But he doesn't spend a lot of time at the

Southwark. He usually takes what he's got and blows it at the theatre. Told us he likes to rent a private box. To watch the dancing."

"Must be quite a show. All right, Bill. You did good. Now I want you to turn around and walk out the turnstiles. And if I see you or your friend at the Centennial again you'd better have your bags packed for Moyamensing. Now get."

Bill nodded gratefully and scurried across the Avenue of the Republic.

I waited a few moments and then headed out myself, making my way to Viola Street and the whorehouse they called a theatre.

16

THE BEERSLINGER AT the Amazon Theatre recognized me from the slum sociables.

"Afternoon, Detective," he said amiably.

The reflections of gas-lamps, already lit, flickered in the stacks of green bottles behind him like pent-up ghosts.

There were a few other customers at the bar, staring into glasses of whiskey or lager-beer and nodding their heads to the minstrel show's fiddle and harp.

"Afternoon," I said, sidling against the smooth counter. I propped my leg against the brass rail and said, "Can you get the woman in charge here for me? I need her advice on a certain matter."

The man smoothed his well-oiled hair and smiled.

"Is that business or pleasure?"

"Shut your mouth and get me the keeper!" I growled at him.

He looked nervously to his left at a large woman making her way behind the bar.

The madam was dressed in a respectable-looking cambric skirt and basque. The only ornamentation on her skirt was a bit of ruffles. There was no need for a corset. Her figure was ancient history. So was her virtue.

She had a very thick board in her hand with large rusty nails poking out of it.

"This fella giving you trouble, Jack?"

She brandished the nail-studded club at me and snarled.

Before the bartender could respond she poked her face into mine and said, "See all them bottles there? I got one with a whole mess of ears in it. I done ripped 'em right off the fuckers' heads when they ran wild in my place. You gonna run wild too, boy?"

"No," I said. "But I just might pry that club from you and nail you into the floorboards with it if you don't take your fat ugly mug out of my face."

"He's a detective," the bartender managed to stammer.

"Well, why the hell didn't you say so, you stupid bastard?" the madam said.

Her booze-reddened face cracked in a facsimile of a smile.

"Did I hear you say you wanted to see me?" she asked, completely disregarding our verbal brawl.

"That's right," I said, playing along with her. "I'm looking for Grand Central."

"You're about two hundred miles off course, blondie."

"That's a good one, ma'am," I said, leaving the last word full of sarcasm.

"Call me Dolly. I don't know what you want."

"Sure you do. His name's Grand Central and he's probably sitting in one of your private boxes right now. I checked at the Southwark Hotel for him and he wasn't there."

"I gotta be professional, mister. I mean, if I went rattling off who my customers were to every dick stumbling in here, what kind of confidence would that inspire?"

"How much for a drink in here?" I asked her.

Dolly smiled again and said, "Two dollars."

"Very reasonable."

"But, Dolly, whiskey's only fifteen cents," the bartender said.

"Shut up, bubby," she told him.

"What'll it be?" he asked me.

"Stick with whatever that fellow there's drinking. In fact, give it to him. He looks like he needs it more than I do. Well, Dolly?"

"I want you to know I wouldn't normally divulge a customer's name . . ."

"But you're going to peach on this scamp anyway."

"He hasn't been orderin' enough champagne when he's with the girls. He don't order champagne, we don't make much of a profit from him."

"He has a lot of gall. Where is he?"

"Third box on the left. You know where they are. Aren't you the one who brings the gents in here some nights?"

"Yes," I admitted reluctantly.

I didn't bother tipping my hat as I walked away from the bar.

The minstrel show was making a valiant effort to inject some atmosphere into the place. But it was late afternoon and the few people there were too sober or too drunk to provide the usual gaiety.

I made my way through the theatre itself, past the permanent haze of blue smoke left by countless segars.

As I entered the hallway where the boxes were it was hard to believe I'd just been here the previous night.

The muffled groans and insincere laughter coming from behind the doors seemed even uglier and shabbier in the light of day.

A girl about twenty years old was stumbling down the hall. Her hair was largely undone and her shoulders and ankles were naked. She wasn't wearing any petticoats underneath the skirt. When she nearly fell into me I could smell the gin on her breath.

"Whatcha waitin' out here for?" she said, her bleary-eyed face confused.

"You gonna dance for the man in there?"

"Dance!" The girl guffawed. "That's one way to describe it."

"Well, go do the can-can somewhere else. I'm handlin' this one on my own."

"I didn't know he was like that."

I pushed her back down the hall and went inside.

There wasn't much to the furnishings. A spindly-legged table stood in one corner with a kerosene lamp flickering on top. There were two chairs, one being empty.

Sitting in the other chair was the same man I'd seen at the Machinery Annex that morning.

I shut the door quietly and stepped in.

"Is that you, pet?" He smiled in anticipation.

His eyes were closed and his head tilted to the ceiling, where a few cockroaches were scampering between the boards.

Grand Central was in a casual mood. His collar was undone, his shirt was unbuttoned, and his pantaloons were ringing his ankles. So were his drawers.

His nether parts waited expectantly.

I took two steps toward him, drew my revolver, and pointed the barker at a crucial area.

When I pulled back the hammer, Grand Central's eyes snapped open.

The first thing he looked at was the barrel of my six-shooter. Then he looked down at his lap. When he raised his head his mouth was wide open in terror, a stream of drool leaking from his lip.

"Let's see how good your memory is," I said to him.

I told him what I wanted. It took several moments before he reacquired the power of speech.

"The p-p-pocket of my c-coat."

"You take it and throw it over to me. Careful now, I'm feeling a little jittery."

That made his eyeballs quiver. With a trembling hand, he extracted a sizeable leather out of his inner coat pocket and tossed it lightly over to me.

"This is everything?" I asked him.

"No," he said, swallowing. "I fenced a few other things this afternoon."

"Is this all you got from the woman at the Hydraulic Annex, I mean?"

He nodded desperately. Sweat was pouring down his face in rivulets.

I bent down to get the leather from the floor.

Then I heard a thud.

Grand Central had fainted.

I left him where he was. He looked pretty comfortable.

The would-be dancer was still lingering in the hall.

As I walked out the door she peered in at Grand Central, whistling in admiration.

"Should I help him get up?" she said.

"I'll leave that to your professional judgment," I said, walking toward the exit.

17

I DUCKED INTO the stables next door to the theatre. There was no one to watch me go through the contents of Hattie Anderson's purse except a sorrel, munching contentedly on some hay I fed him from the floor.

The leather was a small, cheap purse made of alligator. There were three items in it. One was familiar. I'd seen Jesse Wilson pick it off the ground the previous night. At the time I'd paid no attention to it. Now I gave it a good looking-over.

I'd been right that it was a token. It was about the size of a nickel and had a hole punched through the center.

A hole shaped like a heart, with words engraved around it.

GOOD FOR ONE SCREW.

At the bottom of the heart it said, "Ruth Blanchette, Prop."

I stared at the sorrel absentmindedly for a few seconds, as if I were expecting him to comment on the coin.

He blinked an eye and swatted his tail at a fly on his rump.

Next I pulled out a key. The name of a hotel was stamped on it. It was a place I knew, the Star Eating Saloon and Lodging House at the corner of Belmont and Columbia Avenue, a square south.

A paper tag was tied to the key. Although the ink had smeared a bit I could still read the number fourteen.

The last article was the pamphlet Hattie had handed out to some of the swells last night. It looked like someone had been thumbing through it. A good thing, I thought, that Grand Central was a reader.

Like most of the pamphlets passed out at freak shows, it told the outlandish story of the Circassian Beauty's life in lurid detail.

This was more pornographic than others. I skimmed through the dozen or so pages, which described Hattie's initial ravaging in a Turkish slave mart, how she grew to love the caress of man, any man, and the wild pleasures she and these men had attained through opium smoking.

At the back of the pamphlet was, curiously, a trade card—the sort given out by most of the exhibitors at the Centennial as advertisements. This particular one had a picture of Memorial Hall on the front. I had one just like it that I got after I'd visited the Art Gallery during its construction.

Someone had written on the back of the card in a clumsy hand.

"These Delights can be Yours. Back of Museum. Midnight."

I stuck the card in the pocket of my coat, behind my handkerchief.

Then I gave the sorrel a pat on his nose and walked out of the stables.

The fading daylight stung my eyes. I stood on the streetcorner, not sure where to go next, feeling lost. A hack pulled up in front of me and asked me where I was headed. I said I didn't know and waved him off.

I felt like those sailors who'd first crossed the Atlantic, not knowing what lay beyond their shores, but fearing that there was something past where the horizon and ocean ended—a terrible place full of writhing sea monsters, a plummet into an infinite abyss.

I'd reached that point now. There was nothing left to do but let the current take me. I headed toward the Star Lodging House.

Along the way I thought on Hiram King and why Hattie had been so interested in showing the contents of this purse to him.

Which of the items were intended for his perusal? The bawdy house coin? The pornographic freak pamphlet? Or the card inside?

I thought it could very well be all three.

But why would a big bug like Hiram King, a member of the Board of Finance, be interested in the sordid operations of Shantyville?

More importantly, why would Hiram King be interested in a piece of evidence Jesse Wilson had picked up at the site of a murder?

By the time I got to the Star Lodging House I had asked myself those questions half a dozen times each. I remembered the death threat to Hiram King, signed *"B.F. (ha ha)"*. The laughter was ringing in my ears now.

I pushed the door in and walked past a group of travelers from all parts, spoons to their faces, slurping up clam chowder, which surprised me by smelling good.

I was just past the bar when a man ran out from behind it, holding a ladle to his apron with a proprietary air.

"Can I do anything for you, sir?"

I showed him the room key and said, "Friend of mine misplaced her key. I was going to return it for her."

"Well, you can leave it with me. I'm the owner."

His chin jutted out with pride.

"I think I'd rather give it to her myself if you don't mind. Perhaps you've seen her come in to-day?"

I described Hattie Anderson as she'd looked at the Centennial that morning.

"Sure I know the gal. But I haven't seen her to-day."

"Maybe you could've missed her."

"Nope. Wife's been back in the kitchen. I've been up

front. Seen everyone who comes in and goes out."

"Could you show me the register?"

The man's long eyebrow hairs crooked over his deep-set eyes.

"Now why should I do that for you, stranger? Don't see that it's none of your business. Begging your pardon."

I held my star in front of his squinting eyes and said, "I'm a Philadelphia police detective. I'd be obliged if you could get me the hotel register."

When I admitted who I was, there were usually two kinds of reactions. Curiosity or anxiety. You could always tell who had the guilty conscience. This fellow had one.

His head bobbed up like I'd hit him over the head. Then he scurried behind the bar and brought out the register.

"Here she is," he said, a stubby finger with a dirty nail pointing to the name.

Harriet Adams.

"Very clever disguise," I said.

"Come again?"

"Nothing. Listen, did you ever see this woman bring a man in here?"

I gave him a description of Jesse Wilson.

"Now that you mention it, I do remember that fella."

"How many times did you see him?"

"Oh, I don't know. Plenty. I got the feeling they were married."

I gave him a critical look.

"Leastways he was courting her. Didn't ever stay the night."

"Did this woman have other men courting? Who also didn't stay the night?"

The man looked shocked.

"You mean to tell me she was a—"

"No. Just curious, that's all. Were there any other young men calling on her?"

"I never seen any."

I glanced down at the register again and noticed the

date beside her name. July 12. She'd been staying there for quite some time.

"Did she spend every night here?"

"Mister, I don't know. The wife stays up late. You can ask her. I don't ask questions too much, you understand? As long as they keep quiet and pay their bills I don't care what they do or where they go."

"Sound business practice. Okay, where's the room?"

"Up the stairs. I'll show you."

I put a restraining arm against his apron.

"That won't be necessary. I'd like to take a look myself."

The man shrugged and went back to the bar.

There were two floors above the eating saloon with nine rooms to a floor.

No one was making any noise behind their doors. They were probably all eating downstairs or taking in the Centennial. It was the kind of place where mechanics and their families would go—cheap but respectable.

The key fit and I pushed open the door with my boot. My barker entered the room ahead of me. I wasn't going to tussle in the dark again.

It wasn't a large room and the light from the hallway was enough to show me there was no one inside, unless they were hiding under the bed.

I went to the window and drew the curtains. The gray light of the afternoon only made Hattie's quarters seem more drab.

The walls were whitewashed with no paper on them. A couple of wooden hooks were nailed to the wall in lieu of a coat rack. There were four pieces of furniture—a medium-sized bed with a cheap blanket strewn over it, a table with a pitcher and basin on top, a chair, and a dresser set against the wall to the left of the door.

There was nothing threatening underneath the bed except a chamber pot. I went to the dresser next.

There was little in the top drawer. Some hose, handkerchiefs, a dollar in nickels and dimes, and a pasteboard box.

The second drawer had nothing in it except some paper lining the inside. I went to the bottom.

There was plenty to interest me here. A bundle of Hattie's pornographic pamphlets, fresh from the printer. Next to it was a segar box containing a host of trade cards— all of them showing Memorial Hall. I checked the backs of the cards and saw there were no messages written on them. I remembered what the one I had in my pocket said. "Back of Museum. Midnight."

Memorial Hall was the Art Museum of the Centennial. I didn't have much time to puzzle over it.

Toward the back of the drawer was something I'd sought but hadn't found in Hattie's other room.

It was a black tray, like the kind you put before an infant on a high chair, with a pipe, tiny lamp, and needle lying on it.

I took the whole mess out, brought it over to the bed, and scrutinized each object.

They were all familiar to me. I'd seen them before many times at the Oriental Saloon. The Celestials, when they bothered speaking English to me, had called this a lay-out. The tools of the opium smoker's trade.

I cradled the bamboo-stemmed pipe in my arm and examined the stone bowl. The hole for the smoke was about the diameter of a lead pencil. Holding it to my nose I smelled the traces of numerous opium pills, the ones George had said looked like mouse droppings.

The lamp had some peanut oil left in it. It would give off a tiny flame, hot enough to melt the opium pill to a molasses-like jelly that would be stuffed in the pipe and brought to a boil.

I knew now that the needle was used for holding the pill over the flame and then molding it into the bowl of the pipe.

It seemed like a lot of work to me. I caught myself

wondering what it would be like to smoke opium, just to try it.

If it was anything like the morphine I'd had during the War, I didn't want to get near the stuff.

Morphine hadn't made the pain go away, that was the queerest thing about it. The pain was always there, lingering at the edge of my thoughts. But the morphine made me not care about the pain.

The feeling disturbed me.

Pain was not the sort of thing I wanted to ignore.

It was better to find a way to make it stop.

I replaced the opium lay-out on the tray and put it back in the bottom drawer.

I opened the top one again and looked inside the pasteboard box.

It was a lady's undergarment made of bird's eye flannel. The bloodstains, browned and faded, drew my attention immediately. Then I turned away, embarrassed, when I realized what I was staring at. It was probably the only one she owned and was well-washed.

Seeing the garment made me think on her with pity. I felt unaccountably ashamed at finding it, liked I'd seen something that I wasn't supposed to—a glimpse of a deeply private fragility.

I supposed she had some kind of pain that she wanted to ignore. I wondered what might be its cause.

There would be more to come, I was sure of that. She was sharing her bed with a vicious killer. I wonder if she knew. Or cared.

I closed the top drawer and pulled open the middle one, my thoughts somewhere else.

When I snapped out of it, I was staring into the drawer, at the paper there.

Hiram King's august, gray-whiskered face was staring back at me.

It was from a page of *Frank Leslie's Illustrated Weekly*, one of a series that commemorated the Centennial.

There was another engraving from a newspaper, spread out beneath the first sheet.

The masthead had the name of the paper on it. *The Democrat*. Mauch Chunk, Pennsylvania. The date was May 15, 1875.

Mauch Chunk was up north, in Carbon County, coal country. I remembered Hiram King telling me he lived there with his family.

The lithograph showed a young girl's portrait, obviously copied from a photograph. Beneath it was a caption describing Miss Elsie King's numerous donations to a local orphans' asylum and a literary society she was forming to discuss works of poetry.

I had to handle the paper delicately. It was frayed where a hand had clutched it many times. The ink in Elsie's face was faded a great deal.

Someone had written a line in pencil beneath the girl's portrait. The carefully formed words read, "For this alone on Death I wreak/ The wrath that garners in my heart;/ He put our lives so far apart/ We cannot hear each other speak."

I could hear Jesse reciting another poem to me, from last night. A poem about a girl that he'd known once and had lost.

He'd given her another name in the poem—Jenny. But I knew her real name now.

I left the Star House and made my way slowly up Belmont Avenue, toward the Centennial.

Elsie and I were going to have another talk. Let her scream all she wanted to.

18

THE WALK BACK to the Centennial hadn't done much to clear my head.

There was only one place where I could go to get a little peace. I headed for the Tunisian Cafe.

She was not on stage when I walked in. A few of the musicians were playing their instruments—the droning melody quite plaintive and foreign.

I ordered a cup of their thick, strong coffee and settled back in the chair. Then I noticed the girl, behind the counter where the cups and saucers were piled. When she saw me staring at her, she flashed a gleaming set of ivories at me. I doffed my hat to her.

That was the first time we'd ever exchanged any sort of pleasantry. It was a milestone in my infatuation. Of course I expected nothing to come of it. I liked the idea of a beautiful girl whom I could adore from afar—one who would never get polluted like so many of the other things I saw, including myself.

There was something eternal about the Tunisian girl's smile. I thought it was the kind of smile one could have seen in the deserts of Africa a thousand years ago. A smile that had lived through the ages, never corrupted, never stained.

I drained the coffee cup and ordered another. Then I

told myself I was too old for all this wistfulness. But I couldn't help it. Jesse Wilson had brought it out. I didn't like to see the crack in my armor.

The war and prison had made me too hard at too young an age. I had seen so many boys die—dear friends of mine, comrades. There was nothing I could do there but watch them slowly lose their hold on life until one morning I'd wake up and they'd be staring at me without seeing me.

All I could think of after I escaped was the death, the pain, the hunger, the misery. Those seemed to be the only realities, the only things that mattered. I couldn't let myself think about beautiful things when so much ugliness abounded.

When I saw so much evil I began to doubt if a merciful Creator even existed.

But I could not give Him up. I still clung to Him, even when I felt like He'd forgotten the world existed. I decided if He wasn't interested in things like justice and mercy then perhaps maybe I should be. For that job I needed to make my heart cold. Now Jesse Wilson was spoiling all my hard work.

There had been something in him that struck a chord in me. The way he spoke that poetry, the intensity with which he loved that girl, the girl I now knew was Elsie King.

It had reminded me of a love of my own. One that was long gone. I'm sure Jesse's romance wasn't any more impossible than mine. Most of all it was impossible because I made it so.

I had met her on a streetcar five years ago. For a few weeks I knew her and didn't care that she was colored or even that she had, in many ways, betrayed my trust in her. I loved her. Then she went out of my life, fled the city, and I never heard from her again.

So I buried myself in work and scratched and clawed my way into the detectives' room.

I stifled the feelings of loss and regret and hurt along the way. Just when I thought they were gone, I got my first case—the kidnapping of a boy from Germantown.

Before it was over all those painful feelings had come back to haunt me.

What I found in the woods near Eddie Munroe's home had made my existence seem fruitless, my struggle futile. There was too much evil, I could not withstand it.

There was one way to save myself. It was a choice I made to let a guilty person free, to let a killer live.

Mercy had seemed the only way out. My prayers for that killer had never ceased. Every night I prayed that he would escape the evils of his past, that he would never kill again. That somehow, I could take control of the world and its evil for just an instant—and force some redemption into being instead of waiting for it to happen.

I found myself thinking of that killer quite often now.

Not that I thought he would have anything to do with the murdered girl at Shantyville. Instead I thought how much Jesse was like that boy. Or David. Both handsome young men full of life. Yet Jesse chose death.

Was that how he was too—the killer I set free two years ago? Had he chosen death too?

The Shantyville girl's death was my fault, wasn't it?

I let the killer go that time—just like I'd done in Germantown.

This was the result of my mercy. More death.

So was there really no hope at all? None?

If that killer was lost and Jesse was lost, then I knew that somehow I was lost too. Hadn't my face been beneath theirs in my nightmare?

When I let the killer go I was trying to save myself as well as him.

I wanted to believe that I could move past the evil of my own life—the nightmarish memories of captivity, the bloodshed of war, the rampant brutality of my beat—I wanted so desperately to believe that somehow those things could be overcome.

I closed my eyes for a moment, questioning the darkness there. When I opened them I saw the Tunisian girl begin to sift the air through her scarves.

I took a sip of the dregs in my cup and walked out. I didn't have the heart to watch her dance this time.

19

MISS ELSIE KING was nowhere to be found at the Judges' Pavilion. I didn't fancy searching the entire grounds for her. There was no need to since I was meeting David at the Newspaper Building in about an hour. He could tell me where I might find her.

In the meantime I decided to go to Cap's office. We were long past due for a talk on the dead girl and her killer and what they both had to do with Hiram King.

Before I had made it halfway through the door of the station-house a human obstacle placed itself in my way.

"I been looking for you," Bert Pierce said to me.

The detective glared at me with all the jealousy of a scorned suitor.

"What did you do with El . . . I mean, Miss King, McCleary?"

"Who's business is that but ours?"

Pierce's chin jutted out beneath his mustache. I noticed there was a nick in the skin from a hasty razor.

"It's my business because Mr. King says it is. I watch over the family."

He punctuated his sentences by jabbing a finger into my chest.

"You'd think they could've saved a lot of time and

effort by just buying a family dog. Or maybe they did, after all."

"You think you're a funny man?"

I smiled and said, "You don't?"

"I don't like you, McCleary. I said to Mr. King it was a mistake to put you on this case. From the very beginning I said that. I know all about your reputation."

Now it was time for me to raise my hackles.

"What exactly do you know about my reputation?"

I took a step closer to him so our watch chains rubbed against each other.

"You don't have one. The only reason you're still a D is 'cause that Heins owes you. Otherwise you'da been thrown out on your ass after the Germantown case."

"Is that so?"

My face leaned into his.

"Sure," Pierce said, giving me a mock smile. "That's why I don't want Miss King or the others getting near you. Since you have a way of getting people killed. I don't want the same thing happening to Miss King or her father."

I lost my temper at that point. My eyes had been staring straight at his nose. Suddenly my fist followed the path of my gaze.

A thin trickle of blood leaked out of his left nostril. Pierce smiled and wiped it off with a handkerchief.

"Guess I hit a sore spot," he said. Then he laughed, which enraged me even more. And made me feel mighty stupid.

He clamped a beefy hand on my shoulder and said, "Now what did you do with Miss King?"

I answered him because I felt guilty for hitting him. And ashamed for letting him get to me.

"Left her at the Judges' Pavilion."

"She isn't there."

"So what?"

"You were supposed to take her back to their room at

the Transcontinental Hotel, McCleary. Why didn't you do that?"

"She didn't like my company."

"Well, she's gone. Nobody can find her. And you didn't do your job."

"She'll turn up," I said. "Probably went to one of the exhibition halls. I got the feeling she didn't get out much."

"Mr. King doesn't like her going out unescorted. She's in delicate health."

"Then maybe she belongs in a booby hatch where people can look after her."

"What's that? What did you say?"

As he snarled at me, I felt a few drops of spit tickle my cheek.

"I said maybe she doesn't like people protecting her. Is that why you follow around after her, Pierce? Like a cur dog after a bitch?"

This time he grabbed me by my coat and shook me. I didn't bother resisting. It was my turn to laugh.

"Don't you ever say that about her again! If you do, I'll kill you! Do you understand me, you bastard mick?"

"Guess I hit a sore spot," I said.

I tore his hands off me and brushed my jacket. Then I walked past him into Heins's office.

After I slammed the door behind me, Cap looked up from his desk and said, "What was all that fuss about?"

"That Pinkerton dick is mighty protective of the King girl. He was sweating me over what I'd done with her."

Cap leaned back in his chair and began to pick his nails with a pocket knife.

"What *did* you do with her?"

"Nothing!" I said, too defensively. "What the hell's the problem, anyway?"

"You were supposed to take her back to the hotel. We've been wondering why you didn't. Why you've been nowhere to be found for the whole afternoon."

I didn't like the implied accusation.

"Do you have something you'd like to come right out and say, sir?"

Cap slammed both hands on his blotter and said, "I'd like to know what the hell you were doing all afternoon and why the hell you needed to bring a member of the Guard along with you!"

I leaned over the back of one of the chairs and said, "I was digging. I needed his help. He didn't want to help me but I forced him into it. Square it with his captain, okay? I think you can do that for me. The kid made a pinch out of it anyway. A good one."

"You're running out of favors, Mack. Understand me? I can't afford them anymore. Not when I'm playing with the likes of Hiram King."

"Just another rich swell. What the hell do you care?"

"King is not just another swell. He still owns a hefty percentage of the Reading Railroad and he's just bought into Rosengarten and Company in the city."

"Who're they?"

"They make morphine. The largest producers in the Republic."

I took that one and masticated on it for a while. I thought on the opium lay-out I found, the opium pipe, the Oriental Saloon.

There was a lot of—what had they called it?—hop lying around. It seemed to be cropping up wherever I stuck my nose.

So did Hiram King.

I said as much to Heins.

"Where exactly have you been sticking your nose, Mack? Tell me it's not in Shantyville. For God's sake, tell me it's not there."

"What makes you so afraid of Shantyville? Can you tell me that?"

Cap shook his head quickly.

"Then I can't tell you where I've been sticking my nose. Fair enough?"

"Listen to me now," he said, leveling an ink-stained finger at me. "I've had enough of your horseshit, McCleary. I let you in here as a favor. The truth is you are an embarrassment to the force, to me, and to yourself. That Munroe boy would be in his mother's arms to-day if it weren't for you! Do you think I'd trust you with a serious investigation after that? We know I can't force you to leave! No, you can make me keep you on, if you want. Don't think I don't know that. But now I have told you to stay away from the dead girl, and goddamn it I mean stay the hell away from her! Do you understand me, you son of a bitch?"

His face had turned a feverish red. A vein pulsed on his temple.

In all the years I'd known him he'd never spoken to me like this before. I felt like a faithful dog whose master had just kicked him for no apparent reason.

When I spoke next I had to clear my throat.

My voice sounded too soft, but I couldn't control that. I could only take so much hatred directed at me for something I didn't do.

"Do you want to find out who killed her or not? Do you want to know who's trying to kill Hiram King or not? 'Cause I can tell you they're the same person. Jesse Wilson, the swineherd from Shantyville."

Cap wiped his sweating brow off with the sleeve of his coat. Then he gestured for me to keep talking.

"The killer uses opium and so does that freak girl of his. When I searched their room I found an opium layout."

"What the hell is that?" Cap said, his head lowered, fists clenched to gain control of himself.

"Opium smoker's apparatus. Pipe, lamp, tray, and a needle. The same sort of needle I found in the dead girl's neck last night."

Cap's fists started trembling.

"There was no needle, McCleary."

"Sure there was. It was in my pocket while I was talking to you."

"What?"

His voice thundered. With a snap of both arms he hurled piles of papers off his desk, sending them flying in all directions. Those that were left he crumpled in his hands. It was pretty clear he would've preferred to crumple my neck.

"You heard me," I said, suddenly defiant. "I'm one step ahead of you, Heins. Always have been. Don't you think I knew you weren't going to let me within a mile of this? I held on to that thing to protect myself. To ensure that I could run it through on my own. When you brought me over here you pretended you were giving me another chance. You were really putting me out to pasture. But I want that chance!"

I was at the edge of his desk by now with my own two hands on the blotter.

My voice quavering with desperation, I said, "I kept the weapon because I had a feeling it might get lost if certain people took care of the case. It's happened before and it'll happen again. But not this time. Not when I have so much at stake. A man doesn't get too many chances at vindication. I'm not letting go! Not when I've learned so much. More than Hiram King would like, I'll bet."

"What's that supposed to mean?"

"It means his daughter knows the killer."

Cap made a disgusted face.

I raised my voice to get past his disbelief.

"She knew enough to tell me how the girl had been murdered in Shantyville. And she knew his name. Maybe the Christian name was different or the surname. It took her a few seconds. But she knew it all right."

"What else did she tell you?"

I'd gotten through to him. The veins had stopped throbbing.

"When I tried pressing her on this Jesse she wouldn't

talk about it. She threatened to scream and make a scene so I let her go."

"And you haven't seen her since?"

"No. I've been busy."

"In Shantyville?"

"And on the grounds. A Chinamen in Main identified the needle for us. Called it a yen-nock, used by opium smokers to heat up the stuff and put it in their pipes. I went over to the Museum girl's room, the one who was with Jesse this morning, and nearly got my head caved in. Whoever it was took the yen-nock."

"You lost it," Cap said, as if he'd known I would.

"I found plenty more. After Officer Schmoyer and I pinched the buzzers by Agricultural Hall, I got the key to Hattie Anderson's other room. The one where she and Jesse had their assignations."

"Wait," Heins said, confused. "How did you happen to know about this key?"

"Oh!" I said, feigning surprise. "Didn't I tell you? I saw a buzzer lift it from Hattie's back pocket this morning. Right before she and Jesse went to meet with Hiram King."

"Don't you mean, before they went to kill him?"

"No. He was meeting with them. I saw the whole thing. The girl wanted him to see the purse with the key in it and was not too happy to find it gone. They were talking to King for quite a while before Jesse flew into a rage and tried killing him."

"Now wouldn't it be interesting to know what they were saying?"

I had him hooked now.

"Wouldn't it?" I said. "I don't think they were interested in killing him. They wanted more out of Hiram King than his life. His daughter might know what, if we could find her. But if we can't we can always go straight to the top."

I dug my hands in my pockets and got up from Cap's desk.

"As a matter of fact, that's an A-1 idea. I think I'll march over to the Judges' Pavilion and ask Mr. Hiram King what he thinks about a dead girl in Shantyville being killed by an acquaintance of his daughter's. A man with whom he had a not-too-friendly business meeting on the prismoidal railway this morning. I might also ask him if all that opium he imports gets used for strictly medicinal purposes. And hell, I might even ask him why he's anxious to cover up the death of a whore from Blanchette's Amazon Theatre."

Cap said nothing, only blinking at me.

"That's who the girl was, I'm pretty sure of that. There was a coin Jesse found near the body. A token for an evening's or perhaps I should say a quarter hour's entertainment."

I pulled the coin out and tossed it on Cap's desk.

He didn't bother looking at it.

"You don't want to go asking him questions, Mack."

"Why not? Are you telling me he might not want to answer them?"

"I'm telling you he will not answer them. And that he'll take care of whoever does the asking. Make sure they don't have the energy to pose questions again."

"Now, sir, that sounds like a secondhand threat of sorts."

"You can take it however you like. I gave you this job because I thought you'd be discreet. Remember how discreet you were in '71? Remember how nicely you took care of Sergeant Duffy for us? That's what I was hoping for here. But you've disappointed me, Mack. Again."

I walked around his imposing desk. He was still leaning on the back legs of his chair. I put my hands on the armrests and brought the front legs down. We were face to face now.

"You're afraid of Hiram King, aren't you, Heins? I

wonder why. But I don't think I'll be wondering for long."

"Mack, I'm telling you for the last time. Be a good detective. Follow orders. Do what I tell you. Stick close to Elsie or David King and make sure no harm comes to them. That seems very easy, doesn't it? And don't worry over anything else. Can you do that for me? For yourself?"

"I'm worrying about a killer and what he has to do with Hiram King. Are you holding back anything from me?"

Cap vigorously shook his head and said, "I know nothing and I don't want to know. And if you start looking I won't be covering your ass anymore."

I walked to the door and paused before it. I was shocked when the words came from my own mouth, "To hell with you then."

His curses were cut short when I slammed the door shut.

I felt very lonely at that moment.

What I wanted more than anything was to get out of hell. Not the one I'd wished on Heins. The hell I'd been in since the war when I lost most of the things that mattered to me. I'd fought very hard to get back some of those things. Others were lost for good.

That was my definition of hell. Being lost for good.

When I was a boy I used to take walks with my father in the woods near our home in Troy. He would show me the different kinds of birds and trees and insects so there could be something to my life other than the smell of horses and smoke, coal ash and human sweat.

I'd read a poem once about a fellow getting lost in the woods and winding up in hell. I knew just how Dante felt.

It was in the woods at Gettysburg that I was captured by the Rebels. Surrounded by woods, I'd been imprisoned. In the midst of the woods, I found a killer that I had to let go because if I damned him then I somehow damned myself.

But now, in the woods by Shantyville, I'd found a terrible beacon to lead me out. Finding that girl's killer was a way for me to escape, to put some meaning back in the meaninglessness.

To escape was worth any price. Even the one she had paid.

20

THE DEPARTMENT OF Public Comfort was just next door. I went there, hoping David might show up early.

I had to dodge a West End Railway car as I skipped over the tracks before the main entrance. I cursed at the car under my breath, wondering why they made them go so damn fast. People got too reckless when they could go eight miles an hour.

For a moment I stood in the open-air gallery, under the awning with the rest of the crowd, looking for a familiar face among the discharged passengers. David King was not among them. The train quickly pulled out and I was left rubbing the smoke and coal ash it left behind out of my eyes.

I entered the central wing, jostling my way past the tourists standing in line to sign the guest register. The reception room was jam-packed with people reading newspapers, cradling their infants, smoking cigars, or just resting their tired feet on the edge of a pot-bellied stove.

Nudging my way to the lunch counter I paid a dime and got myself some oysters, shelled out by the officious, aproned staff. After squirting them with plenty of sauce I threw them down the hatch and washed the whole mess down with some concoction called ginger ale that I got from a soda fountain.

The food perked me up a bit. I made my way past the water closets, lavatories, boot-blacking rooms, barbershops, ladies' dressing rooms, stamp counters, Chinese corner, and the umbrella stand—which for no apparent reason had two giant wooden cranes perched on the counter.

I was trying to figure out what they were doing there when I heard someone say, "Detective! You looking for me?"

It was David.

The young reporter looked dapper as usual. His evening suit was most fashionable.

"I wish I had your wardrobe," I told him as I shook his kid-gloved hand.

"No," he said. "The lounge look suits you, Detective. Am I late?"

"No, I just got here. Where to now?"

"Why don't we go to the west wing? There's a hall set up for us correspondents. Nice view of the Lansdowne Valley."

David was right. The large, airy chamber certainly had a nice view. Horticultural Hall, barely visible in the distance, was lost amid a cloud of trees.

The scene was so pretty I got lost in it for a few moments. David brought me back by slamming a carefully clipped article on the table.

"Tell me how you like it," he said with a proud smile.

Written carefully on top were the words: "*Evening Bulletin*, September 6, 1876."

Beneath them was the head-line:

ELM AVENUE BY GAS-LIGHT
NEVER-ENDING EXCITEMENT—TRAPS
FOR GREENHORNS—A WORLD OF WONDERS

I read the first few sections with interest, marveling at how romantic Shantyville was, seen through David's eyes.

Then I began reading the second half of the article. The tone was decidedly different. It began:

No Place for Moral People

A man might think himself proof against all the arts and devices of Satan, and feel morally certain that the old boy couldn't get an advantage over him, but let him once get in the polluting atmosphere of one of those free variety shows, and his respectability and honor are at once at stake.

Along come two Centennial District policemen supporting between them a man overcome by the law of gravitation, or in plain English, with "a brick in his hat." His steps are unsteady, his eyes dull and heavy, and as the crowd presses back to let the procession pass, somebody suggests that "he has tight shoes" as the cause of his walking in triangular shapes. It is only one of the many unfortunates carried to the lock-up, and the merry crowd go jaunting along and only stop and giggle at the next funny thing they see.

A Peculiar Excursion

For the past few weeks certain parties have found it amusing to finish their night after the theatre or ball with a trip through Shantyville, well guarded by detectives, of course. Every night the Centennial detectives are called on to pilot such parties through the dives and opium joints and other resorts which make the night life of Shantyville so instructing.

These "slum sociables," as they are called, are very popular with our upper ten. The dudes and their fair friends find an exquisite enjoyment in viewing scenes of immorality which they cannot alleviate and would not if they could. As for vice and misery, they go on in the same old way, reveling and despairing as they will continue to revel and despair long after the "slum sociable" has gone completely out of fashion.

Recently our correspondent had the opportunity to take such a tour with one of our veteran policemen. Everyone in the Quaker City is familiar with the exploits of Detective Wilton McCleary. For ten years this faithful officer has acted as down brakes on crooks who dared to work in our City cf Homes. His reputation suffered during the investigation of the kidnapped Eddie Munroe of Germantown, but this reporter found no cause for censure in the detective's behavior. Indeed, his compassion and integrity were the sole spots of illumination in our descent to the murk of a degraded and wretched world, hidden beneath the glamour of the gas-lights.

I expelled my breath with admiration.

"You really like it?" he asked, rubbing his palms together with anticipation.

"I like the last part, where you stop pulling punches."

"Well, I couldn't come right out and describe the things we saw, of course."

I nodded and said, "You seem unsure about Shantyville. Whether it's wretched or exciting."

With a wink, David said, "It can be both, don't you think? Repulsive and yet attractive at the same time. I certainly know plenty of people like that."

I thought on Jesse Wilson and said, "Yeah. That's true."

"Well, now that I have set the scene, as it were, I think it's time I gave a more detailed account of you and your adventures. Are you going back to Shantyville to-night?"

"I am. But it won't be for any slum sociable."

"Oh?"

"I'll be looking for a killer."

David rubbed his hands together, cracking his knuckles.

Then he leaned closer to me and said, "Go on."

His lips were pursed beneath his thin mustache in an attitude of concentration.

"It's the same man who tried to kill your father to-day."

"The ruffian on the train?"

"Yes. And the same man who you almost came to blows with last night. Remember?"

David's eyes grew wide. His lips parted slightly.

"You mean that was *him*?"

"Uh-huh. Have you ever seen him around before, David?"

"Never," he said, shaking his head vigorously.

"What about your sister, Elsie? Might she have seen him somewhere?"

He propped his lower lip up with his two index fingers and stared out at Lansdowne Valley.

"Why would Elsie have ever seen this creature?"

"You tell me. I got the feeling from my interview with her to-day that she not only knew this Jesse Wilson but also knew about a certain murder in Shantyville last night."

David's face was calm but distracted. He kept his eyes on the window.

"There was a murder?" he asked in a disinterested sort of way.

"I would've thought a police intelligence reporter would be more curious than that. Yes, there was a murder. A young girl we believe was a prostitute."

I said "we" though of course I meant only "I." It sounded more official, more definitive in the plural.

"And you think Elsie had something to do with that?"

There was just the hint of hostility in his placid voice.

"I don't mean to offend. It's just that your sister wasn't too cooperative when I tried asking her about Jesse Wilson."

"Exactly what do you mean by that, Detective?"

"I don't know," I said, shaking my head apologetically.

"It's an instinct you develop. When someone knows something they don't want to tell you—well, it's clear what's going on."

"Clairvoyancy?"

"No, more like the feeling you get when you're in a room by yourself and suddenly you know that someone's come in, behind your back. Elsie knew everything that had been done to that body, David. It was like a story she'd heard before."

"Detective, can I confide in you?"

He motioned for me to lean closer. I did until our hat brims nearly touched.

"My sister is a very *nervous* young lady. In common English she's not quite right in the head. Surely you noticed."

There were plenty of things that were queer about her that I'd noticed. The way she got lost in her thoughts, the poetry she recited out of nowhere, her fear of somebody trying to kill her, the morbid fascination with my job.

I could see that David had something to work with there.

"It may be true that she's disturbed, David. But a policeman kind of gets interested when a handsome young woman like her says somebody's trying to kill her. Especially when that person is her father."

"She *said* that?" David shouted. "Why, that's outrageous!"

"Elsie also told me your father was trying to drive her mad. Would he have a reason for doing that?"

"What do *you* think? Of course not! Oh, Elsie. If she isn't the end! What are we going to *do* with her?"

The boy covered his face in exasperation.

"I've got to find her. She knows something, David. Something you might not want to look at. Maybe she's been looking at it for too long and that's what's driving her mad."

"What could it possibly be?"

"Maybe your father could tell us."

"Father? He couldn't tell you anything except facts and figures relating to strip mining and board meetings."

I thought of the needle in the girl's neck and asked, "What could he tell us about opium, David?"

He wasn't prepared for that one. Something appeared to get in his eyes. For a few seconds he paused, blinking. Then he said, "Why would you ask that?"

"Your father's buying into one of the largest morphine producers in the country, right here in Philadelphia. I've been noticing opium turning up a lot since I found the dead girl."

"I still don't see what my father would have to do with that. Opium is a perfectly legitimate business commodity."

"Sure it is. But how legitimate was the dive we went into last night? The Oriental Saloon?"

"Just some profligate Celestials," David said, dismissing the idea with a wave of his hand.

"I wonder where they get their opium and the license to operate. How they manage to keep American whores, white girls, there without offending somebody or another."

David knotted his brow and prepared to say something spiteful. I cut him off before he got the chance.

"I have it on good authority that Jesse Wilson supplies his lady friend with opium. She herself is habituated to the stuff. I found an opium-smoking tool embedded in the murdered girl. Meanwhile this opium-smoking gal and her man try to throw your father off a train after having some words with him over a purse containing a token to a disorderly house and a pornographic booklet. Do you begin to see the implications here? Or is your reporter's instinct in a state of hibernation?"

"Are you saying my father had something to do with the murder of this, this whore?"

"I'm saying I don't like the way things are beginning to fit together. Do you?"

"No, goddamn it. I don't."

"Now, now. No need to break a commandment over it."

David laughed and said, "I didn't know you were a religious man."

"Some days it's the only thing that convinces me to get out of bed."

"Of course!" David said, trying to snap his fingers then realizing he couldn't with the gloves on them. "You're trying to atone for the kidnapped boy. Manufacturing this whole affair to wipe off your besmirched escutcheon."

I wasn't quite sure what he meant but I denied it anyway.

"I'm only interested in asking some questions. Mainly, I want to know why so many people don't want me or anybody else looking into the death of a girl in Shantyville. And why her death is linked with a young man who wants to see your father dead. A man your sister seems to be acquainted with."

"I don't even want to get into that again, McCleary. And I know nothing about my father's business."

"Sure you don't. I guess things changed for him a little when you were away. Abroad, I mean."

David nodded absentmindedly.

"You know," I said, getting up from the table and looking out at the twilit valley, "it's strange but I seem to remember Elsie telling me you never did go abroad."

There was a silence behind my back.

"I guess her word's not worth much. Her being a cracked nut and all."

I let him think on that for a while. Then I asked him, "Where do you think Elsie went, David? Is she afraid of somebody? Of her father?"

The young man was running his slender fingers through his oiled hair. His voice was laden with weariness.

"I don't know where she is and I don't care."

"No. I got the feeling maybe you didn't. Neither does your old man seem to care much about your sister. Why is that?"

Losing his temper, David crumpled the article I'd been reading and said, between his teeth, "That mad little fool has been getting herself and the rest of us into trouble since she was old enough to wear a long skirt!"

I took slow deliberate steps toward him, my fists clenched at my sides.

"What kind of trouble, David? The male kind?"

"You don't understand."

He covered his face again, as if that could hide him.

I said nothing, waiting.

Finally David spoke after several sighs.

"My sister got into some very bad trouble. You know what I'm referring to?"

"A family sort of problem?"

"Yes," David said wearily. "That's right. The boy was, well, he was unsuitable. Not that I ever met him. I didn't even know what was going on at the time. I was too young."

"When was this?"

"Oh, about ten years ago. Yes, that's right. It was just after the war ended."

"So what happened?"

"The problem was . . ." He searched for a delicate word. "Disposed of."

"And Elsie was not quite the same after that."

"No. She was not. My father had a very difficult time with her. Especially since during the whole affair he had not only to contend with her but with my mother."

I noticed his eyelid was twitching. His whole face was transfixed with pain.

I tried to speak softly, gently, when I asked him to explain about his mother.

"She died," he said. The words were spoken like they were in a foreign tongue, meaningless.

"I'm sorry, David."

"Thank you. Well, you can see that my father and I had a lot of problems already without Elsie making a mess of things by getting herself pr—you know."

"Mmm hmm. Where was her shadow during all this?"

"I don't understand you."

"Bert Pierce, the Pinkerton detective. Where was he during all this?"

David broke away from my stare and looked down at the well-polished table top. Then he turned from his reflection there and gazed out the window at the darkness.

"He was working for my father. He'd made himself indispensable in the matter of my mother's death. He . . . made sure no one heard about it."

"It was a suicide then?"

David's jaw began to tremble.

"Yes, goddamn it. She hanged herself. In her dressing room."

I put my hand on his shoulder. He left it there.

As I turned to stare out at the night with him, David asked himself, "Why am I telling you all this?"

"Because it's been weighing on you, maybe. Because you think it might have something to do with why a man tried to kill your father."

"And the dead girl? What about her?"

"I don't know. But your sister might have some answers for us."

"I thought you said she was gone."

"Well, that's just something we're going to have to do to-night. Find her. After we find out who the dead girl was."

"Do you think she's run off?"

"Your friend Bert thought so. He was mighty concerned about her."

David raised his eyebrows sardonically.

"Bert is certainly interested in my sister. Of course, my father pays him to keep an eye on her. Always has since the unpleasantness."

"Would Bert have a reason for blackmailing your father? To get back at Elsie or something like that?"

It was an idea that had just entered my brain. I was hoping for an excuse to dislike the man other than the fact that he'd said some painfully accurate things about me. Things that had opened up hidden wounds.

But David disappointed me by saying, "Bert's loyalty is unquestionable. He doesn't have the imagination for blackmail. Plus he's madly in love with Elsie. He wouldn't do anything to hurt her or my family."

"Then who is this Jesse Wilson? And why does he use the initials B.F.?"

"I don't know McCleary. He's a madman. What other explanation is there?"

"There's a better one. Your sister was afraid of giving it to me to-day. I need to find her. Make her change her mind."

David wasn't paying attention anymore. He was still looking out the window into the valley, the gas-lights of Horticultural Hall and the Portugal Building flickering dimly in the night.

His voice came to me as if it were an echo from a vast distance away.

"I thought everything had changed when I got back. The past seemed like a dream, a dimly remembered one that I could forget if I chose to. I wanted to, very much. But the dream was a recurring one. Every night it stole into my mind while I slept. It became like a nightmare. The kind where there's something chasing you. Some terrible monster. You run and run but you can't seem to ever run fast enough. After a while I stopped trying. I would turn around and face it. Not to fight it but to go with it wherever it took me."

"You're not going anywhere unless I say so."

The voice came from behind us.

David, startled out of his near-trance, turned with me to the doorway.

Pemberton Pierce was standing there, leaning against the jamb.

"What kind of nonsense is that you're talking, Davy?"

"Bert, do you have to call me Davy in front of the detective here?"

"I've known you since you were a shaver, Davy. I can't help it sometimes."

"How'd you know I was here?"

"Oh." The man smiled. "I used to be a detective once, in the dark ages."

"Did Father send you after me?"

"He did. We want to make sure you're safe with a lunatic running around. My colleague here can't seem to keep track of his charge. The least I can do is keep an eye on mine."

I tried not to let him rankle me again. And failed.

"David and I were just having a friendly conversation. Didn't your mother ever tell you it was impolite to eavesdrop? Of course the mother of a bastard might not be that conscientious."

"Why you son of a bitch, I'll—"

"Gentlemen!" David said, flinging himself between us. "Children! Simmer down. It's all right if Bert heard us talk. He's intimately acquainted with the problem anyway, McCleary."

That surprised me. Pierce didn't seem like the kind to idolize a spoiled girl. But even if her virtue was gone she still had her money. For a fellow like Pierce *that* was worth idolizing.

"You better be careful what you say around people, Davy. You don't know who you can trust anymore."

He gave the boy a smile that had no trace of joy in it.

David smiled back, just as coldly, and said, "No you

don't. I was just talking out loud. Saying nothing of consequence. Right, McCleary?"

"Sure."

I was watching Pierce. He gave me the sort of look a butcher gives a porker right before he puts the cleaver in its neck.

"Don't worry, Bert," I said. "The family secrets are safe with me. For now."

"They're gonna stay that way, McCleary. I buried them and I can bury you just the same."

David lowered his head, embarassed by the threats.

His voice cracking he said, "Bert, will you just shut the hell up! McCleary is not your problem right now."

"He will be, if you keep running off your mouth about Elsie."

"I've told him enough about Elsie. Enough to help us find her and see that she does no harm to herself or anyone else."

"That's fine," the detective said.

Then as an afterthought, Pierce said, "And by the way, Davy. You better keep those dreams of yours to yourself. Someone's liable to think you're as cra—I mean, in the same state of mind as Elsie. You gotta be careful with things like that."

"Yes," David said. "We all have to be careful."

Their conversation seemed to be in a cipher only they could understand. Beneath their artificially calm demeanor I felt a seething, hateful energy.

Both of them became aware of my silent appraisal. David patted his brow with a monogrammed wipe and said, "It's getting late, Detective. Maybe we should be on our way. I have a story to write for to-morrow's edition after all."

"You might not like to print the things we find out."

Pierce glared while David's shoulders hunched in a shrug.

"All right," I said, taking my revolver out of its holster.

I popped the cylinder and examined the chambers. I knew they were loaded already but I wanted them to know. Especially Pierce. The wooden stock felt cold and dry against my moist palm. I thrust the pistol back into the holster and buttoned my coat.

Without a word we departed for Shantyville and Blanchette's Amazon Theatre.

21

NOBODY SPOKE UNTIL we were at the door to the bawdy
house. A variety show was going on inside. A man in
tights was propped on two chairs, balancing a dozen
dishes on either end of a long pole. It made me nervous
just looking at him.

When Pierce spoke I said, "Shhh," because I thought it
might upset the acrobat.

"What the hell are we doing here anyway?" he de-
manded.

"I'm here to ask a couple questions. You're here to
watch over David and stay the hell out of my way."

I walked through the swinging doors and into a murk
of blue smoke.

The slick-haired bartender saw me right away and began furiously polishing a glass.

The room was dank with the smell of closely packed
people. The kind who weren't necessarily concerned with
hygiene.

Any chair that hadn't been broken over somebody's
head was taken. Clusters of men and women, all with, as
David had put it, bricks in their hats, cackled with vapid
wit.

It was the kind of atmosphere that brought out the brute
in me. A place where you could feel the seedy air con-

dense on your skin, covering it with a sticky sheen.

When I was in Andersonville the smoke from our pine fires had turned our faces darker than any negro's. The filthy air had a way of making you look filthy and feel filthy.

Just stepping into this place brought me back to the prison, to the smell of those pine fires.

I had this sudden fear that if I stayed around long enough I might start to look like all the other people here. Worse, to think like them.

I went to the bar and rapped on the counter.

"Hey there. Where's Ruth Blanchette?"

"She's in the office, out back," the bartender said without taking his eyes off the glass.

"Wanna talk to her," I said.

He pointed toward the back door.

I shook my head and said, "You go fetch her for me."

He did like I told him to.

While I waited for him, I leaned with David and Pierce against the bar, scanning the rest of the saloon. The acrobat was off the stage now. A band had taken over, consisting of a debilitated violin and an unstrung piano. They were playing a minstrel tune. I think it was "Devil Take the Blue-Tail Fly." I started humming along as they sang the refrain:

> *Jimmy crack corn and I don't care*
> *My massa's gone away*

The audience was enthusiastic. Some of them even got up and danced in a slightly lopsided fashion. One fellow threw his arms around his lady friend, burying his head in her ample bosom. He nudged her there like a foraging porker.

"Disgraceful," David said, holding his handkerchief to his nose as if to ward off a bad smell.

I laughed. Not at the drunken dancers, but at David's

reaction. It was nice to know his sensibilities were so easily shocked.

My eyes shifted to the back door, where I saw Ruth Blanchette shambling toward me, a segar wedged between her thick, snarling lips.

Then I went back to looking at the room, feigning disinterest in her.

In a smoky, shadow-masked corner, where the two drunks were making a spectacle of themselves, there was someone who hadn't gotten up to dance. She hid herself pretty well, drawing a shawl over her face and wedging herself between two walls.

As my eyes fell on her she adjusted her shawl, but not fast enough.

I saw the hair beneath it—the snarled, outrageously curled hair of the Circassian Beauty, Hattie Anderson.

I sprang from the bar into the crowd of dancers, leaving a trail of swaying, cursing drunks behind me.

Hattie saw me before I could reach her table.

I yelled back at David and Pierce, "Don't let that woman get away!"

I pointed at Hattie as she dusted out the back way, past the private booths and to the rear door.

There were a few tables in my way and I didn't want to take the time to walk around them.

I leaped on top of one, kicking any lager-beer glasses that were in my way. My boots slid over piles of cards, segars, and small piles of coins.

I jumped from one table to another. When I kicked one fellow's drink out of my way he got a little upset and tried grabbing my ankle. I put a heel in his chin to discourage him. Then I made it off the table and was dashing past the hallway of private booths to the rear door, still swinging on its hinges.

Behind me the Amazon Theatre was in complete chaos. I hoped Pierce would take care of David. The whole place was screaming one big curse at me for upsetting their dancing and their drinking. A few were already in pursuit, brandishing splintered pieces of chairs.

That gave me a reason to chase after Hattie even faster.

I ran through the door, barreling right into an ash can and losing my balance. As I swung out an arm to steady myself, I saw Hattie, her skirts hitched way up, running like hell up Tischner's Lane, toward Elm Avenue.

By the time I stumbled past the ash can, she was out of my sight.

I made the bend and ran up the narrow alley toward Elm, hoping I could get there before she got lost in the crowd.

The alley ran up alongside Murphy's Oyster Saloon and emptied me out onto the plank sidewalks of Elm.

There were plenty of people on the street. Streetcars and locomotives ran up and down the tracks, with carriages and wagons darting between them. My eyes went up one side of Elm and down the other. I saw pencil and paper vendors, pretzel salesmen, guidebook hawkers, street arabs I was sure were pickpocketing, and hordes of laborers and their families, out to take in the excitement.

The Museum was too far down for her to have made it. And she was nowhere to be seen on the street.

Behind me, down Tischner's Lane, I heard a policeman's rattle. Then another familiar sound to any copper— a club ringing against a lamppost. Whoever he was he needed help. There was nothing for me to do in Elm Avenue. I'd lost her in the crowd.

Muttering an oath, I ran back down the alley toward the Amazon Theatre.

I was about halfway there when I passed a building on my right. One that I hadn't noticed on the way up.

Allen's Animal Show.

The gas-lights were dimmed and the place looked shut down for the night.

I hadn't paid much attention to where it was the night before. There were too many other things on my mind.

Now I stared up at the canvas paintings of the two great attractions, the learned pig and the five-legged cow. I wondered if maybe there might not be an added attraction this night. An impromptu engagement.

The side door, where Jesse had taken me to meet Allen, led to the animal pens. I could smell the barnyard aroma from the alley.

I walked through the door, overwhelmed by the powerful stench of hay, half-rotten vegetables, and unwashed beasts. The smell of their manure made the usual horse dumpings I encountered on every street seem aromatic.

Jesse's charge, the learned pig, was having a restful evening. His massive bulk rose and fell with the calmness of sleep.

In the next pen was the five-legged cow. She was a pleasant-looking creature, her large brown eyes wide awake, dainty eyelashes fluttering.

I kept my eyes on the ground, careful not to step on anything that might snap or rustle. I made my way carefully to the cow's pen, pausing now and then to listen. The cow took no notice of me, its tail lazily swiping flies off its rump.

Sure enough, the thing did have five legs. I thought the fifth one might be a fake so I scrutinized each of the limbs. They were all proportioned about the same and as far as I could tell this freak of nature was legitimate.

Then, to my astonishment, the cow grew a sixth leg, right before my eyes.

It stretched out from behind her rump, nestling silently beneath a pile of hay.

Fascinated, I watched as the cow grew another leg, in the same position.

What was really extraordinary about this cow was that it could grow two new legs that looked so human. They even had boots and stockings on them.

I wished for Allen's sake that there had been at least someone other than me to watch.

Then I had to shatter the effect by saying, "All right, Hattie. Get up, slowly. And don't try to run or I'll put a ball in your leg."

A voice issued from behind the cow like a mystic oracle. But its word of wisdom consisted of a four-letter word associated with procreation.

The cow's two extra legs detached themselves as the woman rose to her feet. Bits of hay stuck to the bird's nest she called a coiffure.

She held her hands up like I was robbing her.

"Put your hands down and get out of that pen."

Hattie gave the cow a gentle pat on the head and then climbed between two posts, nearly tripping on one of the beams.

I didn't bother steadying her. If she was trying to catch me off-guard it wouldn't work.

"Let's get out of here and get some fresh air," I said, grabbing her by the wrist.

She went about as willingly as last night's dinner had gone to the chopping block.

I pushed her against the wall of the Animal Show exhibition hall.

In the stark light of the moon her face was stripped of all its exotic mystery and sensuality. There was no paint on it anymore.

Just the frantic look of hopeless terror, like an animal thrown to the ground, with its killer's claws already sinking into its flesh.

"You have some explaining to do, Hattie."

"The copper at the Museum. I remember you."

"That's a good memory you've got. How about remembering why you tried to kill Hiram King this morning?"

Her head shook vociferously.

"I didn't try to kill nobody. That was Jesse. He was out of his head. Been out of his head for weeks."

"What were you and Jesse doing there? You better tell me."

The girl looked over my shoulder, hoping there might be someone, something there who could save her from me.

There wasn't.

"We . . . we were gonna try to get some money out of him."

"Uh-huh. For what?"

"It was Jesse's idea."

"I don't care whose idea it was!"

I grabbed some of her frizzy hair and tugged her face a little closer to mine.

She bit down on her lip and started to sob.

"Jesse w-wanted to make King pay for something he done to him. A long time ago."

"Did he tell you what?"

"He didn't tell me nothing. And I didn't ask."

"Why'd he bring you along then?"

"I had a few things on Hiram King too. And I wanted to prove to Jesse that I wasn't afraid. That I'd do anything for him. I wanted him to know how much I love him."

I let go of her hair like it was tainted.

"Your lover's a killer, Hattie. Did you know that?"

"He didn't kill Hiram King. We woulda heard!"

The fear was deepening in her. Beads of sweat collected at her temples. She ran a tongue over dry lips.

"I'm talking about the girl last night. In the woods behind the Museum."

"What girl? Not King's daughter?"

That stunned me.

I thought how I'd left her at the Judges' Pavilion, not watching over her like I was supposed to.

Was that why no one could find her?

Had Jesse taken her to some quiet place and ripped her body to pieces?

The thought made me grit my teeth with rage.

Hattie saw that look in my eye and backed up into the wall, as if she could melt into it.

"There was a girl, probably a whore from Blanchette's Amazon Theatre. Jesse and I found her. Or maybe Jesse led me to her. She was in a bad way, Hattie. More holes in her than a pin cushion. But with most of the stuffing let out."

Her teeth began to clatter.

"No, that couldn't be. Jesse wouldn't . . ."

"The hell he wouldn't! He killed one girl and tried to kill Hiram King! Now tell me why! What's the link? Where's Elsie King? Did he take her?"

My hands were gripping her arms, kneading her flesh.

She was past the point of feeling that pain. There was a deeper pain inside her, beginning to well up.

"Jesse wouldn't kill that bitch! He wouldn't harm a hair on her lousy head, goddamn him! I wish he would! I wish he would kill her!"

"Why, Hattie?"

"She's what caused all this. She used him once. Now she's using him again! As soon as he heard she was at the Centennial, he goes chasing after her. Leaves me alone at that stinkin' Museum. What's he think I'd do without him around?"

Hattie wasn't making much sense. I wanted her to fill in the gaps for me.

But she rambled on, her shouting drawing curses from lodgers in the nearby hotel.

"He went crazy when he saw her! Started talkin' about killing her old man, running off with her! And he told all this to me like I wouldn't care, like I meant nothing to him. So I went along with him. I wanted him to see the kind of woman I am. To know what I'd do for him. So when this little slut betrays him again he'll know who really loves him. Oh, Jesse . . ."

She began to wail now. There was nothing I could do to stop the torrent of her pain.

"Why did you leave me? Where are you, Jesse? Help me . . ."

I relaxed my grip on her arms and then let go of her. She sank to the cobbled ground.

I felt a great deal of pity for her then. I glanced down at my unsteady hands. They'd been so ready to cause her pain. Now I hoped with a guilty wish that they might comfort her for just a few moments.

The woman had been betrayed by him. I knew how she felt.

I rested a hand on her shoulder, gently.

Then a beam of light fell on her tear-stained face.

We both turned around, startled.

There were some Centennial guards there. And Pemberton Pierce, holding the lantern. I wondered what had happened to David.

Pierce laughed and pointed at me saying, "Get a load of him. He looks like someone just shot his dog. What's the matter, McCleary? She put up too much of a fight for you?"

I stifled the urge to wipe his smile off with the handle of my barker.

"That's the one that tried to kill Mr. King, boys," Pierce said to the Guard coppers.

Hattie Anderson stayed where she was, huddling against the cold brick wall.

Two of the guards picked her up roughly.

"Take her back to the Grounds. And put her somewhere where the tourists won't hear her scream."

That made her start struggling, albeit feebly.

One of the guards slapped her across the face.

The sound made Pierce laugh.

"A good night's work, I'd say."

I made to follow Hattie and the guards.

Pierce stepped in my way. It was getting to be a habit for him.

"Where d'ya think you're goin'?"

"I have some more questions to ask that girl."

"No you don't. Not to-night. We're gonna lock her up

and get a good night's sleep. Then you can talk to her to-morrow."

"I don't have time to wait. Neither does our friend Hiram."

"That's Mr. King to you!"

"Elsie may be dead. Jesse, the killer, might have gotten her."

"We've got things under control, McCleary. Now why don't you drag your ass back to the barracks before I kick it there?"

I thought I might have the pleasure of seeing him try. Then I heard someone hollering behind us.

"McCleary! Pierce! The rest of you! Stop standing around jawing at each other and get back on the street. We're still looking for the King girl."

It was Cap. He wore no hat and had a duster thrown haphazardly over his collarless shirt. His half-asleep eyes focused on Pierce and me.

"I need you boys to patrol Elm. One of the vendors saw her outside the Redwood Tree Exhibit just a few hours ago."

"Was she with anyone?" I asked.

"No."

"Then what business is it of ours if a girl goes for a promenade?" I said.

"Because Mr. Hiram King says it's our business. He wants his daughter back. Now."

"And you just jump up to do the master's bidding, eh?"

Cap tried a look of defiance and didn't quite make it. Instead he hung his head.

I shoved Pemberton Pierce out of my way and glared at Heins, who could not meet my stare.

"Get outta my face, Mack," Heins said gruffly.

"Gladly."

I stalked off, hoping he hadn't seen the hurt on mine.

22

RUTH BLANCHETTE'S ESTABLISHMENT was not having a good night.

When I got there, several Centennial District coppers were lining the various whores against the wall of the Southwark Hotel and writing their names down in memorandum books.

I tapped one of the bulls on his broad shoulder. He turned around with a hand on his club.

Before he could give me a dose of it I made sure he had a good look at my star.

"What's going on down here? I heard someone's rattle."

"Big disturbance, Detective. Someone started a brawl in the saloon here."

I tried not to look guilty.

"One of our boys tried to stop the fight but they thrashed him. That's when the rest of us got here."

A few male patrons of the bawdy house were lying on the ground, clutching their guts. Blood ran down their bruised faces.

"Looks like you gave them an eye for an eye."

The copper smiled and said, "We've been spoilin' for a good fight. But they were a little too drunk to make it fair. We didn't even have to use our clubs."

"You didn't have to, but you did anyway, huh?"

The bull squinted for a moment, trying to discern a slight.

I didn't give his brain enough time to go to work.

"Listen," I said, "are you pulling the house now?"

"Captain's orders. We're taking the whole lot to the station-house for the night."

"Ruth Blanchette going too?"

"No," the bull said. "We let her go so she could tele-graph for the lawyer."

I thanked the patrolman and we exchanged salutes.

There didn't seem to be much left for me to do. I was about to go back to the barracks and see if Tad was awake.

Then I noticed, at the edge of the crowd, a woman creeping away stealthfully.

She didn't see me watching her. Neither did any of the other coppers notice her retreating figure.

For a second I toyed with the idea of alerting the bulls. Then I quietly followed her down Viola Street.

The woman was in a hurry, though I didn't think she had any particular destination. She just wanted to put as much distance between her and the coppers as she could.

I passed the shooting gallery, a few night owls still firing away at tin cans with tiny rifles. One fellow won a segar and promptly shoved it into his paramour's mouth, where there were three others.

The woman darted past the Oriental Saloon where the gas-lights were being extinguished by a quaintly clad Celestial with sleepy eyes.

There was a narrow space between the saloon and a hotel for Germans. It was half filled with garbage—soiled undergarments, scraps of tin, and bottles.

By this time I'd narrowed the distance between us till I was just a rod away. I ran up to her, and before she noticed the echo of my boot heels, I had her in a garroter's hold and pulled her kicking and mutely screaming into the dark alley.

Her eyes were filled with mortal terror as I pressed her head softly against the alley wall.

I said to her, "I'm a police detective. I'm not going to hurt you. I just wanted us to be off the street when we had our talk. Now I'm going to take my hand from your mouth and you are not going to scream. Is that understood?"

I had to wait a few moments for her to collect herself. Then she nodded.

"Okay," I said, removing my head. "What's your name?"

She barely got it out.

"Alice."

Her mouth stayed wide open, a few strands of saliva stretching from lip to lip.

"Calm down. I told you. We're just going to have a talk. Like we had this morning. Remember?"

It was clear to me that the girl did not remember me in the slightest. Of course, when I'd met her in the hall-way of the Amazon Theatre she'd been three sheets to the wind.

"I was the one in the buzzer's booth," I said, hoping to stimulate her memory.

She raised an eyebrow and her eyes grew lidded. I thought she was going to vomit.

I twigged Alice still had a few back teeth afloat.

"I don't remember nothing."

"You probably like it that way too," I said gently.

"S'right. Makes life easier."

"Well, you can at least remember your friends, right?"

"You wanna be my friend? Is that what you want?"

Her attempt at seductiveness was perfunctory. She had the lack of emotion of a true professional. Which was saying a lot for a girl who couldn't have been more than seventeen.

"No," I said. "I want to hear about a friend of yours."

"I don't got no friends. Maybe Ruth, when she ain't drunk."

"What about some of the girls?"

"They're all bitches. Don't even belong in a house. They don't have it anymore. They should be walkin' the street. But Ruth has a soft heart."

"A regular angel of mercy."

I tried steering Alice's juiced-up brain back to my original topic.

"I just don't believe a pretty girl like you wouldn't have any friends there. But maybe they're just jealous of you."

There was nothing too pretty about this one anymore. Her plain face seemed drained from all the paint she put on it. Like there had been acids slowly corroding it over the years.

Her lips tried for a smile but all they could manage was a smirk.

"That's right. I could work in a real high-class house if I wanted to! But I like the dancing. Half the time that's all they want, is to watch me dance. If that's all I have to do that's A-1 with me."

"Well, I'll bet you could go wherever you wanted. But they need fresh, young girls like you. I bet Ruth ropes them in regular."

"Not Ruth. Jack, the bartender. He's the one who goes out and recruits in the city."

I made a mental note of that. If I ever went back I'd make sure to slap Jack around a little. Maybe make him less pretty to the kind of girls he picked up at depots and confectioner stands. The kind who succumbed with ease to his blandishments and empty promises.

"Did he recruit any fresh fish this summer?"

Alice shrugged and said, "You saw them all lined up back there. They didn't look so fresh to me."

"No they didn't." I chuckled insincerely. "But I don't think all of the girls were there."

"What do you mean?"

Her bloodshot eyes narrowed.

"I mean there was someone missing. Someone's been missing. Isn't that right?"

The girl's head swayed like a buoy in turbulent waters.

"No, no. I ain't supposed to talk about Susie."

Alice put a hand to her forehead, pinching her skull.

"You can tell me about Susie. Don't you trust me?"

"You're a copper. They told us not to let a peep out. Especially to coppers."

"Who told you?"

She struggled to shake her head.

"I can't . . ."

"Sure you can. You can talk to me. I'm a nice person. Haven't I been nice so far?"

Then I decided to give her a little reminder.

"I could have told the bulls back there when I saw you running off. But I didn't. That was nice of me, wasn't it? I didn't have to do that. I could have pinched you myself. I could still take you back there."

I feigned an attack of conscience and took hold of her arm.

"Maybe I've done the wrong thing. Maybe I should have pinched you."

"No!" the girl said, grasping my arm. "You don't wanna do that!"

"You're right. I don't. But they told me I have to pinch one of you gals to-night. Now, I think you're a very nice girl. I don't want to pinch you at all. Maybe if you told me about the other one—the one who was missing—I could take her in instead? Let you go? How does that sound to you?"

She took a few seconds to wrestle with her conscience. Her conscience didn't win the bout.

"That sounds okay," Alice said. "I never liked Susie Adams anyway."

The outraged, mutilated thing I found last night had a name now.

"Susie," I said to myself.

"She was selling stale pretzels and half-rotten fruit on Elm Avenue when Jack found her," my Magdalen friend said with contempt.

There was a whole cluster of vendors on the corner of Elm and Belmont. Poor bedraggled souls hawking cheap wares like stale bread, fruit, flags, guidebooks, and souvenir coins. They couldn't make much money, but the work was more of a pretense anyway. Especially with the young girls who would sell their bodies as casually as they sold a box of pencils.

"How long was Susie at the theatre?"

"Not long. A month or so. She was a good dancer. I'll give her that. A real pistol."

"Was she an opium smoker?"

I was thinking of the yen-nock I'd pulled from her slit throat.

"Maybe a few times when she went over to the coolies."

"At the Oriental Saloon?"

"Yeah. But she was nothing like Harriet."

"Anderson?" I said, subduing the excitement I felt. "You mean Hattie Anderson?"

"Yeah. That one loved her pipe."

"Was she there to-night when the house got pulled?"

I knew quite well where Hattie had been. But I thought Alice might know more.

"I haven't seen Hattie Anderson around in ages. Not since early this summer. Ruth kicked her out. The opium ruined her. I heard she got a job on Elm Avenue. Dancing, I think."

"With a snake."

Alice wasn't listening to me anymore. She was beginning to nod off. I gave her a tap on the cheek. Then another, hard enough to make her eyes open.

"You're leaving me, dear."

"Sorry. Been a long day. A long life . . ."

"We were talking about Hattie and Susie. Did the two of them get to know each other?"

"I reckon so. Susie arrived just before Hattie went off."

"Alice?"

"Yeah," she said, sleepily.

Her shoulders were slumping beneath her plain black wrapper. She was going to lose consciousness pretty soon.

"Where did Susie go? Why wasn't she there to-night?"

"Went on a job last night. Didn't come back. Musta been some party."

"Where?"

"Ruth sent her." Alice looked blankly across the alley and said, "Lemme see . . . what'd she say? Susie was gonna take a trip to the Art Gallery."

"At the Centennial?"

"I don't know. I thought she was foolin'. I never even been to the Centennial. And it ain't open at night, is it?"

I shook my head.

"See? She was goin' at night. So I know Ruth was foolin'. She just didn't want me to know where Susie was goin'. But I thought it was queer."

"Me too," I said gravely. "Did someone come for her?"

"I saw her, just as she was goin' out. So I ask her where does she think she's tramping off to? And she says to me, 'To the museum.' She was just foolin' with me like Ruth did. Then she just walked off. And I ain't seen her to-day. Maybe she went to the Centennial and got lost. I heard it's plenty big."

"Susie got lost all right. But I found her last night. She was dead, Alice. Somebody killed her."

Alice snickered and said, "You got a sense of humor. Not like most coppers I know."

"I'm not fooling you. I saw Susie's body. Somebody stabbed her. Ripped her throat open."

"No! Did they stab her a lot? How many times? Was there a lot of blood?"

Alice's concern touched me deeply.

I was annoyed enough to say, "I tell you a friend of yours gets killed and you're asking me how many times did they stab her?"

"What do I care if Susie gets croaked? To hell with her. She's just another whore like me. You think any of us live long enough to die of old age?"

"Why would someone want to kill her, Alice? Can you think of anyone who would want to do it?"

"I've almost been killed a dozen times!" She started sniffling. "Nobody cares about that! One used a broom handle on me once. Not to give me no licking neither!"

I tried and failed to keep the disgust off my face.

"That ain't pretty, mister. Lemme tell you. So pardon me for not gettin' all broken up when Susie gets herself croaked. It ain't the first time and it won't be the last."

"Who would do that to her?"

Alice wasn't listening. She stared at the ground, mumbling a litany of sins, the ones done by her and to her. The latter seemed to outweigh the former.

I grabbed her by the arms and gave her a good shaking. I managed to say, "Names."

Alice just laughed and said, "Are you kiddin'? We don't care about their names."

I left her laughing. By the time I'd gotten to the end of the alley Alice had fallen to the ground, hugging her knees. Her laughter had turned to a maudlin weeping.

23

I DON'T KNOW how long I wandered through Shantyville.

My legs ached with every step I took. After I traversed Columbia Avenue and headed up Belmont, I paused in the middle of the empty street.

Closing my eyes, I remembered playing blind man's buff as a child. It was never much fun being the one with the blindfold on. I could still hear my squeal of delight as my brother or one of our playmates sightlessly groped for us.

It had been easy for me to elude the buff.

But now the tables had turned. I felt an invisible blindfold tied tightly around my eyes. Just beyond my reach were the shreds of information that I needed so desperately—links in a chain I could use to bind . . .

Who?

That was another problem. I didn't even know who to grasp in my blindness. There were too many people dancing around me, taunting me.

Jesse Wilson, Elsie King, Hiram King, Hattie Anderson, Susie Adams.

B.F.

Whoever that was. I was not quite sure anymore that it was Jesse.

This morning it had seemed so simple to me.

Jesse Wilson was a homicidal maniac. He'd killed Susie Adams out of sheer blood lust and had a bone to pick with the King family for some perceived slight. Perhaps he had just fixated on them when he happened to see their portraits in *Frank Leslie's Illustrated Newspaper*.

But then why would he have conspired with Hattie Anderson to blackmail Hiram King? And what would they blackmail him for?

Blackmailing was a dirty but decidedly sane proposition.

I asked myself to explain why then did Jesse and Hattie bring along those items in Hattie's purse? What possible significance did they have to the blackmailing of Hiram King over Elsie's youthful seduction and ruin?

The Amazon Theatre had given me some ideas. But the Art Gallery was another matter, one that I would have to look into much more.

Especially after what Alice told me. Susie Adams, the last time they had seen her alive, told them she was going to the Art Gallery. The Museum, she called it.

Yes, I thought. She was following the directions on the back of the card. Where it was written: "These Delights can be Yours. Back of Museum. Midnight."

The blindfold felt like it was loosening, just a bit.

I would have to ask Hattie Anderson about that Art Gallery trade card. And what a person like Susie Adams would be doing making a midnight rendezvous there.

Tad Schmoyer told me there were no guards posted at the Art Gallery on some nights. There had been no explanations for that.

I thought now I might have one.

Suddenly the blindfold seemed to slip down the bridge of my nose. Not all the way but far enough that I could see where I was and where I had to go.

Hattie and I were going to have a talk to-morrow morning, bright and early.

In the meantime, I decided, I had better get back to the barracks to get some shut-eye.

Without even being aware of it, I had circumambulated all of Shantyville, from Elm all the way down to Girard Avenue and back. Now I was on the corner of Elm and Belmont, listening to the cars shuffling into the majestic Pennsylvania and Reading Railroad Depot. Hiram King was a powerful man indeed if he was a boss with that outfit. The rails stretched like arteries from the coal country up north. Those chunks of anthracite in the cars were our city's life's blood.

No wonder King and his cohorts had hired the Big Man to get rid of the troublesome Irish miners, the Molly Maguires. We had to have our coal. Without coal there was no steam and without steam there was no progress. Our Union was shaping up to be an industrial juggernaut, and no one would be allowed to stand in its way.

Across the railways and streetcar tracks was the Centennial, looming like some beautiful unfinished vision of heaven. Everything that we wanted to be.

Here in Shantyville, there were no such illusions. This place was a miniature version of the way the world actually was. Here the bad mingled with the good. Lofty things like redwood trunks and oil wells were surrounded by shooting galleries, saloons, and freak shows.

Two worlds that were so close and yet never seemed to touch.

I thought on our late hero George Armstrong Custer and the far-off world where he was slain. Wyoming, that savage place, seemed a million miles away from the Centennial. But they were part of the same nation. The Corliss Engine could not quite mask the Red Indians.

The Centennial could not shake off Shantyville.

But woe to those who dared to travel from one world to the next.

Susie Adams had tried. She paid a high price for her folly.

Maybe, I thought, that was what Jesse and Hattie were trying to do—force their way into the dream. They were looking in the wrong place and trying to take something by violence that could never be taken that way.

They would fail. It was my job to ensure their failure.

I shook my head with dismay.

I've been hit over the head too many times, I thought. I've forgotten the rules to the game.

The rules were that you didn't worry about their feelings. Nor did you worry about yours. Just like a soldier.

The enemy should never have a face and you should never have a heart.

I repeated that phrase to myself again and again, hoping to drive away a vile thing called pity.

Searching my pockets, I found the tiny bag of honey-roasted cashews I'd bought a few days before.

They were a passion of mine. Back in the days when I walked a beat I always had a bag with me. I craved their sweetness.

Leaning against a lamppost, I watched my shadow stretch over the corner. The shadow waxed and waned with the unsteady gas-light. Crickets were chirping in the woods beyond the depot. Their murmuring made me feel quite peaceful, reminding me there was a calm undercurrent to all the madness I saw, both outside and within.

My eyes were drawn to some moths, banging themselves against the glass facets of a street lamp. They didn't seem to ever give up trying to get at that flame. A flame that would annihilate them.

Then there was the sound of horse's hooves against the cobbles. I turned to my right and saw a New York style cab, the kind that look like little omnibuses. The gas-lamps on either side of the driver's seat flared orange against the sleek, black body. The horse came to a stop, its burly driver resting his crop across his knees.

The man looked down on me and gestured to the cab.

I couldn't see who was inside with the tasseled curtains drawn.

There was a rear door with a tiny metal footstep. I walked over to it and was getting ready to go inside when the door opened quickly, nearly smacking me in the face.

The gas-light stole into the shadowy interior, illuminating the face of Elsie King.

Her cheeks were flushed with excitement. When I looked at her eyes, they were free of the blankness and melancholy I'd seen that afternoon. Now they were alive with joy.

"Mr. McCleary!" she said. "I'm so glad I've found you."

"Elsie! What on earth are you doing running about!"

"Shhh," she said, holding a black-gloved finger to her lips. "This is a secret. No one's supposed to know where I am."

Then she giggled like a schoolgirl and said, "I'm going away!"

I could see that. She was dressed for a trip, her jersey draped with a brocaded velvet wrap, its beaded gimp and lace trimming almost as exquisite as her joyful face.

"Where are you going?" I said. "To an audience with a queen somewhere?"

"No!" she laughed. "But you're close! I've found a prince. My prince!"

Now it was my turn to laugh.

"I mean it!" she said. "He's waiting for me now. I saw him to-day out here. And he was just the same. Just as beautiful."

That invisible blindfold slipped off pretty much all the way.

I said, "You mean Jesse Wilson?"

"Harding! Jesse Harding is his name."

"The same one who tried to kill your father," I said, making to get into the cab.

She barred my way with the delicate fan she bought at the Japanese Bazaar.

"Jesse did not try to kill anyone. He's the one who's been wronged, Mr. McCleary! And I! I wronged him more than anyone! Ten years it took me to find him again. Oh! you don't know how much I've hated him. Wished him dead and in hell for leaving me. But that's all over now!"

"Elsie," I said, grabbing the handle of the door. "You don't know what you're doing. This Jesse Wil—I mean, Jesse Harding is a killer! One woman is dead already. Maybe more. Don't let him fool you!"

She shook her head sadly, like I'd just passed up my one and only opportunity to get into heaven.

"It's you who are being fooled, Mr. McCleary. Jesse and I had a long talk in a quiet place. And he told me all about what happened to him and to us. I didn't want to believe him at first. I just wanted to hate him, to hurt him if I could. For leaving me alone. My father had always told me he was guilty, that he was as evil as they all said he was. After a while I believed him. But I can't keep forcing myself to believe that lie any more. I've seen Jesse and . . ."

She pressed her hands together, enraptured.

"I still love him! I've set him as a seal upon my heart, as a seal upon my arm. Do you know that verse, Mr. McCleary?"

"Yes, Elsie. It's Scripture. The Song of Solomon."

"For love is strong as death," Elsie said, still quoting. "Its flashes are flashes of fire, a most vehement flame. Many waters cannot quench love, neither can floods drown it."

Then she looked past me and said again, "Love is strong as death."

I put a restraining arm on her and said, "Elsie, I'm going to take you back to the hotel. Where you'll be safe. Please, Elsie."

My pleading evoked a sympathetic cluck.

"Mr. McCleary. I'm sorry I gave you trouble this afternoon. You're a good man. Jesse told me so himself. He thinks you can help us. Will you do that?"

"I don't know what you're talking about, Elsie!"

"Help us!"

"When you come with me, I'll see about that."

I pulled her right arm, hoping to get her out of the cab. She looked past my shoulders again, a little sadly this time.

Too late, I turned to meet the driver's fist. It crashed into the side of my head.

I fell on the pavement, stunned. The fellow packed quite a wallop.

By the time I got to my feet and was shaking the pain out of my head, the cab was long gone.

24

My sleep was intermittent that night, punctuated by a barrage of unpleasant dreams. The next morning, after bathing and putting on my other black morning suit, I headed to the American Restaurant for my breakfast. Tad Schmoyer was already on duty by then so I ate alone. There was a copy of the *Ledger* at the table and I was happy to see that September 7 would be a relatively cool day—with the mercury not topping sixty-seven degrees. Upstate, in Hiram King's territory, the Molly Maguire trials had resumed. One of them was sentenced to hang on, of all dates, Hallowe'en. The redskins were getting troublesome out west again and a relative of John Brown of Harper's Ferry fame was eaten alive by dogs. In the city a certain George Koenig "behaved badly" before some children and was sent inside by the magistrate. I had to laugh at the terms the newspapers came up with. I translated behaving badly as exposing his private parts to the shavers. I wished the little scamp the worst of times in Moyamensing.

The news came close to giving me an attack of dyspepsia. There never seemed to be anything good that was fit to print. I washed my catfish down with very black coffee, not nearly as strong as the stuff in the Tunisian Cafe.

I was in a generous mood and tipped the waiter ten cents. He was happy to get it.

Then I headed over to the Central station-house to make my usual ten o'clock rendezvous with Heins.

As I stepped inside the door and nodded to Cap's clerk, I heard a pleasant greeting from behind the door to his office.

"McCleary, where the hell have you been? Get your ass in here!"

I stepped into Cap's office, hung my straw hat on the hook, and said, "A good morning to you too, sir."

Somebody snickered to my side and I saw that David King was already seated in one of the armchairs.

"Hello, McCleary. Glad to see you're in one piece."

He shook my hand without his usual effusiveness.

"What's the matter, David?" I asked. "You look glum."

"If you'd shut yer yap you might hear why," said a voice behind the door I'd opened.

It was Pemberton Pierce. The deep circles under his baleful eyes told me he hadn't gotten a great deal of sleep. His chapped lips scowled beneath his drooping mustache.

"David, show him the letter," Heins ordered, before I could make a retort.

The reporter took a letter from inside his pocket and placed it in my hand.

As I progressed through the brief letter, I could feel the sweat break out all over me.

The words were formed not unlike those I'd seen printed on the newspaper clippings in Hattie's flat.

They were clearly in Jesse's hand:

I almost wish I had thrown you from the train yesterday. But now I'm going to do you worse than death. I've got Elsie. You're going to have to pay to get her back. Pay for ten years of hell. That's a fair trade. Your daughter's life for thirty thousand dollars. You can give it to me to-night. On the

*Grounds. At midnight. Meet me behind the Penn-
sylvania Building. Bring the money if you want to
see Elsie alive again. And bring Hattie Anderson.
If I don't get Hattie first your daughter loses her
life. You'll do it, King—won't you? You remember
how good I was with a knife.*

> *Yours affectionately,*
> *The Boy Fiend*

"B.F.," I said. "The Boy Fiend."

"A killer," David said. "Quite well known back home."

"You ever hear of him, McCleary?" Heins asked.

"Should I have?"

I thought back to last night, remembering I had still
pitied Jesse Harding. The memory was tinged with shame
now.

Elsie was within my reach. And I'd let her go. She
must've gone straight to him after that. Straight into the
arms of a ruthless, bloodthirsty maniac.

Elsie's life was in dreadful danger.

And it was all my fault.

All those illusions I'd had were gone now. I'd foolishly
tried to see the enemy's face—Jesse Harding's supposed
humanity. Instead I projected my own face on him, along
with all my fears and hopes.

Like all the others, I'd fallen for his romantic claptrap.

A horrible mistake. Maybe a fatal one, for Elsie.

I sank to one of the armchairs, thinking what a miser-
able failure I was.

Chewing on a knuckle, I fought back tears of rage and
despair.

I was ashamed to tell them that I'd seen Elsie. It was
the third time I could've had Jesse Harding pinched. Three
chances all blown to hell—a place I felt well suited for
at that moment.

I resisted an urge to break the second commandment and silently gnawed my knuckle.

"Don't take it so hard," David said, resting a hand on my shoulder. I wanted to tear it off—tell him I wasn't worth his sympathy—that his sister was in danger because of me.

"The case is a pretty old one. About ten years," David went on, taking another envelope from his coat pocket. There were some newspaper clippings inside. He spread them on the desktop and motioned me over to read them. "I managed to dig these up at the *Bulletin*."

Someone had printed the year at the top: 1866.

The beginning of ten years of hell for Jesse Harding.

I vowed to give him some more time there.

The head-line of the earliest article got me grinding my teeth:

A YOUTHFUL FIEND
JESSE HARDING CONFESSES
THE ATROCIOUS MURDER OF
DANNY CURRAN

Mauch Chunk, Penn., June 20—Jesse Harding made a full confession of the murder of Danny Curran to Chief of Police Savage to-day, which he read at the Coroner's in-quest. It was in the following words: "I opened my mother's store on the morning of May 18 at 9:30. The Curran boy came in for papers. I told him there was a store downstairs. He went down to about the middle of the cellar and stood facing Broadway. I followed him, put my left arm about his neck, my hand over his mouth, and, with my knife in my right hand, cut his throat. I then dragged him to and behind the water closet, laying his head furthermost up the place, and put some stones and ashes on the body. I took the ashes from a box in the cellar. I sent a boy to Hoyt & Lawrence's store, nearby, and bought the knife a week before for twenty-five cents. The knife was taken from me when I was arrested. My mother and sister never knew anything about the affair. I forgot to tell you that I washed my hands and knife, which were bloody, at the water pipe."

Chief Savage also exhibited to the jury a plan of the cellar which the boy drew from memory. It was remarkably well executed, and very correct. Mrs. Curran, the mother of the murdered boy, was the only other witness examined. The jury then adjourned until Wednesday.

I pulled out my handkerchief and gave my forehead a wipe. The handkerchief was damp when I stuffed it back in my pocket.

I read the second article, feeling my guts contract.

THE BOY FIEND
CONFESSION BY HIM
OF THE MURDER
OF THE BOY MILLEN

Mauch Chunk, Penn., June 23—Jesse Harding, the boy murderer, has confessed that he murdered the Millen boy on the 22d of last May.

The *Democrat* says that the boy has made a full and clear confession of his own free will to two persons at least, and probably to more than two. Although these persons are not at liberty, at the present time, to disclose the whole story, they are willing that the public should know the essential particulars, and these we will give, though not in Jesse's own words.

On the morning of the 22d of May, Jesse rose early and went to his mother's store, and afterward went into town, returning home about 9 o'clock. He remained at the store until 11:30 o'clock, when he told his mother that he was going into town. She gave her permission, and he went over to his mother's house, where he remained a few moments and then started for the town proper. He however went up Race Street, where he saw little Horace Millen, and immediately an evil genius got possession of him, and he determined to torture him, if not to kill him. He asked the boy if he would like to see the old White Haven Canal, and the boy said he would, and both started off in the direction of the river. When they arrived at the spot where the body was found, Jesse told the Millen boy to lie down, and the little fellow, not dreaming of his danger, did so. The young fiend then immediately sprang upon him, clapped his left hand over the little innocent's mouth to stop his outcries, and then, with the same jack knife that had but a month before been used to murder the unfortunate Danny Curran, the monster deliberately cut the throat of the little boy who had so implicitly trusted him. The boy struggled fearfully, and the murderer, desperate at his failure in not at the first blow killing his victim, stabbed him repeatedly in the bowels and chest. He mutilated the body in a frightful manner, but does not know, he says, to what extent, and finally left his victim in a dying condition. He cleaned his knife and person as well as he could, and then went back into town, going to the Narrows where he remained for some time, and then returned home.

The young murderer gives the same reason for committing this deed as he did for killing Danny Curran, "that he could not help it." He had no intention of killing anyone up to the time of meeting Horace Millen, and the nefarious plan entered his head on the instant he beheld the boy. Once, he says, conscience of something made him turn back after he had started and leave the boy where he had found him, but something seemed to draw him on, and "he had to go." Jesse further stated that he made this confession not because it gave him pleasure, but because he feared his mother, sister, or someone else might be suspected.

"Pierce, go get McCleary a glass of water. He looks fit to puke."

I stared blankly at the articles until Pierce slammed a half-filled glass of water on the desk.

Some of the water went down the wrong place. I started choking. It took a few deep coughs to clear things up.

I pretended I had a headache, covering my face with a trembling hand.

I didn't want them to see the anguish in my eyes. Getting control of myself, I said to David, "Tell me the rest of it."

"People were in a panic over their children. They would've brought the Army up to police the streets if they could have. Might have been a good idea considering all the trouble the Molly Maguires are giving us now."

"So what stopped him?" I asked.

David swung his arm with a grandiose gesture to Pemberton Pierce and said, "Our hero."

Heins and I were both surprised.

"*You* nailed the kid?" Cap said.

"You bet I did," Pierce said confidently. "Those hayseeds didn't know a damn thing about finding a killer. It took an old secret service detective to show them their business."

"Pierce is very proud of his military service," David said.

"And why not? I served Mr. Pinkerton in '62. Stayed with him until McClellan got the boot. Got a letter of commendation from him. Then I signed on with Baker till '64."

"Good for you," Heins said. "Now tell us, how did you get the kid?"

"After the war I went back to work for Mr. King. I was supposed to look after Miss Elsie and David—there'd been some threats. And he needed someone to handle certain elements among his workers. I shadowed a man to the Harding store where a lot of them gathered to buy their necessities. I was going to arrest one of them but there were too many of his pals around. So I waited until he went out back to use the water closet. I was all set to collar him when I saw the kid there, Jesse Harding, sticking a knife into the mud. I said to him, 'That's a silly way to clean a blade.' And he tries to hide it. Then I noticed there was blood all over his hands. I asked him if he'd been butchering and he said yes. I went and collared the man after he'd done his business and thought nothing more of the kid.

"Until the next morning when I read about them finding the Millen boy's body. They said he was stabbed and I immediately remembered that boy with the knife. Seemed a little suspicious. So I took some of the local coppers with me to the Harding store and we searched the whole place. I was lucky enough to find a leaden soldier the boy had stolen from Danny Curran. He was stupid enough to hide it in a segar box under his bed, the little bastard. We also found a top that the Millen boy's mother said belonged to her son. Then I did a little more digging in the backyard and there was Danny Curran's body. So I grabbed Jesse Harding and marched him right back to the station-house."

"It sure took a while for the kid to confess."

"That hick son of a bitch Savage kept hemmin' and hawin'."

"The police chief?" I said. "Why?"

"He believed the kid's story—that he was innocent. The kid was pretty convincing, I'll give him that. Shoulda taken to confidence games instead of killing.

"Anyway, we weren't getting anywhere with Harding until one night Savage and I marched him into the funeral parlor where they had Horace Millen. Savage showed him the body, shoved his face right into it, and said, 'Did you kill him?' You shoulda seen how he bawled then. He told us right there and we wrote the whole damn thing down in my memorandum book. Took it to the coroner and that was that. He was set to hang."

"So what happened?" I asked. "What's he doing at the Centennial trying to kill Hiram King and abducting his daughter?"

David was about to talk when Pierce cut him off.

"Mr. King pushed really hard for Harding to hang. Both of the kids were children of his employees. The Governor, that yellow-belly, wouldn't sign the death warrant. Said the kid was too young. So Harding got a life sentence instead."

"That still doesn't tell us what he's doing out," Heins said.

David gathered up his newspaper articles and said, "He was very, very clever, Captain Heins. They had him in a cell at our county prison, right in Mauch Chunk. Once I tried to peek over the wall with some other children to get a look at him in the yard there. We shouted curses at him and threw down rocks until the guards threatened us. Anyway, he was kept in a cell in the basement. Solitary confinement. Harding waited several weeks, right before he was about to be transferred down here to the Eastern State Penitentiary. Then he punctured a gas pipe in his cell. The gas leaked into the air. He must've waited a long time, letting it fill the whole, cramped space. Almost enough to kill him. Then he lit a match. You could hear the explosion a square away I heard. The cell door blew off and three prisoners were seriously injured. Part of the tiny window to the outside had cracked away and there was enough space for him to crawl through. After the smoke had cleared they found he was gone. Somehow he'd managed to scale the wall and clambered into the forest beyond. They never found him."

"Until now," I said. "I wonder why he came here of all places."

"He's a maniac, McCleary," Heins said from across his desk. "What's there to wonder about?"

"Well, what does Hattie Anderson have to say about this?"

"Who?" the three of them said.

"The Circassian Beauty! The one who was with him when he threw King off the prismoidal railway car. You pinched her last night, Bert. Don't tell me you forgot so soon."

The detective looked at me like I was speaking in tongues. Then he turned to the other men with a shrug.

"I don't know what you're talking about. I helped the Guard boys collar some whores at the Amazon Theatre. I don't know anything about this Anderson wench."

"Is that so?" I said, getting out of the armchair. I faced Cap and said, "This man here was with me when I found Hattie Anderson at Allen's Animal Show. Last night. The Guard came and hauled her off to the station-house. Now where is she?"

"Your boy's got his facts messed up," Pierce said to Heins. "I was nowhere near that Animal Show. I had too much going on at the bawdy house."

"What the hell's all this about, Mack?" Cap said, looking at Pierce nervously.

I expelled my breath in an exasperated laugh.

"This son of a bitch is a damn liar, sir. He has that Anderson girl and I don't know what the hell he's done to her but—"

Pierce laid a hand on my shoulder then. There was no use restraining my anger. I picked up a solid brass paperweight from Cap's desk and sent it straight into Pierce's chin.

The man reeled away from me with a groan. When he finally steadied himself there was a pistol in his hand, aimed at my heart.

"Put that damn thing down, Pierce! Now!"

Cap's voice nearly cracked with tension.

Now it was Cap who grabbed my shoulder, from across his desk.

David put his hand on the gun barrel and said, "Bert, stop this!"

"That Anderson girl was pinched last night!" I shouted again. "I saw her!"

"Nobody reported it to me this morning," Cap said.

"What about Hiram King? Did *he* report it?"

"What the hell does Mr. King have to do with any of this?"

"*Mr.* King sent his dog here to watch over David and maybe me when we went looking for her in Shantyville last night. I think he might have heard about my getting a hold of Hattie. I think Bert here probably tells him everything. It's in his blood. He was a spy during the war and he's one now."

"Careful, McCleary. Please," David said, holding down Pierce's gun arm for all he was worth.

I didn't care. I was all too happy to provoke the detective.

"Sure," I said. "I'll bet Hiram King heard about it. He might even have Hattie sitting in his office right now. Maybe I'll go and ask him about her. Maybe he can tell me about the opium she gets from him. Or why she was trying to blackmail him with Harding."

Then the answer manifested itself to me. A lightning-like epiphany.

"I'll bet *Mr.* King would be glad to discuss the subject of a certain young lady's indiscretion. And the father's identity."

David gasped.

"McCleary! Think about our family! Do you think you're doing Elsie any good by disgracing us with such vile slander?"

"David, I don't give a good hot damn about your family honor. I want to save your sister's life! I want answers! The kind of answers your father has! And if he doesn't want to give them to me when I ask nice I'll make him talk just like I bet Pierce made Hattie talk!"

"You do, Mack and you'll get more than you bargained for!" Heins shouted.

"Is that a threat, Cap? My dear old friend? Does Hiram have you in his pocket too? Or is that a stupid question?"

"McCleary, get the hell out of this office! You're through here!"

I stared at Heins in disbelief.

"What the hell are you saying?"

"I'm saying you're finished with us! Pack your things from the barracks and go back to South Philadelphia. And be glad we don't run you in for assaulting an officer."

David was the only one who didn't look like he wanted to kill me.

I thought maybe he had just realized that it was Jesse and his sister who had conceived a child years ago. A child Hiram King had destroyed.

The knowledge was torturing him now. He looked at me, pleading for my help.

My heart went out to him. At least I was safe with this one. He was as lost as I was.

"I'm sorry you had to hear that, David. I'll do everything in my power to get your sister back. I promise you."

"You'll get off the Grounds in an hour or I'll have you locked up!" Heins shrieked.

I kept my back straight as I walked out of the office. When the door slammed shut behind me I started laughing. I didn't stop until I was outside, where the bitterness and pain in the laughter were too awful to bear.

The Judges' Pavilion was next door. After taking a few breaths I headed over there. My hands weren't trembling anymore and I didn't care what might happen after this day.

The only thing I knew was that Hiram King and I were going to spend some time alone.

25

HIRAM KING'S CLERK barely had time to get out of his seat before I brushed past him. I stepped into his boss's inner sanctum, closing the door on the bespectacled clerk's indignant whining.

A lush carpet stretched from the doorway to Hiram King's desk, a gargantuan chunk of mahogany set against one wall. It had more pigeonholes than a small town's post office.

Carmine velvet curtains graced the slender windows. They were inexplicably drawn and the gas-light was burning in a brass chandelier overhead.

The office was well-decorated with architectural drawings of the Centennial Exhibition buildings, as well as a few paintings that looked like they should have been in Memorial Hall.

One of the paintings got my attention. It was hung between the two windows. The meager light that leaked through the curtains bathed the painting in a soft glow. Like a ghostly relic set far away on a darkened altar.

The painting was a portrait of a lady. The technique was almost as good as our Mr. Eakins's work.

The lady was seated primly, her electric blue dress of a style popular during the war. Her hoop skirt covered all traces of the sofa she sat on. I was impressed by the way the light seemed to really shine off her dark hair, parted in the middle and smoothed flat, without a trace of the curls that were all the go now.

For a moment I stared at her elegant, handsome face, wondering if I'd seen it before.

Then I realized that I had, of course. In a slightly different, younger version.

"This is Elsie and David's mother, isn't it?"

Hiram King hadn't even noticed me. He swiveled around from his desk and said, "What do you think you're doing barging in here like that? If you wish to speak to me, sir, I advise you to make an appointment with my secretary."

He wheeled back to his desk and began dipping his nib in a bottle of ink.

My laughter made him spill a little of the ink, which he blotted with a sigh of annoyance.

Once again, he turned around to face me.

"Did you forget me so fast, Mr. King?"

"Eh?"

He extracted some spectacles from his coat pocket and carefully perched them on his nose.

The man was hesitant to put them on. Perhaps he thought they made him less formidable-looking. To make up for it, he scowled at me, his well-sculpted mustache stretching nearly to his lapel.

"You're the police officer. McClaherty, was it?"

"McCleary. Wilton McCleary. I'm flattered you should remember me so well. Considering I saved your life yesterday."

"My apologies, sir. As your Captain Heins told you, I'm sure, I've been preoccupied with this madman's threats."

"Not to mention your daughter Elsie being abducted by a murderer."

"Ah! So you're aware of our predicament."

"You make it sound like a minor annoyance."

"I don't quite care for your tone, sir."

"Good for you. I don't quite care for liars."

"And what the devil is that supposed to mean?"

The old man's arms perched on the rests of his chair. The gesture was meant to be threatening, as if lightning and thunder might erupt if he actually got to his feet.

"It means you've been hiding things from us, Mr. King. About you and Elsie and the Boy Fiend."

"I've said what needed to be said. I don't have to answer to you. Need I remind you that you are all on the board's payroll. And that means my payroll."

"Well, consider this my letter of resignation. Because Heins discharged me when I told him I was coming over here."

Heins relaxed a little, smoothing his gray hair.

"If you've been divested of your official capacity then I certainly have no reason or wish to speak with you. You're just another Irish hooligan like the ones we get in the mines. I know how to deal with your kind. If you don't leave my office this minute I'll have you arrested."

I walked over to his desk, swiping the papers on it to the floor. Then I planted my rump on the blotter.

He made to get up but I pushed him roughly back into his seat.

"You take your hands off me, you ruffian!"

"When I'm good and ready," I said. Then I unbuttoned my coat, resting my hand on my right hip. The pistol there was in plain view.

"Is that supposed to frighten me?" he said defiantly.

"You're already frightened."

"Is that so?" he said. Then, as if to prove me wrong, he pulled a segar from his pocket and lit it. Tendrils of smoke oozed out of his mouth and into my face. But through the wall of fumes he'd erected I could see the sweat begin to shimmer on his face.

"I want some answers from you. Let's start with Susie Adams."

"Who?"

"A whore from the bawdy house in Shantyville. She was killed two nights ago, right behind the Museum on Elm Avenue. You told Heins to keep it quiet."

"I did no such thing," he replied haughtily.

Ignoring him, I went on.

"There was a device opium smokers use planted in the girl's neck. With some Chinese characters on it that correspond with two initials in English. B.F. That's Boy Fiend to you and me."

King raised his eyebrows in a gesture of boredom.

"Of course I don't expect you read Chinese. But you didn't have to. I bet Bert saw the body. He must've recognized the handiwork of our friend Jesse Harding. Tipped you off that you had a situation on your hands. So you put a clamp on Heins and the rest of us. How come, Hiram? Why didn't you want us to know there was a monster out there?"

"That is no concern of yours," he said, sucking the smoke between his yellowed teeth.

Seized by a fit of rage, I reached down to his chair, picking it up with him still in it. After I'd lifted it a foot or so, I let it fall to the ground. Then I smacked the segar from his mouth and said, "Elsie's with him now, Hiram! You don't seem to care one way or another if she lives or dies."

King stared at me, visibly shaken. My rage galvanized the space between us like an electric charge.

"Is that what you want to do? Let her die?"

Then I took verbal aim below the belt and said, "Like you let your wife die?"

With a bestial shriek, Hiram King lurched at me, hurling fists at my face.

I caught both fists in my hands and pushed him back into his seat.

"Don't you talk about my wife! You don't know a damn thing about her!"

"Oh, but you're wrong. I know all about your wife. She hanged herself. People usually have a reason for doing that, Hiram. A woman can be pushed to suicide. Were you pushing her, Hiram?"

"My whore of a daughter was pushing her! The little slut got herself pregnant by that piece of trash Jesse Harding! When her mother found out the news nearly killed her."

He banged his impotent fists against the leather-upholstered armrests.

"It was all her fault! She's been an albatross around my neck ever since then! I wish she'd never been born!"

"Why Harding? Why the Boy Fiend?"

"How in hell should I know?" he thundered. "She was the most beautiful girl in the whole county. She could've had anyone. She chose that boy to spite me and her mother! To spit in our faces. And after all that we lavished on her! The ungrateful harlot!"

"Are you trying to tell me that your wife killed herself rather than admit her daughter was seduced by a laborer's son?"

"That's exactly what I'm telling you, boy. Elsie could've had her pick of nobility! But Harding ruined her."

I surprised myself by saying, "Very convenient he turned out to be a killer."

"Oh I knew he was no good, from the minute I found out about him."

"How did you find out? No, let me guess. Elsie had a little shadow. The glorious spy for the Union, Pemberton Pierce."

"Yes," King said, straightening his collar. "Bert did me a great service in ferreting out that little rat."

"A pity he couldn't do the same thing here."

"Bert has done an outstanding job of protecting me and my family. He is very valuable to me. And loyal."

"So I've seen. If he knew I was here now he'd probably kill me."

"What a tragedy that would be."

I smiled ironically and said, "Are you so afraid for your family's honor? Are you willing to risk your daughter's life for that?"

"I still have David. He's all I need."

"Is it him you're trying to protect from all this dirty linen?"

"Oh yes, Mr. McCleary. I will do anything to protect my son. Anything."

"Including sacrificing Elsie?" I said, feeling the veins in my forehead throb.

"No one is going to be sacrificed. We have the matter thoroughly under control."

"Is that so? Then why do I get the feeling you're scared right now?"

"Why shouldn't I be afraid of a gun-toting brute threatening and assaulting me?"

"You're not afraid of me. You're afraid of what I might learn. Or already know. Like Hattie Anderson, for instance."

"Who?"

We stared at each other with our best poker-playing faces.

"Come on, King. Bert and your Guard boys stashed her someplace last night. I was there! Have you talked to her yet? Did you find out from her where Jesse is?"

"I don't know what you're talking about. I've never even heard of such a person."

He went back to smoothing his gray hair and mustache. It was a good attempt to look calm and collected. Except his hand trembled.

"Bloody hell you don't. She was trying to blackmail you on the prismoidal railway. You got a good look at her face, I'm sure of that. She wanted to show you something but it wasn't in her pocket. A pickpocket had buzzed her. I found him later and got her purse back. The contents were very interesting. Would you like to hear what was inside?"

He said nothing, turning to look at his wife's portrait.

"A very indecent pamphlet and a trade card of the Art Gallery with an appointment written on the back for some sort of assignation. You'd be surprised to learn that Hattie used to be a whore before she took to dancing with snakes at the Museum. And she was an opium smoker too. Funny how much opium turns up. You know a little about opium, don't you, Mr. King? Oh that's right"—I slapped my hand against my forehead—"I forgot. You're one of the owners of a huge morphine-producing firm. And here's Hattie, habituated to opium, and her young man, Jesse Harding, going around sticking pieces of an opium lay-out in young girls' necks. Did he do that just to gall you, Hiram? Did Jesse know something about you and the opium trade around here in Shantyville? I guess it wouldn't do for the family honor if folks found out the great Hiram King was selling hop to lowlifes. And not for medicinal purposes either."

I wasn't sure how well I was hitting the mark. Not until Hiram King said, "You said these articles are in your possession?"

"That's right."

"What would it take to make you part with them?"

I looked at him quizically.

"One thousand dollars, perhaps?"

I shook my head, hoping he hadn't seen the hunger flash briefly in my eyes.

"Two thousand dollars? That's quite a nice bit of money for a fellow like you. How much does a policeman's salary run these days? I mean, not including the usual bribes you take from each and every low character you come across. A few hundred dollars a year? Think about it, McCleary. Two thousand dollars. Everybody could use some money."

"Keep your greenbacks, Hiram. All I want is to get your daughter back and nail Jesse Harding."

"So you're not going to hand over those articles to the proper authorities?"

"I am the proper authorities."

"Oh, I don't think so. You yourself told me Captain Heins threw you off the force right now. All I'm trying to do is help you."

"Help me? That's a laugh."

Hiram King stood up from his chair and walked to the window facing the Avenue of the Republic.

"Laugh all you want, McCleary. It would be better for you if you handed those things over to Bert. I can send him over to the barracks to retrieve them. Otherwise they might be too hot for you to handle. I wouldn't want to see you get hurt. Or even killed. You did save my life after all."

"Just one of many mistakes," I said.

I could see past him to the avenue. He watched with a smile as a row of Centennial guards clambered through the entrance to the Judges' Pavilion.

I didn't think they were paying us a social call.

As I left his office, I heard him say behind me, "You're dead, McCleary!"

Before I headed for the rear entrance, I leaned back through the doorway and said, "That only scares a man with something to lose."

26

I TOOK THE curving road behind the Judges' Pavilion, passing the small pond there. A crowd was standing in front of the Lafayette Restaurant. The appetizing fumes wafted my way. I told myself to go inside, what did anything matter anymore. Then I yanked out my bag of cashews and devoured them on the way to meet Tad Schmoyer.

He was patrolling the Main Annex area to-day. On the note he'd placed on my pillow Tad said he would be in the vicinity of the American Kindergarten around midday.

My watch told me I still had a few minutes before noon. I joined a crowd of tourists shuffling into the schoolhouse. It was better, I thought, if I was seen as little as possible on the Grounds.

I took my seat at the back of the four rows of benches set up for visitors. A fancifully carved barrier separated us from the schoolroom proper. Eighteen children were seated around a U-shaped table, dressed in uniforms. The pamphlet I picked up at the door said they were from the Northern Home for Friendless Children. They were happily engaged in assembling puzzles with the letters of the alphabet on them.

Two women were supervising them, both young girls

in plain suits with not a trace of bows, ribbons, or lace. Their bustle skirts were the only bit of fashionable attire on them. Even their hair was plain, not curled but merely tied in slightly disheveled buns. They both wore spectacles.

Yet despite their severe demeanor the two young ladies treated the children with an unusual kindness and patience that was a far cry from my old schoolmaster.

Every now and then, one of the women, who introduced herself as Miss Burritt, told us about the system.

"The kindergarten system," Miss Burritt said, "does not allow for corporal punishment."

I heard a few members of the audience cluck with disapproval.

I smiled down at my knuckles, which had received their share of whacks from a ruler.

"Instead exclusion from one of the games is considered sufficiently severe. You will notice that Miss Steiger and I have few problems with them, for the games which Mr. Froebel has devised engage their infant minds much more than the tired, repetitive exercises of old."

I was certainly impressed and almost envious. I wondered how my life might have been different if I'd learned like this. The children giggled and talked to one another, completely absorbed in their studious play.

For a few moments I lost myself in their smiles.

Then a tap sounded on one of the windows across the room. Tad Schmoyer was there, motioning me to go outside. I was reluctant to go. It had been a long time since I remembered what it felt like to be innocent and unafraid.

Tad shook my hand solemnly and said, "They were talking about you at the mess hall to-day."

"And saying what?"

"News travels fast. They said Heins kicked you off the force. Is that true?"

I hesitated for a moment before I nodded. I was afraid of what Tad might do.

"Griffin told us he heard from Pemberton Pierce that you were threatening him and Captain Heins, that you were liable to attack Hiram King. You were on some kind of rampage. It sounded like you'd gone out of your head. What's going on, Mack?"

"Before I explain the situation to you, tell me what Mulford said about leaving your post yesterday."

With a look of annoyance, Tad said, "He docked me a day's pay. It would've been worse but I collared that buzzer. Your Captain Heins never did talk to Mulford about it, like you said he would."

"No," I said apologetically, "I didn't think he would. Not after what I said to him."

"What could you possibly say that would make him throw you out?"

"I told him he was a corrupt son of a bitch. That he was covering up for Hiram King. Trying to hide some pretty ugly stuff that I think should be brought out into the light."

"Like what?"

"As I left Hiram King's office he told me I was a dead man. Now, are you sure you want to know about all this? I don't want my condition to get contagious."

Tad bowed his head and I feared the worst.

He was the only friend I had left but I understood his position. There was no percentage in it.

Tad said, "Mack, I've listened to what other people have said about you. None of it good. I listened to-day too. All the things they said didn't amount to a bucket full of spit. Because I know you. And I'm proud to call you my friend."

I said nothing for a while. Then I clasped his shoulder and squeezed it.

It took me a good half-hour before I was finished telling him everything.

We walked along the Art Annex, pausing near the

Singer Sewing Machine Building, removed from the larger crowds.

Tad listened without a word. When I finished he asked me, "Tell me what you want me to do."

"Help me find Hattie Anderson."

"You think they've got her somewhere on the Grounds?"

"Where better? Hiram King wants her hidden—especially from me. And like he told me, the whole Guard's on his payroll. So he can pretty much arrange whatever he wants around here."

"I still don't see what he has to do with that business at Memorial Hall. The trade cards and all."

"I don't either. But I have a feeling Miss Anderson might be able to clear things up for us."

Tad made a puzzled face and rubbed his thin blond mustache. A chill wind brushed against us, rattling the trees overhead. I watched the shadows of leaves wash over his face. Suddenly I saw how young he was, just a boy really. I thought I might be asking too much of him.

Then I remembered how old I'd been sitting in the Andersonville stockade. Younger than this lad by a year. I decided then to put as much trust in Tad as he'd put in me.

He looked west, toward Lansdowne Valley. The ornate glass skylights of Horticultural Hall loomed over the treetops.

"Two men searching the whole grounds? That's a tall order, Mack."

"I think we can narrow it down. Last night, when Pierce took Hattie away, he had some guards with him. Some of the faces were familiar."

"From our barracks?"

"Yes. Can you remember offhand anyone talking about going into Shantyville last night?"

"Nobody talked about it this morning at roll call. Or at the mess. But I saw something last night . . ."

"What?"

Tad tipped the visor of his cap back and said, "Well, I don't remember exactly when it was but it was sometime before midnight . . ."

"Don't worry about the time. Tell me what you saw."

"It's not what I saw. It's what I didn't see. Or rather who. I was making my rounds at the Photograph Gallery, on the Avenue of the Republic. Right across from Main."

"I know where it is," I said, trying to keep the impatience out of my voice.

"The first time I went by I looked across the avenue and saw Eric Copper standing guard by the north entrance of Main. I remembered from roll call that that's where he was stationed for the evening. Well, the second time I came around, he wasn't there. And the third time and the fourth time. In fact, I didn't see him till this morning."

"Did anyone come to take his place?"

Tad shook his head.

"Wasn't this Copper the one you were telling me about before? The one who drinks on duty?"

"Yeah, that's right."

"And I think you also said he talked a lot about the gals at the Amazon Theatre."

"From his wealth of experience. He got the clap twice since opening day. He was very proud to tell us all that."

I grunted, crossing my arms over my chest. With the toe of my boot I began stirring the dust at my feet. The fine flakes of dirt swirled off with the wind.

"Let's go talk to Copper. Maybe he can tell us another dirty story. The kind that might interest us. Where's he at?"

"Now this is queer. Horticultural Hall."

"What's he doing there? That's out of your district, isn't it?"

"Sure is. But that's where Griffin sent him, just the same. On the orders of Mulford himself."

"Any reason given?"

"Nope. And none of the other boys were assigned out there."

"Well, now. I think it's time we paid a visit to Horticultural Hall, don't you?"

I started off toward those glimmering skylights. Tad cracked a smile and fell in beside me.

Horticultural Hall was the smallest of the principal exhibition buildings. This did not detract from its magnificence. It stood on the other side of Lansdowne Valley, opposite Main, on a hill overlooking the Schuylkill. Like Memorial Hall, it had been built to last and would remain a part of Fairmount Park long after the Centennial was over.

Twenty-five acres of ground surrounded the hall. These were devoted to an immense ornamental garden, shimmering with flowers from the other side of the world and colors I had never dreamed of seeing in nature. A gigantic fountain stood before the entrance, at the base of a sunken garden with promenades teeming with people, some sitting on benches breathing in the narcotic scents of the blossoms while others strolled up and down, umbrellas shading them from the sunlight.

Standing like a citadel behind the fountain was the hall itself, a palace of iron and glass, painted in variegated colors as if to reflect the garden. Someone had told me the design was Moorish, like palaces in Mohammedan Spain, but this seemed more like a fairy castle than anything else.

Tad and I climbed blue marble steps to the entrance, emerging into the main conservatory. The interior looked like something from the Thousand and One Nights. The roof was of glass, its iron framework decorated in fresco. Around the roof ran a gallery with railings of open fretwork, fancifully ornamented. Beyond the arched portals lay the collections of plants. I saw palm trees and fern fronds, heard the trickle of hundreds of hoses, and felt the humid air creep along my skin.

"See our Mr. Copper around anywhere?"

"No," Tad said. "And I don't see where they would put that Anderson girl either."

"When we find Copper we'll find her."

"Maybe they're both hiding under that thing over there."

He pointed to an odd-looking tree which gave off a pungent stench.

"A eucalyptus," I said, reading the placard beneath it. "I've heard they clear the air of malarial miasmas."

"Hmm. They should put one behind the latrine in our barracks."

"Why don't we split up and cover these greenhouses on either side here? Tell me what Copper looks like."

"He's about as tall as me, but a lot older. Maybe fifty or so. With a gray beard down to here," Tad put his hand on his chest. "No mustache. Looks like a prophet."

"A false prophet maybe. He'll be in his Guard uniform, I imagine."

"Yeah. I'd hate to have to stand around here too long in this woolen jacket."

"Well, let's get going and find him quickly then."

The green-houses extended for two hundred feet down either side of the conservatory. I headed into a forcing-house for tree-ferns from all over the world. Every now and then I took a look at one of the specimens. A maple from Japan caught my eye. I was amazed by the deep red color of its leaves.

After running up and down the aisle, past ferns and sago palms, flamingo plants and Norfolk Island pines, I met up with Tad back where we started.

"No luck?" I asked him.

"None."

"Let's try the galleries."

We went to the east first, stumbling into a crowd of

people straining to see the Electro-Magnetic Orchestra on exhibit there. The machine was playing "The Blue Danube" all on its own. The exhibitor was talking about the music being printed on sheets which, once they struck certain feelers, telegraphed to the corresponding performance magnet.

"Ingenious," I said. "Takes up less space than a human band. And you can take it anywhere."

"Human musicians are better," Tad said, taking me seriously. "How impressive would a parade be if you just wheeled one of these things down the street?"

"That's a good point."

While everybody else stared at the music machine, Tad and I went to the windows overlooking a breathtaking view of the Schuylkill.

"You can see all the way to Laurel Hill," Tad said.

"Further. I see the State House," I said, pointing toward the horizon.

Tad squinted and said, "Well, I'll be. And there's the Art Gallery over there."

I peered toward Memorial Hall, my eyes drifting over the greenery of Lansdowne Valley.

Nestled among the boughs was the Bible Society Pavilion and the Cuba Building. I was about to give up and go to the western gallery when I saw something.

"What's that?" I said pointing northeast.

There was a field there with a tent pitched over it.

"That's for flowers in bloom," Tad said. "Saturday last I took my parents to see the rhododendrons there."

"No," I said. "Not that one. The two little brick buildings next to it. About three or four rods to the east. You see them?"

Tad pressed his face against the warm glass. He squinted and said, "Look like miniature hot-houses. Or maybe they're for storage."

"Just keep looking and tell me what you see."

Tad waited expectantly for a minute. Then he gasped.

He saw, as I did, the figure of a man circle around one of the little brick buildings. A man in a Guard uniform with a long gray beard.

"Son of a bitch," Tad said. "What's he doing there?"

"Is that him? Eric Copper?"

"You bet that's him."

The two of us walked hurriedly toward the blue marble steps leading outside, the Strauss waltz reaching its crescendo behind us.

27

I TOOK ERIC Copper from behind. Grabbing his coat collar, I pulled him into the path of my revolver. It crashed down on the back of his skull with a dull sound. Copper fell to the grass, dead to the world.

"Why'd you do that?" Tad asked.

"I don't want this Copper giving anyone our description."

"He's bleeding."

"I don't think it'll kill him," I said, unconcerned. "Put him on his back so he can breathe."

I had to help Tad turn the guard over. Grunting with the effort, we both looked around us, hoping that no one was watching. Then we dragged Copper behind one of the little brick sheds, where he'd be out of sight.

That gave me an idea.

"You stay out here, Tad and tell me if anyone's coming. Rap your club against the door or something. Don't holler. If we have to we'll head for the Schuylkill."

"Mack?"

"Yeah, Tad."

"You weren't serious about them wanting to kill you—us, were you?"

The boy looked nervous for the first time.

"Stay sharp," I said, trying the door of the shed on the right.

Peering through the window I saw nothing inside but some flowerpots lined up against a metal sink. The floor was covered with white tiles like a fancy water closet.

I walked a few rods over to the other shed. There was nothing in there either. I was beginning to get worried that we'd made a big mistake. My palms grew slick with sweat.

Then I thought to look up at the tiny scroll-sawed dormer. For an instant, the black curtains behind the glass fluttered with movement.

The door was secured with a new Yale lock, probably bought from their pavilion in the Main Building. Stooping over Copper's prone body, I found what appeared to be the right key attached to a loop on his belt.

The key fit. I stepped inside and immediately started coughing. A thick fog of opium smoke curled around me like a phantom fist.

A rickety ladder was propped against one wall, the top leaning against an opening in the ceiling. I took the ladder, the bittersweet stench of opium growing stronger with every rung I climbed.

The crawlspace above was just large enough for the human being stuffed into it to sit up.

There was a small opium lay-out beside her and a feeble lamp. It was a wonder she hadn't set the whole place on fire.

I carried Hattie Anderson down the ladder, her body limp in my arms.

With a grunt I laid her against the cool white tile floor. She was deep in a temporary, opium-stoked oblivion.

I went to the sink and grabbed a coiled, metal hose.

Her paradise was lost when I showered her wan face with frigid water.

She sputtered back down to earth from the stars. Her

transition from the dreamworld was marked with a string of creative obscenities.

"It's good to see you again, Hattie," I said.

Her eyes fluttered and then stayed open. She smiled and said, "It's nice to see you, too."

"How do you feel?"

"Very . . . comfortable," she said, resting her outrageously curled hair against the tile wall. The two words came out of her in long sighs.

I took my place beside her, the cool floor numbing my rump. She didn't seem to mind that or anything else.

"They've been missing you at the Museum."

"Can't go back there now. Gotta find Jesse."

"Jesse's going to find you," I told her. "He wrote a ransom letter to Hiram King demanding that he bring you to-night in exchange for Elsie and thirty thousand dollars."

Hattie gave me the same idiotic smile and said, "I knew he'd save me, somehow."

"Did the Guard do anything to you last night? Did they hurt you?"

"I don't remember." She sighed. "And I don't really care if they did. I'm goin' home now, to Jesse. Hey, mister? You have any candies on you? My sweet tooth's actin' up."

I gave her some of my honey-roasted cashews and said, "You know I'm worried about Jesse."

"Why are you worried? I'm not. Nothin' worries me right now."

"Because of the opium?"

"Of course, because of the opium. You oughta try some. You look like you need to relax."

Then she made a disappointed face and said, "I wish I had some left over. But Copper only gave me one pill."

"You know Officer Copper then?"

"Sure I know Eric Copper. And he knows me. We knew each other quite often. That's in the biblical sense."

"Uh-huh. When you were working at the Amazon Theatre, you mean?"

She put a pale hand on my sleeve and said, "That's right! You're a good detective. You know all about me. Well, I left that line of work."

"Why was that, Hattie?"

"Ruth Blanchette didn't care for the lamp habit."

"Huh?"

"The lamp habit. You know, opium smoking. I don't think she woulda hired me if she knew I was a hip."

"A hip?"

"Sure. Experienced with hop. From leanin' over to light the pipe, you know. My hip's pretty sore now," she said, then laughed at the thought of even trying to move.

"How long have you been a hip?"

"For centuries and centuries. Since before you was born. Maybe a year. A girl in a house where I used to work showed me how."

"That was good of her."

"Yeah, it sure was. Jesse tried to get me off the stuff. Nothing doin'. It takes an effort you know. Why make an effort to do anything?"

"Sure. So Jesse didn't supply you with opium?"

"Hell no. Who told you that? The Professor? That little weasel would say anything to turn you against Jesse. One time the Professor said some things to me—dirty things. Jesse was there and he hit the Professor, hard. They didn't get along too well after that."

"What about the opium then?"

"I used to buy mine from the same place as everyone else in Shantyville. At the Oriental Saloon. Then, when I started work at the Museum, I didn't even have to pay for it."

"Why is that?"

"'Cause the boss gave it to me for free. For leaving Ruth and going to the Museum."

"Wait a minute. I thought you said Ruth kicked you out on account of the opium."

Her lidded eyes blinked a few times. She tried smiling again but even that was an effort.

" 'Course that's what I told you. I was supposed to tell people that."

"Because the boss told you to?"

"Not the boss. The lackey."

"The lackey?"

"Sure. He told me the boss had some work for me at the Museum. Said the pay was better than what I got on my back. I was ready for a change. And it was so easy. Just meet with some swells every few nights of the week and make sure I put on a good show for them. And make damn sure some of them bought my life's story. With the invitations inside."

The opium was loosening her lips, releasing the secrets. I hope its effect lasted long enough.

"You mean," I said, "the Memorial Hall trade cards? The ones that said 'Back of Museum. Midnight'?"

"Yeah, that's right. Did you go?"

"No I didn't. Did you?"

"That wasn't my job, mister. I just had to pass out the cards."

"Susie Adams. Remember her?"

"Sure I do. Cute kid. Had a mouth like a sailor, though."

"Did Susie go to the Museum?"

Hattie's rational brain struggled against the opium. A vague glimmer of suspicion lit up her glassy eyes.

"I don't know nothing about that."

"Sure you do, Hattie. That's why I'm here. I want you to tell me about Susie and your boss and the lackey."

"I think I'd rather sit here and stare at the ceiling. It's a nice white color."

"Yeah, it's nice. Nicer than the inside of a jail cell. That's where you're heading, Hattie. Jesse won't even get the chance to go inside. They'll shoot him down like a mad dog the first chance they get."

"You'd like that, wouldn't you?" she said, her face grimacing in halfhearted spite.

"I'd like to see you come out of this ahead."

"That would be a change."

"All you have to do, Hattie, is tell me about Susie Adams. And the rest."

She peered nervously out the window.

"Is Copper coming back?"

"He's taking a nap right now."

"You think you can get me some more pills?"

"We'll see about that later. First tell me about Susie Adams."

Hattie started scratching herself, like she had fleas under her petticoat.

"What's the matter?" I said.

"Itching all over the place. Did I ask you if you can scare up some more opium pills for me? There ain't much to do here."

She was scratching her teased hair. I pulled her hand away and squeezed it.

"Susie. Remember her?"

"Sure I do. Cute kid."

"Yeah, you told me that already. Did she ever go to Memorial Hall?"

There was a sudden silence between us. I heard water leaking from a faucet into the metal sink.

"Damn that thing's noisy. Why don't they get that fixed? I've been listening to that all day. Drives me crazy."

"Listen to me now, Hattie. Susie's dead. Ripped to pieces by some maniac. They think Jesse did it."

"My Jesse wouldn't hurt nobody."

"I don't think throwing Hiram King off a train was a gesture of good will."

"He had it coming, that bastard! If you knew the things he done . . ."

"I'd love to know all about them. All you have to do is tell me."

"You should know already. You're good enough friends with the lackey."

"I am?"

"I seen the two of you together last night."

I felt my body tense up like a predator ready to strike. "Pemberton Pierce."

"So you *do* know him," Hattie said.

"I know he arrested you but kept it secret. That he's holding you against your will, without any legal authority. Why would he do that, Hattie?"

She put a hand on my knee and said, "He can do anything he wants to, sweetie. He's the boss's man. And the boss runs the show."

"What show?"

"Every damn show. The whole fucking Centennial. And Shantyville."

The truth hit me like a dimly remembered dream.

Then I asked her, "Tell me how you know this."

"Pierce used to come by Ruth's when I was working there. He was the one who collected the rent. Not just at our place, but everywhere else—all the dives and bucket shops in Shantyville. He was the one who told me to go find work at the Museum. I got the pamphlets from him and the trade cards. Pierce told me what to write on 'em. And when I was a good girl and did what he told me, he satisfied my yen-yen."

She giggled and closed her eyes.

"What's that mean, Hattie?"

"My yen-yen," she repeated, as if I were an imbecile. "That's what the coolies call it when you got a hunger for hop."

"Pierce gave you the opium?"

She nodded, her chin nearly reaching her chest.

"Who'd he get it from?"

"I didn't know. Till Jesse told me."

"How did Jesse know?"

"Jesse knows a lot of things. I never met someone who knew so much. Or talked so pretty."

"Tell me what he said about Pierce."

"Oh, Jesse hated Pierce. Hated him like hell. Used to know him from somewheres else. I forget where, though. Anyway, Jesse was tellin' me one time about how this Pierce arrested a poor little boy for somethin' he didn't do. Had him sent to jail and nearly hanged. Jesse hated him for that. The boy must've been close to Jesse or somethin'."

"Yes. Very close."

"I wish I'd never said anything to Jesse about Pierce."

"Why is that, Hattie?"

I sat a little closer to her, putting her hand between my own.

She liked the attention and said, "You're nice, mister. I wish they had you guardin' me instead of that fat bastard with his greasy beard."

"You were telling me about Jesse and Pierce."

"Jesse was so good to me. Just thinkin' on him makes me blue. I don't wanna be blue right now."

"There's no reason to. You'll see him soon enough."

"Oh, I hope so. I love that boy. I really do."

Her itching was contagious. I took off my straw hat and ruffled my oiled hair.

I was beginning to get impatient with her. We'd been sitting there for a good quarter of an hour. I hoped Tad was doing his job outside.

There was nothing I could do but keep gently coaxing her. If I started getting rough she would shut me out with all the other bad things. I had to be as nice and gentle as the opium.

"Why do you love him so much, Hattie?"

"Because he treated me good. Read poetry to me sometimes even. Do you know how romantic he was? He bought me some flowers from a vendor on Elm Avenue one day. Can you believe that?"

We exchanged smiles and she said, "I met him right after I quit at Ruth's. One day I was bored and went to see the Animal Show. I saw him hangin' around the animal pen and started talkin' to him. I invited him to see me perform at the Museum. That night he came. And the next and the next. Then he asked me to go for a walk with him, just along Elm Avenue. I nearly burst my gut! Like I was some rosy-cheeked little girl or somethin'. But I liked the way it felt to lock my arm in his. I asked him why he was being so nice to me. You know what he said? He said, 'You need to be loved as much as I need to love someone.' I thought that was poetry or somethin'. Jesse is so sweet."

"Tell me more about Jesse."

"We were so happy, mister. You wouldn't believe it. I didn't even stay around the Museum no more. Especially not with that slimy Professor pawing me whenever I wasn't on the stage. Jesse and I got our own place. A little hide-away, he called it. And it was perfect. Until I told him about Pierce."

"What exactly did you say?"

"I was just talkin' about Ruth's. He didn't mind that I used to be a . . . you know. One day I told him how I got the job in the Museum. And when I mentioned Pierce's name he looked at me so wild I thought he was gonna have a fit. He made me tell him all about Pierce, every little thing. When I asked him why he wouldn't say. Not until I found a newspaper hid in his drawer."

"The one with Hiram King's picture on it?"

"Yes, did he show you?"

I tried thinking of a way to answer that but she kept going, thrilled to be talking about the love of her life.

"I went to Jesse and asked him what that was doin' there. He showed me Hiram King's picture and said, 'See that man? That's the one Pierce was working for when that boy I was telling you about got arrested.'

"So I says to Jesse, Well I reckon he's still workin' for him here at the Centennial. That's when I remembered somethin' I heard Susie say months ago. She was entertainin' this captain of the Centennial Guard. Mumford or somethin' like that."

"Mulford?"

"Yeah, that's it. Well, he was lyin' around drunk as hell in her bed braggin' to her about how important he was. And Susie told me later he said he could do her a good turn if she was lookin' to make some extra money. When she asked how, he said Mr. King had put out the word that certain young girls would be needed on the grounds on certain nights. For some kind of entertainment. You can imagine what kind. Susie said, 'What would the Board of Finance man have to do with us?' This Mulford laughed and said, 'You silly bitch. Who do you think's in charge of this shit-hole?' She said she surely didn't know. Mulford said, 'Why, Hiram King, of course. He's got both ends covered.' "

"The Centennial and Shantyville?" I asked, my voice hoarse.

"That's it," Hattie said. "He's runnin' the whole show. That's what Susie told me. I'd forgotten all about it but then Jesse made me remember with that newspaper of his. I got to thinkin' on the trade cards I wrote out. Setting up assignations for swells and Ruth's girls at the Centennial, after hours. And the opium Pierce always had for me. There was hop all over Shantyville. When Jesse read to me the article about Hiram King ownin' a morphine-making company, even I could figure out where all the hop came from."

I had to get up at that point. My stiff joints ached as I began to pace around the room.

"You all right, mister? You look sick as a dog."

"I'm okay, Hattie. Keep on with your story."

"Well, when Jesse and I put it together he came up with the idea of, uh, blackmailin' this Hiram King."

"Not a very good idea, was it?"

"We thought it was gonna be fine! Jesse was sure King would pay up. We were gonna use the trade cards as proof that we meant business."

"But that would've tipped him off that you were involved. Did you think of that?"

Hattie pursed her lips in concentration.

"That didn't occur to me, I guess."

"How'd you get the death threats typed up, Hattie?"

"Oh! That was easy. Jesse knew a way into the grounds. We went to the Main Building and—"

"Wait a minute," I said, holding my hand up. "How did you get in there?"

"Well, Eric Copper was standing guard. I just sort of preoccupied him while Jesse snuck through the door. Good thing I brought my gloves with me."

"There were many letters. Did you sneak in on different nights?"

"Sure. Once we got lucky and Copper wasn't even there. Nobody was."

"There weren't any Guards?"

"Not around the plaza between Memorial and Main. It was spooky there. But I loved it. Jesse and I had the whole place to ourselves. Like it belonged to us."

I was still curious about the type-writer. When I asked Hattie why Jesse used it instead of just writing the letters she said, "He told me he heard this author he liked just wrote a whole book on that machine. Mark Train, Twain, something like that. Jesse was always tellin' me how much he wanted to write books."

"I don't know of many authors who get their start writing death threats."

"He didn't mean it! We weren't gonna touch that Hiram King. But when we were on the train, King said somethin' to Jesse, somethin' I couldn't hear, and Jesse just flew into a rage. I tried to stop him but he was out of his head."

"Did Jesse have a habit of getting violent?"

Hattie shook her head with effort. "He's the sweetest."

"Susie Adams wouldn't agree."

"Jesse didn't even know Susie Adams! He wouldn't waste his time with a piece of trash like her anyway!"

"Somebody did, Hattie. Right behind the Museum, where you worked and where I saw him that night."

"So what? He mighta been tryin' to find me. He loved me, you know! I know he did! We were fine till he started in on that little bitch."

"Elsie King? Hiram King's daughter?"

"Yes," she snarled. "He seen her picture in the illustrated newspaper and couldn't stop thinking on her. I could see the change. I'd start talkin' to him and he wouldn't mind me. Whenever I tried gettin' him to talk about her he'd just say I couldn't understand, that he was sorry for everything he'd done or would have to do. That he cared for me deeply."

Tears began to leak down her pallid bony face.

"What the hell does that mean? I asked him. Does that mean you don't love me anymore? Is that what you're sayin'?"

It was like I was out of the room and she was back in their flat, arguing with the love of her life. Except this was a love she had lost to another and she knew it. Hattie had lost him to the mother of his child. A child that had never been born, thanks to Hiram King.

Hattie stared through her tears at me.

"You gonna bring Jesse back to me, mister?"

"I'm going to find him, Hattie. I don't know what'll happen after that. It would help if you told me about Susie Adams."

"I don't know nothin' else! She told me right when I was leaving Ruth's that she had work inside the Centennial, like I told you."

"You told me she was the one who met the men with the trade cards. Behind Memorial Hall."

"That's not what I wrote, mister. I wrote, 'Museum.' That means our Museum. On Elm Avenue."

I wanted to kick myself. I just assumed that "Museum" meant Memorial Hall, since that was the picture on the trade card.

But it made much more sense now. The place where the murder took place was where Susie would meet with her customers.

Confused, I said, "You told me she was working at the Centennial? So what was she doing behind the Museum?"

"That's where she went to get into the Centennial."

My patience was at an end. Gesticulating wildly, I cried out, "Hattie, what the hell are you talking about? How can she get into the Centennial from behind the Museum?"

"The tunnels," she said.

I froze where I was, stunned.

I swallowed to wet the inside of my mouth and said, "Tunnels?"

"How'd you think Jesse and I got into the Centennial? He was on a crew that laid gas and steam pipes. There're underground tunnels stretching right across Elm Avenue, go right into the Grounds. I'd get lost but Jesse knew right where he was going. Nobody sees you go in or go out that way. Keeps things a secret. The swells who take Susie in there like things to be kept secret. That's what Pierce told me. I thought you knew, mister. You were the one bringin' the swells around in the first place. Pierce told me you or some other copper would. They had it all planned out."

The list. I didn't have to wonder where it came from anymore. There was probably a copy of it lost in the pigeonholes of Hiram King's desk.

"Where's the entrance to the tunnels, Hattie?"

"I don't know. Somewhere in the woods there behind

the Museum. It was always dark. I never remembered where it was exactly. I didn't care. I didn't care about anything except Jesse. Did you mean what you said, mister? Is Jesse gonna come back for me?"

Without waiting for me to answer her, she grasped my arm and said, "I'm afraid! I'm so afraid he's going to leave me here! They want me to tell them where he is but I don't know! I wouldn't even if I did!"

Hattie clung to me, hiding her face like a confessing sinner.

"Copper said if they caught Jesse they were gonna shoot him on sight. Don't let them do that to my Jesse! He done nothing wrong! They're the one's who hurt him. He didn't think I was smart enough to figure it out but I knew when he told me about that boy who went to jail that he was talking about himself. All I wanted to do was make him forget about everything and just think of me. I wanted him to feel the way I do when I'm with him. If I could just put my arms around him again I could make him forget everything. I know it . . ."

The tears flowed from her face onto the sleeve of my suit jacket. I watched them soak into the checkered fabric, spreading like ripples in a pond.

There was a sound behind me. A club rapping against the window pane.

I heard Tad's nervous voice through the glass.

"They're comin', Mack! Get the hell out of there!"

I caressed Hattie's snarled hair and wiped the tears from her cheeks.

"I have to go now, Hattie," I said, detaching her hand from my arm.

"Are you gonna find Jesse?"

"Yes."

"You won't hurt him, will you?"

I left Hattie Anderson resting against the white tiles. She was holding herself tight, trembling before a loneliness that only those who had been knee-deep in despair might understand.

28

TAD AND I were long gone before the guards arrived at the shed. When we were sure no one was following us, we headed into the closest building, the Women's Pavilion.

Everything on display inside had been made by women. Perhaps it was their way of saying they were just as good as men were. Certainly there were many women pushing for the vote. One woman named Susan B. Anthony even had the audacity a few months ago to interrupt a reading of the original Declaration of Independence at the State House by standing on the platform to read a Declaration of Independence of Women. Naturally we arrested her.

Despite such peculiar sentiments, I was impressed by the work of women's hands here.

Tad and I wandered through the exhibit, not saying anything to each other. On the way down I explained to him what Hattie told me. It took the wind out of him.

We walked around aimlessly, like greenhorn troops after a bombardment of grape. Tad was struggling, as I was, to regroup and prepare for what came next. Both of us knew that one way or another we would have to attack.

In one showcase I saw some drawings prepared by the Women's Medical College. I closed my eyes and thought on Arabella Cole. It took some effort but I buried the feelings that came with her memory back down where they belonged—a distant place, where they couldn't hurt me.

A large engine was employed to power some carpet-weaving machines. Tad and I were amazed to see a woman engineer operating the thing. She told us she came from Ontario. I had to tell Tad where that was. Neither of us had ever seen a female mechanic before. She showed us how she ran the engine, her sleeves curled up over muscular arms. We stared at her for a few moments, more awed by her presence than by any other thing in the pavilion.

Then we came across a showcase of women's undergarments. We spent a certain amount of time scrutinizing this display. To cover his embarrassment, Tad finally asked me, "What do we do now, Mack?"

"Forget it, Tad. Get back to your beat. With any luck, your Sergeant Griffin is still emptying lager-beer into his belly across the street. We've only been gone a half hour. They might not even miss you."

The boy looked hurt.

"You got another think comin' if you think you can get rid of me! I've helped you plenty and I want to see this thing through!"

"Don't work yourself into a lather, Tad," I said. "I know how much you've helped me. I appreciate that. And now you can help me a whole lot by going back to your beat. I'm going over to Shantyville to have a look around the Museum. We don't want a Guard uniform over there attracting attention. It's better if you stay here for now."

"What about to-night? The exchange. You're going to be there, aren't you?"

"I plan to crash that party, yes."

"They might not like it, Mack. I got a feeling the Avenue of the Republic's going to turn into a shooting gallery."

"That's why I'm bringing my partner with me."

"Your partner?" Tad asked.

I patted the revolver at my side and said, "Get back to your post."

Then I turned to leave.

Tad laid a restraining arm on me and said, "I'm going with you to-night. I'll bring my partner too."

"The hell you will. You've risked enough as it is. I don't have a job anymore. Think with your head, Tad. You let me handle this alone. I'm going to need your help again soon when I get Jesse Harding and Elsie King. Because after I find them I'm going to nail Hiram King to the wall. And I'll need your help to do that. In the meantime I won't risk your life. Now get your ass back to your post."

I patted him on the back of the neck and walked away without looking back.

It was relatively easy to slip out of the grounds unnoticed. There were plenty of crowds that Thursday, waiting to catch a glimpse of President Grant, who was in attendance.

I left the Grounds through an exit as far away from Mulford's district as possible. That way I figured there would be less of a chance of anyone recognizing me.

The exit at Belmont Avenue was the closest. It would mean a longer walk to Shantyville but I had plenty of time. It was only about four thirty.

As I neared the turnstiles the aroma of the Southern Restaurant proved itself irresistible. I decided to put something more than cashews in my stomach.

A colored waiter—they were all colored in there—took me to a small table. I was probably the only Yankee in the whole place. My former mortal enemies sat at tables with their wives, playing cards, joking, or filling the air with segar smoke. Their accents seemed as exotic as the eucalyptus tree in Horticultural Hall.

When the waiter brought me my fried chicken, okra,

corn, and biscuits, I sat there savoring the steam coming off my plate. I closed my eyes, remembering the men and boys I'd known eleven years ago. I thought on those endless days in prison where we'd sought to assuage the hunger gnawing at our insides by spinning intricate yarns about the table fare at our grandmother's dinner or the local hotel. We lingered over every imaginary drop of gravy, grain of salt, juicy shred of succulent roast beef. And every morning there would be fewer of us to listen. Scurvy, gangrene, fever, pneumonia, diarrhea, and starvation killed us faster than the Rebels ever could.

I heard the Southern men spinning their own yarns now in the room around me and I wanted to hate them. I wished that they all might've had sons killed as their brethren had slain my friends.

Then I cast the evil thought from my mind and covered the old, ugly wounds with forgiveness.

I had a hard time reminding myself the war was over. That we were sitting all in the same room, Yankees and Rebels, with one flag flying over the restaurant.

I told myself that there were other wars, more noble ones, left for me to fight. One waited for me in Shantyville.

Opening my eyes I mumbled grace over the food and began to eat with abandon. I didn't think I would have the chance again for quite a while.

I sat there for a good half of an hour stuffing my belly and then left the colored boy a good tip. It was novel having a colored waiter. Restaurants in the North wouldn't even think of letting them work the tables.

After that meal I was ready to sit down and sleep for a few hours. Instead I got up and went through the turnstiles and headed down Belmont Drive, a winding dirt road that skirted the Centennial. On my left was the George's Hill Reservoir, where the Centennial got its water from. To the right were the buildings of State Avenue. Twenty-six of the thirty-eight states had built small meeting houses for their respective citizens. Some of the newer states like Oregon and Nevada shared buildings.

I kept off the road and walked along the grassy embankment. Despite the precaution I still got caught in clouds of dust thrown up by passing carriages. I wound past the Spanish Government Building, the Catholic Total Abstinence Fountain, the Saw Mill, and the Boiler House. Finally I made it to Elm Avenue. Taking out my pocket watch I saw the time was a little past six o' clock.

Staying on the south side, I proceeded down Elm, past the squares of hotels and the railroad depot. I braved the chaotic traffic, nearly amputating a limb thanks to a reckless hack driver. Right at the corner was the triangular-shaped, mansard-roofed Transcontinental Hotel. I looked up at the five stories of windows stretching across half a square of space. Sure enough, men were dangling their legs from many of those windows to relieve themselves from the warmth of the day. A few of those men, no doubt, would be raining segar ash on our heads.

The Transcontinental was the largest hotel at the Centennial, with five hundred rooms accommodating one thousand two hundred guests. Half of them were being disgorged onto Elm Avenue, right in my way. Their luggage was stacked about as high as the second story. I was negotiating my way around them when I felt someone touch my back.

One hand dropped to my barker while the other tore the person's arm off me.

The revolver was halfway out of its holster when I turned around and saw David King, smiling at me apologetically.

"Didn't mean to startle you again, McCleary. I saw you from the second-story ice cream saloon. Had to rush through the crowd to get to you."

I made a noise that was something between a grunt and a snarl.

"What do you want, David? I don't have any good stories for you to print just yet."

"Oh, I don't know about that."

"Have you spoken to your old man?"

"Yes," he replied. "That's why I wanted to see you. But you dashed out of Heins's office too quick for me to catch up with you. By the time I made it to Father's office you were gone from there too. He looked like a tornado had just paid him a visit."

I snorted with amusement and said, "What made you come to Shantyville?"

"Oh, I figured you might wind up here, eventually."

"And how did you figure that, David?"

The young reporter gestured for me to follow him into the Transcontinental Hotel.

We entered the lobby. I paused on the threshold of the public parlor.

David made no move to sit down.

"I have a room upstairs. It's private. I need to talk to you."

He could see my reluctance. I was afraid it was some kind of trap. After all, he was Hiram King's son.

"I'm sorry for what's happened to you. Heins gave you a raw deal. And my father . . . well, he's part of what I wanted to talk to you about."

We paused by the Western Union window, the wide staircase leading to the upper floors a few steps away. The smell of the laundry nearby made me conscious of the dirt on my suit. I began brushing it off, feigning disinterest in David.

"Mr. McCleary, I know I have no right to ask for your help. Not after what happened to-day. But I do ask you for my sake and for Elsie's."

David seemed to have gone through an emotional about-face in the space of a few hours.

I wondered why.

"What I told you last night I spoke in anger and weakness. Things have changed now. I'm afraid for her. For both of us."

Whatever that fear stemmed from, it was making his eyes twitch. David was trying to give me a brave face, but underneath the facade I could sense the turmoil inside him.

"There's more to tell about Elsie, isn't there? About Mauch Chunk?"

"Yes, Mr. McCleary. If you'll listen."

I looked toward the staircase and said, "Lead the way."

David's room was on the fourth floor. Inside it was pretty much like any other fancy hotel room.

It consisted of a water closet and bath, with a miniature parlor room and a bedroom. The door to the bedroom was open and I saw a host of papers scattered across the desk inside.

I took a seat on the leather-upholstered divan. David pulled a rocking chair over and set the chair in motion, teetering nervously. Evidently he was waiting for me to say something. I was more interested in hearing what he had to say. Doffing my boater and ruffling my hair, I started playing with some dominoes left on a marble-topped table to my side.

Finally I said, "It's getting dark in here, David. You should turn on the gas."

His heels came down on the floral-patterned carpet and the chair swung to a halt.

"Forget about the gas. I need your help. They're going after Harding to-night."

"I know that. Half the Guard will probably turn out to arrest him."

David unloosened his cravat and said, "Oh, they're going to do more than arrest him, McCleary. They're planning to kill him."

"On whose orders?"

"Whose do you think? My father's. And he told them it doesn't matter who gets in the way."

I stopped playing with the dominoes and said, "What the hell's that supposed to mean?"

"I think it means that if Elsie gets shot in the process, my father won't lose sleep over it."

I swallowed audibly.

"Did you talk to him about this?" I said.

"I overheard him giving Pierce instructions. I waited for Bert to leave. Then I had a word with him."

David took a pencil from his jacket and began tapping it against his shirt.

"I asked him how he could do such a monstrous thing. Not just murder a man. *That* I could see my father doing."

"Has he done it before?"

"No, no. But in a roundabout way he has. He and Pierce were behind the arrest of many of the Molly Maguires in Carbon County. Men who are going to hang, mark my words."

"I thought you were against those men yourself. You called them terrorists."

"I've altered my position on a lot of things to-day. Anyway, I asked him how he could be so cold, so full of hatred for Elsie. Do you know what he told me? That he was doing it to protect me."

Cold, hollow laughter contorted David's face.

"I said to him, 'Protect me from what? My sister?' Then I accused him of blaming Elsie for our mother's death. And he agreed with me. He said, 'Every time I look at Elsie I see your mother's face. And it's gotten worse since she grew up. Whenever I look at your sister now I see my dead wife's face staring back at me. I picture her mouldering away in that lonely grave in Mauch Chunk. If it hadn't been for Elsie playing the whore with that Harding boy your dear mother would be alive to-day!' "

I lowered my head, letting his pain wash over me.

"Father doesn't seem to remember that Elsie lost her

too. And she didn't play the whore with Harding. She loved the boy, God help her."

"Why, David? What was it about Jesse Harding?"

"He loved her, McCleary. He wrote her poems, some of them copied, others original. Father called him the Gentleman Breaker Boy once, to mock him. I only heard about this much later. I was too young when it all happened. But even I could see that my father didn't love Elsie. He made no secret that he always had wanted a son. When my mother gave birth to Elsie he held it against her that she wasn't male. Always has too. When I was born it was like God had come to earth for him. There was nothing he wouldn't do for me. He gave Elsie plenty of things."

"Except his love."

"Yes. Perhaps Elsie got pregnant to punish him or herself, or both. I don't know. I don't think *she* knows. If she couldn't get love from him she looked for it somewhere else, from someone as different from him as possible. What a tragedy that was. For all of us."

I waited for him to say more but he was lost in his memories.

To jar him out of his melancholy, I said, "So you want me to watch out for her to-night."

"Yes," he said. "I want you to make sure she's not hurt. The Guard will be armed. And I know she won't leave Jesse willingly."

"David, have you thought anymore on the things I told Heins this morning? About Susie Adams, the girl who was killed behind the Museum?"

"Yes," the reporter said quietly.

"David, I think your father had something to do with her death."

"No!" the boy said, repulsed by the suggestion. "I know how low he can sink. But even he is above that horror."

"Then why did he tell Captain Heins to make sure it wasn't reported or even investigated?"

"He's afraid of Jesse Harding. What Harding knows about him."

"You mean Elsie and the baby?"

"More than that, I'm afraid. With Elsie under his spell he's liable to coax anything out of her. All the ugly little secrets we've nestled away over the years."

"How many more ugly little secrets can a family have?"

"Oh, Mr. McCleary. Bless you, sir. A seasoned police-man like you can still be naive."

I leaned back in my chair and started playing with the dominoes again. I was leading him out to where the ice might crack. We had to step carefully.

David got up from the rocker and went to a small side-board. He pulled out some brandy and drank it, in a most ungentlemanly fashion, from the bottle.

"Sorry," he said, wiping his mouth. "This whole thing's got me in a hellish state."

"That's entirely understandable," I said.

He sat back on the rocker and scrutinized me. I could see a flush begin to spread on his cheeks.

"No," he said. "I don't think you do understand."

"Help me then."

David stared at the window behind me. The sky was darkening outside. A pigeon perched on the window ledge like an obese gargoyle.

We watched the clouds turn from a fiery orange to a dark purple and then to black.

The gas had still not been turned on. I sat with him there in the darkness, listening to carriages rattling over the street outside and the pigeons cooing on the window.

When there was enough darkness between us, David began to speak.

"My father forgets sometimes that Elsie was closer to our mother than any of us. She was never the same after Mother died. Elsie was hit very, very hard. Over the years her condition got worse. By the time I was out of short pants Elsie was . . . well, I think the doctors would call her mad. It wasn't always obvious. But I'd catch her from time to time talking to herself, having a conversation with some invisible person. Some days it was her baby. Other days it was Mother. Father didn't do anything about it. Just ignored it, like he ignored everything else about her. As soon as she was old enough to graduate from the school she would sit around our parlor knitting doilies, day after day. I'd hear her speaking to her dead baby from behind the closed door.

"One night she woke me out of a deep sleep. I could see she was in a state of the utmost excitement. A panic, really. Her nightdress was torn and it looked like she'd been stumbling outside. There were cuts and bruises all over her arms. You should have seen her eyes. There was no life in them, no light. As if the spark of her soul had been suddenly snuffed out and she was unaware of it. I remember the way the moonlight came through the latticed windows and lay on her face. Like a shroud. She stood there ranting at me for some time."

"What did she say?"

"All sorts of mad things. The usual delusions. Someone was trying to kill her. Had outraged her even. I wasn't too experienced with that sort of thing but I knew she had to tell Father right away. You should have heard her laugh at that! It was a terrible sound, McCleary.

"I let her sleep beside me and she lay there quivering, though it was humid as hell outside. I must've closed my eyes and I suppose Elsie thought I was asleep. Then she whispered something to me. I don't think I should forget it, though I wish I could. She said, 'I won't let them hurt you, Davy. Not like they hurt our mummy. You saw her and they know you saw her. They're afraid that you'll remember, Davy. Remember that she didn't die from her own hand. Don't ever remember that, Davy. Forget what you saw forever.' "

David began to chuckle then. I was glad the shadows obscured his face.

"But I never forgot, McCleary. Why in God's name did she have to say that to me?"

"It could have been a mad girl's raving. But maybe not. That sort of knowledge is a hell of a burden for a girl to bear on her own."

I was beginning to see why Elsie had changed. The madness was a good disguise. A place to crawl away and hide from the truth.

I wasn't sure how much more I wanted to hear. But David needed me now as much as she had needed him then.

"Hell is a choice word, McCleary. I've read somewhere that the theologians say hell is merely the absence of God. Well, that's my condition in a nutshell. I stopped believing in God after she told me that. I didn't care if it was true or not. Just the hint that it was possible was enough to shatter my belief in any ultimate goodness. I decided if I was living in hell that I should map out its geography. Did you ever wonder why I want to write police intelligence? It's quite simple really. I think I called it reality when we were speaking a few days ago. What I really meant to say was filth. Isn't that reality after all? Suddenly I was aware of the evil that flitted everywhere about us. I thought perhaps I shouldn't hide from it. Perhaps it wouldn't have any more power over me if I decided to wallow in it instead."

"Why, David?"

"To drown myself. To drown those goddamn words Elsie said to me that night! I did my best to heed her, McCleary. Have you ever known what true forgetfulness is? Not unless you've sampled opium."

"You've tried opium then?"

"Tried! We were intimately acquainted. How did de Quincey put it? 'I have sat from sunset to sunrise, motionless and without wishing to move. For it seemed to me as if . . . the tumult, the fever, the strife, were suspended, a respite granted from the secret burdens of the heart.' "

"When did you stop taking opium, David?"

"Long before I came to Philadelphia, I assure you."

"You took some sort of cure, didn't you? That story of going abroad was—"

"A lie. Yes. I suppose Elsie told you. That's precisely what my father fears. He doesn't want anyone knowing how low I went. I never did anything really harmful. There was always Bert around to prevent me from doing that."

He took another swig from the brandy bottle and smacked his lips.

"You see," David said, "Father doesn't believe the upper classes are susceptible to the low impulses opium brings out in its devotees. He wants to elevate its status, make it a pleasant recreation for the elite, like croquet or lawn tennis."

"Is that why he bought the morphine-making company here in the city?"

"I suppose so. His goal is to make opium the national stimulant of choice instead of tobacco or coffee. But to do that it has to be respectable. Gentle folk like us have to be gently persuaded."

By the slum sociables, I thought. By Susie Adams and opium and risk-free sin.

The swells on those slum sociables hadn't been just anyone. They must've been men in the position to further Hiram King's goals. Men he would want in his pocket.

The whole thing sickened me. I was thinking of Hattie Anderson's empty eyes. And the even emptier ones of Susie Adams.

"I wish I could see your face now, McCleary. It might look something like mine did on that night Elsie came to my room."

"No, David. I've seen evil plenty of times. It doesn't

frighten me anymore. I won't let it. That way I still have a chance to fight it."

"I stopped fighting a long time ago. Now I'm content to just watch it do its work."

"Except where your sister is concerned."

"Yes," he said, his words a whisper. "At least her soul's intact. I'd like to keep it that way."

"What does Elsie know about you that's so harmful? That would make your father want to kill her and Jesse to bury it?"

"Ask Elsie when you see her. Give her my love."

David got up then and drained the rest of the brandy.

There was no sound in the room except when David's hand struggled to replace the glass cap in the decanter.

I got up from the armchair and said, "David, I admire you for telling me all this. I think we can find a way to make things—"

He laughed in the darkness again.

"Mr. McCleary! I understand how you feel. Being tantalized is a terrible thing. I didn't mean to do that. I only told you what I did because I wanted to see if it were possible for me to tell the truth. It was an innocent experiment. I chose to tell it to you because I know that you will not be alive much longer. And that makes me very sorry."

Stunned, I let him walk past me and into his bedroom, where I heard him turn the key in the lock.

I drew my revolver and opened the door to the hallway, expecting an assassin to strike at any moment. There was no one there that I could see.

Fear crept into me then. It came not from what David said but how he said it. Like my imminent death was as certain and as boring a fact as the sun rising the next morning.

My hand, trembling in spite of my efforts to control it, reached into my vest pocket and took out my watch.

I watched the second hand ticking away. The exchange

was set for less than an hour from now. There was no time for me to waste.

But I did waste it, staring down at the black and white face of the clock, wondering how many hours I had left. The hand shuddered its way around the numerals, pushing me closer and closer to that final second.

I snapped the lid shut and hurried down the stairs. Outside the air was cool and smelled of rain.

I sucked it into my lungs, savoring it while I could.

29

I TOOK THE back way to the Museum, via Columbia Avenue. There was nothing down this way except a few hotels and long, squat wooden stables for the horses of the Chestnut and Walnut streetcar company. They were separated from the carriage repositories facing Girard Avenue by a lot. As I made my way across the stretch of open space I took my revolver out and kept my thumb on the hammer. Every now and then I'd freeze up at the sound of something crashing through the brush. But it was never anything more terrifying than a groundhog or a rabbit.

It was twenty minutes before I was behind the Museum. There was no lantern to illumine my way so I had to go by the faint blue haze of the moon. The stars seemed too vast that night, their feeble light mocking reminders of the absent sun.

My progress was painfully slow, lest I alert anyone who might be lingering about to my presence. For all I knew some of Hiram King's men might be conducting swells into their private opium dens to-night. As it was, I had to find the place on my own.

At least Hattie Anderson had pointed me in the right direction. But there was too much ground to cover. My pocket watch told me I had a little over a half an hour to find my way into the Grounds before the shooting started.

Part of me wished I had Tad along. I wouldn't have felt so much of the pressure that tensed every muscle and sinew in me, making my neck and shoulders throb with pain.

After what David told me, however, I knew I'd made the right decision in shooing him off. With any luck Tad would sleep through the whole thing to-night. And if to-morrow he learned I was shot dead I hoped he wouldn't feel any foolish regrets over not being there.

The irony of the situation appealed to me. The purpose of a copper was to beat down the untamed elements that threatened respectable, civilized society. To club them into submission. I was proud to be a part of that.

Except over the past few days I saw the veneer stripped off that cultured, genteel world.

I used to think that there was a difference between the two worlds that Shantyville and the Centennial represented.

But there wasn't, of course. One world simply covered up its lusts better than the other.

To-night, David had stripped away the world's comforting illusion of safety.

I was back in the war. But a different kind of war, where there were no hypocritical rules to make it seem noble or civilized.

There was no sign of an entrance to the tunnels at the place where I'd found Susie Adams's body. Neither was there any trace of her there. Thankfully, nature was already busy obscuring the horror of her last moments, covering the spot with bramble vines and weeds, tremulous in the night wind.

After a time I began to get careless and started making noise. Midnight was encroaching.

Pretty soon I was crashing through the brush, hoping my foot would get caught on some piece of metal piping or grating—some sign, any sign, that Hattie Anderson hadn't handed me some opium-stoked fantasy.

I got nothing for my efforts except burrs and thorns stuck all over my suit.

Frustrated, I resolved to give up the search and see if I could find another way into the grounds—over the fence, through the turnstile—anything.

I stumbled through the serpentine weeds to a backhouse that leaned at an awkward angle behind an elm tree. Leaning against its side, I paused to catch my breath.

Then I noticed something queer.

There was another backhouse, not more than three rods from the rear of the Museum.

I wondered what they would need two backhouses for— and why the second one would be placed in the middle of the woods here.

I didn't think it was for greater privacy.

The door had warped enough that I had to tug it open.

There was the usual hole. Except this one was large enough for a person to fit into. To make the descent easier, someone had placed a wooden ladder there.

I said my silent thanks to Hattie Anderson and started climbing down into the tunnels.

After twenty feet or so I hit the ground. As I took a step forward into the blackness, I tripped over something and went sprawling on tightly packed earth.

Groping around in the dark, my hands fell upon the unseen cause of my stumble. My fingers ran over its smooth tubular surface of metal and glass. When I probed down the glass tube I felt something coarse.

Reaching into my coat pocket, I pulled out a match and lit the wick of the kerosene lamp. Someone had trimmed the wick and there was enough kerosene inside to keep me from running into anything else.

With that meager light, I began searching for the way to Memorial Hall, where Jesse Harding and Elsie would be waiting for Hiram King's men.

I couldn't see more than a few rods past me. The tunnel

was narrow and I had to bow my head as I went.

The cramped quarters didn't bother me a bit. Long ago I'd participated in a tunnel-digging project with some boys from Pennsylvania. We were trying to dig our way out of the prison stockade. Thanks to an informer we didn't get very far.

After the Rebels forced us to plug it up we got a hold of that informer, a sailor from Ohio. One of my friends took a rusty knife from his cherished mess kit and carved the letter S for spy on the sailor's forehead.

If the scar bothered him he didn't have long to endure the anguish. He was stabbed a few nights after that by a man who didn't care for the sailor's sexual proclivities.

I pictured myself digging that tunnel now, with the dream of freedom looming just beyond the stockade walls.

Except I wasn't sure what I was digging for this time.

As I stared into the darkness ahead of me, watching the sewer pipes extend into infinity, I began to notice the particles of shadow moving like minute creatures beneath a microscope. Now and then they'd assume a recognizable shape. Their favorite seemed to be the face of Eddie Munroe.

This was nothing special. There had been many nights when the moon had taken on his face before the clouds rushed to disguise the fact.

I wondered if people could be haunted, like houses were. If I were a house I would have to have plenty of rooms for all my ghosts. I'd have to be a mansion. Maybe even a city.

Each one of my ghosts—the memory of the first limb I saw blown off a man by grape, the first time I smelled a human corpse, the first touch of another man's warm blood on my face—all these things and more would not relinquish their hold on me no matter how much distance I put between me and the memories.

I knew some people who had lived through the war and

had gotten over the carnage, the brutality, and the loss.

In the moments when I was honest with myself I admitted that I was not one of these people. I'd never gotten over the realization that evil exists in the world. Exists like a living, breathing, hungry thing.

The first day I really saw it was in prison. Not long after I reached Andersonville, I witnessed a young boy beaten to death because he wouldn't hand over his woolen blanket to a Raider. Beaten to death in broad daylight, with a crowd of passive, curious, fearful onlookers giving the Raider plenty of space.

I was here now because I would not become like David King. I would not stand around and just watch it work.

I still had this crazy idea that if I cried in the dark, lonely silence, my weeping would be heard, my anguish shared, and my fearful questions answered.

So far nothing had quite convinced me otherwise.

All these thoughts swirled through my brain like shooting stars in the surrounding night. I had long since given up wondering how far I had to go. By my estimation I was probably halfway past the Main Building now.

At irregular intervals the tunnel broke off into smaller shafts with bewildering complexity. As far as I knew, I had kept forging ahead in a straight line. But I was not sure. I didn't even want to think about what would happen if I got lost down here.

I pulled out my watch as I went and checked up on the time. There were only about ten minutes till midnight. Quickening my pace, I hoped I would reach an exit before Jesse Harding and Elsie encountered the amateur firing squad.

I went a few more paces and then I smelled something.

It was a distinctive scent. There's nothing quite like whale oil.

Peering ahead of me, I saw one of the branching shafts flicker with a feeble light.

As I poked my head around the corner I saw the source, not more than a rod away. I left my lantern where it was to mark the intersection. Then I made my way toward the whale oil lamp, my revolver out of its holster now.

The lamp stood in a small space beneath some dirt-encrusted piping. Just beyond it were several blankets, full of human odors—the kind you encounter when you don't bathe.

On the floor was a half-opened package of butcher paper. There was some partially eaten cheese and bread inside. Nearby was a bottle of water.

I looked at the way the blankets were arranged and pictured the two lovers lying on them, limbs entwined. I caught myself wondering if Elsie had surrendered herself to him as she had ten years ago. From the disorder of the blankets and certain marks on them I decided there wasn't much to wonder about.

There was a book on one of the blankets. I could read its spine in the dim light. It said *The Collected Poems of Lord Byron.* Pretty racy reading from what I'd heard. Inside on the title page, was an inscription. It said, *"For Jesse, Let these verses be reflections of my undying love for you, for your beauty and the joy you unlock within me. With love forever, Elsie. 20 October 1865."*

I shook my head, thinking on the poor, opium-addled girl who had also loved Jesse. The Circassian Beauty never had a chance.

One of the poems was bookmarked. Out of sheer curiosity I opened to that page.

I didn't bother reading the opening verse. I was far more interested in the bookmark.

There were two of them actually. They were a pair of tickets on the Philadelphia and Reading Railroad. One-way fares to Mauch Chunk, Pennsylvania. The date stamped on them was September 7. That was to-night.

Did that mean they weren't going to the Grounds after all? I wondered. Were they simply going to elope and run as far away from her father as they could get?

Why then would they be going to Mauch Chunk, where Hiram King wielded even more power than he did here?

I didn't have the time to answer these questions.

Retrieving my kerosene lamp I began to run down the tunnel as fast as I could without upsetting the fuel in the lamp.

I didn't think Jesse Harding was the sort of man to abandon Hattie Anderson. She had loved him and believed in him. Perhaps she had a reason.

The hand of my watch was past the numeral 11 by the time I came upon the metal rungs leading upward.

It was the end of the tunnel. Above me, I saw a wooden door, with no light seeping through the cracks. Hoping the door wasn't locked, I extinguished the lamp and ascended the rungs till I reached the door.

With my revolver in one hand I twisted the knob.

The door opened and I saw the night sky beyond.

A gigantic shape stood black against the starry background. It took me a few moments before I recognized it and the building beyond.

It was the standpipe of the Centennial Waterworks. I had emerged from a row of water closets adjacent to the Art Annex.

Memorial Hall's beautiful statue-capped dome stood against the star-encrusted sky like a dark blossom of copper and glass.

Even from this distance I could see the figures silhouetted on Memorial Hall's rear promenade. And the rifles they carried.

There were more men in the area between the Hall and the Main Annex. I counted a whole company.

I stayed in the shadows and wound my way toward the Education Department Building, where Tad and I had seen the kindergarten that afternoon.

There was a gazebo there, between the Main Annex

and the Lafayette Restaurant. I hopped inside and crouched low enough to remain invisible.

I made myself as comfortable as possible. There was enough space between the lattices to give me a good view of where the exchange was set to take place.

I propped the barrel of my revolver on one of the slats and waited.

It was about ten minutes before I noticed two shadowy figures creeping along the Annex. They paused, surveying the company of Guard coppers. I could see one of the figures had a dress on. So he had brought Elsie with him, I thought.

Perhaps Elsie thought they wouldn't harm Jesse with her along.

She was very much mistaken.

I heard Jesse call out, "Show me Hattie!"

The only answer he got was a volley of gunfire.

As the smoke cleared, I saw the Guard coppers racing after Jesse and Elsie. When they ran past the gazebo, I could hear Elsie whimpering in terror.

Revolvers thundered after them.

One ball slammed into the post I was leaning against. That was my signal.

I fired into the crowd of them, emptying all the chambers.

I didn't wait to see if it stopped any of them.

With the smoking revolver in my hand I vaulted over the side of the gazebo and ran after Jesse and Elsie, a tattoo of bullets crackling behind me.

30

By THE TIME I reached Agricultural Avenue I had my
barker reloaded. I pointed it behind me at nothing in particular and squeezed off a few more shots. A spark flashing out from the cylinder singed my hand, already covered
with tiny powder burns. I stopped firing and ran for the
intersection ahead, rubbing my gun hand. There were
shouts in the distance and something like a moan.

The Guard returned fire just as I ducked behind the
Sweden Building. I looked ahead of me into the darkness
for Jesse and Elsie. The boy, I thought, must have some
sort of escape plan—another entrance to the tunnels. Or
it could be that he was leading them on a wild goose chase
just long enough so he could double back to the standpipe
closet that I'd used.

I wondered if Jesse realized, as I did, that he wasn't
the only one who knew those tunnels. That whoever was
conducting swells and whores into the Centennial for
Hiram King used that same network.

I had a pretty good idea who that person was. I was
looking forward to meeting him here to-night. If I could
only save enough cartridges for the occasion.

Ahead of me I saw two figures scurrying past Agricultural. They disappeared between the Japanese Bazaar and
the Department of Public Comfort.

There were plenty of shadows to hide them. The Centennial grounds, labyrinthine enough in the daytime, were bewildering at night. As long as they stayed off the wide-open Avenue of the Republic, there was a good chance they could evade the guards.

I hoped my chances were as good. I stared at the massive Main and Machinery across the avenue. They were like gigantic walls barring my escape. To my right the complex of smaller buildings, so still and darkened now, reminded me of a silent city of mausoleums.

I had no intention of becoming a permanent resident of such a city. Not yet at least.

Crouching as low as I could, I dashed across Agricultural Avenue and followed Jesse and Elsie. The path they'd taken led behind the Judges' Pavilion and the Pennsylvania Railroad Building.

The shouts of the guards echoed from all points. I couldn't tell if they were quite close or distant. It was like being lost in a cave, with sounds issuing from unseen passageways all around you. And no light to show you the right way to go.

I wasn't sure where Jesse and Elsie had gone but the most logical direction seemed toward Belmont Avenue. If they'd headed to Fountain, they would be out in the open on the terraced gardens—easy pickings for the guards.

As I burst out on Belmont, staying close to the wall of the Centennial Photographic Association, I saw them.

They were only a few rods ahead of me. They hesitated at the corner. I thought I heard Elsie whimper with fear again. Jesse said something to her I couldn't pick up and had to stop her from running back the way they came.

I figured it was as good a time as any for me to grab them. What I would do after that I wasn't too clear on.

Just as they were about to cross over to the lake, I hollered, "Jesse Harding, stop where you are!"

He did just that. But I don't think my words were the cause.

Jesse saw, as I did, the dozen guards who were racing down the Avenue of the Republic with their guns drawn. They were just past the Washington statue and were closing in fast.

With a snarl of rage, Jesse dashed across Belmont. Only when he was halfway to the lake did he realize that Elsie was not with him.

The girl had stumbled over the West End Railway tracks and lay sprawled across the asphalt.

Jesse cried out, "I'm coming!"

But the guards drowned him out with their pistols.

By this time they were rounding the bend. If Jesse tried to go back for Elsie they would have both of them for sure.

He stood in the middle of Belmont, an easy target, trying to make up his mind what to do.

Before the guards could shoot him dead I cracked off a few shots at them. I wasn't too fussy over my aim. I just wanted to give them something to think about.

The shots bought me enough time to scramble across the train tracks. Jesse was gone by then, lost amid the copse of trees surrounding the man-made lake.

I picked Elsie up and ran after him, hoping the guards would be confused enough over who I was to not shoot.

Then I heard a familiar voice scream, "It's McCleary! Let him have it, boys!"

I squinted enough to see Pemberton Pierce a few rods off, leveling his revolver in my direction.

When they shot at me I was close enough to smell the smoke. Something stung my back, right below the shoulder blade. There wasn't enough pain to stop me from running. I waited a few moments and sighed with relief when I realized the bullet had just grazed me.

As Elsie and I raced past Frank Leslie's building, I wasted some breath and said, "You both were crazy for coming back here! Your father wants him dead and he doesn't care if you get in the way."

All I got out of her was a grunt. The sound was familiar enough for me to know that things were quite suddenly very wrong.

I stopped running and swung the girl toward me so I could see her face beneath the dim starlight.

Tears were streaming down the terrified face of Iola, the Wild Australian Child. She whimpered at me like an infant, her teeth clattering against each other.

Jesse had done a good job of dressing her in Elsie's clothes. His plan must've been to get Hattie back without sacrificing his paramour.

That made me wonder where Hattie was right now. I hadn't seen her among the guards by Memorial Hall.

My ruminations were cut short by a few bullets slamming into the oak tree we were standing under. I thought it prudent to get moving.

Tugging Iola along, I circled the lake, staying beneath the cover of trees.

Ahead of us, I heard more guards coming from the direction of Fountain Avenue. They were flanking us, like a pair of pincers. And there was nowhere for us to go.

My eyes darted from side to side, desperately searching for a way to escape.

I didn't even notice the massive copper arm bearing a torch until Iola and I ran past its concrete base.

Bartholdi's colossal limb glistened against the heavens. *Liberty Enlightening the World* was far from finished, but it was already majestic enough. Its electric torch, now dimmed, reached toward the sky, waiting to be ignited by the dawn.

Along the base of the Liberty Statue were some paintings showing what the statue would look like upon completion. Iola lingered over them, pointing excitedly. I was more interested in the door at the base of the statue. There was no lock on it.

I gave the child a gentle tug and made a sign for her to keep quiet. Then I pulled her inside the statue with me.

The giant arm was hollow, like the rest of the statue would eventually be. Centennial tourists waited in line for up to a half an hour to be able to walk up the iron stairs to the platform just beneath the copper burst of flame.

During the day, the stairs were easy enough to climb with the daylight leaking down on them. But now the inside of the arm was pitch black. I moved slowly. The last thing I fancied was breaking my neck.

Slowly we creeped upward, my free hand running along the inner surface of the arm to guide us.

I whispered soothingly to the girl the whole way, hoping she wouldn't fall and alert the Guard to our hiding place.

At last my head peeked out over the platform. I pulled the girl up with me and motioned her to sit against the base of the torch.

Meanwhile I crawled along the platform to the railing. Below me I saw a beautiful vista—a glorious dream city—all dark and hushed. I saw the gothic spires of Agricultural Hall glisten with starlight. Horticultural's glass roof reflected the setting moon like liquid crystal. The U.S. Government Building towered just past the lake, where the fountain was still in operation. I could hear the bubbling jets as they sprayed water upward in the shape of a canopy, with a thick stream shooting up from the middle.

I realized then that I'd never really taken note of the Exhibition's beauty—a fragile beauty, for most of the buildings were set to be torn down by the end of the year. Only now did I appreciate their magnificence—dreams in iron and glass and stone of a future that I might never live to see.

There were a few cartridges left in my pocket. I loaded them into the empty chambers and peered down below.

A few dark figures moved slowly along the banks of the lake. I counted five. There were more men farther down the Avenue of the Republic. From their shouting I figured they had Jesse on the run. I lost sight of them once they passed the Pennsylvania Building.

My only hope was that the guards would pass us without bothering to look inside the statue, thinking we'd head toward Fountain Avenue.

The iron platform was cool and reassuring against my sweaty palm. I held on to it like a lifeline. The beautiful vision of the Centennial dissolved as suddenly as it had appeared.

I was back on the colossal arm, trapped beneath the darkened metallic flame.

I felt like a man lost at sea, with the sharks beginning to circle and no land in sight.

I stared up at the stars and past them. I tried not to be frightened of death.

There was a scream from behind me.

It was Iola. Someone else was on the platform now, struggling with her.

As I edged along the torch his face came into view.

I heard him say, "You silly little fool! Did you think I would ever let you go?"

Then he slapped the girl loud enough for me to wince. Her beating was cut short when he saw her face.

I aimed my barker at him and said, "Hello, Bert."

Pemberton Pierce dropped the girl like a dead thing. I could see she wasn't that hurt. Just terrified. She began clawing toward me.

The detective had his own gun pointed at my head.

I said to him, "It takes quite a man to beat on an imbecile child."

"Come closer, McCleary," he whispered. "I got a present for you."

I mustered what little bravado I had left.

"Why don't you call your friends? Let's make a party out of it."

"Oh, they're coming," he said, looking down the dark

staircase. "I just wanted to take a piece out of you myself."

I got to my feet and backed up against the railing.

"Tell your boys there's no one up here."

"Not a chance," he said. "Mr. King wants you erased from the slate. And I'm gonna have a ball doin' it."

"I'll bet you always do."

A guard stumbled out on the platform just then. Pierce turned his head for a split second.

I squeezed the trigger and sent a pill at him.

I waited just enough to see it tear into his shoulder. He started cursing a stream and shot at me, wildly.

The other guard opened fire but I had dropped over the side of the railing by then. My fingers clawed at the platform, my feet kicking back and forth in open space. I tried in vain to find a solid surface to jump down on.

More guards began crowding onto the platform.

"Where the hell'd he go?" I heard one say.

Then someone saw my fingers clutching at the platform's edge. I heard their boot heels clicking toward me.

I let go then and fell through space, my heart reaching into my throat, beating so hard I felt my neck ready to burst.

Something cold and metallic slammed into me and I wrapped my arms and legs around it like an awkward lover.

I was on the smooth surface of the giant statue's hand. Below me the arm stretched a long way to the ground. I didn't know exactly how far. My brain was not in perfect working order.

It seemed too far to jump.

Above me the guards began to lean over the iron railing.

I was too terrified to move and upset my balance.

There was no way I could go up or down without breaking my neck.

Suddenly that didn't seem to matter much when bullets

began to ricochet off Liberty's wrist, just a few feet below me.

I closed my eyes and started to scream. I was back on the field at Gettysburg, with the Rebels mowing us down. All the terror of that day slammed into me like a granite fist.

As I screamed, I felt my damp palms slowly lose their grip and I began to fall again.

I kept my body pressed against the statue and let gravity slide me down the massive hand, its wrist, and its forearm.

Bullets careened on all sides of me. A few bit into my clothes. One missed my head by a few inches. I didn't mind. I was too busy screaming.

I slid down Liberty's arm all the way until my heels hit the concrete base, sending me sprawling backward.

My back hit the ground hard enough to make me groan. I blinked a few times and stared at the stars, too stunned to move.

Then I noticed there was no one on the platform. I could hear a din of profanity coming from inside the arm as they clambered down the stairs.

Before any of them had got through the doorway, I was running across the Avenue of the Republic toward the main entrance.

My laughter echoed off the towering walls of Main and Machinery. It was a queer sort of laughter. More shrill than usual, and as hollow and mirthless as a madman's.

I was still laughing when I sprang over the wooden turnstiles and stumbled onto Elm Avenue. The streets were relatively quiet but the gas-lights of Shantyville were still aflame. I stood in the middle of Elm for a moment and took in the gaudily painted frame hotels, saloons, and variety shows. I breathed deeply and got a whiff of grease and horses.

Nothing had ever seemed so beautiful as that shabby little corner.

My back was throbbing with pain as I ran through the

light traffic of broughams and wagons and into the Transcontinental Hotel.

David King seemed like the only one who could help me now. The only one interested in the truth.

And the only one who didn't want me dead.

I clambered up the stairs to his room with the desperation of a man at the gallows who had the rope break on him once. Chances were they'd tie it tighter the next time.

THE CARPETED HALLWAY was clear, illuminated by a few
gas-lamps. I reached David's room and knocked lightly
on the door. There was no answer.

I knocked again, a little louder this time. It wouldn't
do to make too much noise, I thought. The fewer guests
who saw or heard me enter David's room the better.

After a minute of waiting I got impatient and tried the
door. I wasn't surprised to find it unlocked. There was
little chance of a hotel sneak operating in a place like the
Transcontinental Hotel. It could afford enough private detectives to keep the scamps out. I'd seen two of these
dicks looking me over when I passed through the public
parlor.

David's room was dark inside.

The window sash was open, the lace curtains fluttering
lightly. Outside was the dim sound of locomotive whistles
and the glass-clinking gaiety of the nearby variety shows.

I didn't see the reporter lounging on any of the parlor
furniture. My feet fell softly on the expensive carpet as I
made my way to his bedroom door.

"David?" I called as a warning.

There was no answer. I went in, thinking he might have
retired.

Sure enough, there was someone in the bed. The window shades were down and I could barely see where I was going.

I walked right up to the bed and tapped the form lying prone beneath the sheets. The face was covered but I didn't think it too odd.

Then my eyes adjusted to the darkness a little better.

That was when I saw the stains on the bedsheets.

The chest was not rising and falling like it should in sleep.

"Oh no . . ." I said. Only when I'd spoken did I realize the unearthly silence in the room.

The stains were a dark color. They were still soaking into the white linen, growing like ugly crimson blossoms.

I tensed my face and ripped the sheet off.

There wasn't much recognizable. The mutilation to the face was hideous. Like someone had tried carving a jack-o'-lantern out of it.

But there was one telltale sign left.

An explosion of hair, teased to the extreme, half covered the stained pillow and bleeding face.

Hattie Anderson's face.

My head ached and sweat streamed down my face and sides. I tried not to look at the tongue jutting pathetically between what was left of her teeth.

The killer had ripped open her throat like a wild beast. The blood was still pulsing out of the ruptured arteries.

I heard a whimpering noise and realized only after breathing deeply a dozen times that it was myself.

My loins felt weak and my legs trembled. I didn't bother pulling the rest of the sheet off Hattie's body. I didn't want to know how bad it truly was.

She was far, far worse than Susie Adams had been. Like the killer had had all the time in the world with Hattie, enough to vent upon her all his diabolic fury.

As I stood there, praying for her, I felt the horror of her last moments. I hoped that she had had enough opium to not feel too much of the pain. But that was a vain hope, I knew.

I struggled to think clearly. There were certain questions I kept repeating to myself to give my brain something to do other than focus on Hattie's mangled corpse.

Did Jesse Harding do this? The Boy Fiend?

He had the time. The flesh was still warm and the bleeding not yet staunched.

How in hell had she gotten here?

Most importantly where was David King?

I very much wanted to ask him what a dead girl was doing in his bed.

The dark silence amplified the sound of my breathing. The air came in and out of me at a frantic pace. I almost wished I was back on the Liberty statue.

I didn't know to whom I should go. Would Heins even listen to me anymore? I wondered. Not unless I could bring him some proof. For that, I needed Jesse Harding or David King.

One of them was going to answer for Hattie Anderson. I didn't know what to think of either of them anymore.

Then something helped my cogitation along. I had backed up against the dresser by the bed. Inadvertently I walked into it, sending a box perched on the top falling to the carpeted floor.

I crouched to pick up the contents. One of them was familiar to me.

The yen-nock.

The needle with the initials B.F. in Chinese on the tip. The same one used to kill Susie Adams.

There was blood on it now. My fingers were moist with it. Hattie's blood.

Other instruments had spilled from the box. I'd never seen any of them before. But I'd seen things like them.

They were part of an opium lay-out. A pipe and a little lamp devoid of fuel. The box appeared custom-made, lined with velvet, with compartments for the opium-smoking apparatus. Each bore the distinctive Chinese mark on them. The initials B.F.

On top of the case was a brass plaque with a different set of initials, engraved with fanciful Western flourishes.

D. K.

With clammy hands, I put the instruments back in the box and fastened the lock on the outside. Then, with the box under my arm, I backed out of the bedroom and opened the door to the hallway.

I had to get this to Heins. He'd have to believe me when he saw this.

Just as I stepped out David's door, the one directly opposite me swung open. A man in his bedclothes, his sparse hair ruffled with sleep, looked like he was on his way to the water closet.

At first he didn't take much notice of me.

Then he saw my disheveled suit, tattered with bullet holes.

His squinting gaze fell on my hands. There was still some of Hattie's blood on them.

I managed the most idiotic of smiles and said, "Good evening."

Then I proceeded down the hallway, trying to walk as calmly as possible.

When I was about halfway to the exit door, I heard some noise at the other end of the hall.

A door opened and shut. A few moments later, when I was just a few paces from the exit, I heard someone shriek, "Murder! Help, help! Murder!"

"Look, there he is!"

"Stay where you are, McCleary!"

My head turned just in time to see Pemberton Pierce, his arm in a sling, pointing his finger down the hall at me.

There were about a half-dozen guards with him. The man across the hall was already telling a copper with a memorandum book all about the blood he'd seen on my hands.

I broke into a run and kicked open the door to the staircase. I leaped down them, taking five or six steps with each jump. The Guard coppers were still on the second floor when I made it out into the lobby.

I walked at a brisk pace past the telegraph office and public parlor. The hotel dicks were nowhere to be seen. They had probably joined Pemberton Pierce by now.

Some people were coming in the Elm Street entrance. I swiftly changed directions and took the other exit. Once I was out on Belmont, I scanned the streets, looking for any trace of the Centennial Guard.

Sure enough, a large band of them was congregating on the street outside the main entrance to the Centennial.

There was no chance of me getting inside and to Heins. At least not right away.

I started crossing Belmont, just to keep moving. Pierce and the other coppers would hit the street pretty soon.

I was about to turn down Belmont and head past Doyle's restaurant when I saw someone with a Guard uniform step out from between two of the buildings. He was far enough away that I couldn't see his face. But he stood there on the wooden walkway, appearing to take quite an interest in me.

That left only one place to go. Across the street to the open lot reserved for the souvenir hucksters.

No one took notice of me from the group on Elm. Then I glanced over my shoulder and saw the guard from Doyle's stepping over the tracks laid in front of the Hotel.

If I ran I might alert the coppers to my right. Each step I took made me wince. My hands were trembling. There was still some blood on them. I wiped it off with my handkerchief. When I reached the lot I threw the wipe into the gutter.

My shadow was about halfway across Belmont.

We both turned around when a voice cried out, "There he is! He's getting away!"

Pierce and his detachment of guards had just burst out of the Transcontinental Hotel.

The hollering got the attention of the idle coppers outside the Centennial. I had no choice but to run. They saw me right away and gave chase.

Clutching David's box, I ran past the Soda Water Saloon and into the open fields of the Pennsylvania Railroad Depot. A locomotive whistled a few miles away.

I crossed the first set of tracks and looked around for somewhere to hide. There was nowhere. Just flat open space covered with track.

Then I spotted a small shack fifty rods away, probably for the brakemen. I had no choice but to make for it, hoping they'd lose me.

There wasn't much of a chance of that, I realized. One of the coppers, I didn't know which one, had just crashed through some freshly trimmed bushes and into the railyard. I thought he shouted something to me but I couldn't hear it. Just then the train whistled again, about ready to roll into the station. I saw its lantern flashing way down the stretch of track.

I made it past the next set of rails with no problem. My free hand reached for the revolver at my side. But there was nothing there. Only now did I realize I must've lost it at the Liberty statue. Without it I didn't stand much of a chance against the guards.

My brain had stopped working by now. The only thing keeping me in motion was fear. The blind terror of a hunted animal.

I fought against the weakness and remembered Hattie Anderson. The anger I felt gave me a burst of speed that took me right to the shack.

But before I could even think of finding a way inside, someone grabbed me from behind. His good arm got hold of me by the waist and threw me to the ground.

Pemberton Pierce leered down at me, panting.

"I'm getting tired of chasing after you, McCleary."

I took a swipe at his wounded shoulder. He swatted my fist away with the revolver in his left hand. The hammer scraped against my knuckles, tearing off a layer of flesh.

Then he pressed the barrel against my forehead. I closed my eyes, wondering if I'd hear the shot first.

"Keep your eyes closed."

Pierce whispered it, in between heavy breaths.

I opened my eyes and stared at him defiantly. I was too interested in the barrel of his gun to pay much attention to the movement behind him.

Before his thumb could pull back the hammer something cracked across his skull. Pierce collapsed on top of me, a thin stream of blood leaking from his scalp onto my already soiled shirt.

The detective's body rolled off me then and a hand pulled me to my feet.

"Tad Schmoyer," I said. "I could kiss you."

The boy returned my grin and said, "I wish you wouldn't."

While Tad replaced the club in his belt, I picked up Pierce's revolver, only to find that it was my own. I put the little traitor back in my holster where it belonged.

Then I said, "Am I really dead and dreaming this? You are Tad Schmoyer, aren't you?"

That made him laugh. "You didn't think I'd really let you have all the fun to-night, did you?"

"Was it you who came after me out of Doyle's?"

"Of course," he smiled. "I've kept my eye on you the whole night. Since they started taking potshots at you from the Liberty statue. As soon as I heard the shooting start I got myself outside. Didn't let anyone see me either. When I saw you make for the main entrance and Elm Avenue I followed you."

"Listen," I said. "We don't have a lot of time. This is very important. You've got to get this box to Heins. Understand? There's a murdered girl in David King's room at the Transcontinental Hotel. The same one that Hiram King's boys arrested last night. The yen-nock, that needle they used on Susie Adams? The one they took from me? It's here in this box. Hattie's blood is all over it."

"Why don't you take it to Heins?"

"Hiram King wants me dead. Hear those boys back there? I think they've got instructions to shoot me on sight. David King told me so, in so many words."

"What are we gonna do then?"

A locomotive moaned behind us, pulling into the station. It ground to a halt and threw out a gust of steam.

I shoved the box into Tad's chest and said, "Take this. I gotta catch that train. Make sure Heins sees it before our friend here finds you."

Before he could react, I slapped his cheek and ran off into the darkness, toward the train. It was just beginning to pull out of the station. The conductor had to help me up the platform.

I rode it all the way to the West Philadelphia Depot. I bought a round-trip ticket at the window and then waited for an hour or so. I cleaned myself up as best I could in the washroom.

Then, a little bit before two in the morning, I caught the train for Mauch Chunk.

32

BEFORE WE WERE out of Philadelphia, I fell dead asleep.

I was suddenly alone in the darkness. There was a swaying motion, as if I were still in the railcar. Except that now instead of a comfortable seat I was lying down on a metallic floor. Slowly I became aware of the faintest light, coming from far above me. I saw that the light fell down through slats.

It took me a few bewildering moments till I understood that the cold, hard surface I rested on was sheet iron. And those slats, iron bars.

I was in the Black Maria.

The van used to transport prisoners from court to the penitentiary.

But what, I thought feverishly, am I doing in the prison van?

Where am I going? To trial or to jail?

There was no way out of the van. Just enough space between the bars for a little light and air to leak through.

I groped in the darkness to find a latch for the back door. Instead, I brushed against something alive, a body lying right beside me.

There were more of them, countless numbers of men and women. I couldn't see them but I could feel them there, huddled close against each other. It reminded me of many station-house basements I'd seen, where those who had nowhere else to go could sleep for the night.

I think I asked some people what we were doing there and where we were headed. No one knew any more than I did.

I thought there had to be at least one person with that knowledge. But the van seemed to stretch into an infinity of darkness, with hundreds of people inside its iron walls.

The air was stagnant and miasmic. It had the reek of a thousand centuries in it. The silence was deathlike. Every now and then I thought I heard echoes of familiar voices—ones that I had not heard in years.

Soon the faint echoes rose to a din and I felt the throng pressing against me. Someone had decided to bribe the driver into letting us all out. They were rushing to the front end of the van to hammer on the walls, hoping he would hear them before the van reached its destination.

But something told me it was futile. That we had already somehow arrived.

The crowd was far away from me now but I could hear them imploring the driver to listen to them.

That was when I noticed that the van had come to a stop. I wondered how long it had been since we had moved and realized it must've been ages ago.

I began to doubt if we were even in the Black Maria anymore. Or had ever been.

Perhaps there was no driver at all. And no prison to get to.

That didn't stop me from clambering for the back door, again hoping against hope that it was still there. I kept running till I struck something solid. Then my hands ran up and down its metallic smoothness, searching for an opening of some kind.

It was only when I realized that there was no inside latch, no means of escape, that I heard a bolt drawn from the outside.

The door swung open and I was blinded. Just before

that I saw the silhouette of someone standing there, the one who'd opened the back door of the Black Maria.

I put out a hand to grasp him. Then I was jolted forward and down into that blinding light.

The shriek of locomotive brakes woke me as the train pulled into South Bethlehem.

I stared at the horizon, glowing blue and orange with the dawn.

The memory of the dream came back to me then.

In Allentown I stepped off the train to purchase some of the mineral water that town was famous for. A butcher boy sold me a piece of tasty sausage. I stepped back on the train as it pulled out and kept my eyes on the lush countryside.

The train rolled slowly past a string of slate mines, stopping at only two villages, named Catasaqua and Slatington. I watched the farmers already at work in their fields, their barns painted the color of fire engines and covered with queer designs of swirling color. A man seated in front of me noted my interest in them and said they were hex signs. I asked what a hex was and he told me in the old days it meant witchcraft. The designs were special symbols to ward off bad luck.

I watched my reflection in the window and thought on how much I'd like a personal hex sign. Anything to drive away the memories of last night.

But there was nothing supernatural about what happened to Hattie Anderson. The devil had used a middle man.

I cast my eyes to the cornfields streaming past my window. I wished I could leap into their midst and lose myself in them like country people did for sport around harvest time. But there was nowhere to hide from the answers to my questions—answers I knew I would find in Mauch Chunk.

As the train sped north through the Lehigh Valley, civilization dwindled and the tracks were surrounded on all sides by verdant hills, towering above the serpentine Lehigh River. The pristine beauty of the scene awed me. The woods seemed eternal and impassive.

We entered into the Lehigh River Gorge and I felt the mountains on either side of us closing in. I pictured Jesse Harding and Elsie King reaching this same spot, just a few hours earlier, and thought how this place had drawn us to it, with the ineluctability of a whirlpool.

It was a journey not just in space but in time. To the prison of the past, that neither of them had ever been able to escape.

I thought on Andersonville and the war and realized that I too was an inmate.

It was time for all of us to break out.

I made that promise to Hattie's tear-drenched face as I saw it in my memory. She had not stopped believing that she might make Jesse Harding forget the past.

There was a great deal of meaning in that for me.

From the windows I could see the jagged mountains of the gorge towering above the Lehigh. The hills glowed purple in the morning sun, covered with slate and heaps of slag. Beneath those hills, buried in the dark recesses of the earth, were the veins of anthracite, the black blood of our Republic.

I thought on those tunnels under the earth's surface and of the men down there even now working with only the feeble light of candles on their helmets to stave off the darkness. At that moment I felt a strange sort of kinship with them.

The train tracks curved along the river and soon bore us to the tiny squat depot. The brakes shrieked as we came to a stop.

Once I was outside of the car I brushed the coal dust off my already well-soiled suit and headed inside the depot.

The usual loungers were grouped around the brass cuspidor, their legs propped on the pot-bellied stove. One man was reading the front page of the newspaper to them. They listened to the story about the Hayes and Tinsdale presidential race in reverent silence.

I approached the ticket window and waited for the old man sitting there to stop chewing on a drumstick. He was licking his fingertips when I cleared my throat.

"May I help you, sir?" he said, adjusting the visor over his bald head.

"I hope so. I'm looking for a man called . . ." I tried to remember the name in the article David showed us.

The ticket man waited patiently. He was an old fellow and I was moving at his speed.

"Savage," I said, remembering. "Used to be the chief of police. I guess it was about ten years ago."

"You're looking for John Savage, eh? Well, sure, I can tell you where to find him. The county lock-up, just four squares up Broadway."

Confused, I asked him, "You mind telling me what he's doing in jail?"

That got a chuckle out of him.

"Well, he don't do much, I think. The liquor kinda ruined him. Used to be a fine figure of a man in the old days."

"So you're saying he's a prisoner? What did he do?"

"Johnny's no prisoner. At least he ain't behind bars. He's a guard up there now."

I shook my head, exasperated, and headed for the door. Poised on the doorstep I turned around and asked, "Where's Broadway?"

The newspaper reader pointed in the direction without missing a syllable of the Vermont primary results.

There wasn't much to Mauch Chunk. From the train I saw the town was divided into two parts, the industrial center skirting the Lehigh River while a smaller section of newer homes nestled on a natural terrace above. Coal shutes streamed from the mountains to the river, where in the old days the canal boats had borne the anthracite south. Now the railroads held sway and the air was full of their smoke and steam and strident whistles.

Broadway was pretty hard to miss. It was just about the only street in town.

Like most villages and boroughs, Mauch Chunk's public buildings were crammed into half a square's space. After that were the usual hotels and saloons, goods stores and marketplaces.

The dirt streets were a little damp from rain during the night. Horses, hitched to milk and meat wagons, plodded through the mud.

Buildings that looked like they weren't more than a few decades old stretched down Broadway for a few squares. Their rain-dampened, red brick walls glistened in the morning light. A woman was leaning out of her window, beating a carpet that sent huge clouds of dust into the air. Out of one saloon I smelled the unmistakable scent of oysters. I couldn't resist. When I had washed them down with a pot of coffee I stepped back out on the wooden walkways, navigating my way through teams of mothers, cooing over one another's bundled-up infants.

I took my time, enjoying the walk. I stepped inside a general store and bought myself a new straw hat to replace the one I'd lost the previous night. And a much-needed new linen coat. There was space in the back for me to put it on. I fastened the top button and exited the store. Outside, I didn't don the boater right away. The wind felt nice rustling my hair.

After I'd gone four squares I was beginning to breathe a little heavy. The whole way had been an uphill climb. Then I saw it on the corner, just ahead.

I rested against someone's front porch and caught my breath.

It was worth stopping to look the place over.

The new Carbon County Prison was an impressive

sight. It looked new and reminded me of our own Eastern State Penitentiary.

Set into the side of the mountain, its thick walls and watchtower were of hewn stone, stark and imposing. It was as majestic as a church, but with none of the church's grace. Its beauty was cold and hard, made not for worship but punishment.

Inside were some of the most notorious criminals of the day, the Molly Maguires. Men that Hiram King, and many others, were hoping to hang.

A series of low stone walls separated it from the street, like petrified moats. I climbed the stairs through them and reached the massive wooden door.

A plaque over the arched doorway told me that the prison had been built only six years ago, and by the son of the man who designed Eastern State. A quaint family business.

It took me about a quarter of an hour to introduce myself to the Keeper of the Jail and his subordinates. I told them I was a city detective from Philadelphia looking for an escaped criminal. I didn't mention the name Jesse Harding. All I said was John Savage might be able to help me find him.

My appearance didn't lend itself to trustworthiness. But when I produced my star they were willing to take me at my word.

After a few minutes' wait, a man shambled in.

"Savage," the warden said, "this man is from Philadelphia. He wants to talk to you about an old case."

John Savage straightened his back and pulled his chin up, giving me a looking-over.

He was still a handsome man, his thick brown hair flecked with gray. A graceful, well-kept mustache curled over his stern lips. Just the hint of a belly protruded over his thick leather belt, from which a club and key ring dangled.

I didn't see the telltale signs of dipsomania. His lucid

eyes looked at me sharply and with intelligence. The lines of his face were rigid and far from the puffy, sagging look of the drunkard.

"What can I do for you, sir?"

Not wanting to speak any more in the warden's presence, I asked, "Is there a place where we could talk?"

"I was about to have my breakfast in the kitchen."

I thanked the warden and followed him to the entranceway. As soon as I shut the door I said, "It's about Jesse Harding. The Boy Fiend. I've seen him at the Centennial Exhibition. And I think he's come back to Mauch Chunk."

Savage lowered his head. A veil seemed to pass over his face, casting a dark pall.

Then he said, "What will you do if you find him?"

"Take him back with me. And Elsie King."

"She's with him?" he said, startled.

"There's more than that. Two women are dead. With their throats ripped open, beaten savag—"

I smiled.

"That's all right," he said. "I know what you mean. And you think it's Harding's work?"

"I think the Boy Fiend did it. Whoever that is."

With a barely perceptible nod, Savage said, "You're not sure it's Jesse Harding."

I sighed and said, "No. I'm not."

"Forget about breakfast," the ex-police chief said. "You and I need to talk privately. Lemme see . . ."

He rubbed his hands together a few times, then snapped two dry fingers together.

"The dungeon! Perfect! This way, uh, Mr. . . . ?"

I told him my name.

"McCleary, I'm pleased to meet you. I mean that too."

Gesturing me to follow him, Savage led me to a series of doors, each covered with a complicated sequence of locks. He deftly and quickly twisted his set of keys into them and ushered me into the cell block.

"Twenty-eight cells," he said, waving at the two levels of quiet cages. A platform ran along the upper story, its ironwork carved in fanciful designs that looked like cathedral windows.

"Pretty artful for a prison," I said.

"That cast-iron staircase to the upper level was made right here in town. So were the oak handrails," Savage said proudly.

"Fine piece of work."

We stepped around the staircase and headed down the corridor. The vaulted ceiling echoed our footfalls and the quiet murmurings of the prisoners.

Savage showed me down a set of stairs leading to the basement.

When he shut the door behind us the darkness was total.

"This is where we have the solitary cells. Sixteen of them."

"Any people in there now?"

"Three of them are occupied. But they won't hear us."

He lit a small lantern and set it on the concrete floor.

From its dim flame I saw the doors to the solitary cells, studded with an array of fat bolts.

"Like armor plating," I said.

"Sheet iron, three eighths of an inch. All the doors have holes in them for the air to go through. I'm sure you smell that air."

"I've smelled worse."

"Well, I won't keep you down here too long. The miasmas are enough to prostrate a man."

"I take it there are no toilets in the cells."

"We shackle them to the wall. Where they do their bunk is their business."

Savage walked me over to the end of the dungeon. There were some boiler pipes there that offered a little warmth. Holes built into the walls conducted heat to the rest of the prison.

We sat there and began to talk.

I didn't want to waste time telling him the whole story.

Instead I asked him, "You don't think Jesse Harding was the Boy Fiend?"

"Well, the Boy Fiend is just a name, Mr. McCleary. A name the press conjured up to sell newspapers. He was branded with that name. But I don't think Jesse killed those children."

"Tell me why you think he's innocent. Convince me," I said.

With a sigh he said, "Mauch Chunk is a very small place. About four thousand souls. When we found Horace Millen's body it hurt us . . . the whole town. Like we'd all lost a child. I tried my damnedest to find the one who did it. But there wasn't any trace of the killer. I spent weeks going over every detail, the whole time under this enormous pressure from all sides. Then Danny Curran disappeared. The town was ready to string anybody up at that point. I had the feeling it might be me if I didn't bring someone in and soon. I kept looking and finding nothing."

"Until Pemberton Pierce broke into the Harding store and just happened to find a body hidden behind the privy."

"Mr. McCleary, I went over every inch of Mauch Chunk. I did a house to house search. Everyone was glad to let me into their homes. Jesse's mother let me into theirs. And I found no trace of the Curran boy. Not even by the rubbish heap out back. That body wasn't there. You understand what I'm telling you?"

"I think so. The body was put there on purpose by someone else."

"That's it! That's it exactly. You see, anyone could've gotten in the backyard of the Harding place. There wasn't even a fence. And the rubbish pile stank so bad nobody'd get too close to give it a careful examination. Not after I already poked through it myself. I would've seen something. I know it . . ."

His voice cracked at the very end. I watched his face, half-cloaked in shadow.

Without looking in his eyes, I said, "You can see the Millen boy's face at night, can't you? And Danny Curran?"

For a few seconds I listened to the sounds of his irregular breaths.

"I know how it is, Savage. I've seen faces like that too."

When the man had regained his self-composure he said, "It's not just the children. It's Jesse too. You don't know how many times I've thought on him these past ten years. Wondered if he were dead or alive."

"Even though he confessed to the murders? Didn't that prove his guilt to you?"

He shook his head.

"If all you know was what the papers said, you know next to nothing. The confession sounded good in print, didn't it? But not when he said it to me. Ever since Pierce and Hiram King's boys brought Jesse in, the boy denied everything. He even had a good alibi for the afternoon that Millen was killed. You don't know how stunned I was when one morning a week after we brought him in Jesse comes to me with his confession. Read it to me like he was reciting a lesson at school. No trace of emotion in his voice or anything. Like he was far, far away from me or anything that could touch him.

"I was furious. With him, and with myself for believing in him. The worst part was, I still believed he was innocent. So I marched him over to the funeral parlor where the Millen boy was. Pemberton Pierce was with me on Hiram King's orders. I shoved Jesse's face right into the coffin and said, 'Did you kill him?' You should've seen his expression when he saw the corpse. I'll never forget it. Like he was someone who never believed in hell and just suddenly got a sight of it. He confessed his murder to me again, right there. Really softly, with that flat, cold tone of his. I thought then he might be mad. Like those lunatics you hear about who confess to crimes they didn't even commit."

"But the judge and jury weren't convinced of that."

"Oh no! Hiram King made sure of that. He convinced the other railroad bosses, Packer and Gowen to push for that boy's execution. They wanted to give the people a little bloodsport to take their minds off what was going on in the coal mines. I reckon they thought Jesse's hanging might divert their attention from their own misery. It's too bad they can't find a Jesse now. They wouldn't have so many problems with the Mollies.

"I know what you're going to ask next. Why pick an innocent kid like Jesse?"

"I already know. He was the father of Elsie King's unborn child."

Savage blinked in the near-darkness.

"How the devil do you know that?"

"I'm more interested in how you know about it."

"I was told by someone . . . very close to the matter."

He seemed reluctant to discuss it further. I could see I'd have to prompt him.

I took a guess and said, "Someone who's no longer living."

Shaking his head in bewilderment, Savage said, "Maybe I'll tell you since you seem to know so much already. And you know what? I've been wanting to tell someone for a long time. But I was afraid. That was the only reason I kept my mouth shut. I was a coward. It's her face I've seen night after night."

"Elsie's mother?"

I heard him sigh.

"Elizabeth. She came to me when it all began with Elsie and Jesse."

"Why you? From what I've seen of the King family they're pretty close-knit."

"Well, you see, Elizabeth and I were very close too. We grew up together here in Mauch Chunk. She was just a few years older than I. Such a fine woman. Beautiful beyond belief . . ."

"Yes, I've seen her portrait in King's study."

"I know that portrait well. That was the way she looked the day she told me Hiram King wanted to marry her."

"She was in favor of it?"

"Oh yes. He was dashing back then. And rich. Beth told me everything about it. She didn't know how I felt, you see. I was like a brother to her. But . . . I wanted to be much more than that.

"Once she was married to King she still called on us. Which was pretty extraordinary, considering how poor my family was. Just workers in the mines. But she never forgot me, through those years. My mother received baskets of food and gifts at the holidays and when I was old enough, Beth saw that Hiram King appointed me to the new police force. My life was good then. I was out of the mines and making a good wage. Then Beth had her children. Aside from the holiday greetings I rarely saw her after that. You know how it is. People grow apart. Beth made a new life for herself, centered on her children and a horde of social causes. Abolition, temperance, even the plight of the laboring class."

That made Savage chuckle.

"She had the nerve to give a speech at a town meeting in favor of the ten-hour day! We heard stories about the quarrel that erupted with Hiram that night. Neighbors said it went on all evening. That didn't stop her though. Beth volunteered as a nurse and wound-dresser during the war. Went down to the capital for months at a time. I liked to think that she'd seen the light by then. That she wanted to be rid of Hiram. If she had said one word to me I would've run away from here—gone to one of the territories. I stayed up plenty of nights thinking on that."

We stopped for a moment to listen to the boiler pipes, rattling with heat. Some vermin scurried farther back in the tunnel, disturbed by the racket.

"But she never came to me. Not until after the war, not long after the Curran boy disappeared. One night she paid a call on me at my home and asked for my help. She said she needed someone she could trust. And I was the only one left in Mauch Chunk."

"Did she tell you about Elsie and Jesse then?" I asked.

"Yes," Savage said. "She was afraid that Hiram might do something to the boy. And his daughter. She . . . wanted me to look after them. I got the feeling the whole thing appealed to her romantic sensibility. By that time it was pretty clear to us that Hiram and Beth were estranged. The servants gossiped that they didn't even talk to each other anymore. And had long since given up sharing a bed. Anyway, she wanted me to make sure nothing happened to Jesse. Or Elsie. Beth told me Hiram knew about the whole mess and wanted the child dead and the whole matter hushed up. Elsie confided to her mother that she was going to run away with Jesse."

"Then Horace Millen's body was found."

"Not more than a week later. Beth called on me again. I took her in my break way out to the country, where no one could see us. Beth was terrified of something. She wouldn't tell me what. But it had something to do with her son, David. I thought then maybe someone had done something to him that she couldn't tell anyone about. All she said was she knew what really happened to Danny and Horace. Then she promised to call on me the next night. I couldn't let her leave me like that, McCleary. I was afraid for her. There was that same look on her face like I saw later on Jesse's. I couldn't bear for her to suffer like that. She told me she'd be all right, that she'd see me the next night. Then she let me kiss her hands. I'll never forget that."

Savage lost control of himself again. The sound of his quiet weeping stirred my own store of anguish.

"The next day," he said quietly, "David found his

mother hanging from the ceiling of her bedroom. They called me and I . . . had to cut her down."

"They told me it was a suicide."

"An ugly word for an ugly crime. I've wondered over and over what it was she learned that drove her to that. And I can't help thinking that it's somehow my fault. If I had just had the strength to keep her with me that night, to wrest the truth out of her . . . She might've found some strength in sharing that truth with me. I could've helped her! I could've saved her from . . ."

I placed a hand on his quaking shoulder and said, "Tell me what happened after that."

Fists clenched to bring himself under control, Savage said, "I spoke up at her inquest. Said I thought the death was suspicious. That she'd come to me with certain information. Of course, the paper never printed that. The *Democrat* was Hiram King's tool. By then, it didn't really matter. Jesse Harding had been arrested for the two murders. Beth's suicide was an . . . embarrassment that everyone wanted to forget. All they wanted now was blood. Harding's blood. Jesse's escape was the perfect excuse King needed to take my job away from me. There wasn't much else I could do. I went back to the mines. There were some accidents then. I came close to getting killed twice. A charge going off too close, that sort of thing. One day in the shafts a voice started speaking behind me. I didn't look to see who it was. He said if I ever spoke out about what Beth told me that I was a dead man. That if I kept my mouth shut I might not meet with a fatal accident one of these days."

Savage stared down at his open palms as if he was reading a list of sins off them.

"I've kept my mouth shut. I wanted to live, Mr. McCleary. There was nothing I could do for Beth anymore. Elsie . . . well, you can ask Dr. Solt what happened to her. David I heard became something of a prodigal. Had to be sent away to an asylum for some years. And I had a ten-year fling with the bottle. Then they pulled me out of the mines and gave me a job at the prison here. I guess they figured I was pretty harmless by now. It was like climbing out of hell and into purgatory. I started remembering what I was and the way Beth had made me feel. I remembered all the temperance parades she'd marched in. So I signed the pledge for her. That was one thing I wanted to do for her."

He took my hand in his own and said, "This is the other thing. She told me to look after Jesse and her Elsie. The only way I can do that now is to tell the truth. And not be afraid of the consequences."

"You did good, Savage. She would've been proud of you."

The burly man appreciated that a great deal. I turned away so he could vent his emotions.

Then he walked me back up to the cell block, where I said goodbye to him. Savage shut the prison door behind me, his keys jangling against his hip.

Repeating the address he'd given me, I turned a corner and headed down High Street, past a Presbyterian cemetery. The sun was beginning to set and the only sound I heard was the strident chirping of blue jays in the burial ground.

I went about two squares more till I found Dr. Jacob Solt's residence.

33

TO MY DISMAY, Dr. Solt was indisposed, still suffering from a stroke he had three days before. I got the feeling he wasn't going to get better.

After taking my leave of the doctor's harried wife, I went for a walk around town, savoring the fresh air of the dusk. It gave me the time to work some things out. I went back to the oyster saloon for supper. Forty cents bought me a nice prime rib supper.

At around seven thirty I made my way to the second address John Savage gave me.

It was a boardinghouse along the river, on Susquehanna Street. I had to pretty much walk all the way out of town, till I reached an iron bridge linking the row of hotels and saloons with a canal that led down to Easton. I walked to the edge of the street and peered down at the black water. Closing my eyes, I traced the progress of the river down through the Lehigh Valley till it emptied into the Delaware, sliding past Philadelphia and into the bay.

I stared at the river for quite a while. Then I went to Mary Owens's boarding house. Owens was her married name. I got her maiden name from Savage.

Harding. Mary was Jesse's sister.

I didn't want them to know I was looking for Jesse

right away. When Mary answered the door I told her I was looking for a room.

She didn't look an awful lot like Jesse. Perhaps when she was younger she had. Now childbirth and widowhood had taken their toll on her. She looked almost old enough to be his mother.

"We don't usually rent by the night, mister. This ain't a hotel."

"Well, all the other places are booked up. Don't you have one room vacant? I'll pay you up front. Will a dollar do?"

It would indeed. My greenback vanished beneath her batter-stained apron.

Mary Owens brought me into the dining room where six men, their faces smeared with coal soot, were devouring a custard pie.

"You hungry?" she asked me. "We still got some left over from supper."

"No thank you. I got something on the way here."

"Won't cost you anything extra."

"Thank you, but I'm all right."

I feigned casual curiosity and asked her, "How many rooms do you have here?"

"Seven. You're in luck. One of the boarders just left yesterday morning. You looking for a job in the mines?"

"No. Just passing through."

I settled into an armchair next to a small melodeon. Some sheet music lay open across the bench. It was a new song, incredibly popular—"I'll Take You Home Again, Kathleen." There was a book there also. A book of Byron's poems that I recognized.

"You play?" I asked Mary.

The presence of a stranger was putting her on edge. She hovered around me as if, left alone, I might break something valuable.

"No, my mother bought that for my brother."

"Is he going to entertain us with some music before we go to bed?"

The question startled her. It took her several seconds to reply, "My brother's dead."

"Oh?" I relaxed in the chair and glanced at the wallpaper, darkened by years of coal smoke. "I'm sorry to hear that. Looks like your brother was very cultured indeed."

I picked up the book of poetry. Mary gripped the mahogany-finished side of the melodeon, her knuckles white.

A slip of paper fell out of the book. I leaned over and took the ticket from the carpet. The punch-hole cut off some of the letters but not enough.

"Were you in Philadelphia?" I said congenially. "I'm just from there myself. At the Centennial. Did you get a chance to see it?"

Mary shook her head like I'd just announced the death of a close relative. She managed to fake a smile and said, "Why don't I bring you some custard pie? I was just making some tea in the kitchen. You make yourself comfortable and I'll be right back."

Her smile collapsed before she turned away from me, her arms pressed rigidly against her sides.

I waited for a minute and then followed her.

There was no one in the kitchen when I got there, just like I expected. Mary hadn't been completely lying though. A tea kettle was whistling on the range. I took it off and poured myself a cup. Then I went out the back door, which lay slightly ajar.

It took me a few moments to adjust to the darkness. Then I saw Mary Owens stepping around a pile of firewood stacked so high it almost hid the shed behind it.

I walked stealthfully toward her. She opened the door of the shed and began talking in hysterical tones.

"There's a man from Philadelphia here! I think he might be a policeman. He found the ticket in your book.

I told you not to leave it out there where everyone could see it!"

I waited until I was just behind her. Then I said, "That's all right, Mrs. Owens. I think Jesse and Elsie will want to see me."

Before his sister could shriek with terror, Jesse rushed through the doorway and clamped a hand over her mouth.

His sister mumbled with terror beneath his grip. Jesse patted her hair and said, "It's all right, Mary. You did the best you could."

Mary Owens walked away from us slowly, dabbing her eyes with her apron.

Jesse ran a tremulous hand over his face, covered now with a few days' stubble. Beneath his calm veneer, he looked as frightened as his sister.

Elsie King appeared behind him, her delicate hands gripping his shoulders.

"Mr. McCleary!" she gasped. "I thought that was you."

"It's me, Elsie. I've come to take you back."

"No!" the girl snarled, shoving Jesse behind her. "You won't take him away from me again!"

She lunged at me, her nails clawing the air. I caught her wrists before she did any damage to my vision. Then I threw her into Jesse. The two of them stumbled back into the shed.

I walked in after them and shut the door.

"Now sit down!"

They did like I told them. Elsie was weeping now and Jesse held her face to his breast.

"Wh-what," Jesse asked, "are you gonna do with us?"

"I'm takin' you both back to Philadelphia."

Jesse nodded solemnly. Then he pulled a bottle from behind him and uncapped it.

I watched the two of them stare at each other.

They said their silent goodbyes and then Jesse asked me, "You mind if we have a drink first?"

I didn't see what was wrong with that. Not until Elsie said to Jesse, "I'm afraid."

"It's all right," he said. "I'll show you."

He was about to tip the bottle back when I kicked it out of his hands.

There was no shatter when it bounced against the far wall. I watched the liquid drain into the floorboards.

"What'd you have in there?" I asked them.

"Laudanum," Elsie said. "Enough to kill us both."

Then she put her hands on Jesse's face and said piteously, "I've ruined our chance. Our last chance to be together forever."

I sat down on the floor across from them, took off my hat, and sighed.

"Neither of you is going to die if I can help it. There's been too much killing already."

Before Jesse or Elsie could protest, I said, "Hattie Anderson's dead, Jesse. I found her in David King's bedroom at the Transcontinental Hotel. She wasn't a pretty sight."

Jesse flinched, like each word was a stab. Then he hid his face behind his trembling hands, mumbling something I couldn't make out.

"But you can't think that Jesse . . ." Elsie stammered.

"No, I don't. I don't want to think it. Not about Hattie or Susie Adams. Or Danny Curran or Horace Millen."

Stunned, Jesse gripped for his heart beneath his shirt.

"You mean you think I'm innocent?"

There was a hysterical half-smile on his face.

"I mean," I said, "that I'm willing to listen to you now. So talk. And don't hold anything back. I want to hear all of it."

The two lovers exchanged near-ecstatic glances. Then Jesse began to talk.

"I met Elsie at a temperance party her mother gave for the town. That was, when Elsie?"

"10 June '62."

Jesse smiled now, his lidded eyes gleaming with the memory. "We were just twelve years old then. She showed me how to do a quadrille that night. That was only after she spotted me hiding out by the water closet, too terrified of girls to even think of dancing. Guess she took pity on me. Elsie never had a problem getting any boy to go anywhere, or do anything with her. She had a magnetism, you know? Anyway she danced with me and all I needed was that one dance.

"I was just a mine boss's kid. But my father was pretty shrewd with money. And he wouldn't let me work in the mines. He would tell me horrible stories about what went on there, just to frighten me. Father wanted me to go to school instead. Thank God he didn't live to see what happened in '66."

"Wait a minute," I said. "You told me that night when we looked for the pig . . ."

"I told you a story, Mr. McCleary. That's all it was. A patchwork of truth and lies."

"What about now? Is this just a story?"

"A truthful one, I promise. Two years after the dance I went with some boys to Elsie's school to have a debate. She and I started talking at the pic-nic afterward. She remembered me . . ."

He caressed her cheek, completely unembarrassed by my presence. Then he said, "I started writing to her after that. I was a good letter writer. We must've written a letter to each other just about every other day. About a year later, when we were sixteen, we started meeting at the reservoir on Pine Street. Her mother let her pretty much go where she pleased in those days. Her father didn't care.

"We had our special tree that we sat against and I read her all the poems in my book and we talked and talked. And then one day, we stopped talking for just a little while."

Jesse turned away from her, staring at the laudanum still seeping into the floor.

"It was almost a month before she knew. When she told me how it was I asked her to marry me right away. I wasn't sure what to do about school or getting a situation somewhere. But I told myself I'd do what I had to. My father was gone by then and maybe my mother wouldn't mind sharing the house with us."

A bitter laugh came out of him. "That tells you what a young fool I was. I believed that nothing would change— that nobody would care. I was wrong. Another month went by and I'd heard nothing from Elsie. I was getting worried. By that time her father found out about it and sent his man, Pemberton Pierce to talk to me. All he did at first was offer me some money and a ticket out of town. But I said no. Then he whipped the tar out of me and said if I ever came near Elsie again he'd kill me, on her father's orders.

"I never saw her again. I stopped going to school. I didn't care anymore. About anything. Most of my time was spent helping mother and Mary at the store. The Curran boy disappeared about a week later. And one day after that I resolved to write a letter to Elsie's mother, pleading with her to let me see Elsie. I told her I would never let Elsie go. That I would do whatever I could to make sure that we were together for the rest of our lives.

"A few days later Pemberton Pierce and some policemen came into our house, saying they were looking for a boarder of ours. We let them look wherever they wanted, we had nothing to hide. Pierce found Danny Curran in the rubbish heap in our backyard. Another of his men found his things in my room. They took me in that day. I never got a reply from Mrs. King. In jail I learned the reason—long after the fact. She'd killed herself the night before I was arrested."

His clenched fists trembled in his lap. Through gritted teeth, he said, "Do you know what that's like? How powerless, how scared I was? The worst part was I kept asking myself, What if Elsie thinks I killed those boys? I wanted her to know the truth."

"But you never got to talk to her again," I said.

"Not after I confessed. I knew that would end it forever. But I wanted . . . our baby to live."

As Jesse's voice cracked, the two of them clung to each other fiercely. Elsie wept again and Jesse patted her hair with a look of utter devastation.

"Who made that deal with you?"

"Pemberton Pierce came to my cell one day. He told me Mr. King was willing to send Elsie away so she could give birth to the baby in secret. But the only way he'd do that was for me to confess to the killings. Pierce said Mr. King would fix things so I wouldn't hang. I was young enough to go to a reform school and maybe to the penitentiary for a few years. But that was all. If I didn't agree with King's terms, Pierce told me I would hang. And Elsie would go to the abortionist."

"Dr. Solt, the family physician," I said. "The same one who did the autopsy on her mother."

Elsie nodded, as if noticing me for the first time.

"But they lied to you."

"Oh yes. You can say I was a stupid fool for believing them. But I had no choice. If I could save the baby, then at least something good would come out of all of it. That's what I thought then."

"So you confessed. And then when you went to trial things didn't happen the way you thought they would. You were sentenced to hang."

"Elsie's father would've bribed everyone in that courtroom if he could. But he didn't have to. A few polite reminders of favors or indiscretions here and there and all the evidence that contradicted my confession was thrown out. The town wanted my blood by that time anyway. Nobody ever used my name anymore. They just called me the Boy Fiend. I was a monster, not a person."

"Didn't you try to tell Chief Savage about what you'd done? Couldn't you trust him?"

"I wanted to tell him. But I was afraid for our baby.

After the trial when I went to prison . . . well, I didn't trust anyone anymore. All I knew was that I had to escape."

"So you rigged the inside of your cell to explode from the gas pipe. Blew your way right out."

"Yes, and I climbed onboard a car filled with coal and rode it all the way to Philadelphia. I've been there ever since, hoping I might see Elsie and our child someday."

"Why didn't you try to contact her?"

He shook his head as if I were an idiot. "I knew she believed I was guilty! I didn't want to face them, knowing they thought I was a killer. So I worked on jobs here and there. Eventually I signed on to do construction for the Centennial. By that time I had found a way to bury my past and let it moulder."

"Hattie Anderson?" I asked.

Jesse looked at Elsie questioningly.

"It's all right, Jesse," she whispered, looking away.

Harding turned to me and said, "It wasn't just Hattie. It was liquor too. They both made it easier for me to forget. Hattie needed me and I needed someone to need me again. I needed to know that I wasn't a monster.

"Things went as well as they could for us. Then I saw Hiram King's portrait in *Frank Leslie*'s. And I saw Elsie again. All my pitiful attempts to forget were reduced to nothing."

"And you wanted revenge. So you decided to blackmail her father."

"No, not right away. I didn't know anything about her father. Not until Hattie told me."

I leaned closer to him and rubbed my suddenly moist palms against my pantaloons.

"What did Hattie tell you?"

"That a man had offered her a job at the museum, steering men to some kind of assignation house inside the Centennial. I didn't believe her. Then she told me the name of the man she'd spoken to."

"Pemberton Pierce."

"Yes," he said, seething with anger. "I knew right away if Pierce were around, Hiram King had to be involved. So I did a little digging and so did Hattie. It didn't take us long to figure out who was backing all the seedy spots in Shantyville. But I wanted something more to smear in his face. So I had Hattie warn me the night they were planning on taking swells into the Centennial. I waited behind the Museum like she told me to. Then I watched Pierce lead three men down the shaft that went to the tunnels. I knew the shaft well. Most of those tunnels I'd helped built. I'd been using it for weeks so Hattie and I could see the Exhibition without the crowds. It was fun, you know? Like it was our own private fair."

Elsie looked uncomfortable as Jesse began to reminisce. I decided to bring him back to business.

"Tell me about what you saw that night."

Jesse closed his eyes as if assembling the words in his head before he spoke them.

"Pierce took them right under Memorial Hall. There's an entrance to the tunnels from the basement there. I waited until they were all out then I followed them upstairs. There weren't any guards around anywhere. All I had to do was follow the sound of their footsteps. There's a staircase leading to the promenade on the roof, the one that faces the Art Annex."

"Yes," I said, remembering. "There are two enclosed sitting rooms up there, set up by the base of the dome."

"Exactly," Jesse said. "Well, I crept up to the roof and poked my head out just far enough to see what was going on. There were some girls there. Two for each man as far as I could see. They stepped out of the two sitting rooms and I caught a whiff of opium smoke. Then I heard Pierce say, 'Compliments of Mr. Hiram King, gentlemen. Enjoy.' The girls tugged the men back into the sitting rooms and Pierce stayed to watch. I thought I'd seen enough by then. I crept back to the basement and met up with Hattie at the Museum."

With a deep sigh, I leaned back against the door of the shed.

Elsie did nothing but hold Jesse's hand in her own, squeezing it from time to time.

"I'm sorry you have to hear about all this mess, Elsie," I told her.

"I'm not," she said. "It just makes me love Jesse even more. I can't even believe there was a time when it hurt to know my father loathed me. Now I feel almost proud of his hate. And proud of my own—for him."

She laughed, nervously.

"Is that when you started sending your letters, Jesse?"

"Yes. Hattie and I thought it would be fun to use the type-writer in the Main Building to write them. She . . . distracted the guard while I printed the letters."

"How long did it take for you to arrange that meeting on the prismoidal railway?"

"About a week. He was supposed to bring money with him. I guess I decided by then that I would take as much money from him as I could. A sort of compensation for ten years of hell."

"But something went wrong that morning."

"Hattie didn't have the articles we were going to exchange with him."

"The pamphlet and the coin and such."

"Yes. Hiram King wouldn't give us the money."

"So you threw him off the train? That was pretty dumb, Jesse."

"No! No, I didn't. Not yet. Not until he threatened Hattie and me. Said we should get out of Philadelphia if we knew what was good for us. I was scared enough of him to go along with it."

"What stopped you?"

"He pulled me close to him as if to say goodbye. Then he told me the baby . . . our baby was dead. That he'd been dead long before they forced me to confess."

"There wasn't much of a reason for you to stay away from Elsie then, was there?"

"No. I found her that day. It was easy when I tried."

"What was that ransom letter about then?"

"Elsie and I thought Hiram King owed me some money. For restitution. And I wanted to get Hattie back."

"You thought they would actually go along with your terms?"

"I wasn't sure. That's why I brought Iola with me. I still had a key to the Museum back door. I was always kind to her and when I said I was taking her to the Centennial she was happy to go. Didn't mind wearing Elsie's clothes either. I wanted them to think I was bringing her. But she was safe the whole time—waiting at the depot for our train. The plan was I would get Hattie to a safe place and then meet Elsie at the depot."

He turned to the girl and smiled, "I was still wondering whether or not she'd call the police on me. She wanted to when I first got hold of her."

"What made you change your mind, Elsie?"

The girl patted Jesse's face with her ungloved hand and said, "He told me why he'd made the confession. And who put him up to it. Things fell into place in my mind after that."

I was experiencing the same thing.

I took a sip of tepid tea and asked, "Why did you call yourself the Boy Fiend in the letters Jesse?"

"Because sometimes I felt like that's who I was. That the only reality in my life was that brand. In prison I started having a nightmare. I was with Savage in the funeral parlor and he was holding me in Horace Millen's dead face again. Except when he asked me, 'Did you do it? Did you kill him?' the little corpse opened its eyes and stared right at me. Then he spoke to us. He said, 'Jesse did it!'"

Harding shivered in Elsie's embrace.

We sat there quietly for a while, listening to the katydids.

Elsie was the one who broke the silence.

"What are you going to do with us now, Mr. Mc-Cleary?"

"I'm thinking on it."

"Don't you believe us?"

"I said I wanted everything. You haven't given me that yet."

"What do you mean?" the girl asked.

"You haven't told me why you think your mother was killed."

Jesse gasped and stared at her, incredulous. Elsie looked like the breath had just been sucked out of her.

"Who . . ." she said, nearly choking on the words, "told you?"

"David did. Last night, in his room. A few hours before I found Hattie's body there."

Her name escaped Jesse's lips. He let it trail off into the air like smoke.

"But how? How could David know that?"

"Because you told him Elsie. You thought he was sleeping but he heard you. Is that what sent David to an asylum? Made him turn to opium?"

"No! No!"

She clamped her hands against her ears to shut me out.

"How did you know, Elsie?"

The girl wouldn't answer. I had to ask her again. Jesse still held her to him but there was a look of fear on him now.

"Why did you tell David your mother was murdered?"

Elsie screamed then, her piteous wail silencing even the vast army of insects in the darkness.

Then she grew very quiet and said, "I told David because Bert told me himself. The night he tried to outrage me."

Jesse snarled with rage, shaking the girl in his arms.

"Stop it, Jesse!" I said. "He outraged you, Elsie?"

The girl chuckled and said, "Tried to. I told my father, of course. He laughed at me and said I should stop throwing myself at him. But Bert never touched me again. I know you think I might be mad. I certainly try to act it. But I have good reason. What he did to me, what he told me, is the reason."

She made a noise again that was something between a chuckle and a sob.

"He said that my father murdered my mother to keep her mouth shut. That's what he told me after he . . . did what he did. And he said I'd better keep my own mouth shut or I'd wind up like her."

Jesse pulled her closer to him with trembling arms. She laid her head against his chest, a cold empty look in her eyes.

"The only thing that's kept me sane is to not think about what Bert told me. To not think of what my father did."

"How could that pig do this to her?" Jesse asked me. "How could King let that piece of filth molest her and get away with it?"

I remembered something Hiram King told me the last time I saw him.

For a moment I kept quiet, hoping the sound of the katydids could drown out the memory of his words.

But they could not.

I looked at them across the darkness and said, "Hiram King told me he would do anything to protect his son."

THE THREE OF us spent the night at Mary Owens's house, though I think none of us got much sleep. The next morning, Saturday, 9 September, we climbed on board a train for Easton. There was a wait of a few hours in that city and we didn't arrive back at the West Philadelphia Depot until half past two o' clock.

Tad Schmoyer was there to meet us. I'd telegraphed him from Easton.

I was surprised to see who he brought along with him. Captain William Heins.

I didn't bother to greet them. Instead I waited for Heins to speak his piece.

He fidgeted with the brim of his bowler hat and shifted his segar from one end of his mouth to the other.

Then, hands clasped behind him, he said, "I'm sorry, Mack."

That didn't quite satisfy me. I kept silent.

Tad finally interjected, "I showed Captain Heins the evidence you gave me. The box. And I told him the whole story. As much as you told me."

"Your boy here brought me over to the Transcontinental Hotel. I didn't want to go, understand."

"Of course not," I said. "That might upset your master."

Heins flushed with anger. "He's not my master, damn

327

it! He's just a man with an awful lot of pull around here. A man I don't like to cross swords with if I can help it. I've heard of what happens to people who do."

"People like the Molly Maguires?"

"And others. Pardon me, miss," he said, turning to Elsie. "But I wasn't about to risk my neck for the sake of a Shantyville whore. That's just what would happen if we started sticking our nose into it. We'd come up with who was really running things down there. And a lot of good people would get hurt in the process."

"You're a credit to mankind."

"Stop it, Mack," Tad said. "The point is he's willing to help us now."

I crossed my arms over my chest and said, "So you want me back now?"

"Yes," Heins said. "We need you. *I* need you. Schmoyer took me to the hotel. We both saw the Anderson woman's body. I began to see that maybe it was better to let some so-called good people get hurt."

It took me a few seconds to subdue my anger and pride. Then I uncrossed my arms and said to the two men, "Where's David King?"

"That's what I came to tell you," Heins said. "We've got all of our detectives looking for him plus a few from the city. He's disappeared."

"Did you go to his father? Search his room at the Transcontinental?"

"Yes, we did all that. Hiram King was not especially helpful, as you can imagine. But he let us look wherever we wanted. David's gone, McCleary. I don't think he's even in the city anymore."

"I think he most definitely is. You just didn't look in the right place. Who else knows about this?"

"We're keeping it very quiet. Nobody from the press caught wind of it. Had to shut the Professor up when we returned that deformed girl to him."

"Was she all right?" I asked.

"Sure. But the Professor wanted to tell the papers that she'd run rampant through the Centennial and eaten one of the guards. Would've brought in droves, he told us. Offered to give us a piece of his admissions if we went along with him. Naturally we didn't. I told him he'd better keep his mouth shut about that night if he wants to keep his Museum."

"What about David? You going to keep that quiet too?"

"If we find him we're going to see he gets put away quietly somewhere, out west, if we can help it."

"What about me?" Jesse said, stepping forward. "I have a right to my innocence. To a good name, at least."

"Young man," Heins said. "If I were you I'd take what I could get. When this is finished you and Miss King here had better fade away quietly. Forget about your good name. Find another one. There are plenty to choose from."

"All right, all right," I said, holding up my hands. "Enough of this. Why don't we meet the two of you back at the Grounds in a few hours? We need to find a place to stay for the night. I don't think I'd be too welcome back in the barracks. Not with Pemberton Pierce around. By the way, Heins, have you brought him in?"

"Hiram King told me Pierce was out looking for David. He didn't care to say more."

"Well, it can wait. Jesse, go get us a hack to Shanty-ville. Why don't we try the Globe to-night? On Captain Heins here."

The older man grumbled and stalked off. I let Jesse and Elsie go on so I could talk to Tad.

"You did real good, boy," I said, squeezing his arm. "I thought Heins and I were—"

"So did I. But the box was enough to get him out of bed. When he saw the girl's body . . ."

Tad shivered with the memory.

"He called the coroner right away. And he arranged things with Mulford. Mack, he made me a detective!"

"I wondered what you were doing in plainclothes. Well,

at least Heins's done something right this week. Congratulations, Tad."

"It's on account of you, Mack. Don't think I'll ever forget that."

"Tad, how would you like to help me nail Hiram King and David?"

The boy got a hungry look on his face.

"First, tell me something," I said. "Has Mulford taken some guards away from Main and put them on Memorial Hall? Like you told me he did sometimes?"

Tad thought for a moment and said, "Last night. I noticed them when Heins and I got back after looking over Shantyville. They were at every corner of the building. And they're still there. I checked this morning. I thought it was queer. Do you think Hiram King's still bringing whores into the Grounds?"

Ignoring his question, I asked, "Did you happen to look up at the promenade, right beneath the dome?"

"No. I didn't bother. Nobody's been going up there. They closed the promenade yesterday. Said the roof was leaking. In fact, they closed the whole place down today."

I cracked a wide grin and said, "Bring a few boys you trust to Memorial Hall this afternoon. Let's say around four thirty. That gives me about two hours. I might have a surprise for you by then."

"You think he's there? David King?"

"I'll see you later, Tad."

I waved and trotted off toward the hack where Jesse was helping Elsie into the cab.

It was four o' clock before Jesse and I made it to the back of the Museum.

As we walked down Elm Avenue, he said to me, "I can't believe it's only been two days since I left this place. Feels like centuries. It doesn't even look the same to me."

"Shantyville hasn't changed. You have."

"Yes, you're right. While I was living here these past few months I felt only two things. Fear or despair. Now I have Elsie again. Those things don't seem to matter anymore."

He bowed his head and said, *The world is weary of the past. Oh, might it die or rest at last.*"

"Is that poetry?" I asked.

"Shelley. He's one of my favorites. And Elsie's."

"You know the past doesn't always pass away like that. Nice and softly. Trust me, I know. Sometimes you have to kill it. Before it kills you."

"Is that what we're going to do to-night?" Jesse asked, searching my eyes for a promise I could keep.

"We'll see which it is."

When we got to the back of the Museum, Jesse navigated his way through the brush to the backhouse.

"I keep thinking of Hattie," he told me, his hand poised on the warped door. "And it makes me feel guilty, somehow. But I don't want to forget her. I wanted her to be safe. That's why I went back there that night."

I laid a hand on his shoulder and said, "She told me you would come back for her. She never stopped trusting you."

"This will be for them," Jesse said. "For her and for the other one Hiram King took away from me."

"Just show me where to go," I said, following him into the tunnel.

Jesse wanted to go with me into Memorial Hall. It took some doing to make him turn around. I didn't want him there. It would be difficult enough to worry about my own neck without being preoccupied with his. I told him to go back to our room at the Globe and stay with Elsie.

I waited until his footsteps had receded into the darkness of the tunnel. Then I opened the door leading to Memorial Hall's basement.

The skylights and tall arched windows let plenty of light into the galleries. As I made my way to the north end of the building, I avoided those windows, lest the guards notice me.

Halfway there, I reached the central rotunda, its massive dome looming over my head like a man-made sky.

I didn't like being alone with all those statues. They were too lifelike and I got the feeling that when I turned my back they might move, ever so slightly, or whisper, just loud enough for me to hear.

As I made my way through the hushed galleries, I felt like I was wandering inside a massive skull. The paintings were like dream scenes, beautiful fantasies pasted over the cavernous walls, distracting my attention from the eerie silence.

At the north end of the gallery, I found the staircase leading up to the grand balcony. I paused on the ornately decorated stairs, my hand gripping the thick oak bannister. No one was following me. At least I didn't hear them.

The door to the roof was open. My revolver preceded me outside.

The promenade extended the length of the hall, about two hundred and seventy-five feet. On either side were the east and west pavilions, their skylights reflecting the low-flying, ominous clouds.

Set next to the pavilions were the enclosed sitting rooms for people to take in the view of the grounds behind the hall when it was raining.

I walked over to the roof's edge and stared down to the ground forty feet below. A few guards wandered through the trees by the annex, swinging their clubs.

Both of the sitting rooms were large enough to fit at least a dozen people. When I opened the door to the one set against the east pavilion, I saw David King looking quite comfortable lying on the floor. There were several bottles propped against the back wall.

"Good afternoon, David," I said.

His eyes came open and something like a squeal came out of his throat.

"Don't mind me. Pour yourself another drink. Though I don't think it'll do much good."

"You're right," David said. "It probably won't. But I'll drink some more anyway."

"The memories will come back. They always do."

"I should have stayed with opium. Lasts longer."

"Your father could help you out with that, I'm sure."

I tried to keep the anger out of my voice and failed. I stared down at the revolver in my hand and wished it had a will of its own, that I could shoot him in cold blood and not have to wrestle with my conscience over it.

David's head nodded slowly. When he spoke again, the slur in his voice was pronounced.

"My father's not too happy with me. He shut me up here like a prisoner."

"You've made life difficult for him, David. He's tried to protect you all these years."

"Yes," David said, with a sigh. "I suppose he has done his best."

"He certainly did a good job in Mauch Chunk when you killed Danny Curran and the Millen boy."

David's smile sent a chill through me. When he spoke next his voice reminded me of something Savage had said about Jesse sounding like he'd just seen hell for the first time. Except David seemed well acquainted with hell. I got the feeling he might just like it there.

"I tried to stop it once. But I gave up on that a long time ago. You can't stop death from coming. You have to learn to accept it. To sit back and watch it happen."

My hand tightened on the stock of my revolver. I looked into the corner where David sat and watched as he suddenly changed. His face was no longer his own but another's—a murderer I had let go years before.

I'd been foolish enough to wage war without breaking the rules. My mercy had counted for nothing.

I lost all sense of feeling in me except the awareness of my finger on the trigger of my revolver.

I don't know if I would have squeezed it or not. I never got the chance.

A voice behind me said, "Put your pistol down, Mr. McCleary."

Hiram King stood at the open door, his abnormally long whiskers straying from his upper lip at odd angles. He looked like he'd been napping. His gray hair was tousled and he wore no collar around his shirt.

The other sitting room door was ajar. He must've been sleeping there, keeping a protective eye on his child.

I noticed he was unarmed. I said to him, "Give me one good reason why I shouldn't put a pill in the both of you."

"I'll give you eight reasons," Hiram King said. "All of them are surrounding this building. If they hear a shot you won't get out of here alive."

"Well," I said, relaxing the grip on my revolver and lowering it to the ground, "I guess we have a stalemate."

The man brushed past me and stood towering over his drunken son.

"What did you tell him?"

"Oh, not much," I said. "But enough to convince me I'm looking at the real Boy Fiend."

Hiram King made a gargling noise and crushed his son to him.

He said, "I'll have you skinned alive for this!"

"Like your son skinned those children? And the two girls in Shantyville?"

"You don't understand, damn you!"

"I understand enough. Your son's a killer. And you've known it all along. Sending Jesse Harding to the gallows was a good idea. You got rid of your daughter's lover and you made sure no one ever suspected your own son for the killings. Your precious family honor came out of it without a smear in sight."

"Not quite, Mr. McCleary. My wife didn't survive the ordeal."

I almost laughed at the sight of his eyes watering.

"Beth couldn't bear the shame of Elsie carrying a bastard in her. Is that what you're trying to push on me?"

"You're not worthy to mention her name!" Hiram King sputtered indignantly. "She was the only decent thing in my life. I loved her. Loved her dearly. After a time she ceased to return that love. I kept hoping that I could make her change into the person that I used to know. I never got the chance. When she . . . killed herself my whole world fell apart. I had nothing left. Nothing except David."

"And your money. You had plenty of that. Enough to make Jesse Harding hang."

"He got what was coming to him. I was only doing what any decent man would do. Protect my women from seducing swine."

"The same kind of seducing swine you patronize? The ones you and your boy Pierce parade up here? Don't you get sanctimonious with me, you son of a bitch!"

Hiram King reached to straighten his collar. When he found it wasn't there, he smoothed the whiskers, a haughty look coming into his eyes.

"Those men aren't seducing anyone. I supply them with whores and opium. In return they help me with my project. Which was going beautifully until this whole ugly mess reared its head. Men were making a great deal of money and I didn't hear anyone complaining. Especially you, who led those folks around Shantyville night after night. Did you ever stop to think, you silly bastard, that you are a part of this? That if you open your mouth about me or my son that you'll be dragged through the filth too?"

"What are you talking about?" I said, confused. "What project?"

"Shantyville! What else? I own it. As surely as I own

part of the railroad and the mines of Mauch Chunk. It's an experiment in commerce, McCleary. A sort of trial run in miniature."

"You mean you want to control all the criminal operations in a town? Just one man? That's impossible."

"Impossible?" King sneered. "I've done it! The Guard collect from every quiet game, whorehouse, opium den, and saloon. And it ends up in my pocket. If I can do it here I can do it anywhere, slowly. First I had to make friends, like I'm making friends here. Divide and rule, Mr. McCleary."

"Is that your ambition, King? To rule a kingdom of shanties and whorehouses?"

That made him laugh.

"I didn't create those things. Or the rabble's lusts. Do you think I care if I profit from their depravity?"

King laughed out loud and said, "Call it my revenge. For what the world did to Beth."

I was beginning to think that David had no control over who he was—that Hiram King's own madness tainted his blood from the very beginning.

"I stopped caring about those people, McCleary. I cared for no one anymore. Except David.

"Elsie sold her virtue to a miner's son. After that she was dead to me. If I let her stay with me it was only for her mother's sake. But David—he was the only thing I had left that wasn't ruined after Beth's death. Then Pemberton Pierce came to me only days after that. Bert told me he'd spotted David wandering around a dangerous section of town. He wondered what he was doing there. Before he could act, he saw David kill the Curran boy. Bert was horrified and did what he could to quiet the whole mess up. Cleaned up the place and got rid of the body. And a good thing he did it too or David might've been seen and caught. Unfortunately Bert hadn't been following David when Horace Millen was killed. But he had no doubt that David had done it.

"I didn't want to believe him at first. But he had proof! The knife and Danny Curran's things. I almost followed Beth that night.

"Then I thought of David and knew I could not abandon him. If I let him go then everything I'd worked for would be for nothing. He had to grow into manhood and assume the power and position that I built for him. It was my one hope, sir. A faith for a man who had learned to scorn the puny myths of the rabble. A hope that my son could heal. It gave me something to live for. Replaced the meaning I'd lost when Beth hanged herself in her room."

"It was worth it to ruin Jesse Harding's life? An innocent boy?"

"I ruined him like he ruined my daughter! That part was simple. So was buying Bert Pierce's loyalty and silence. It's worth it to keep him around to ensure that silence if it gives my boy a chance to heal—and forget."

King looked at me with pleading eyes, hugging his boy to him.

"He's sick, can't you see that? I sent him away hoping he'd get better. He stayed away too, for years. I thought the time and distance would do him good. I thought he might be ready to come back and take his place at my side."

Carressing his son's ruffled hair, King said quietly, "He wasn't ready. Thank God Pierce was looking after him like I told him to. If only he could've prevented those deaths . . . But it's clear to me now that David must go away again. Far away. I just have to keep believing that my only hope isn't in vain."

I watched father and son, locked in a desperate embrace. Then I lowered my head, my mind full of memories of two years ago. Of a killer I'd hoped might someday redeem himself.

Not unlike Hiram King.

I hated recognizing that I had something in common with this evil man.

It made me angry. Mostly at myself.

"You can't keep protecting David, Hiram. Not any-more. I won't let you bury what happened. Not without a hell of a fight."

Hiram King laughed again.

"You don't frighten me, McCleary. You just annoy me. You're a problem that needs fixing. And I have men who can fix any problem."

"I'm sure of that. Pemberton Pierce has done a lot of fixing for you over the years. Like the way he fixed it with your wife?"

Hiram King smoothed his gray wisps of hair over his glistening scalp. He winced with confusion.

"What are you talking about?" he asked.

"You heard me! Like Pierce fixed it with your wife. When you killed her!"

His voice cracking, King screamed, "You're mad! My wife committed suicide!"

I took a threatening step toward him, my whole body surging with hate.

"She didn't hang herself, you lying bastard. You killed her! Are you so mad you've forgotten it? Did you fix that memory too? It's too bad you couldn't do the same thing with your friend Pierce. Bert told Elsie all about it the night he tried to rape her. You broke your wife's neck and then strung her up so it looked like she hanged her-self. Because she knew the truth about David, didn't she? She knew he was the Boy Fiend—that you were sending an innocent boy to the gallows. Did she threaten to tell her friend Savage about it, Hiram? Was that when you put your hands around her throat and squeezed the life out of her?"

David began to smile at the same time his father groaned.

"No!" Hiram King cried, turning to the soiled window panes. There was nothing to stare back at him but the overcast sky.

I didn't know which one of them was worse. The sight of both father and son sickened me.

Training my revolver on them, I said, "Both of you get up. We're taking a walk."

I wasn't concerned about the guards anymore. If they started firing at me, I'd make sure to empty my gun into Hiram and his son. I told him so.

Despite my revolver staring them in the face, they weren't persuaded to get to their feet.

"Get up, damn you! Now!"

They stayed where they were, crouching against the wall of the sitting room.

I heard the grunt behind me just a little bit too late. Something hard landed on my skull, right below the left ear.

The next thing I knew I was on the floor. My face was covered with some sticky liquid. It was draining into my mustache, making my lips itch. I tried to move. The effort sank me back into the darkness.

I heard voices, coming to me as if from across a chasm.

"No, leave him for now. We've got to get out of here."

"I hear something going on down there."

There was a pause. Then I heard footfalls.

Pemberton Pierce's voice said, "Some other guards are down there. Not Mulford's boys. We better go through the tunnels."

"David's in no shape to go that way!"

"We don't have a choice, Mr. King. You want him arrested? We'll take him to my room at the Ross House. He'll be okay there until we can get him on a train."

"All right, Bert. Let's get out of here. Then I want to talk to you."

"Not now, sir. We have to go! Hurry!"

I heard a door slam from miles and miles away.

Then I sank back into oblivion, blood gluing my eyelids shut.

35

I FELT SOMEBODY'S hand on my head. The most I could do was groan.

"Mack! Are you all right?"

I rubbed a hand over my face, dried blood flaking off my fingers.

"Got . . . hit from behind."

Tad Schmoyer gave my head a cursory glance and said, "It ain't bleeding anymore. Can you stand up?"

"Here goes nothing."

I got to my feet, my legs a little wobbly.

I looked at the sky outside and noticed the sun was going down.

"How long have I been out?" I asked.

"I'm not sure," Tad said. "We just got here. Mulford's boys weren't about to let us into Memorial Hall without a fight. We gave them one. Three of theirs and one of ours is in the infirmary now. I remembered what you said about the promenade and got up here as fast as I could."

I took my watch out of my vest and observed the time: four fifty six.

"The three of them dusted out of here," I told him.

"If they did we would've seen them. We had all the exits covered."

"No you didn't. There's a tunnel leading from the Art Gallery into Shantyville."

"How—"

"Don't worry about it. I think I know where they're heading. Let's get out of here."

"You oughta go to the Medical Department yourself and have that cut taken care of."

"The hell with that. They're hiding a killer over there. Let's go smoke him out."

That was when we heard the bells ring.

"That's queer," I said. "It's not yet five."

The bells were still ringing when we emerged onto the Avenue of the Republic.

I peered across the way at the Main Building and suddenly understood.

Behind Main, thick coils of black smoke rose into the overcast sky, its gray clouds burnished with orange light.

I stood there in the middle of the avenue, stunned.

"Oh my God!" Tad cried. "The Main Building's on fire!"

"No" I said. "It's Shantyville."

The paint on the main entrance was beginning to blister as we ran through it.

Elm Avenue was teeming with the terrified and the curious. It was a twenty-five-cent day at the Centennial so the crowd was larger than usual. I read later that a hundred thousand people were on hand.

Four Centennial steamers were already on the scene and the Centennial Guard was having a hell of a time keeping the crowd out of their way. All of them had streams on the fire by now, which raged just a hundred feet east of the Transcontinental Hotel. The flames were close enough to singe the hotel's eaves. Guests issued out of the lobby in a steady stream, each man and woman laden with trunks, coats, chairs, caskets, and tables. The furniture and luggage stood in chaotic heaps on the street while spectators seethed around the deadlocked streetcars, eager to watch the firemen at work.

Just as Tad and I arrived, a city engine pulled up, the horses nearly trampling a few gawkers. The freshly polished boiler, looking like a huge milk can, gleamed with reflected fire. As the firemen leaped off their wagon, the crowd cheered.

The horses were quickly unharnessed and led far away from the fire, with blankets over their backs to protect them from falling ash. The animals were soon feeding in their nosebags, unconcerned with the blaze around them.

In the meantime several men had taken a force hose that led back into the grounds and attached it to their intake pipes. The pressure head on the pump began to shake, like an egg about to hatch. Six hundred gallons of water per minute steamed into the blaze.

They were too late to save Murphy's Oyster Saloon, where the fire started. It was already gutted and crumbling by the time we got there. Behind it, the buildings facing Viola Street were taking fire. To the east and the south, the cheap frame saloons and hotels along Elm Avenue were beginning to smoke.

I stood watching a fireman shovel coal into a boiler, gusts of smoke spewing out the top to join the thick black pall coating the sky. Cinders and glowing embers fell on us like red rain. The crowd began to look across Elm at the Main Building, fearing the worst.

My eyes followed the progress of the fire down Elm Avenue, watching the roof of the ice cream saloon disintegrate before clouds of steam from the hoses obscured the sight. Next to it was the Main Halle saloon and variety show. A man in striped tights and a satin cape burst through the front door, a carpet and what looked like a crystal ball tucked under his arms. Just as he came out a trunk was pushed out the third story window and crashed to the street, missing the magician by inches.

The next three buildings—Crawford's drinking saloon,

Bomeisler's Hotel, and Ullman's eating and drinking saloon—were partially on fire. Flames licked up their flimsy
wooden walls, their gaudy paint boiling and blackening.
Windows burst apart with the heat. Tad and I could hear
the creaking timber floors give way and crash to the
ground below, their thunderous impact like the sound of
a far-off bombardment.

The building next to Ullman's had not caught fire yet.
Its brick walls resisted the flames.

The Ross House seemed safe.

Several people on various floors of the hotel were poking their heads out, evidently undisturbed by the fire but
curious to see what was going on.

From the top floor, I saw a gray-haired head lean out
of a window. I knew it was him as soon as I saw his
outrageously long whiskers.

"I'm going in there," I told Tad.

He grabbed my arm and yanked me back.

"Like hell you are! You'll be nothing but a piece of
charcoal in seconds."

"It's not on fire yet. And they're inside! Hiram and
David and Pierce!"

There were a few people staring out the windows of
the hotel, waiting until the last moment to evacuate.

"The brick should hold it off for a while," I said. "Go
round up some bulls. I might need help getting them out."

Before he could stop me, I tore away from his grip and
dashed down Elm, leaping over the snaking coils of hose.

A few people were clambering out of the Ross House
already, steamer trunks across their backs. Two boys
rushed past me, squealing with delight at the sight of the
firemen and their engines.

Behind the front desk, the manager was busy filling a
canvas sack with receipts and currency. He stopped for a
moment to frantically undo his collar, cursing under his
breath.

It wasn't a good time to ask for assistance. But I didn't have much choice.

"Listen," I said. But he didn't. I heard him counting and mumbling prayers for the safety of his building.

"Listen," I shouted at him again. The noise made him jump, the spectacles sliding down his perspiring nose.

"Not now, damn it!"

"I'm a policeman. There's a murderer in here. In Pemberton Pierce's room. Tell me where it is."

He turned to me, his lower lip trembling, and said, "I told Mr. Ross he should have paid the extra few hundred dollars for the full insurance. But he didn't listen to me."

As an afterthought, the manager threw the guestbook at me and resumed stuffing his sack.

My finger ran down the flowery lines of script till it hit on Pierce's name. The room number printed next to it was thirty-eight.

I took the stairs three at a time.

When I reached the third floor I had to stop to give my aching lungs a respite.

Suddenly a loud noise echoed down the hall, startling me.

It sounded like a gunshot.

Then there was shouting.

I couldn't hear what they were saying clearly until I came to the door to room thirty-eight.

A voice screamed from inside the room.

"Look what you made me do, you stupid son of a bitch! You couldn't leave it alone, could you?"

The only answer was an anguished moan.

My hand turned the knob. With a sharp kick, I flung the door open.

Pemberton Pierce stood with a smoking pistol in his good hand. Hiram King lay at his feet, blood seeping out of a hole in his side.

David leaned against the open window, his youthful face sobered now with fear.

As soon as Pierce saw my barker, he swung his own from Hiram King to David.

"You take one more step and I'll kill him," he said breathlessly.

There was blood spattered over the detective's cream-colored vest and pantaloons. With his free hand he wiped a smear of it from his cheek. His sallow face contorted in a grimace of anguish and desperation.

"Put the gun down, Pierce. You can't save them anymore."

"Save them?" Pierce sputtered. His lips twitched in a spastic smile. "What do I care about them? There's only one . . ."

Hiram King was still moaning on the ground, "Oh my god . . . Beth . . . all the time . . . You bloody bastard . . ."

Before he could say more he squeezed his side and whimpered in agony.

My gaze stayed right where it was, on the sights of my revolver, aimed at Pierce's throat.

I could smell the acrid stench of smoke filtering in from the open window.

Fire crackled the timber next door.

I wished I could hear the roar of the flames wash over the words in my mouth, trailing them into the air like smoke.

But there were no flames yet and I spoke the words.

"You murdered his wife," I said to Pierce.

David shook his head as if to jar the words from his memory.

"Elsie was right," he said. "But I always thought it was Father. That he did it for me. That her death was on my head."

Hiram King gasped, calling his son's name.

David tried to get off the windowsill but Pierce shook his head, poking the gun toward him for emphasis.

I felt my eyes narrow and the truth crowd into my brain, choking it like black smoke.

"There never was a Boy Fiend. There was only Pemberton Pierce."

Smoke began seeping beneath the cracks of the door.

Pierce was blinking the smoke out of his eyes, his lips parted in a leering smile.

"Tell our friend what you saw that morning, Davy. I want to hear you tell that story again."

Tears coursed down David's cheeks. But I didn't think it was from the smoke.

"I went out to play in the backyard. There was a large pile of timber there with some cracks in it so I could see to the other side. I heard Pierce making noises, like he was struggling with something. I peeked through and saw Bert with a little boy. I knew him from school. Danny Curran. Danny was on the ground—and it looked like Bert was hurting him . . . Danny made no sound—but I screamed. I went around to where they were to make him stop. I thought he would listen to me like he listened to my father."

Pierce chuckled as David pressed his face against the windowsill, clinging on to it like a suicide steeling himself for the jump.

"He had him down on the ground. There was a huge knife in his hand. I tried not to look but I . . . couldn't help it. Then Bert saw me watching him. He said, 'Hello, Davy'—like he knew I'd been there all the time. And then he put the knife to Danny's throat. I didn't see any blood . . . I think I fainted because the next thing I knew I was in bed. I didn't speak for a few days. They thought I had a fever. But I was too scared to talk. One night, Pierce came into my bedroom and whispered in my ear that if I told on him he would do to me what he did to Danny."

"You tell the story so good, Davy. Like we were doing it all over again."

Pierce walked closer to David, his eyes still on mine. Then he began to pat David on the head, saying, "Tell him the rest Davy."

David spit in the man's face and said, "Go to hell, Bert."

Pierce stuck his revolver into David's nose and said, "Again."

I kept my mouth shut, relaxing my grip on the barker. Pierce wasn't interested in shooting me. At least not now.

I stared at the two of them by the window. Outside the sky was afire with an apocalyptic glow.

David spoke to me, struggling not to show his fear.

"Bert took me for a walk a week later like he sometimes did when my mother was at a meeting. He took me to the Narrows and showed me where the other boy was killed. Bert said he found the boy in the confectioner's and bought him some licorice. Outside on the street, he asked the boy if he wanted to see the canal. The boy said yes. Bert took him there in his carriage. When they got there, Pierce told the boy to lie down and then he . . ."

"He did it just like Jesse Harding said in his confession?" I asked.

Without turning his eyes from David, Pierce said, "Where do you think Harding got his confession from, you stupid jackass? I fed the whole thing to him!"

Then he addressed the reporter again, as if I weren't even in the room.

"You left some things out Davy. You forgot to mention what I did to the Millen boy. Where I stabbed him. Remember what I told you—about his face? And his belly and below that . . . I stabbed him a lot, right Davy? I counted fourteen times. Remember I made you count with me?"

David slammed his fist into the window, breaking a small piece out of it. He let the blood run down his hand and soak into his cuff.

He said, weeping, "All my fault. You were wrong McCleary. I was the Boy Fiend. I was there."

David turned his face to the shattered window, his voice only a whisper.

"I couldn't stop it. And I never told."

"Except when you told your mother," I said.

"The little brat tried to spoil our fun. Hiram's bitch was going to the police that night," Pierce said. "I wanted to do more than I did to her. But I thought it might be fun to hang her from the ceiling. At least the children got to see her before Savage cut her down."

There was something in my eyes that I tried blinking away. The smoke perhaps.

"I still wasn't sure if she talked to Savage, told him anything. So I decided the killer had to be caught. I went to King one night and told him I found Danny Curran's things in David's room—and that I saw him kill the Millen boy. You should have seen his face! It was priceless!"

"Hiram King owed you everything after that, didn't he?" I asked.

"Oh yes. There was nothing he couldn't do for me. After all, I saved his son from the gallows. Of course, when Davy got sent away I had to be careful."

"But that didn't stop you then, did it?"

"No." He smiled. "Not a bit."

"It wasn't good enough to destroy their lives though, was it? You had to destroy Elsie too. By telling her Hiram killed their mother."

"No! I never hurt a hair on her head! I only said that after—"

"After you tried to rape her?"

"You don't understand! I had a right to take whatever I wanted. I'd earned that right!"

He snorted again, swallowing his words. "Then Davy came back to be with us at the Centennial. You should have seen the way King fawned over him! Treated Miss Elsie like nothing! Like David might break if you breathed on him! For ten years he lived in fear that someday someone would learn the truth! Ha ha! The truth! That David was the Boy Fiend! And I made him swallow that!

"Hiram was getting a little stingy about his money. And

he had so much more of it with Shantyville."

"That money's going up in smoke now," I said.

"Oh, he can set up shop elsewhere. Mr. King has plenty of resources. He was raking it in here—that's for sure. And I didn't want an underling's wages. I thought maybe he better be reminded of what might happen.

"So I decided to be much less careful than usual and sliced up a whore one night when I brought her back from Memorial Hall. I made it look just like Mauch Chunk. And I planted David's needle in her neck. But you took it before anyone else could see it! That wasn't very sporting of you. So I had to get it back. For the next time."

"When you killed Hattie Anderson in David's bed. That wasn't too subtle, Pierce."

"No . . . ," he said, his words coming out hesitatingly— as if he were carefully choosing the right ones to say. "But I didn't much care. She was available and I . . . couldn't help myself. And I wanted King to see that David would have to go away again. And of course I offered to help David escape, for a price."

"Did you make David watch it that time?"

Pierce smiled, slapping David's cheek. "Davy boy wasn't there for that party. A little too drunk this time. He was lying passed out in the parlor while I did it."

David didn't respond, keeping his eyes tightly shut.

Pierce's gun hand began to tremble. He blinked away a drop of sweat.

"That was good, anyway. I had plenty of time to do it just the way I always wanted to. Plenty of time."

My mouth was dry when I swallowed. Breathing was uncomfortable.

Behind me the door was smoking as flames licked up its boiling surface.

Then a gust of heat burst through the window, sending David and Pierce sprawling to the floor. I felt it on my face, stinging my eyes and scorching my flesh.

I was across the room in a second, kicking the gun out of his hand.

David stumbled to his feet, while I planted a boot on Pierce's heaving chest.

The ceiling was beginning to crumble, the plaster and wood smoking and crackling. I watched pieces of it flare up and drop to the wooden floor, setting it ablaze.

"David, go help your father out the door while I keep an eye on Bert here."

The two of them stared at each other, locked in a last struggle.

"Don't forget, Davy! She was worth ten of you! I know! That time you watched me . . . you liked it, didn't you? Didn't you?"

Pierce burst out laughing. I cut it short with a kick to his jaw. His head fell back on the floor. He didn't move after that.

I tore my jacket off and covered my hand with it. Then I went to the blisteringly hot door, the lower panel already on fire, and pulled it open. A burst of flame poured out from the hallway and set my suit ablaze.

David wrestled me to the ground and beat the fire out while I screamed in terror. Then he tore Pierce's coat off and draped it over my smoking shirt.

We both struggled to get Hiram to his feet. He left a trail of blood behind him as he stumbled out the doorway.

Just as I got both of them out the door, a piece of the ceiling crashed down on Pierce's bed, igniting the sheets.

The hall was filled with smoke and fire that darted from every conceivable angle. The carpet was alight, its fibers shriveling and giving off a putrid smoke.

Inside the room, Pemberton Pierce was groaning, his head twisting from side to side. Another piece of the ceiling crashed just beside him, a few sparks landing on his pantaloons. As they caught fire, he awoke from his stupor with a jolt.

Overhead blackened pieces of smoldering plaster began

to fall. In a few seconds the entire roof would collapse.

Pierce sluggishly got to his feet.

He hadn't taken a step before he noticed his pantaloons were on fire. He brushed them with his hand and stared at me as I stood in the doorway.

The ceiling began to groan like a thick branch swaying in a hurricane. Then it trembled, like the earth itself was shaking.

He stood in the middle of the room, frantically brushing the fire out of his smoking clothes.

I stepped away from the doorway.

In that last moment I saw Pierce's face grow pale as he saw something I couldn't see. A terrifying thing. He shrieked as I kicked the door shut, making sure the lock caught.

His anguished screams mingled with the popping, crackling noise of the hotel's burning innards.

I started running then, stopping only once when I heard a tremendous crash. Behind me I saw the door to Pierce's room blown across the hall and a heap of flaming rubble pile out, all that was left of the caved-in roof.

The screaming had stopped.

I found David King on the stairs just outside the third floor. He carried Hiram on his back, his father's arms draped around his shoulders in a feeble embrace.

"Let me take him!" I said, grabbing hold of Hiram. "Follow me down! Quickly! The roof's already gone. The rest of the building won't last much longer."

I stumbled down the stairs, groaning with the weight of the old man on my shoulders.

I tried to keep my eyes open, though they were swollen and stung like the devil. The bannister was gone by now and I had nothing to guide me down but the wall, the paper on it beginning to boil from the heat.

Every now and then I tried to make sure David was right behind me. We were on the last flight of stairs before the lobby when I looked back for him and saw he wasn't there.

Just then a cinder got into my eye. I cried out with pain and fell halfway down the stairs. The old man rolled off of me but I couldn't see where he fell. My hands searched for his bulk across the stairs and found him at the bottom. I didn't know if he was dead and I didn't care. With my watering, burning eyes tightly shut, I got him across my shoulders again and burst out of the front door and onto Elm Avenue.

I landed in the arms of a fireman.

"Good God, man! You're lucky to be alive!" I heard him say.

Then I felt water pouring over me. I caught some of it and rubbed it in my eyes. In a few seconds I could see.

Hiram King was already on a stretcher, being borne to an ambulance. I stared down at my smoking clothes, hoping I wouldn't have any permanent burn scars. Then I called David's name.

There was no response.

"David?" I called again.

The fireman said to me, "You looking for the man you came out with? They're putting him in an ambulance now. He'll be all right."

"No! There was another!"

"Mister, only the two of you came out."

With a snarl I tore myself out of the fireman's protective grasp and headed back into the inferno of the Ross House.

I found David two flights up. He was sitting calmly against one wall, his eyes closed.

"David! Get up and come with me! Now!"

His eyes opened hesitantly as he said, "I'm not leaving!"

I ran over to him, pulling him away from the smoking wall.

"Are you out of your head?"

"I have been! For ten years. But not anymore. I know what I have to do. Stay here and atone for what I did."

I grasped his slender arms and shook him.

"You did nothing David!"

"Nothing? I watched while a boy was killed! I was too afraid to tell and when I did my mother paid for it with her life! Bert visited me every night for a year and made me tell him what I'd seen in the backyard that day. Until I couldn't stand it anymore! I couldn't stand thinking of them anymore and wondering if the reason I didn't try stopping Pierce was because I wanted to watch him do it! That I liked it!"

He burst into tears, collapsing in my arms.

"No David," I said. "You were afraid, that was all. And you were a child. There was nothing you could do."

"He killed that boy so I could watch. I never let myself forget that! Not even when I was taking opium all those years. Even when I tried to escape, I needed a reminder. To punish myself."

Remembering the opium-layout, I said, "B. F."

"That's who I am! Not David King! I'm the reason those children and women are dead!"

I began moving him toward the stairs, trying to keep the panic out of my voice.

"Damn it, no! You're a victim like they were. His greatest victim."

We stood on the flaming stairs, the roar of the fire and the smoke curling around us.

"You want him gone? For good? You have to kill him then."

David King turned to me with tear-streaked eyes and asked, "How?"

"Follow me out of here."

He didn't stop me from dragging him down the stairs then. We emerged onto the street, our clothes and hair smoking, my skin covered with a host of burns.

I felt someone throw a blanket over me. Then my legs gave way and I fell to the cobbled street. I sat there for a long time, watching Shantyville burn to the ground.

36

BY THE TIME the fire was under control I had enough energy stored up to get to my feet. I forced my way through the teeming crowds and headed for the Globe Hotel. With any luck, Jesse and Elsie were still waiting there for me. I wanted to play the harbinger for them, delivering the news that meant release from the past that had held them prisoner for so long.

As I made my way down Elm Avenue I couldn't help noticing the twilit sky. It should have been a deepening bruiselike color. Instead the darkness was tinged with the glare of a dying inferno. If hell had a sky, I thought, it would look just like this.

The Globe Hotel was practically empty. There were only a few reporters in the lobby. They stood in a cluster, their derby hats cocked, memorandum books out, all struggling for control of the telegraph.

A quick peek at the register told me where Elsie and Jesse were staying. I shambled up the carpeted stairs and found their room. When I knocked on their door I noticed for the first time that the coat I was wearing was not my own. I couldn't remember where I'd gotten it from. It stank of smoke and ash, like the rest of me.

I knocked again. There was no answer. I was too tired to care if they were asleep or finding other uses for the bed. The knob twisted all the way and I walked in.

The room was empty. It looked as if the maid had just finished sweeping it clean. Jesse and Elsie had left no trace of themselves. Nothing except a note resting by the wash basin.

It was written on hotel stationary. I recognized the handwriting. I'd seen it twice before—in Hattie Anderson's apartment and on a ransom note delivered to Hiram King.

Jesse wrote:

> *Dear Mr. McCleary,*
>
> *Elsie and I cannot thank you enough for all that you have done for us. We wanted to stay long enough to say this to you in person. But perhaps your Captain Heins was right. It is better to fade away quickly and quietly. Ashes to ashes, dust to dust.*
>
> *I can't tell you where we're going. We'll decide when we get to the depot. I can tell you it will be somewhere far away from here—where the past can't reach us. Neither Elsie nor myself care what it is that you will find. We have each other again.*
>
> *That is all the peace or justice or restitution that we need.*
>
> *Yours sincerely,*
> *Jesse Harding*

I managed a brief smile and wished them well. It had taken ten years for them to work themselves out of hell. I wished them godspeed wherever it was they were going.

Then I moved toward the window and watched Shantyville smolder. I thought on the things that Pemberton Pierce told me at the Ross House, just before he was buried beneath flaming rubble.

The sickening horror of it made my eyes water, though perhaps it was from all the smoke. I rubbed them against my sleeve. That was when I remembered whose coat this was.

Pemberton Pierce's.

It was a little large on me but now, in the darkening room, it felt constricting. Quickly I took it off and threw it across the room in disgust, wishing I could blot out any trace of Pemberton Pierce's existence—even from my own memory.

I watched the coat crumple to a heap in the corner of the room. It lay there in the shadows like a giant cockroach. Outside I heard the sound of firemen's axes hacking away at the remnants of Shantyville.

I saw it then.

The edge of a small book leaning out of Pemberton Pierce's coat pocket.

Curious, I stepped into the shadows and pulled the book all the way out.

It was about the same size as many a wartime diary I'd seen—the sort that fit well in the pockets of your uniform, ready for a last scribbled valediction as you lay bleeding to death on the battlefield.

I couldn't think of any reason why I shouldn't read it. I wish I had been more resourceful.

My hands quivering, I held the first page to the window, where the Shantyville fire gave me enough light to read by.

Pemberton Pierce had been keeping his diary since the war—when he was mustered out of the Secret Service and began working for Hiram King in Mauch Chunk. But it was far from a chronicle of his life.

Instead it was all about Elsie King. What Miss Elsie wore, what Miss Elsie ate, the way Miss Elsie walked, the few words that Miss Elsie had spoken to Pierce that particular day.

She was fourteen when he first noticed her. After that

she was not just his boss's kid anymore. She became Pemberton Pierce's obsession.

The more I read his nearly illegible scrawl, the more I wanted to either laugh at it—or shudder.

I'd been ready to relegate Pemberton Pierce to oblivion. But now I was looking at his face and it frightened me. Because I found myself pitying him.

It was hard not to pity when I read passages like this:

February 24, 1865—Danced with her to-night—in my arms—one arm encircling her slender waist— (satin)—nice green gown—during King's ball, which he allowed me to attend. She said to me, "You always seem happy." I wanted to tell her that was because I was near her. Instead I looked into her eyes—large and wondrous—Fate has brought me to this wonderful place to be with them right now. The touch of her hand—the closeness of her body—the chance to talk to her and her alone. She is full of life, vibrant as a morning in April. Elsie—I invoke her name here—Elsie.

March 16, 1865—After supper, I caught her in the garden reading a book. Tried everything I could to get her to stay there and talk to me and she did. Spoke in whispers—leaning her face toward mine— trying to fathom the color of her eyes—a color I can't describe—something rare that no one ever sees. Let us meet there forever, surrounding ourselves in the mystery of our lives and none is more mysterious than your beautiful face, my darling Elsie, and voice and eyes all focused on me and mine on yours—we envelop one another in the embrace of our lonely minds and hearts and involve one another in our search for something unknown to either of us. The touch of your hand, the moment you put the coin in my palm, didn't you linger there for just

*a moment longer than normal?—lean closer to me
as we walked through the peopled streets and mar-
ket? And I will never forget your face in the sunlight, how it revealed you—so beautiful, graceful,
full of happiness. I saw something that I could love
forever.*

I made sure that the name written at the beginning of
the journal was indeed Pemberton Pierce's. Somehow I
couldn't believe that this articulate voice belonged to the
brutish thug I'd sentenced to death in the Ross House. I'd
looked into his eyes there and thought I saw the depths.

But I had only seen what Pemberton Pierce wanted me
to see.

I wanted to smile at how cleverly he'd played me. But
the muscles in my face refused to move. I tried clearing
my throat but it was too dry. It felt like something very
essential had just drained out of me. Whatever it was, I
wasn't sure if I'd ever get it back.

I put my hand to the windowpane, running the tips of
my fingers against the glass. The surface was still warm
from the dying fire.

Page after page, I read through the history of Pierce's
infatuation. Then it stopped abruptly. Several pages were
torn out.

The next passage had no date on it. All that was written
was:

*Found out about Elsie to-day. From her father. I
offered to dispose of the boy. King said it wouldn't
come to that. Solt will take care of the problem. I'm
in hell. King said if the girl dies, so be it. She means
nothing to him. Never has. Not since he got himself
a son. I wanted to kill him for saying those things.
And that brat he calls a son. Elsie is worth more
than his life—ten times over.*

It's done. I was the one who brought her back

*from Solt's. Even now I can't stand seeing her suf-
fer. King doesn't talk to her. Doesn't even look at
her. He's taken David fishing for the week.*

*She's changed so. I can see it in her eyes—those
eyes I thought so beautiful once. They're dead now.*

What I read next made me take the flimsy pages and
crush them in my soot-stained hands. Then, with a cry of
rage, I put my fist through the window. The jagged glass
cut me only when I tried pulling my hand back in. Blood
ran down my fingers, dribbling onto the floor. I opened
my mouth to make a noise but nothing came out of it.

My eyes fell to the page and saw, to my dismay, that
the words had not disappeared in the interim. They
damned me now as they did the first time. I understood
now the source of Pemberton Pierce's final anguish. He
knew that I would read this. Knew that his work had
ended in failure. I pitied him more than ever when I read
the words:

*Elsie killed a boy to-day. I'd been following her
ever since she was well enough to go out—just to
make sure she didn't see Harding. First she stopped
in town, wandering around like she was looking for
something. She went into a store and came out a
quarter of an hour later with a boy. Elsie knew him
I think, from her school. A little boy, like her
brother. She could ask them to do anything, go anywhere and they would do it. Didn't matter how old.
Or young. I know. I watched them—wished it was
me holding that hand of hers. Followed her all the
way to the Narrows. She never knew I was watching. Then I saw her do it. Just slit the child's throat
like she was slaughtering a pig. I made a sound—
guess I screamed. But a locomotive whistle drowned
it out. By the time I made it over to her, she had
stabbed the body a few more times. But he was*

dead. I took the knife out of her hands and slapped her. I asked her why. She was hysterical, just kept saying her brother's name. Then she began to cry and asked when she could see her baby, if it was all right. Elsie walked away from the body like she didn't know what it was. Or what she'd done. I had a lot of work to do. I hid the boy. Went back for him that night and put him in the root cellar of my house. And waited.

Maybe if I do this for her—maybe then she'll know. Maybe then she'll understand. I love her still. She's sick. She didn't mean it. I know she didn't. She couldn't have. It was the shock. Of course, that's what it was. She didn't even know where she was, what she was doing. It's all right, Elsie. I'll protect you. I'll make sure no one ever finds out. Then you'll know how much your Bert loves you.

Damn it to hell—another—I should have been there—instead of fussing over King's goddamn labor problems—the pompous bastard—he doesn't know a damn thing. Will never know. They've found the body now. It's out of my hands. What to do?

A plan. To make Elsie stop. To make her mine, forever. I'll get her revenge and mine. I don't understand her—but I remember what she said at the Narrows. She said, "David." She wanted her brother dead. I understand that, at least. She wanted to hurt her father. Hurt him as he's always hurt her. To destroy what he loves—the only thing. But she didn't know how. Well, I do. And I'll do it for you, my love. To prove myself to you.

It was all there. As complete a confession as I would ever hope to get.

Pierce had taken the body of the boy in his root cellar and dumped it in Jesse Harding's backyard the night before his search. He made sure that David happened to see him with the body that afternoon before he moved it.

David's life was ruined from that moment. Pierce pretended to stab the dead boy again and again, making David watch, telling him it had all been his fault. That he must never tell anyone, that he would die if he did.

David was too young to see through the deception. He believed that he was witnessing a real murder.

The evidence was easy enough for Pierce to plant in Jesse Harding's house. No one seemed to notice that the detective knew exactly where to look for all of Danny Curran's things.

Pierce got his revenge—for Elsie and himself. He implicated David and Jesse at the same time and nearly destroyed them both. In the meantime, Elsie plunged even further into madness.

He had lied to her about their mother. And to me.

Elizabeth King had not been murdered. At least, not directly. Pierce gave a brief account of it in his diary.

He went to her with the news that Elsie was the real killer. That he was covering up for her, protecting her. In return he wanted Elizabeth to promise him that Elsie would be his.

She couldn't make that promise. He gave her till the next morning. Sometime during the night David had gone to her with his own story and Elizabeth King had finally felt the true depth of the horror around her. It struck her like a tidal wave, and it pulled her under. She didn't have the strength to fight against it.

Elizabeth King had taken her own life.

When Pierce went to her for an answer the next morning, he found her hanging from the gas-lamp. Finding David, he forced the boy into the death chamber. David didn't have much of a chance after that.

Neither did Elsie. Bert saw her as his property. The spoils that he, the victor, richly deserved. He cheerfully damned Jesse and David to a lifelong hell. All for Elsie.

Except she wouldn't give herself to him. Finally one night, he decided to take her anyway, whether she wanted it or not. But she fought him. Pierce told her some lies, so she wouldn't talk about his attempt at rape. That was the night she told David the story that he would need opium to help forget.

The darkness of the room was closing in on me like a stranglehold. There was just enough light for me to read the end of Pierce's diary—which ended soon after the account of Elsie's near rape. He was writing exclusively about Elsie again, as he did in the beginning of the diary—as if nothing had ever happened. Her sickness, he insisted was in the past. He'd made it go away—changed what happened—erased it and reinvented something in its place. Elsie was not to blame for anything. Just David and Hiram and Jesse.

The diary resumed at the Centennial.

The next page was dated just a few weeks before.

Elsie says she saw him. I don't know if it's another of her hallucinations or not. She says she saw him with another woman. A freak, she said. I should never let her wander around Elm Ave. by herself. I don't know what she saw or didn't see.

She told me to-day she's been watching him for some time. I just laughed. Let her play these games with me if she wants. She thinks she owns me. Maybe I have to remind her. I should've killed Harding when I had the chance. But a ghost is even harder to kill. There's a look in her eyes I haven't seen since . . . those days. I don't like it. It scares me. She's talking that queer way again—the way she used to. I'm worried about her. Worried about what she might do. No. It's impossible. She never did anything. Remember that.

Harding's no ghost. I found out to-day. He's here. Working at Allen's Animal Show. He's been sending King letters—wants money. I've been watching him. Waiting. But not just yet.

Elsie—oh my God—why in hell did I believe her when she said she was all right? Why did you—No no no no—can't be—after what I did, how could she? Killed a girl—in back of Museum on Elm. Thought it was Harding's woman. Told me she'd watched them meet in the same place. It was dark and she'd been waiting for them. When she saw that whore, she acted hastily and . . . what the hell difference does it make? It's done. Elsie told me the whole thing as if it had happened to someone else. Why doesn't she tell me in time for me to do a good job of cleaning up? Dear God in heaven, what am I going to do? How much will it take?

I took one of Davy's souvenirs from his opium-smoking days. One that he'll recognize—and Hiram too. I don't want there to be any question this time.

A policeman's involved in it. I've been playing an act for him—me, the stupid bully—just to intimidate him. He doesn't see past the disguise, doesn't know I have a brain or a heart. Let him underestimate me. Like they all have. Even her.

He's getting too close. To her. I can't control her anymore. I'm losing her. For good I think. At least I got the thing back from him while he was searching the woman's room.

Elsie's gone to him. We got the letter. It's out of my hands. Goddamn her, I wish she were dead.

And I love her so—goddamn me.

Lost McCleary. It's all right. I've fixed things good now. Seen Elsie again. The bitch found me in Shantyville. Wouldn't say where she was. But I told her what she wanted to know anyway. Should never have told Elsie where the freak show woman was. But I knew what would happen. I know Elsie, after all. Know what she's capable of. Know that look in her eye when she's about ready for it. Is that all it takes? Her jealousy? I would give anything for that. Anything.

He'll find them up there. I know it. What will she tell him? Will he find out how much I've protected her? Will she even bother to tell him? Does it matter to her all the sacrifices I've made?

I'm writing this just before I go over to Memorial Hall and check up on David and King. Something's going to happen. I felt that sinking feeling in my gut this morning. He's coming back with them, I think. I bet she thinks I'll tell them. Tell them everything. I bet she thinks that's the kind of man I am. As if I mean nothing to her. As if all my life I haven't done everything for her—even when I knew I couldn't have her. I'd let her kill again. I'd protect her again. Maybe if I get lucky it'll be Harding next time. And she'll have no one left but me, this poor stupid bastard—who will never betray you, my darling Elsie. Not in this world.

I reread the whole thing. Just to make sure. The room was completely dark by the time I was finished, my eyes straining in the blackness.

When I was finished I walked over to the wash basin, and looked at Jesse's letter.

I stared at the laces of my boots for a while after I was done. Then I stared out the window again. There was no glimmer of fire left. Just darkness. I don't know how long I kept my eyes on the window—long enough for the lattice of the panes to show up when I closed my eyes to weep. Except there were no tears, no matter how much I wanted them to come. I cowered in the room there with my failure, repeating to myself that she was gone. That I would never have the chance to make her pay.

I had killed Pemberton Pierce in cold blood. A man I thought was a cold-blooded killer. Now I was the one with blood on my hands.

This time I'd let a killer go and there was no chance of mercy or redemption or any other damn thing.

There was just an empty feeling in me. The kind you get when you know that there's not going to be any answer.

I stepped over to the broken window. My elbow cracked off the remaining shards.

For the next quarter of an hour, I tore each sheet out of Pemberton Pierce's diary, ripped them in shreds, and scattered them out the window like ashes.

I thought on a great many things and people. Most of all I thought on a force of nature called cruelty.

It seemed as permanent an element as wind. Or fire.

There was no way for me to quench it. No matter how I tried. I knew that now.

I understood, perhaps for the first time in my life, the devastating extent of my powerlessness.

It closed in on me in the room there and did not let me go, even as the last shred of paper flitted away on a gust of wandering smoke.

Epilogue

BY THURSDAY 28 September, the ashes of Shantyville had been disposed of. A charred empty space stretched between the Transcontinental Hotel and the gutted Ross House.

Tad Schmoyer and I stared across at the ruins as we stood just inside the main entrance.

Heins had wanted two detectives in place of one that morning. It was Pennsylvania Day and the crowds were enormous—fertile ground for the pickpocket's touch.

"How does it feel," Tad asked me, "to be a hero?"

He was talking about the letter of commendation I received for pulling Hiram and David out of the burning hotel. Suddenly the city was proud of me again.

"A-1, Tad. I even got a little honorarium out of the whole thing."

"What are you going to spend it on?"

"Fire insurance."

He chuckled and said, "Have you heard from Jesse and Elsie Harding?"

I hoped he didn't see me wince.

"Not since the day of the fire."

Tad shook his head.

"Wonder why they just ran out like that?"

367

"I guess they had their reasons," I told him. "Anyway, wherever they are they have each other."

I nearly laughed at the platitude. I wondered if Jesse Harding would ever find out that the reason for his ten years of hell was the very girl he loved.

It was the cruelest of many ironies.

"Has Hiram King called up the Big Man to go look for them?"

"I think it's best we lose them. For good. But if he wanted to find them, I guess he could. If he was stupid enough."

"Yeah, I'll bet he could get 'em found. That old boy has a lot of pull, doesn't he?"

"Enough to get me back on the city force after the Centennial closes. And you."

I looked at the open lot where souvenir vendors gathered by the site of the Animal Show.

"From what he tells me that's the last bit of politicking he'll do for a while. He's going to rest up in Mauch Chunk. And keep his hands out of certain business ventures."

"Like Shantyville?"

"Yes," I said. "He lost a pile of money. The Amazon Theatre, the Oriental Saloon, the Animal Show, the saloons and hotels—he was collecting a fair share from them all. Anyway, he has more important things to worry over. Like his son."

"How is David?" Tad asked, looking over a shabbily dressed man who was eyeing a gentleman's watch chain.

"He's doing well. It was pretty hard on him, you know. The statement to the police. The whole ugly mess out in the open."

"Sure."

"But he survived. And I think he'll keep on doing just that. Whatever happens next."

I would do my best to ensure that survival—by never telling him what I knew.

"Uh oh, Mack," Tad said, squinting towards the turn-stiles. "Look who just mosied on in."

"Grand Central," I said. "The mollbuzzer."

"That's him, all right. Oops! You see that?"

"Bumped right into her bustle. Her pocketbook's half-way down his drawers by now."

Tad cracked his knuckles and said, "I'll take care of him."

"You need any help?"

"Hell no! I'll pinch him and meet you later."

"It's about luncheon time. I guess I'll go to the cafe."

"Okay," Tad said, and pushed his way through the crowd. I watched him clamp a thick hand on Grand Central's stooped shoulder, the buzzer's top hat teetering with the impact.

Then I made my way to the Tunisian Cafe.

She was just coming on stage when I arrived.

The musicians finished tuning their instruments and be-gan the frenzied, exotic tune I was familiar with now.

The girl stepped lightly on the carpets, trailing scarves through the air. I watched her ankles and let my mind wander.

I thought on the time I'd first met David King, seated at this very table.

The memory of him that day flooded into my mind, to join the other images there—the spectral faces of Jesse Harding and Eddie Munroe.

And the face of a very young Wilton McCleary, starved and scurvy-ridden, beginning to lose everything that mat-tered while he rotted inside a towering fortress of pine.

The faces of my ghosts. Elsie had joined the inmates by now. She shared a room with another killer—the one I'd let go in Germantown two years ago, hoping I could will some redemption into being, on my own.

But that night of the fire I found out how powerless I was to redeem anyone or anything. Especially myself. I knew now that if I were merciful it must be for no other purpose than to show mercy. Certainly not in the hopes that someone might be saved.

That was not up to me. Or anyone else on this very cruel earth.

Accepting that truth made it easy for me to let those ghosts fade from my mind like the dusk.

As I sat sipping my coffee, I felt them vanish—without much of a trace. That was when I began to smile again for the first time in many weeks.

It caught the eye of the Tunisian girl as she fluttered her scarves through the air.

She returned the smile, thinking it was meant for her.

That made me laugh, with a child's joy.

Afterword

THE CRAZE FOR world's fairs began in London in 1851, with the Crystal Palace Exhibition. Over the next several decades, a host of cities followed suit, including New York, Paris, Dublin, Moscow, and Vienna. The fairs were the theme parks of their day. The Centennial Exhibition in Philadelphia outdid them all in grandeur.

Far more than a fair, the Centennial was a city in itself, with the largest building in the world at the time, and other gigantic structures that housed the world's largest engine and fountain. Monstrous specimens of produce were heaped in Agricultural Hall. The colossal arm of the Statue of Liberty stood on the banks of a vast man-made lake.

Along with size there was volume—thousands upon thousands of showcases displaying everything from the first high chair to a gilded coffin. And anything else a man or woman might need or want in between.

It was America's coming-of-age party. The first sign after the devastation of the Civil War that the re-United States would take its place on the grand stage of world power.

The Centennial was also the symbolic beginning of the modern age. Most of the great inventions that revolutionized production, information, and communication were introduced here for the first time—including, as McCleary noticed, the telephone and the type-writer. Adding machines, the forerunners of computers, were on display, as well as mechanized farm equipment that would change agriculture forever.

And with the citizens of every civilized nation on the earth in attendance, the Centennial heralded what would be known a century later as the global economy, with the United States at its epicenter.

It was one of the most monumental events in American history.

To-day it is largely forgotten.

Most of the buildings were destroyed after the Centennial closed. Of the main exhibition buildings, only Memorial Hall and Horticultural Hall were left standing.

To-day there are scant traces left of the Centennial in Philadelphia's Fairmount Park. Horticultural Hall was ruined by a hurricane in the 1950s and demolished. Memorial Hall, once the city's art museum, escaped a similar fate when park officials converted most of it into a gymnasium. To-day a makeshift boxing ring stands where the glories of nineteenth century art were exhibited, the paintings gone and replaced by posters of scantily clad women advertising beer. In the basement of Memorial Hall is a wonderful model of the Centennial. Unfortunately it was partially ruined when a water pipe burst over it. At the time of this writing the model was still being restored.

To research this book I took a visit to Memorial Hall. I stepped through the cavernous rooms in shock. For months I had wandered through these same halls—but always in their glory, while reading numerous guidebooks and viewing faded stereographs. As I saw the great rotunda, the floor spotted with puddles of rain leaking from the once-majestic dome, I felt for a moment like a traveler from the past stepping forward a hundred some years. I have never been more keenly aware of the ravages of time.

One of the most significant buildings in Philadelphia's history, Memorial Hall is in a sad state of disrepair and neglect. Perhaps this book will, in part, bring more attention to this piece of our national heritage. The last great building of the Centennial Exhibition deserves to be restored to its former glory.

The only other structures from the Centennial that I was able to locate were the Catholic Total Abstinence Fountain and the Ohio State Building (still on their original sites) and the two brick sheds—one of which I used for Hattie Anderson's hiding place. Shantyville, of course, no longer exists. Where the Oil Well, Allen's Animal Show, and the Museum once stood are now rather lovely Victorian row homes. One of the archivists of Fairmount Park tells me that when it snows you can see the outlines of what was once the Art Annex behind Memorial Hall.

The rest of the Exhibition is dust.

So is the Boy Fiend. He was a real person and his name was Jesse Harding Pomeroy. He committed his crimes in Boston, not Mauch Chunk, Pennsylvania. For the sake of a good story I altered the time frame as well as the locale. During the Centennial, the Boy Fiend was behind bars, having murdered his two victims in 1874—the same year Charley Ross was kidnapped. Even back then the children of America were not safe from each other.

The newspaper accounts of the case are factual and were culled from a variety of nineteenth-century papers. A serial killer before the term was invented or the concept understood, Pomeroy was only fourteen when he was tried for his life. Because of his age he was spared the hangman's noose. After several escape attempts he was put in solitary confinement for a record fifty-eight years until his death.

Although the Boy Fiend was never incarcerated there, the Carbon County jail is a real place. Now a museum it is open for tours in Jim Thorpe, Pennsylvania, formerly known as Mauch Chunk—worth a visit for its decidedly Victorian atmosphere.

The fire in Shantyville really happened when I said it did, having got its start when a cook in Murphy's Oyster Saloon spilled some grease on an open flame. The Centennial itself managed to escape destruction thanks to the diligent fire companies. Most of Shantyville, however, was burned to the ground—including the Ross House, which was owned by a relative of the world-famous kidnapped boy, whose whereabouts were still unknown in 1876.

Sometime during that Centennial year my great-great grandparents, William Graham and Martha McCleary, met. They married a year later. Their son Wilton was born in 1879. I like to think that William and Martha met at the Centennial, or because they were in town to see it. As I read the accounts of the exhibits and the marvels there I felt an incredible closeness to these long-dead ancestors of mine.

Their resting place is an unmarked grave in West Philadelphia. This book is a living memorial to them.